The
Garland
CLASSICS OF
FILM LITERATURE

REPRINTED IN PHOTO-FACSIMILE
IN 32 VOLUMES

THE GOLDEN EGG

James S. Pollak

GARLAND PUBLISHING, INC. ● NEW YORK & LONDON ● 1978

Copyright, 1946, by
Henry Holt and Company, Inc.

Library of Congress Cataloging in Publication Data

Pollak, James S   1909-
    The golden egg.

    (The Garland classics of film literature ; 25)
    Reprint of the 1946 ed. published by Holt, New York.
    I. Title. II. Series.
PZ3.P7604Go10   [PS3531.O274]   813'.5'4   76-52124
ISBN 0-8240-2890-2

Printed in the United States of America

THE GOLDEN EGG

JAMES S. POLLAK

THE GOLDEN EGG

HENRY HOLT AND COMPANY

To You, with love,
and to Russell whom we both adored.
To my family,
my friends,
and all those who helped
by waiting patiently.

BOOK 1

THE FAMILY

1

POPPA LEVINSKY died fourteen years after coming to America. He left a widow Sophie, a son Louis, and a small jar filled with the few dollars he'd salvaged from the ragpicking business.

Few people remember exactly how it happened because it was a casual thing. Casual in a street filled with major and minor catastrophes. And yet Poppa's was a glorious death. It started a dynasty.

The legend grew as the family became more important. They tell it now along the stoops of Rivington Street and spin it out for hours. It's a story that seems to keep the kids quiet on hot nights. It's personal and American, and it happened right here in front of number 417.

First Poppa came down the street, giving a little push with his elbows now and then when the sidewalk got too crowded. Poppa never looked to right or left and never talked to neighbors. Only on Shabbos after Schul, then he grunted a little bit and shrugged his shoulders.

When Poppa walked down the street his whiskers jiggled in the breeze. His lips were always moving and he didn't see the bedding hung over the fire escapes, or the children running in between his legs. He didn't even scowl at pushcart peddlers who grabbed his elbows and tried to sell him dry goods at bargain prices. Poppa had his mind on other things. Poppa was going to cross the street and collect a dollar ninety-eight from Horowitz the tailor. Horowitz the tailor, who hid behind the counter and never saw it happen; Horowitz the tailor, who looked up when he heard the scream and ran out and took the number of the big Rolls-Royce standing in the middle of the street; Horowitz, who cried when he saw Poppa, a mass

3

of broken bones and bleeding flesh floundering against the curbstone; Horowitz, who pressed two crumpled dollar bills in the old man's hand and, having paid his debt, cursed out the liveried chauffeur who towered over Poppa and frightened him with questions.

When Poppa looked up and quivered again at the sight of a uniform, Horowitz knew why. He, too, had been born to a cowering respect of brass buttons. It was a respect born of bitterness and the futility of rebellion, for in Russia brass buttons had identified the Law.

"What's your name?" the chauffeur asked.

"Isaac Levinsky."

The chauffeur scribbled Poppa's answer in his notebook.

"Where d'ye live?"

"Four tvanty-two Rivinkton Stritt."

"Ye married?"

"Yaah."

"Any kids?"

"Vun."

"Name?"

"Louis Levinsky."

"I'll call an ambulance."

The chauffeur shut the notebook, jammed the pencil in his pocket, slammed the car into gear, and drove down the street toward the corner drugstore.

Poppa Levinsky, suspicious to the last, propped himself up on what was left of his elbow, looked toward the receding machine, waved his arm in a gesture of defiance and gave voice to his long pent-up contempt for the privileges of authority.

"Nah," he groaned, as the breath ran out of him, "vot can he do me?"

The ambulance came too late. Horowitz held Poppa in his arms until the widow Levinsky arrived.

The old man's heirs collected $5,000 in damages, which was more than Poppa could have earned in a lifetime.

4

2

THE ELEVATOR stopped on the ninth floor of the Mar-Ben Building. It was late at night and when the door opened no salesmen
surged out of the car to scurry down the corridors and lose themselves in the caverns of a building dedicated to the cloak and suit
business.

Joe, the night service man, had just come on duty. It was a warm
June night and the streets outside were already sticky with the stupor
of summer.

Joe folded his paper. The headlines were about some archduke
guy who had stopped a bullet down in the Balkans. Joe was bored.
Bored and lonely. He knew that Dominic, the sign painter, was
changing names on one of the glass doors somewhere in the building.
And when he found him on the ninth floor he hooked open the
door of his elevator and pushed his chair into the corridor. Then
he sat down and lit his pipe. Dominic was glad to see him.

"Who's through now?" Joe asked.

Dominic looked over his shoulder and shook his head. He was
already applying the gold leaf to a new name on the door of Strauss,
Levy and Co.

"Nobody she's a go," Dominic explained. "Somebody she's a
come!"

"New partner?"

Dominic nodded.

"Levinson. . . . Eight letters. . . . Good, eh?" he asked, drawing away from the door to survey his work.

"Yer an artist, Dominic. An artist," Joe said.

Dominic beamed. "Costa guy fi' tousand dollar," he said. "He's

5

a name Levinsky, he just work here. Now's Levinson, partner of Strauss and Levy."

"Ya mean Louis Levinsky, the guy's been cuttin' fer them fer ten years?"

"Says here," Dominic nodded, pointing to the order from the superintendent.

"Whadda ya know!" Joe said. "Even changed his name!"

"Maka da mon, chainja da name." Dominic grinned. Then he asked, "Nice fella?"

Joe shrugged his shoulders. "He don't talk much. How'd you know it cost him five thousand bucks?"

"Da super, he told me."

Joe's pipe went out and he put anotner match to it.

"Wonder where Levinsky ever got ahold of five thousand bucks."

"His'a Pop. Lasta month dey turn his feets to window."

"Insurance, eh?"

"Mebbe so. How she look?"

Joe read the sign. "Strauss, Levy and Levinson. Looks all right," he said. "Don't make no difference to me, though. I only see them guys at Christmas when I come around to collect me presents. Ya goin' down?"

"Just a minutes," Dominic said, stuffing his equipment into his work kit.

Joe put the chair back in the elevator and unhooked the door.

Dominic waved his hand toward the pane of glass and said, "Gooda luck, Levinsky-Levinson." Then he stepped in the elevator and went home to his wife.

3

THE NAME LEVINSON rang like music in Louis's ears, but Momma shuddered every time she heard it.

"Levinson," the old lady would groan as she set about making the beds, "Levinson." Then she would suddenly shout, "Levinsky!" and slam the mattress over on its other side.

Three months later Louis Levinson and his mother Mrs. Levinsky moved into one of the new apartment houses that were springing up all over the Bronx.

Mrs. Levinsky liked the Bronx. If only Poppa had lived to see this magnificence—two bedrooms plus a bathroom, kitchen, and living room. It was such a change from Rivington Street that, mourning or no mourning, she couldn't help bragging a bit.

At the grocer's or the butcher's, while the ladies of the neighborhood were busy squeezing melons or sneering at the meat, they would inquire, as good people do, "How's by you?" To which query Momma would invariably answer, "By me is fine."

Then she would plunge into a description of Louis's latest financial schemes. These tales, calculated to shake the very foundations of Wall Street, produced in the women of 176th Street an apathetic admiration, tempered somewhat by their preoccupation with the day's purchases.

Momma Levinsky liked living uptown, but she wished Louis would stop yelling at her not to lean out of the windows. She stood it as long as she could and then one night she turned on him and suddenly shrieked, "Vot's a lady goink to do on a hot night? Sveat?"

"A lady, Momma, should have some class," Louis insisted.

"Cless!" Momma groaned contemptuously from the window

7

sill. "Vot's cless? A lodda fency vimmin keepin' dere hads inside vindows? Dey dun't even know vot dere missin'!"

Louis just sighed. So Momma winked at him and went about her business.

In time the living-room window became Momma's office. A clearinghouse for gossip, good tidings, and commiseration. Strangers were shocked into friendship by the sound of Momma's cheery greeting from the second floor. "Hallo," she would shout, "I'm Mrs. Levinsky! Who're you?" And Momma remembered their names, and the next time they passed she told them how well they looked and how happy she was to see them again. And pretty soon they waved and spoke to her before she spoke to them. And in the late summer afternoons when the women gathered beneath her windows she talked to them for hours while they sat in the sun knitting and jogging their perambulators.

And then one day Momma informed them that she and Louis had joined the 176th Street Beth Israel Temple, and she closed her office and took her racy tongue to Schul.

Momma, who had immediately become a member of the Ladies' Auxiliary, nagged Louis into delivering a speech at their next meeting. Present, and by far the prettiest of them all, was Rebecca Korn, a dark-eyed, quiet girl in her early twenties.

Louis's talk was called "How Judaism Helped My Business," and he told them about his kindly dealings "even with those who are not of our faith."

As though religion or creed had anything to do with it, Rebecca thought irritably. He was just an upstart, and after all, she was a second-generation American. But when the lecture was over she found herself congratulating Momma Levinsky while her eyes rested on Louis. This embarrassed her, and when Louis smiled she resented it and dashed away. But Louis had somehow been awakened by that look and after many indirect references managed to get her address from his mother.

8

He sent flowers and called up the next evening from the corner drugstore.

"Hello, Miss Korn?" he asked.

"Yes?"

"This is Louis Levinson, you remember, I made the speech the other evening at the Ladies' Auxiliary?"

"Yes, Mr. Levinson?"

This question proved too much for Mr. Levinson's conversational resources, so he hung up. Rebecca frowned at the phone and turned to her father.

"That upstart Louis Levinson just called," she said.

Jacob Korn looked up from his paper. "That kike?" he asked laconically.

"He's *not* a kike!" Rebecca replied with a fervor over which she had surprisingly little control.

Jacob scratched his beard. The stubble was a day old now and the sound was pleasing to his ear. It pleased him because it would have annoyed his wife, *olav hasholem,* who used to make him shave every day in the year. After her death, Jacob, who had been a thin man, began to put on weight. His face was chubby now but his eyes were still inquisitive and sad as though he were searching for a happiness he never had.

Jacob looked at his daughter. She was a good girl, but a fool. Like most women she didn't know what was in her heart until it was too late.

"Many years ago, your grandfather told me that every Jew other than the one using the word was a kike. Now, may I read my paper?"

"Who's stopping you!" Rebecca snapped.

"I'm glad you like him," Jacob said softly.

"I hate him," Rebecca murmured with no conviction at all.

Jacob put his paper down for good. "Wait till he meets that brother of yours," he chuckled.

"He won't meet him. He'll never set foot in this house!"

"Listen, Rebecca, when a man like Louis Levinson sends flowers you can bet your last dollar he's coming by to make sure you got them."

"Then he's coming?" she asked, quite like a little girl.

"If you're the only one that's going to keep him out, he's here already," Jacob answered.

4

BETH ISRAEL was an orthodox temple and the women sat in the balcony. The pulpit was in the middle of the floor where it belonged, and not at one end as it was in those reformed synagogues built like churches. Here things were as they should be, as they had been for thousands of years. Men with their heads covered in the Presence of God, wearing their prayer shawls, chanting in Hebrew, not in an alien tongue. After all, one spoke English, or what passed for it, every day in the week and Saturday was different. Saturday was Jehovah's day. Jehovah's and Rebecca's and Louis's.

It was the one day they could be sure of seeing each other and when the service was over, the first one out lingered on the steps until the other came and said, "Good Shabbos." Then they'd walk home together. Slowly. Awkwardly. Half-ashamed and conscious of the fact that Momma and Jacob were nudging each other and pausing at shop windows to stay behind them.

Inevitably they were drawn closer together. Walking home from Synagogue led to movies twice a week. Movies led to daily phone calls. Daily phone calls led to a casual intimacy and lots of kidding from Momma and Jacob.

All of them knew it was just a question of time. All of them, that is, except Rebecca, who wasn't quite sure. She wanted her brother to meet Louis before she said yes.

And for months now, Louis had heard about Moe who, as Jacob put it, "in all his twenty-nine years never asked me for a nickel or told me how he earned one." But they had never met, because Moe came home so seldom.

Rebecca knew that he had an apartment. She had gone there once to see him when they needed cash, and he had given it to her without a word. She also knew perfectly well what went on in his place, but nice girls didn't think about such things, much less talk about them, and what Poppa didn't know wouldn't hurt him. Besides, she always kept Moe's room in order so that if he did come home he wouldn't feel they'd forgotten him.

She never told her father that she had called Moe and asked him to meet her "gentleman friend." It was better that way. It would look like an accidental meeting.

One evening just after they had cleared the table Rebecca heard Moe's key in the door. She looked at Louis and her heart skipped a beat. Jacob frowned.

Moe came in and sat down without saying hello to anybody. He looked at Louis.

"This him?" he asked Rebecca.

Rebecca nodded.

Jacob cleared his throat. "Moe, this is Mr. Louis Levinson," he said.

"He's a partner in the firm of Strauss, Levy and Levinson," Rebecca added, hoping to impress her brother.

"Cloak and suiters?" Moe asked.

"The best." Louis grinned amiably.

"Dope," Moe said and he got up and walked off to his room.

Rebecca bit her handkerchief to keep from crying. Jacob shrugged his shoulders.

"Nice boy," he apologized, "but difficult to get along with."

"Half the time I can't believe he's your son," Rebecca cried angrily.

"You didn't know your mother well," Jacob sighed.

Moe came back a few minutes later. He had a cigar in his mouth. "Wotsa madda ya changed Levinsky ta Levinson?" he asked between puffs.

"Why shouldn't I?"

"He's got a perfect right," Rebecca flared up.

"I didn't ask you. I asked him."

"How'd he know?" Louis frowned. Rebecca stared at the floor.

"I know everything," Moe snapped. "Well, why?"

"Levinsky's no good for a man in my position," Louis explained with dignity. "I gotta think about things like that. How'd Levinsky look in gold letters onna door, alongside Strauss and Levy?"

"A herring's a herring," Moe countered. "Inna pickle barrel they all smell."

"But lots of people are named Levinsky," Jacob protested quickly. "Nice people. And if you ever become famous they'll be proud of being Levinskys."

"I'm sorry, Mr. Korn, the name is Levinson, and Levinson it stays."

"Maybe so, Louis, but I don't think you'll be any the happier for it. It's one thing to be proud of a name, but it's something else again to make a name proud of you."

"Don't you worry," Louis said. "I'm gonna be a big man all right. An important man."

Moe began to grin. "Levinsky, Levinson, wotsa difference if you're gonna be a big man?" he demanded.

"Lotsa difference. Levinson's got class. Sounds like Park Avenue."

"Park Avenue to you, Flatbush ta me," Moe said with a shrug. "Inna cloak and suit business they shoot ya, ya take one step east of Central Park West."

"Not me. I'm gonna be somebody. I'm gonna make Levinson a name everybody'll know. A name they'll remember!"

"Waid a minute. You gonna do all that inna cloak and suit business?" Moe heckled him.

"You got any sudgestions, Mr. Smart-Meyer?" Louis snapped.

12

Moe blew a cloud of cigar smoke toward the ceiling.

"Sure," he said, "come over and see me in Fort Lee. I'm workin' in movin' pitchers over there."

"Moving pickchas!" Louis snorted contemptuously.

Moe just shrugged his shoulders. He knew.

5

LOUIS AND REBECCA were married a month later. They left for Fleischman's in upstate New York with the good wishes of the neighborhood ringing in their ears, and Moe went home to live with his father. "Just ta keep the old man from blowin' his brains out," he explained to his friends.

After the honeymoon, Louis and Rebecca settled down in the apartment with his mother. The bride and groom were becoming used to each other, but Momma was not reconciled. The Americanization process brought about certain social reforms that invariably annoyed her, such as the one forbidding her to hang the bedding over the window sill any more.

The feud continued until Rebecca finally took Momma to one side and confessed, with great seriousness, that she thought there was going to be a grandchild in the family. Momma tried to share the secret solemnly, but suddenly she gave in to herself and great round gusts of laughter spilled over her face.

"She vaits til she gets like a house," she heaved, "den she tells me a secret I know four months awreddy! Dun't tell Louis, she says. Is blind de poppa? He shouldn't know? Is in fronta you like a balloon and de poppa should tink is sumpin' you ate, maybe? Louis knows is anodder Levinsky coming! Hokay, hokay, Levinson. Should be tvanty Levinsons someday en' by me couldn't be better. Tvanty Levinsons!"

Then the old lady's excitement turned to tears and Rebecca went over to her. And the two women hugged each other and Momma murmured very softly to herself, "But only vun Levinsky."

Momma finally dried her eyes and got down to business. "Vot's he saying, de duktah?"

Rebecca blushed; she hadn't been to a doctor yet—she knew it from other signs.

"Ai!" Momma exclaimed. "Is no duktah in chotch? Four months awreddy en' no duktah!"

"It's all right, Momma. I'm all right," Rebecca reassured her.

"Nah, sure! Is pea-green de color fomm de chicks, en' by her is ull right!"

Rebecca suddenly pressed her hand against her temple. She felt strangely dizzy.

"You ull right, Becky?" Momma cried anxiously.

"Morning sick . . ." Rebecca sighed. Then her eyelids fluttered and she collapsed in a heap at Momma's feet.

The old lady gasped, dragged her daughter-in-law to a chair, left her there and ran across the room. "Dun't move!" she yelled before she closed the door. Then she tore out of the house and dashed down the street screaming at the top of her lungs, "Duktah!—Duktah! I nid a duktah!"

A large automobile pulled over to the curb. "What's the trouble?" a man asked.

"You a duktah?" Momma panted.

"Yes."

"Comm opstairs. Is mine boy's vife. Qvick!"

Dr. Richard Lansburgh had a case; one of the few cases he ever acquired without an appointment. He had stumbled across an emergency call and he was grateful for it. It interrupted the deadly routine of sitting in an office and carving a brilliant career for himself out of the elderly patients he'd inherited from his father and the middle-aged neurotics he'd unearthed for himself.

Here, he was sure, he would find a person who needed medical attention quickly, desperately, one who wanted to get well in contrast to the desires of his own patients, whose happiness seemed to depend upon their being assured that they were merely quite comfortably ill.

Dr. Lansburgh chased up the stairs after Momma and encountered his first maternity case since his internship. She was weeping quietly in an overstuffed chair.

6

FIVE MONTHS LATER Dr. Lansburgh brought a new baby into the world.

Rabbi Maibrunn himself, from the Beth Israel Temple, attended the circumcision and toward the end of the ceremony Louis's son was formally given the name of William Levinson. Presents and felicitations were numerous, but Moe pulled the biggest surprise of all when he gave the baby a ten-thousand-dollar life insurance policy with premiums all paid up for the first five years.

"Anything ta annoy Louis," Moe announced at the party following the circumcision. "He'll have ta meet premiums fa fifteen years more before my nephew earns a dime."

A few nights later Jacob cornered Moe and asked him if he didn't think he was spending too much money.

"I'm earnin' it, ain't I?" Moe snapped back at the old man.

And he was. The motion-picture industry, while still in the growing stage, was already beginning to pay its technicians good salaries and Moe had, by deft finagling, become the studio's chief cameraman. His check was seventy dollars a week and as Papa Korn sighed wistfully, "Just for taking pictures, that's a lot of money."

Strangely enough, the new nephew strengthened family ties in

Moe, and he came regularly to check up on his progress. To be sure, the baby invariably greeted his approach with a scream of protest that began before his uncle even reached the crib, but then Moe's face, when lit up by affection, assumed the saturnalian expression of a laughing moose.

One Sunday morning while William, now a happy half-year-old, lay gurgling in his crib, Moe barged into the apartment and told Louis he had an idea. He'd like to take a few shots of the kid so that the Levinsons would always have a motion picture of their son as a baby.

The following Sunday the Levinson family ferried over to Fort Lee. Moe put William through his paces and the Levinsons, gushing proudly, expressed their gratitude and went home.

Little William more than lived up to Moe's expectations. The child emoted with such natural unconcern before the camera that Moe experienced the satisfaction of seeing his scheme succeed beyond even his wildest hopes.

7

"HOW MUCH?" Rebecca shrieked from the bathroom.

Louis sat on the edge of the living-room sofa and rubbed his chin. Then he held up the check again and shouted incredulously, "Says here, seventy-five dollars!"

"Where from?" Rebecca inquired breathlessly, pulling her robe together as she ran into the room.

"Amalgamated Films, where Moe works. It's made out to him and he's indorsed it to me."

"Vye so motch noice?" Momma demanded, barging out of her bedroom. "On Shabbos so motch noice? It ain't respeckful."

Rebecca snatched the check from Louis.

"Momma darling! Look! Seventy-five dollars we got from Amalgamated Films."

Momma glanced at the check and handed it back to Louis. "So?" she asked suspiciously. "Vye?"

"We don't know yet. But we will," Louis said. Then he stood up and put the check on the mantel. "Where's the paper?"

Rebecca handed it to him. He put it right back on the arm of a chair and shrugged his suspenders off.

"You through in there?" he asked.

Rebecca nodded distantly. She was busy with a vision of an evening dress bought in a Fifth Avenue store.

"Then get Moe over here," Louis continued. "Excuse me. I gotta think this out."

He was halfway down the hall when Rebecca called him back.

"What is it?" he asked impatiently.

"The paper," she said.

He tucked it under his arm. His suspenders slapped against the seat of his pants as he disappeared toward the Levinson lavatory.

Moe arrived soon after the family returned from Temple. He carried a package under his arm because he knew that by this time they would be crazy with curiosity and the package was a kind of protection. It was a present for Willie. A very noisy present. One that would certainly drown them out when they all started jabbering at once. He knew it would work. He'd tried it out in the store.

This particular afternoon Moe wanted to do the talking.

Louis met him at the door and took his hat. Moe walked down the hall and yelled, "Good Shabbos!"

"Good Shabbos!" his inquisitors echoed suspiciously.

They were gathered around the dining-room table.

Moe paused in the doorway.

Momma looked up. "Comm in," she said. "Hev a grape."

"I brung sump'm fa the kid," Moe said, putting his present on the table.

17

Rebecca and Louis glanced at it and murmured thanks. Moe cut the string with a fruit knife and lifted the toy out of the box. He held it up so they could all see it. It was a tin grenadier with a drum.

"Like it?" he asked.

The Levinsons nodded impatiently. Moe sat down and held the toy in his hand. Then he began inspecting it very carefully, turning it over from side to side as though he expected to find a flaw in its mechanism.

"Wotsa madda?" he said, without looking up. "I kill somebody?"

Rebecca nudged Louis with her elbow. "Go ahead. Tell him," she whispered.

"Moe, we got here a check from Amalgamated for seventy-five dollars. Why?"

Moe began turning the key in the toy's back. "See," he said, "ya just wind it up like this. Put it onna table and let go."

The Levinsons' dining room suddenly sounded like a shooting gallery on a Saturday night. Momma, Louis, and Rebecca froze to their seats and stared at the drummer. It was the most infernal racket they had ever heard. They looked up and scowled at Moe, who smiled back at them and pointed proudly at his gift.

"Some fun, eh?" he shrieked. "Wyncha get the kid up and let him see it?"

"My child sleeps after lunch!" Rebecca shouted, looking anxiously toward Willie's bedroom.

"He ain't sleepin' now!" Momma volunteered.

"Shut that thing off!" Louis shouted.

Moe shrugged his shoulders. Louis lunged for the toy and grabbed its arms. They all sighed and shook their heads.

"Moe, you crazy?" Momma asked.

"Ya don't like it?" Moe said, and he looked very sad.

Rebecca took command of the situation. "Of course we like it," she said. "And you were sweet to bring it. Wasn't he, Louis?"

"Sure." Louis smiled gingerly. He was afraid to let go of the grenadier, so he pushed it at Moe, who took it and turned the switch to "Stop." Then he set it back on the table.

"Now, about that check?" Louis asked. He sat back and opened his vest.

Moe flicked the switch again.

"Turn that thing off!" Rebecca screamed.

Moe shook his head. Momma jumped up and clouted the grenadier. It skidded into Moe's lap.

"Qviet!" she blazed. "Is Shabbos!"

The grenadier subsided.

"Answer me, Moe," Louis insisted, loosening his tie.

"Ya gotcha money. Askin' questions ain't smart."

"Moe Korn, you answer Louis!" Rebecca snapped angrily.

"Okay. So ya kid's an actor now. The boss liked the scenes I took last month and he says give the kid sevenny-five so's he'll onney work fa us and we'll make a star outta him. He dunno it's my nephew. I give him a name—Billy Lane."

"En ectah, my grennson?" Momma shouted, by this time thoroughly aroused. "Not so lonk I should teck anodder breath!"

"Keep tsivil de tongue, Momma!" Moe grinned at the old lady. "Sevenny-five bucks is a lotta money fa a coupla hours' work."

"Moe! Don't talk like that! Where's your respect?"

"Respeck, my backside! Listen, Rebecca, I'm tryin' ta make a big shot outta ya husband but he can't see in front of his Yiddisha nose!"

"Moe!" Rebecca's face dripped dignity as she rose to her feet in defense of her own.

Louis reached up and gently pulled her wrist. "Sit down," he begged. "Sit down. Let's hear what he has to say. Moe's a bright boy even if he is a bum."

Moe shook his head at Louis and dropped his voice.

"A bum?" he asked. "A fella drops sevenny-five bucks in ya lap and ya call him a bum?" His voice began to rise again. "Louis, listen, fella, get wise ta yaself. Ya kid gets that fa an *hour's* work. Thass

19

almost watchu make a week! If a fella kin afford ta pay salaries like that, what kinda money is *he* makin'? Yer askin' me? I'm tellin' ya. Fabulous. Fabulous! An' the dumb sonuvabitch never has a dime!"

Rebecca started up again. Louis hauled her down without a word.

"Ya got money," Moe continued. "Ya put it away fomm the first day ya gotcha hands on it. . . . Don't looka me like that. I know ya got it! And listen, Louis, fa two, three thousand bucks ya get an innarest inna firm. Yer a podner! And if ya put away watcha make on each pitchure ya'll end up on top. Let Bloomfield run the joint awhile. You hannel the mazuma."

"Who's Bloomfield?"

"He's za boss," Moe said, winding the toy up again. "And when the time comes we'll get ridda Mr. Bloomfield and you and me's gonna own a pitchure company."

"Moe, Moe, wait a minute! With you everything's gotta be right away yes or no."

"A reglah hurry-upnick," Momma nodded sagely.

Moe and Louis looked at her and grinned.

"Listen," Louis continued, "I'm making a respeckable, Grade A income right now. So, okay, smile; by you it's a second-class Grade A income. It's still a living. A nice living. You see Momma, maybe, begging in the streets? Rebecca, maybe, she's got no close onna back? Willie's maybe a charity patient? Whatsa sense, Moe? Why should I give up a partnership in Strauss, Levy and Levinson for an idea you got in your head? You think that's good business? You think that's smart? I got my name onna door, Moe, in gold. For as long as I want, my name can stay on that door. Who knows, someday maybe it'll be the first name, not the last. I got security in the dress business—and I got a family to support. I'm set for the resta my life. Women gotta have dresses. So we make 'em, the dresses. That's sense. That's money in the bank. And that's the kinda life I wanna live."

Moe tapped the head of the grenadier against the table. "Ya got it in black and white they're gonna buy *your* dresses?" he asked.

20

"You got it in writing they're gonna see *your* pickchas?"

"Nope," Moe answered.

"See!" Louis appealed triumphantly to the judgment of the family. "No guarantee!"

"All I gotta say is this," Moe said slowly, "*if* they see our pitchures, you'll make fifty times the dough ya'd make *if* they bought yer dresses."

"Fifty times is a lotta money."

"Louis," Moe said quietly, "someday fifty times'll be buttons."

Louis shrugged his shoulders.

"I'll speak to Bloomfield Monday," Moe said. "Tell him I know where I can get some quick dough. Think it over."

He got up to go, and put the kid's present back on the table. Louis took him to the door.

"Whadda you think, Momma?" he asked when he came back.

Momma shrugged. Rebecca stared into space. The grenadier gave a spasmodic jerk and suddenly started banging away all by itself. Louis reached over to stop it.

Momma touched his arm and shook her head. "Vait," she said. They waited until it ran down.

"Ull by itself it vent!" Momma exclaimed. Then she looked up at the ceiling and sighed, "De finger uf God!" She smiled at Louis. "Could be," she said. "You and Moe. Could be."

Little William woke up and began to cry. Rebecca bundled him in her arms and brought him back to the living room. She sang to him softly while Momma and Louis dreamed of the future.

8

FORT LEE was just a ferry stop on the motion picture's path of progress. But to Louis, Fort Lee looked like another Ellis Island. It was the gateway to a new adventure that began in George Bloomfield's office.

Mr. Bloomfield sat at his desk alternately scanning the contract and Louis's check. But Louis, looking out the window over Mr. Bloomfield's head, saw only the shimmering reflection of the sunlight on the Hudson River, and for a frightening second he became sick with fear and wanted to run as far away from the Amalgamated Film Company as possible.

Moe, who was sitting on the edge of Bloomfield's desk, sensed Louis's panic and nodded reassuringly.

"It's too late now," he said, and he leaned over and took a cigarette from the box on the desk.

Bloomfield looked up sharply. "Too late for what?" he asked.

"Fa him ta pull out." Moe winked. Then he lit the cigarette and threw the match on the floor.

Bloomfield looked from the match to Moe and sighed as he signed the contract.

"For three thousand dollars you can throw a match on the floor. Just one. No more."

Moe put his tongue between his lips and spat out a tobacco crumb. "Poddon me, boss," he said.

The boss sat back, crossed his arms, and looked at his new treasurer. Louis smiled impatiently. Mr. Bloomfield liked to make snap decisions and stick by them. His snap decision, encouraged by

22

Louis's meek smile, was that Moe had found him a picture-struck sucker. His gratitude was short-lived.

Mr. Bloomfield rose and extended his hand across the desk to Louis. "Well, well," he said, "if your check's good, it looks like we've got a new treasurer. Congratulations, Mr. Levinson, congratulations!"

Mr. Bloomfield played the scene as he always had, with the giddy insincerity of a banker about to extend a client's note. He turned and patted Moe on the shoulder. "Of course, he doesn't realize he's the fifth new treasurer in five years, does he, Moe?"

The question was purely rhetorical.

"The others quit," he explained to Louis. "They bought their way in and when we couldn't show a profit, they quit. Very unfortunate."

Moe smirked at his brother-in-law.

"Well, Mr. Levinson," Bloomfield continued, "you just run along and we'll mail you a pay check every month. That is, if our pictures make money, which, unfortunately, they seldom do. But you know what show business is like, Mr. Levinson, a seventeen-to-one shot against you. But you can't tell, this may be the one!"

"What's the name of it?" Louis inquired. He was still smiling.

"*A Woman's License*. And say, the cutest kid's going to be in it. Billy Lane. Did you see *The Sinful Moment*? He walked away with it. Yessir. And I'm gonna get him for this one if we have to pay him a thousand simoleons a week. We got him cheap for seventy-five in the last one. The boy's a natural, a gold mine. He's got a great career ahead of him, a great career!"

"Could be," Moe nodded quietly. "But it ain't gonna cost us no thousand bucks."

"Who said it would?" Mr. Bloomfield demanded. "His folks don't know what he's worth. As a matter of fact, you brought the kid, you make the deal. You know the family?"

Moe looked at Louis. "Nope," he said. "He does."

"You do, Mr. Levinson! What a coincidence! Maybe you can handle it for us?"

"Maybe," Louis answered, hesitating momentarily. "Maybe I can." He changed the súbject abruptly. "Where's my office? I'd like to start going over the company's books."

Mr. Bloomfield came around to the front of the desk. "Mr. Levinson, you don't understand. You don't have to work. I'll run the company. You just run along and loaf. You'll get your checks from time to time."

"For nothing?" Louis asked.

"For nothing." Mr. Bloomfield smiled.

Louis saw Moe reach over and slip the contract into his pocket. They were safe now. Safe enough to become belligerent.

"Mr. Bloomfield," Louis bellowed, "as treasurer of Amalgamated Film, I *demand* those books!"

"Mr. Levinson," replied Mr. Bloomfield blandly, "there *are* no books."

"No books?" Louis repeated, the bombast blown right out of him.

The president of Amalgamated shook his head.

Louis turned green. Moe had tricked him. Betrayed him into throwing away his savings. Persuaded him to invest his money in a bankrupt firm. Rebecca was right. She'd been against it from the start. Moe was no good. She'd said so herself. Louis looked at his brother-in-law and muttered hopelessly, "Now what?"

"Now," said Moe, crushing out his cigarette, "as an officer of the company, you can demand a public accountin'."

Louis came out of the coma fast and snatched at the straw Moe had thrown him.

"That's a good idea!" he shouted. "A good idea!"

"You wouldn't want to do that. It's not ethical," Mr. Bloomfield said.

"Who said anything about ethics?"

"He don't make ethics," Moe explained; "just little pitchures."

Bloomfield ignored him. "You'll find it quite unnecessary to have any accounting, Mr. Levinson," he said.

"What're you worried about?" Louis countered shrewdly. "This is a reliable firm, isn't it?"

"Five treasurers in five years, it must be." Moe grinned.

"You stay out of this," Bloomfield snapped. Then he smiled at Louis. "I assure you it is, Mr. Levinson. Certainly you don't doubt my word."

Louis stared at the president. "The books, Mr. Bloomfield," he insisted quietly.

Mr. Bloomfield sat down behind his desk, looked up at Louis and shook his head. "There are none. Remember?"

Moe leaned over and swiped another cigarette from the box. Bloomfield frowned at him. "Fa three thousand bucks, Mr. President?" Moe asked.

Bloomfield nodded and waited for Louis's next remark. But Louis was stymied and looked anxiously at Moe. Moe pursed his lips and very carefully began inspecting his cigarette, which he held lengthwise in his hand.

Then he turned and grinned at Louis. "Okay," he said, "here we go." And he looked over his fingertips at the boss. "Feins . . . Corrigan . . . Weaver . . . Rosenheimer . . . and Sachs." Bloomfield blanched perceptibly as Moe slowly intoned each name.

"The treasurers?" Louis asked.

"One by one." Moe nodded. "The slobs he busted. And he's tryin' ta tell us they walked outta here without seein' any books. Chris', theydda burned the joint down first!"

Mr. Bloomfield made a mental note to look up all of them and give them token payments on their investments before Levinson got to them. But in order to do that he'd have to keep Louis's check.

"Mr. Levinson," he said, "I don't think we can come to any pleasant working agreement. Supposing we call the deal off and I'll refund your money."

Moe, who saw his brother-in-law hesitating, suddenly groaned, "Don't let him bull ya, Louis, ya got him goin' now."

"Moe Korn," Bloomfield suddenly shouted, "you're fired!"

"That's fine, Georgie," Moe answered complacently, "and before we leave ya'll take me back at a fifty-buck-a-week raise. You got commitments, aincha, fer another pitchure?"

"What's that got to do with it?"

"Whadda ya gonna shoot it with?"

"Cameras, naturally."

"Sure. Ya got two cameras. Special ones I had ya make up. Fine, fancy cameras and onney four lenses inna country fits 'em."

"So?"

"So, they're with the cameras, those four lenses, Mr. Bloomfield?"

"Sure," the president said hopefully.

Moe shook his head very slowly.

"Where are they?"

Moe shrugged his shoulders. "I should know? he said.

"You're the head cameraman. Who else should know?" Bloomfield inquired angrily.

Moe shrugged again. "Ya fired me, remember?" he said, imitating his boss.

"Twice," Bloomfield snapped. "This is the second time."

Moe leaned over the desk and looked Bloomfield square in the eye. "Got it all figgered out, haven't cha?" he snorted. "You're gonna rent cameras. You, with your credit, you're gonna rent cameras! Don't make me laugh!"

Oh, God, Bloomfield sighed to himself, if he only knew the trouble I had getting film from Eastman the last time. Jesus—maybe he does. Maybe he knows the lab isn't even paid for yet. Goddamn him!

"Moe Korn," he said very slowly, "I'm going to sue you."

"Go ahead, sue, Mr. Bloomfield," Louis interrupted, "and maybe me and my brother-in-law won't institute a countersuit?"

"Your brother-in-law!" Mr. Bloomfield gasped.

"Yeah, me brudder-in-law, Georgie. Me brudder-in-law and five ex-treasurers. And, Georgie, them guys don't *like* you."

Bloomfield collapsed quickly. "I can imagine," he suddenly sighed aloud.

"The books, Mr. Bloomfield, now!" Louis said firmly.

Bloomfield got up and walked across the room. "All right, god-damn it!" he said. "Go ahead, look at them!"

He opened the safe and gave the books to Louis, who put them on the desk, sat down, took out his glasses, and began to pore over them.

Georgie glowered at Moe, who grinned right back at him.

A half hour passed.

Louis closed the books, placed his spectacles back in their case, looked accusingly at Mr. Bloomfield, and calmly stated a well-known fact.

"Mr. Bloomfield," he said, "you're a crook."

Bloomfield shrugged his shoulders.

"Moe, do you know what this guy's done? Each pickcha shows a net profit of about eight thousand dollars. All the statements show no profit at all."

"What's that mean?" asked Moe.

"That means he faked his accounts to the stockholders, lied to his creditors, and stuck the profits in his pocket. He ain't no piker, your Mr. Bloomfield. But listen to this, alluva sudden he gets scared, so on his last pickcha, *Sinful Moment,* he puts aside the tremenjous sum of five hundred dollars for payment to his stockholders. Maybe that's because the pickcha seems to be making twice the money the others did to date."

"That," shouted Mr. Bloomfield, swapping a trade secret for a kind word, "is because of the Lane kid. He's the works. If we can get him for the new show we'll make a fortune, and I'll tell you what I'll do, boys, I'll cut you in on it."

"Mr. Bloomfield," Moe sighed, "you ferget, I'm fired."

"Never mind cutting us in on it," Louis interrupted. "Just give Moe another fifty a week, make my salary the same, and from now on I'll take care of the books of the Amalgamated Film Company.

But first I'm going to let a C.P.A. go over them and you'll pledge yourself to pay your stockholders and creditors every nickel you owe them."

Mr. Bloomfield sat down slowly. "That's all right with me, boys," he said. "I'll have the contracts ready for you in the morning."

"*I'll* have them!" Louis objected, pausing at the door with Moe. "and, by the way, if that Lane kid is so good, how much do you think we ought to pay him?"

"One hundred fifty, tops."

"Ya said a thousand!" Moe yelled.

"We'll make it a hundred and call it quits," Louis said. "I'm his father."

Louis closed the door.

Mr. Bloomfield looked out the window. "Jesus," he muttered to himself, "they could have had two hundred."

9

WITHIN SIX MONTHS Messrs. Korn and Levinson were practically sole owners of the Amalgamated Film Company.

Moe was certain that if honesty had got them into the business, then the mere impression of honesty was all they had to maintain to gain control of it.

He was quite right. Mr. Bloomfield ran out of funds shortly after the start of *A Woman's License*. In itself a perfectly normal occurrence, this time the fact that he could raise no further cash filled him with misgivings, and much against his better judgment he found himself forced to turn to the boys. Their credit was good, or at any rate unknown, which in the motion-picture business amounted to the same thing. So he suggested that they figure out a scheme to raise the needed money. Something within the law, if necessary. But something that would do the job quickly, efficiently—

"And honestly," Moe had added.

Mr. Bloomfield shrugged his shoulders.

The boys asked for a half hour to think it over, during which time they made arrangements with a stockbroker to buy up all the shares of Amalgamated that would shortly appear on the market. Then they returned to the president's office and suggested that he sell more stock to the public. Mr. Bloomfield asked if they thought that a safe procedure. When they nodded their heads he said, "Let's do it, then!"

Moe was in Louis's office a week later when Bloomfield dropped in and announced, "Just to show you what the public thinks of Amalgamated—the stock's a sellout! They snapped it up as quick as they could get their hands on it. There's nothing like being on the level after all, is there?"

He laughed and left them alone.

Louis looked at Moe. He wasn't sure, but he actually thought he saw his brother-in-law blush.

10

IN THE MIDDLE of the production of *A Woman's License* the leading lady died. And although Mr. Bloomfield walked off with the mourner's laurels at the funeral he saved his real tears for the office. He sat himself down and had an honest cry because he felt genuinely sorry for himself.

"Why me?" he groaned, as Moe and Louis wandered into his office.

"That's a helluva question to ask us!" Moe snapped. Then he looked at Louis and asked, "Why him? I dunno why. Do you?"

"He makes moving pickchas."

"Oh." Moe nodded wisely. He sat down on the edge of the president's desk.

"Wotsa madda, G.B.? Stuck?"

"Get off my desk!"

Moe slid to his feet. "Okay. Okay. So get sore. So what good's it do ya?"

The boss began to cry again.

Moe handed him a handkerchief. "Here," he said, "stop snivelin', will ya? It makes me sick."

Bloomfield blew his nose. "Sorry," he mumbled.

"Well, whadda ya gonna do? Ya can't shoot the resta the pitchure inna coffin. Fa Chrissake stop that yappin'!"

"I don't know," Bloomfield moaned. "I don't know what to do."

"We do. Tell him, Louis."

"It seems to us," Louis said, "the thing to do is write her death into the story, fake it in a scene and build the rest of the pickcha around a woman who looks like her and takes her place in society."

"That's it," Moe interrupted. "And the hero, who's a dope anyway, can't tell the difference between them. Onney this second dame's a bitch and leads him a helluva life. So at the end of the show he walks out to face life alone."

"Disillusioned by love," Louis added, swatting a fly that had settled on his neck.

The boss slowly came out of the weeps and grinned.

"Boys," he said, and there was admiration in his voice, "you're geniuses. I've got an idea," he continued. "We won't kill her off. She's been taking care of her sister's baby. The baby dies and the shock's so great she ages thirty years. That's romantic as hell. Think of it, thirty years! And in love with a young man. I've got just the girl for it."

And he had, too. That very week a famous French actress finished her New York engagement. In France she was still considered a glamor girl, because the French, feeling as they do that age is a

30

matter of the spirit rather than a chronological catastrophe, readily accepted her as a perpetual ingénue. But America had been a different experience and she was about to sail home when George Bloomfield approached her with a contract to finish *A Woman's License.*

He knew very well that her acting lacked the sparkle of her earlier days, but more important, he recognized the value of her name as a household word throughout America. And realizing that he was dealing with a temperamental prima donna, he had hired the best cameraman in town to make a test of her.

But he had forgotten to tell Moe and Louis about it.

The two of them barged into the projection room one afternoon and when they saw her face on the screen, Moe shrieked, "What is it? A crocodile?"

"Ssh!" Bloomfield cried, waving his hands frantically in a futile attempt to convey the fact that the lady was in the room.

"Deaf and dumb stuff," Moe confided to Louis.

"Ssh!"

"Don't shush us!" yelled Louis.

"Sit down," Moe said, and they slipped into seats at the rear of the projection room.

"Where'd you get her?" Louis demanded.

"Quiet, boys, please!" Bloomfield pleaded.

By this time he was so mad that he shook like a hyperthyroid leaf, but he was still gallant enough to keep reassuring the great tragedienne who sat beside him.

"*C'est bon,*" he repeated mechanically. "*C'est bon.*"

"If you got her for *License* you're wasting our time and your film," Louis said.

"She stinks!" Moe shouted as the test ended and the lights went on.

"Zey like it?" the new star inquired with Gallic innocence. She spoke very little English.

"*Mais oui,* madame. *Mais oui.*"

The star stood up and smiled at the boys.

31

"Jesus!" Moe said. "Look at them gums."

Bloomfield got up very slowly. Then he smiled, and he kept smiling while he said softly, "You're fired, boys."

The boys jumped to their feet. "We're fired?" they shouted together.

Bloomfield nodded and said. "As of this moment."

The boys looked at each other. Moe broke the silence with a command. "Tell him, Louis!"

The tragedienne, sensing battle, stalked out of the room as haughtily as her limbs permitted.

Louis spoke very slowly. "Bloomfield, *you're* fired," he said. "We own over fifty-four per cent of the company's stock."

"I don't believe it."

"Who keeps your books?" Louis asked.

"Oh," Bloomfield said. "Sure. But I'm still the president. It says for five years in the new incorporation papers. So, okay, I can't fire you, you can't fire me. We've just got to get along together."

"It says in them papers"—Moe started.

Louis put his hand on Moe's arm. "Let me handle this," he said. "It says that the Board of Directors has the final say in all matters pertaining to the company. We are the Board of Directors, Mr. Bloomfield. You and us."

"How about a little meeting, Louis?"

"Let's do it strictly legal, Moe."

"*Strickly* legal!"

"Okay. The meeting will now come to order."

"Those in favor of tyin' the can ta Bloomfield raise their hands."

"Hey, wait a minute," Louis interrupted. "We gotta have a witness. Hey, Sam!"

"Don't need Sam," Moe said. "Don't need nobody, not even a sekketary fa minutes!"

"Now look, boys," Bloomfield protested, "this is no laughing matter. You guys know goddamn well you can't make pictures without me. The contracts, for Christ's sake, are signed in *my* name!"

Sam, the projectionist, walked into the room. "Yeah?" he asked. "Stick around," Louis told him. "Board of Directors meeting."

Sam shrugged his shoulders and lit a cigarette. He was used to anything. He didn't even grin when he heard Moe say, "We got that covered too, Georgie. The contracks are signed in yer name as *president* of Amalgamated Films. Fa that we got anudder paper. Anythin' else on ya mind?"

"The vote!" Louis said.

He and Moe put their hands up.

"All those against?" Louis asked.

Bloomfield was too mad to move.

"Two ta nothin'!" Moe yelled. "Get the hell outta here and clear ya crap outta the desk."

"You haven't heard the end of this," Bloomfield muttered, by way of announcing his retirement from Amalgamated Films.

"He dunno from the time a day," Moe said, the moment the door closed behind the ex-president.

11

BLOOMFIELD TAKES POWDER
Amalgamated Film Prexy Resigns
Louis Levinson and Moe Korn to
Continue Production at Fort Lee

THE VARIETY SQUIB created only the barest ripple among the vaudevillians and "legits" of Longacre Square. In the Bronx, however, Momma became a walking billboard, shouting the praises of her boys. She had adopted Moe, with reservations, ever since the night he suggested that Louis become president. They were to share profits and salaries on a fifty-fifty basis, but Moe preferred to be vice-president so long as he had complete charge of production and the making of pictures. It gave him a front guy to blame things on.

Louis's responsibilities were financing, distribution, advertising, and addressing ladies' clubs.

"He's good at that," Moe said to Rebecca, who blushed and answered. "Never mind, Louis's going to be a great help."

She was right. They made a good team, although Louis was still occasionally frightened by his sudden rise to eminence. He wasn't so sure of himself as Moe was.

It was better, he thought, to let Moe handle things. Moe had been right from the very start and Louis felt a little ashamed of himself for not having trusted him. Ashamed and startled because his judgment had been wrong. But Rebecca had influenced him and made him forget that Moe really knew this business. He was a smart man. They would go far together. Moe had promised him that. And the more security he got for Rebecca and Willie, the better he'd feel. Security, to him, was a storybook legend—something his father hadn't given him and something that could be planned.

To Louis, marriage was a sacred trust personally handed down to him by God; and he felt that nothing must ever be allowed to interfere with that obligation, not even the very business that might give him the security he so desperately wanted. But, then, that could never happen. It wasn't the kind of business that seeped into a man's blood. He could keep it a thing apart from his personal life. With Moe's help it wouldn't be difficult, and besides, Moe would understand.

Their first problem concerned the French star who had been signed by Bloomfield without their knowledge or consent. No amount of bargaining or persuasion could dissuade her from complying with her part of the contract. So, much against their will, the new bosses continued the picture.

Willie had long since finished his original part in it, but now they

34

had to make additional scenes with him. The instant Rebecca learned that her son was to be in the same picture with a French actress, she put her foot down on Willie's acting career.

"Ya can't do that!" Moe yelled. "We got a lotta dough on that show. All he's gotta do is die in her arms—ya wanna ruin us?"

Rebecca was grim, but one look at Louis's face convinced her.

"Just this once," she conceded grudgingly. "But no more pictures after that."

"What's eatin' you?" Moe demanded, glaring at his sister. "You an execkative of the company alluva sudden? We build the kid up, overnight he's a star, then you come along and tell us no more pitchures. Wotsa madda with you, Becky? He means money inna bank fa us!"

"Money's got nothing to do with it," Louis snapped. "I wasn't going to let my son go on acting in pickchas anyway. I got better things planned for him."

"Name one, fa Chrissake!" Moe snorted.

But Louis and Rebecca finally won the argument. Shooting was resumed and Willie performed in front of a camera for the last time. Three weeks later the picture was finished.

As suggested by Moe, the story had an unhappy ending, and after the first screening Moe was discovered weeping wildly in a corner of the projection room. At this point the director of the film congratulated himself and on the way out called to the sobbing vice-president, "It's gotta be good to make you cry!"

Whereupon Moe turned his tear-stained face to the ceiling and shouted, "Listen, dope! I ain't cryin' because it's good! I'm cryin' because it stinks!"

Louis agreed with him and they decided the best thing they could do was to hire an excellent title writer and stay away from the studio to avoid process servers. The title writer went to work as soon as he got over his initial shock at being left alone and he turned in such a good job that the picture proved to be a minor hit.

Running in what few neighborhood theaters there were at the time and in direct competition to the first two-dollar motion-picture attraction, *The Birth of a Nation*, it clicked far beyond their expectations largely because of the popularity of their much-maligned French star.

Moe and Louis, with the help of some high-powered press-agenting, became known as artistic producers and superb showmen and the financial position of Amalgamated Films was at least temporarily improved.

Now it was Momma's turn to have fun. At first she requested passes for only a few of her intimate friends, but one Thursday evening the old lady precipitated a family riot at the dinner table when she blandly inquired if she could have "vun hunerd feefty-two teekets fa Vensday mat-in-hay."

"Whaaat!" Louis exploded.

"Matinee," Jacob explained quietly.

Louis had just finished dunking a piece of coffee cake. It was halfway up to his mouth when he let go and it dropped back into the cup, splattering coffee all over Rebecca. She jumped to her feet and grabbed a napkin.

"Momma leben, you're sick!" she cried, as she began daubing away furiously at the coffee stains.

"Is too motch?" Momma asked innocently.

"A hundred and fifty too much," said Jacob, lighting his cigar.

"Watcha wanna hunerd and fifty-two tickets fa, Ma?" Moe demanded.

"De Ladies' Auxiliary fomm de Temple."

Louis pursed his lips. He genuinely hated to deny his mother anything. "That's thirty dollars and forty cents' worth of tickets at twenty cents apiece, Momma."

"So fa toity dollahs you're a hero to de Ladies' Auxiliary."

"Fa thirty bucks they kin go to hell!" Moe said.

Momma glared at Moe. "Ladies fomm de Schul?" she asked indignantly.

"Fomm de Schul," Moe repeated.

"Why don't you boys have a benefit performance that after-noon?" suggested Jacob.

"Yes, and buy me a new dress," Rebecca grumbled. Louis looked up at her. "Schlemiehl!" she said reproachfully.

"What good's a Temple benefit gonna do us?" Moe asked.

"Lotsa good," answered Louis unexpectedly. "Listen, we plaster the whole Bronx with paper announcing Levinson and Korn of Amalgamated Films are giving a benefit matinee for the Beth Israel Synagogue at the Orpheum on Eighty-sixth Street. That's a big house. We give Momma her hundred and fifty tickets—"

"Feefty-*two!*" Momma interrupted, holding up two fingers.

"All right, a hundred and fifty-two tickets, and we charge fifty cents apiece for the rest of the house, balcony and all. So it's a charity and the Ladies' Auxiliary sells all the other tickets for us. Momma gets hers for nothing and we get a packed house. What can we lose?"

Moe got up and kissed the top of Momma's head. "Okay, sweet-heart," he said. "Next time ask fa two hunerd and we'll charge a buck."

"I got a good femily," Momma sighed proudly. She knew that af-ter the benefit she would be elected chairwoman of the Ladies' Auxiliary Entertainment Committee.

12

THE BRONX proved its loyalty to her philanthropic sons by travel-ing down to Manhattan in droves to see *A Woman's License.* The boys' success had become a matter of local pride. The New York *Times* in-terviewed them, their pictures were published in the papers, and wherever they went people began asking them for jobs. Everybody they knew bowed to them deferentially. Only Jacob Korn's glance became more and more quizzical. One night he called Louis to one side.

"Louis," he began, "you're a smart boy and a nice one. Moe? He's a bum. Nah, sure he's a success, so what? He's got Yiddisha gumption and little else. But you? You can be a gentleman. Now I want to tell you something."

"What is it, Jacob?" asked Louis, deeply touched because he at once admired and envied his father-in-law's wisdom.

"When I was a little boy, my father, Rabbi Korn, was asked what were the three things he most desired from life. And he answered, 'Gentility, humility, and economy.' When they next asked him why he chose such odd virtues instead of health, riches, and the conventional things, Father answered, 'My friends, I chose gentility because it holds the key to power, humility because that is the only approach to knowledge, and economy to enable me in my declining years to be providentially generous.' . . . And I think that even today those are pretty good precepts for us to live by. Now look at you, blustering around like a smart, important man. You know you're lucky and you know I know it. I want you to do something before it's too late and before they find you out. I want you to go to theaters and see plays —to concerts and hear good music. I want you to read books and acquire some measure of learning. My God, boy, people think you're a genius and you know nothing, absolutely nothing about fifty centuries of culture that have gone on before you. Take my advice, Louis, and remember I give it to you because I love you even better than my own son."

The old man's eyes filled with tears and he momentarily touched Louis's sleeve. Louis gulped quickly, took Jacob's hand and said, "I will, Father, I will."

13

THEN IT WAS that after purchasing the proper apparel, a dress suit for himself and evening gowns for Rebecca, the Levinsons, innocently enough, entered the magic world of the theater. It was a thrilling experience. Here on the stage their dreams had found the trappings of reality. Here at last they saw themselves across the footlights and listened to their unexpressed ambitions, hopes, despairs, embellished by the wit of Shaw, the grace of Schnitzler, the talents of such troupers as Laurette Taylor, Arnold Daly, Margaret Anglin, and a newcomer named Lynn Fontanne.

They were amazed that the world of culture contained such grand excitement because the very word itself struck fear into their hearts. Somehow culture in their minds had previously been identified with showing off, with being highbrow and superior, and it had embarrassed them.

Now they were free. Free to indulge a hitherto unrealized thirst, and they quenched it with spectacular abandon. They sampled other arts, attended exhibitions, lectures, concerts, but for the most part painting and music and the vast storehouse of literature left them cold.

The theater and its allied art, the motion picture, appealed to them more vividly.

And it was a motion picture that changed their destiny.

Louis took Rebecca to see *The Birth of a Nation*, and while they were in the theater Louis began wondering how his own picture managed to make as much money as it did. It was such a little thing in comparison with this—this epic. There on the screen, he thought, is something as vast as all America, something big, exciting, real. Something he never knew pictures could do before.

And suddenly he realized why other motion-picture companies were moving out west. There were too many difficulties connected with making movies around New York. Stage actors looked down upon the moviemakers. They felt that working in pictures jeopardized their theatrical standing. Out west, Louis had heard, actors came "a dime a dozen," living was cheap, the climate excellent, and the opportunities as great as the varied scenery he had been told slumbered unphotographed beyond the Rockies.

He decided to talk to Moe about it and when he did he was surprised that Moe agreed with him so readily.

"Hell," Moe said, "stage actors ain't no good fa pitchures. They won't move foiniture, paint scenery, or build sets. All they wanna do is act. And who the hell wants actors? Let's blow!"

"When do you think we oughta break the news to the folks?" Louis asked.

"After Thursday night dinner," Moe said. "Hit 'em when they're fulla wind. It's easier then. Their nerves is resting."

They played poker every Thursday night after dinner. It was a family ritual interspersed with blasphemy. But on this Thursday night the cards were never touched.

Louis rose to his feet just before Rebecca gathered up the dishes. It was the moment he and Moe had both agreed upon—a moment of destiny when he, Louis, was about to become the head of the family, to assume a great responsibility.

He looked around the table. Moe was the only one who noticed him. Momma, Rebecca, and Jacob were babbling away like mad. Like little children. They never even looked at him. Not once.

Louis waited with quiet dignity and closed his eyes. Moe smiled to himself and nudged Momma's elbow.

"What's with him?" he whispered, nodding toward Louis.

Momma glanced up sharply over her glass of tea. The spoon jiggled and the glass came crashing down.

"Votsa metta, Louis? You sick?" she cried.

Louis opened his eyes, but before he could answer, Rebecca, who felt that Louis's health was her concern and not his mother's, added, "You're white as a sheet. You better go to bed."

"Uh-huh, and me with him," Moe grinned. He was enjoying himself immensely. This wasn't at all what Louis had expected. Moe liked that. Liked it a lot. Louis was stuck, standing there with his dignity crammed down his throat by their affection.

They love the poor bastard, Moe smiled to himself. Listen to Jake. For Jacob was full of good counsel.

"She's right," he was saying. "Rebecca's right. You've been working too hard. You ought to take a rest."

"Maybe we better get a doctor," Moe suggested and he took a long, hard puff on his cigar. He had to, to keep from laughing.

"I'm all right," Louis protested weakly.

"Wyncha sit down then, dope?" Moe said. "Cantcha talk with yer ass in a chair?"

"Moe!" Momma swung at him.

Louis began to laugh and sat down. "Now, listen! All of you," he said. "Moe and me, we're leaving here. We're going out west. Our future lies out there."

"Cull Duktah Lentzboig—qvick!" Momma whispered to Rebecca.

Rebecca, tense, pushed her away. "Might I ask where, Louis?"

"Hollywood."

"And why, Louis?"

"I'll tell you why. Because it's cheaper to make pictures there. We gotta pay too much for stage actors here and out there we can make our own stars—at our own price. The lease is up on Bloomfield's studio, and we cleared twenty thousand on *A Woman's License*. In other words, we got the money and this is the time."

"And what happens to us in the meantime?"

"You and Momma and Jacob live here together, and after Moe and me's settled, we'll send for you."

41

"Don't be silly," Rebecca said. "Momma and Jacob can't live in the same house."

"Vye nod?"

"It's not right."

"Listen, Rebacca, at his age it's ull right," Momma said.

"At my age it's wonderful," Jacob said, and even as he laughed he sighed a little because he knew it wasn't true.

14

TWO WEEKS LATER Moe and Louis arrived at Los Angeles. They took rooms in a cheap hotel and began scurrying around town. Within a few months they managed to become moderately intimate with five independent, or "quickie," producers. They induced these gentlemen to sign a contract with them whereby Moe and Louis were to set about building a chain of distributing centers or exchanges in the fifteen leading American cities. This distribution corporation was henceforth to be known as Miracle Pictures, Inc., and the picture product of the five affiliates was to be released solely through the new organization.

Now, the establishment of exchanges postulated the presence of sufficient funds to rent offices, pay salaries, and acquire the necessary equipment to facilitate the shipment of film. The affiliates took this fact for granted. It was an illusion, however deviously arrived at, that Moe and Louis took pains not to destroy. They had no intention of risking their own twenty thousand in the venture. So they issued stock. Ten shares to each producer at a thousand dollars a share. Louis's eloquence and Moe's magnificent prodding gave the project the necessary impetus.

There are no national distributors for independents, they argued, and the small profits of their own picture, *A Woman's License,* could have been tripled if they had had a corporation like this behind them.

The five producers, who ranged from an erstwhile pants presser to a genuine college graduate, gradually fell in line and pretty soon Miracle Pictures, Inc., Louis Levinson, President, and Moe Korn, Vice-President, became an embattled tyro scavenging what business it could from the larger exchanges already established by the major companies in America's key cities.

For three months, aside from dividends and percentages paid the producers, Moe and Louis split twenty-six dollars apiece. And then the unexpected happened.

George Tilden, the college-bred picturemaker, produced a rip-roaring, full-length Western starring Buck "Hard-Hitting" Barrett. It had plenty of what the trade ads call "B. O. SOCKO" and it gave Miracle's exchanges their first taste of the extra profits in preferred bookings. These preferred bookings, the producers learned in no time at all, protected the "play dates" of first-run theaters by prohibiting neighborhood houses in any given territory from showing the picture until the expiration of a two weeks' protection period.

On the wall behind Moe's desk there was a title card that read:

PREFERRED BOOKINGS BRING
HIGHER FILM RENTALS

He pointed to it at least once a day.

Meanwhile, in New York, little Willie came down with pneumonia. Dr. Lansburgh wired Louis to come home, which he did, leaving the field to Moe. Jacob was of the opinion that Willie had been going about so long with the rear of his pajamas unbuttoned that the pneumococcus germ finally caught up with him. Willie recovered slowly and it was five months before he was able to make the trip to California.

In the meantime, Moe set about raising funds to build an entire motion-picture studio, completely equipped to handle six pictures simultaneously. This maneuver required all his vaunted ingenuity, as well as the assistance of George Tilden, who rapidly sensed that the Levinson-Korn duo was one of those unusual combinations that, through the grace of God, good fortune, and the dexterous manipulation of their own wits, would always manage to survive the constant unpredictable upheavals in the motion-picture industry.

Moe's plan was simple enough. He discovered that every time a producer planned a new picture he needed money to finance his production. That is, all but Tilden, who had amassed a considerable sum on his successful Western. Moe took Tilden into camp and they loaned the other four gentlemen the necessary funds. The only collateral they asked was an option, at a ridiculously low price, on their individual shares of stock in Miracle Pictures. The producers themselves, gratefully aware of this opportunity to produce the "Epic Sensation of the Season" without first mortgaging their homes, cars, and wives' jewelry, snapped at the offer. And when the pictures just managed to clear their negative costs, the Messrs. Korn and Tilden, acting in the interests of Louis Levinson, snapped up their options on the stock and in return gave each of the boys a contract to produce pictures for Miracle at a flat weekly salary.

This made the trio sole owners of Miracle Pictures. "But what," Moe asked Tilden, "is a pitchure company without a stujio?" So they took the balance sheets to the American Bank, convinced the gentlemen behind that venerable institution that Miracle Pictures was an excellent risk, and with their assistance issued enough common stock to enable them to break ground for the new plant.

Moe, as evidence of his good faith, invested their twenty thousand dollars in the venture. The bank, however, conceded his right to call that twenty-thousand-dollar investment preferred stock.

Building began in a moderately deserted valley about seven miles from Hollywood. Within four months, construction being what it was around Los Angeles, the studio was practically finished. Steel was seldom if ever used, and the moment the carpenters finished the skeleton of a stage, plasterers appeared and slapped stucco on the framework. This virtually completed the building. Motion-picture stages were then built without roofs so that the sun could pour down to light the scenes being photographed indoors. The intensity of this sunlight was controlled by rectangular streamers of white muslin suspended from the ceiling. These "reflectors" could be so manipulated as to deflect the light rays to almost any given corner of the stage.

The Administration Building, with its magnificent offices for Louis, Moe, and George Tilden, its suites for the now-abashed producers, its stenographers' cells and publicity offices, took somewhat longer to complete. But the building itself had already been erected and a bust of Louis Levinson had been installed over the front gate by the time Louis, Rebecca, Momma, Jacob, and little Willie arrived in California.

15

FROM THE BEGINNING it was obvious that Momma had no use for palm trees.

"Dey look like God fahgot to finish 'em," she complained. "A liddle dingus on top and a coppla bomps to de bottom, like a nekkid voman vid her hair op."

Willie squealed with laughter from the back seat.

"Ssh, Ma!" Rebecca admonished, pointing to her son.

But Momma just scowled and shouted "Look!" at the rattiest trees on their route from the station.

It had taken her too long to become chairwoman of the Beth Israel Ladies' Auxiliary Entertainment Committee to relish being whisked away to a new locale. Even Louis's bust over the gate failed to reconcile her.

"Vot good is it," she wailed, "ven I ken't tell nobody?"

All Louis's pleadings and Moe's exaggerated promises of big money proved useless. It was only when Jacob took her to the Los Angeles Synagogue that she responded, and then only begrudgingly.

"Sure, it's a high-kless Schul," she admitted, "but dey chotch fomm fife hunert dollahs a seat, vidout holidays. Beth Israel vas a boggin. A cut-rate Schul. Same God, too."

Jacob shrugged his shoulders. He loved the sun and the southern laziness of the place. And although he warned them all that "hot climates are no good for honest men," Rebecca still thought it was a grand adventure and little Willie thrived placidly in the garden of the middle-class hotel that was to be their home for the next five months.

Louis in the meantime went to work in the new Administration Building. Once his excitement and gratitude had worn off and he had become accustomed to the opulence of his office, George and Moe prevailed upon him to call in his producers.

They sat in a circle facing the mahogany desk behind which Louis sat, flanked by George and Moe. Louis nodded quietly to his producers.

These, then, were his "boys." To be sure, their new contracts guaranteed them a great amount of independence in the choice of stories, actors, and directors. And he would never encroach upon that freedom. Nevertheless, they must be kept constantly aware of the fact that only Louis Levinson had the right to renew or refuse the options on those contracts. And above all, they must be made to feel a certain pride in Miracle Pictures.

He suspected a few of them of being impractical dunderheads, but he firmly believed in an impartial trial—tempered, he admitted privately to Moe, by personal prejudice. He distrusted the aesthetic yearnings of most men, yet respected these same instincts in people like Richard Morse, whose reputation as a dramatic critic had preceded his entry into the motion-picture business.

To Louis, men like Morse were born to culture, and this assump-

46

tion, however erroneously arrived at, filled him with envy. It was his first personal contact with a man of even moderate fame and under Jacob's tutelage he had begun to confuse brains with breeding. Accordingly he found himself beaming at Morse, who was just finishing his speech welcoming Louis to the studio on behalf of the producers.

In reality, Richard Morse was a self-educated press agent and playreader who had eventually become the dramatic critic for a prominent New York daily. However, his reviews proved to be so bitter and biting that most of the theatrical producers pulled their ads out of his paper. This loss of revenue convinced the publishers that Mr. Morse was not their man. But Morse wasn't the type to be intimidated easily. He promptly produced a play that was, in his own words, "devoid of the sentimental balderdash that distinguishes our stage today." The play failed and Mr. Morse, unable to interest more capital in the premature wisdom of his conceits, lit out for the west where, after expounding his theory that "the difference between Sentiment and Sentimentality is the difference between Romeo and Casanova," he proceeded to produce the most sentimental epics on the screen.

Morse saw nothing paradoxical in this fact. He was a man of good taste with a keen instinct for luxury. The one naturally necessitated a compromise with the other. And compromise, he had learned, was the essence of good business.

He had made a good speech, he thought as he sat down. The kind of speech the boys had expected of him. It polished the apple without rubbing the skin off the damned thing.

He nodded to Moe.

The producers turned their eyes toward the new boss and waited.

The new boss suddenly felt intensely nervous and unsure of himself. Although speechmaking was nothing new to him, his tongue felt strangely thick and heavy.

He stood up slowly and surveyed the room.

"Gentlemen," he said, and he only vaguely remembered how he

had planned to begin, "we's got here the nutriment of a swell organization."

"Nucleus!" Tilden prompted.

"Look," Moe whispered hoarsely, "if he ain't talkin' it right, how come you know what he's tryin' to say?"

"I love him," George whispered back.

Louis paused. The mumbling behind his back had disturbed him. He turned around momentarily before resuming his speech. "George, who knows you better, disagrees with me," he said. "But I think you're a pretty good bunch of boys. You're smart. Smart enough to sell out to Moe and Tilden. . . ."

"We dint have a chance," Manny Adelstein grumbled in his beard.

"What did you say?" Louis asked, turning toward the former pants presser who now specialized in producing sex dramas.

Manny looked up at the new president, his heavy eyelids drooping as usual, so that he always appeared to be looking out from under them.

"I said Miracle Pictures was okay!"

"Yer a goddamn liar!" yelled Moe, pounding on the desk.

"Gentlemen," interrupted Louis, "please!" His mind was clear now and his thoughts came back to him with amazing clarity. "What I was about to say was that with our capital and your knowledge of production Miracle can't miss fire. And I must add that while it says in your contracts you have a complete choice in stories, directors, and actors, I think I ought to remind you at this time that there's nothing in those contracts that says we'll advance the money. However, if your choices are acceptable to our story committee, consisting of Moe Korn, George Tilden, and"—he coughed self-consciously—"myself, then I assure you, your backing will be unlimited."

And it virtually was, for Moe and Louis were selling stock to the public again.

16

LOUIS RODE HOME alone. He had begun to realize that one is infinitely more apt to find solitude in crowds than on solitary walks through the city. He always took the bus to the hotel and did his most constructive thinking in those thirty minutes to and from the studio.

This time his thoughts lingered not on the future of Miracle Pictures but on the reliability of his "boys."

In George Tilden he felt absolute confidence. After all, hadn't George joined forces with Moe? And wasn't Moe's judgement always good? Besides, Moe had said that in due time they could and would buy out George's interest in the business and he could remain as general manager. But some of the others—Manny Adelstein, for instance, with his perpetual leer, pockmarked face, and sullen expression. Who could trust a man like Manny? A man who had never really looked at people but sort of peered out at them from under his eyelids. Moe had said the guy was practicing for his deathbed, so's he could look out from under the pennies and watch his creditors. And while there was no doubt that Adelstein's sex dramas brought him notoriety and cash if not fame, Louis wasn't certain that he wanted Miracle Pictures identified with what he considered the most personal of human passions.

He felt vaguely apprehensive about Tim Sullivan, the burly, genial Irishman who had been making comedies ever since he deserted the mining-stock racket. Louis suspected that Tim's breath occasionally indicated a disposition toward the barroom.

Finally, aside from Richard Morse, there was T., for Theodore,

Monte Cooper. Cooper was the reigning director of the day. He produced and directed one spectacle a year. These spectacles never approached in humor or color the picture of Monte Cooper himself, in puttees and riding breeches, bawling stentorian, florid commands to assistants who shuddered with fear the moment they heard the great man's voice.

Louis, who knew that Cooper's latest epics had lost enough money for the larger studios to make him leap at the opportunity to tie up with a small one, was still proud to have the director associated with Miracle Pictures. He knew that Cooper's name alone added a great deal of prestige to his list of producers.

"They're a strange bunch," Louis muttered to himself. "If only I can get them to pull together . . . for me," he added as a cautious afterthought.

17

WITHIN A FORTNIGHT five productions were under way. According to the press notices released by the new publicity director, Jock Merington, whose employment was suggested by Richard Morse and approved by Louis, these productions were:

1.

Betrayed! . . .
By the Man She Loved!
ARLINE ARDEN
in
"LOVER'S ECSTASY"
A Manny Adelstein Production

2.

Passion!—In the most sumptuous elegance
ever devised by man!
T. Monte Cooper
presents
His Latest Lavish Spectacle
"SAINTED SINNERS"
featuring a cast of thousands.

3.

You'll Howl! You'll Roar! You'll Scream!
as Effie The Flea edits a fashionable magazine!
Tim Sullivan
presents
"LOUSE AND GARDEN"
A Comedy Cartoon

4.

Nothing More Tender
has touched the hearts
of a million moviegoers!
Richard Morse
presents
"ENCHANTED PARADISE"
featuring
The Beautiful
BELLE LA FOLLETTE
and
GREGORY MANFREDO

5.

A Rootin'! Tootin'! Shootin'! Drama
of the Plains . . .
Featuring America's Favorite Cowboy Star
BUCK "Hard-Hitting" BARRETT
Directed by JOHN DODGE   Story by HANK IVES
Tentative Title: "LORD OF THE RANGE"
FINAL TITLE: "KING OF THE WEST"

Headaches all of them. Louis had never been beset by so many difficulties. Arline Arden, the star of Manny Adelstein's production, *Lover's Ecstasy*, complained that the whole studio stank. "There ain't a man in it," she groaned. And she had firsthand information.

From the beginning of the picture she had taken a different grip home every night. When the director demanded an explanation and she answered, "I gotta *feel* my roles," he laughed at her and snapped, "Never mind that business . . . lay offa my crew! They come in here flopping around like drunk ducks after you get through with them."

"I know," she said. "It's getting so their legs can't carry their own weight in the mornings. It's awful, ain't it?"

She finally managed to land Manny Adelstein and at the conclusion of the picture sued him for twice her salary. She had Manny by the ears and when she won the suit Manny demanded that Miracle pay the judgment. "After all, I was on Company business," he told Louis.

Louis conferred with Moe, who took Adelstein out and socked him on the jaw. Adelstein sued Miracle Pictures. The court dismissed the case, claiming Moe Korn hit the plaintiff off the lot, therefore the company was not liable. Manny finally dropped his suit.

The pulse of power began to flow through Louis Levinson's finger tips. His five "boys" consulted him daily about their knottiest problems. Could they exceed the budget allowance on the number of extras employed in the mob scene? Oh, yes, they felt quite certain they'd balance the books by scrimping on the star's wardrobe.

Didn't Mr. Levinson prefer a humorous ending to *Lover's Ecstasy*? No? Why not? . . . Well, it was just an idea. . . .

Louis knew most of the answers and Moe generally anticipated those that were likely to embarrass him. However, through constant exposure, Louis himself became qualified to settle their most outlandish disputes. And it was only after he realized his own competence that he displayed the first symptoms of arrogance.

After all, there was a sort of logical reasoning to all this nonsense.

And if it was up to him to make decisions, he'd make them, and furthermore, make them as final as possible. Gradually the pronoun "I" crept into his opinions. And it must be honestly recorded that the use of the first person singular, as befitting a Hollywood Executive, gave him a certain eminence around the lot. Moe was the first to congratulate him, Rebecca the last. She intuitively sensed that a forceful male was a necessity in business and a nuisance around the house. Jacob warned her the transition would be one she wouldn't like, but she was a dutiful wife; therefore, while she outwardly admired his success, she never voiced her personal resentment toward his career. But they became slightly estranged. The camaraderie that had prevailed in the early days of their marriage became a thing of the past. Her affection for Willie increased. She began to worry about him. He had been coughing again.

18

SHE HATED to tell Louis that she feared for her son's health. Things had been going so well at the studio that it was a shame to worry him. But the better the future looked, the stranger Louis became toward her. Even his speech began to change. She noticed it gradually. Where he had once conscientiously tried to improve it, and barring the misuse of a big word here and there, he had managed to master the language rather well for an immigrant, now he didn't seem to care, and his studied English gave way to the jargon of the studio, particularly when he was excited or interested in his subject. It wasn't important. But Rebecca hated to see it.

They had started out right. But now something dreadful was beginning to happen. He needed her only when he had been disappointed or crossed. And Jacob had brought her up to feel that a wife played an integral part in a man's life. Sometimes she found herself hoping for a slight disaster that would bring them together again. Then she would become ashamed of her disloyalty and retire to the safety of monosyllabic replies to his stories about the picture business. He usually waited till they were alone in their bedroom, then while they were undressing he would regale her with the day's gossip. She almost betrayed herself one night, the night he told her about *Enchanted Paradise*.

"Well, ya shoulda heard Adelstein this morning," he said. "We looked at Morse's new pickcha, *Enchanted Paradise*. You know, the one with Belle La Follette. We just finished it, and honest, Rebecca, it's a beautiful thing. Such a sweet story, and so delicate! We're all sitting around thinking here's a tear-jerker that'll just clean up and alluva sudden Adelstein makes with the mouth. 'It stinks!' he says. That guy who knows from nothing! *He* pans it yet! Well, I didn't want to get too tough—after all, the whole gang knows what a dope Manny is—so polite-like I inquire, 'And just why are you of that opinion, Mr. Adelstein?' And he says, 'It's too fine.' Can you imagine that, Rebecca, 'too fine'! . . . One of my pictures is so good it won't make money. Ain't that something! Well, George Tilden sure shut him up. He looks at Manny and says, 'The only fines you know anything about are the kind you pay,' and you shoulda heard that bunch laugh. Well, we got a bet on, Manny and me, I say the pickcha'll gross more than anything we made except the spectacle and the Western—say, you oughta see that Western, it's a peacherino. . . ."

"Louis! What kind of fancy language is that?" Rebecca snapped.

"That's show-business talk," Louis answered proudly, dropping his shoes on the floor.

"It may be show-business talk, but it's bad English."

"So what! . . . Say—what the hell's the matter with you, anyway? You been driving me screwy for the last three weeks. Here I am, working like a horse, and all you do is sit around and feel superior."

54

"I'm sorry, Louis."

"Sorry . . . nuts!"

"Louis, I won't stand for such talk!"

"Tsk! Tsk! And what are you going to do about it, Miss Fency-Schmency?"

"You'll see!"

"Yeah, that's what Adelstein said and you're both wrong. I know a good picture when I see one and a stuck-up wife when I gotta live with one—and that's that!"

"Louis!"

There was no answer. Wearily she turned out the light. Tension, ever the daughter of darkness, stood between them and sleep. She stared blankly toward the ceiling waiting for him to say something. But he only tossed nervously in his bed. She wanted to say, "Louis, I'm sorry," but she couldn't speak. So she lay there resenting the power of the emotion that betrayed her into silence. It was really so simple. She had apologized. He should have sensed that. But she knew he didn't. She had earnestly begged his forgiveness, but because she couldn't say a few simple words he'd never know how she felt. And it was so dark, so lonely, so stupid to be excited by such nonsense. Tears slowly rolled down her cheeks and dampened the pillowcase. Louis finally turned.

"Are you all right, Rebecca?"

"Yes," she answered weakly.

"Then go to sleep."

"I can't."

"Why not?"

"I'm worried about Willie. He's been coughing lately."

"Don't worry about him. Go to sleep. He'll be all right."

But as time went on, Willie got worse.

19

GREAT CHANGES had occurred at the studio. The stage roofs had been closed over and Kleig lights installed. The semiannual stockholders' report showed a substantial profit. And Miracle Pictures was a going concern. Only one thing irked Louis. Manny Adelstein had been right. All the productions except Morse's were box-office successes. While critics paused to approve and express their gratitude to Miracle for *Enchanted Paradise*, the customers, as Manny raucously pointed out, never paused in their parade past the theater. And that, insisted Oracle Adelstein, was bad business. Louis disagreed with him on principle. He paid his bet and interrupted Manny's broad grin by calmly stating, "A producer who can make highbrow, good-will pictures within a limited budget is an asset to any studio, and I think Dick Morse is our man."

Then once again Moe Korn changed Louis's destiny. He and Tilden strolled into the president's office one sunny afternoon and glumly draped themselves in his best chairs.

"Now what's the matter?" Louis asked.

"We're not making enough money," answered Tilden.

"And tell me the name of the studio that'll pay you more?" Louis demanded.

"It ain't that," growled Moe.

"I know. You're not happy here. Well, I'll give you both twenty-five bucks more a week."

Louis was playing at being the boss, but Moe interrupted him. "If there's any salary raisin' to be done around here, I'm the guy to do it." He came over and sat on the edge of the desk. "Now lookit,

Louis, what we mean is Miracle Pitchures ain't makin' enough money."

"A hundred thousand dollars in six months! That ain't enough?"

"It ain't enough, Louis."

"Whadda ya talking about, Moe?"

"Simply this, Mr. Levinson," George Tilden said, "six months ago we released five pictures. On those five pictures we showed a net of a hundred thousand dollars and that's not enough."

"He's right!" echoed Moe. "We shoulda coined a hunerd thousand on *one* of 'em."

"And we think," continued George, "we've found the difficulty."

"Where?"

"Distribution."

"What's the matter with that? We've got exchanges all over the country just like the big companies," Louis protested.

"Yeah," replied Moe, "but their distribution centers is in New Yawk and thass where ours is gonna be!"

"And who's to take charge of the New York office?"

"You," Moe answered casually.

"And who runs the studio?"

"Me. With George," Moe added. "We buy George out and make him general manager for good. It's okay with him."

"Give me time to think it over."

"Sure," answered Moe, heading for the door. "We'll give ya a week."

Louis finally agreed. Still president of the company, he would control the main office in New York and make business trips to the Coast only when necessary. Moe and George would spend two months of the year in New York so that the production and distribution branches of the business wouldn't become entirely divorced from each other.

The family greeted the announcement with much hoopla. Momma began to yell for sturgeon, which could not be purchased in California. Jacob said he would be glad to leave a land where they

57

thought only in close-ups and long shots, and Rebecca was grateful for a chance to take Willie to Dr. Lansburgh who, she was sure, could cure him with a look.

20

DR. RICHARD LANSBURGH

PATIENT'S RECORD

DATE: Oct. 1, 1920

NAME: Levinson, Wm......ADDRESS: Hotel Carnegie, 79 St. & CPW
(temporary)

PHONE: Schuyler 3900

AGE: 6....BORN: July 1915....HEIGHT: 3 FT. 11 IN. WEIGHT 47 LBS.

PREVIOUS ILLNESS: Bronchial pneumonia ....

PRESENT AILMENT: Lobar pneumonia. Pleurisy in both lungs......

TREATMENT: Incision. Pleural cavity now draining ....

NOTES: Patient at Mt. Sinai Hospital....Room 401 ....

THEY SAT SILENTLY around the room. The shades were drawn. Their eyes roamed from the white walls to the bed and back again. Whenever the doctor of necessity left William's bedside, their vigil became a nightmare of anxiety. Even the vigilance of Rosa Kurtzmann, a scrawny, efficient German nurse, brought no reassurance.

The doctor had said, "Prayers for the sick are seldom heard, and if they are, it's mostly by the patient."

But the Levinsons knew better. Generations of futility had taught them the sanctuary to be found in the ritual of words and if what the doctor had said was true, Willie heard many prayers.

Dr. Lansburgh had told them to expect the crisis tonight. There was nothing to do but wait. To watch the fitful seizures, the rattling cough, the sweats and racking gasps for breath. For two days now they'd waited. This, then, would tell the tale. The doctor entered. They sat there dumbly, their senses heightened by physical fatigue, and watched him count young William's pulse. He injected a sedative into the boy's arm, patted Rebecca on the head, touched Momma lightly and whispered, "I think he'll be all right. Go in the next room and get some sleep. I'll be back in an hour."

"He always says, 'get sleep . . . get sleep.' How can one sleep?" Rebecca cried in anguish.

When the doctor finally returned he brought three husky interns with him. "Let's have an end to all this nonsense," he said. "Rebecca, drink this!" Meekly she drank. Then he dosed Ma, Jacob, and Louis before he examined William. Finally he turned and saw their sagging bodies.

"Take them out, boys. Get them undressed and into bed." He sat by William's bedside.

At nine in the morning the doctor went into Rebecca's room. Wearily he pulled up the shade. Rebecca opened her eyes. She recognized him. Her face grew taut.

"Doctor," she cried brokenly, "I know it. He's dead. . . . My only boy. . . . He's dead . . . I saw him die. He was asking for me. . . . I dreamed all night . . . he was asking for me . . . and you —you drugged me and I wasn't near him when he wanted me. . . ."

"Rebecca," he said, stroking her forehead, "your boy's alive, and well. Now get some sleep."

21

THREE TIMES the taxicab stopped uncertainly on its journey through East 95th Street. Finally Rebecca shouted, "That's it! Twenty-six—and it's beautiful!"

One by one the Levinson family emerged from the cab. Only Louis was missing—he had had to go to the office. His place was taken by Willie's nurse, Rosa Kurtzmann, who had been persuaded by means of fruit, excess flowers, and an old dress of Rebecca's to join them in their new abode.

Momma put her hands on her hips and watched Rosa carry Willie across the sidewalk and into the big brownstone house. If only Poppa could have lived to see this day. "Ve come a long vay, Poppa leben, a long vay!" she sighed.

Rebecca wondered what it would be like inside. She had rented it sight unseen on Dr. Lansburgh's recommendation. He has described it as a large, spacious house belonging to a patient of his, a Mr. Holden, who was being sent to Europe for his health. If they liked it, the house was theirs indefinitely on a yearly basis and he felt they'd be very happy in it.

Rebecca took the key out of her purse, but before she could use it the door opened. Startled, she looked up and saw a smiling middle-aged Negro framed in the doorway.

"I'm George," he said. "You're Mrs. Levinson?"

Rebecca nodded. Momma's face broke into an astonished grin and she nudged Jacob. "See," she said, "vite coat en evvy-ting!"

"Dr. Lansburgh's waiting for you in the drawing room," George said.

"Dr. Lansburgh!" Rebecca cried in surprise. She turned to Rosa. "You'd better get Willie to bed," she said.

"Second floor rear, ma'am." George smiled at Rosa. "The bed's all made up."

Rosa started up the stairs to the parlor floor, followed by the family. "Hello!" Dr. Lansburgh called down to them from the landing. "Welcome to your new home."

They crowded around him and he led them into the living room. Rebecca took a quick look at the bay window, velvet draperies, and overstuffed chairs, and sighed a deep, slow, satisfied sigh.

On the coffee table in front of the couch was a magnificent silver service. Beside it stood a rather large Negro woman, beaming at them.

"This is Fanny," the doctor said. "George's wife. Mr. Holden recommended them very highly. They worked for his sister for many years, and Fanny's an excellent cook."

"She cooks kosher?" Momma asked suspiciously.

Fanny's smile vanished and she looked to the doctor for guidance. "She certainly does," he said quickly. "Southern-fried kosher."

"That I don't want to miss!" Jacob laughed.

"Don't worry about the dietary laws now, Momma," Rebecca said.

Lansburgh led Momma to a chair beside the fireplace. "Sit down," he said, "all of you. I thought you'd like some coffee. Fanny, you and George help the nurse put Willie to bed, and I'll pour. Cream and sugar, Mrs. Levinsky?"

"I dun't care if I do," Momma said elegantly.

Rebecca sank into the cushions on the couch and sighed again. "This is like a wonderful dream," she said, "a wonderful dream."

"It's absolutely first-class!" Jacob agreed.

When Lansburgh handed her the coffee, Rebecca looked up at him and murmured, "We owe you so much it's almost impossible for us to thank you enough."

The doctor smiled. "I have to see that my patient's well taken care of, don't I? If anything happens to Willie I'll have all of you on my hands."

"Is a reglah femily man, de duktah," Momma announced. "Vyncha gaht married? Is no good a man nod merried."

"You find me a girl." The doctor grinned. "A nice one, like your daughter-in-law. Unfortunately, all the people I know are rich here," and he flicked his thumb against his index finger. "Not here," he added, touching his chest.

"No richness in their souls," Jacob nodded.

"Mr. Korn, they've got no souls—they've just got dinner parties."

"Vot he neets is a femily," Momma insisted.

Dr. Lansburgh shook his head. "My family's growing every day, Mrs. Levinsky. The babies I bring into the world for other people— they're my family. And Willie was the first. He'll always be my favorite."

22

TWO YEARS passed. Rebecca rode around town in a limousine and Momma complained about the stairs in the 95th Street house. Moe came in from California for a short visit, sneered at Rebecca's fashionable furniture, and trundled off without so much as a word of parting. To be sure, he gave Louis a quizzical glance just before he left, but then Louis's life was his own business. Moe just wanted to get back to the giddy informality of the west. He hated anything stuffy, whether it was shirts, sofas, or people. Furthermore, he liked being called "the big little executive" at the studio, and under the guidance of George Tilden and Moe, Miracle was producing a goodly number of acceptable movies that were sold and exploited to the hilt by Louis and his staff in the New York offices in the Times Square district.

Willie was growing up. He was beginning to cast envious eyes at the neighborhood gang that gathered on the corners of 95th Street and Madison Avenue in the middle of the afternoon. This gang was drawn out of the aggregation of tenements, apartment houses, and private dwellings that framed 95th Street from Fifth to Third avenue. There were about fifteen youngsters of diverse colors, creeds, and instincts. That they got along at all was one of those inexplicable miracles of youth. They were bitter, cruel, and instinctive artists at mayhem, but somehow the mere fact that they lived in the same locality served to hold them together; that, and their hatred for governesses.

Willie knew intuitively that he'd have to get rid of Rosa before he could become a member of the gang.

It took him two months to convince Rebecca and Louis that few of the youngsters attending the public school were deposited and collected there by nurses. And when Rebecca had pointed out that Mrs. Stein's children (heirs to Stein's Scintillating Two-Reel Comedies) were not only called for by their nurse but were also driven to school in the family car, it looked as though William had lost his fight for independence. But Jacob came to his rescue.

"If the Stein children are so excessively chaperoned," he said doubtfully, "then I feel sorry for them. They must hate school because the other pupils must laugh at the very things you find enviable about the Stein children. They would probably like to drown their nurse and walk to school. I think it would be a good idea to let Rosa go. It's about time William was left somewhat to his own devices. A dozen children in this neighborhood go to that school and he might easily run down there with them."

So Rosa was given her notice and Willie gradually found himself accepted in the gang.

One afternoon after a hockey game broke up because some of the older boys had to go home to do their homework, the rest of the athletes retired to a neighboring stoop and began to rehash the World War. Eventually the discussion drifted toward the fascinat-

63

ing subject of "How My Father Won the War." Those who were fortunate enough to have had a parent in uniform hogged the conversation and stuck out their chests. Those who didn't conceived elaborate tales concerning their fathers' having been in the Secret Service, or having been sent on secret missions by the President.

Louis Levinson would have been somewhat surprised to learn that his son had, in the space of a few moments, created him Colonel in Charge of Entertainment for the whole A.E.F. But Willie was merely defending his family's honor. It was Jacob who bore the brunt of the afternoon's discussion. He got quite a turn when Willie bounded into his room and asked accusingly. "Why weren't you in the war?"

The old man, realizing the flood of questions that might follow were he to do the simple thing and answer, "I was too old," fell back on the teachings of the Talmud and growled, "My son, I have always been suspicious of glory. . . . Now, go!"

His inquisitor frowned and left.

Two days later in the middle of a stickball game Willie struck out with the bases full. The next lad up poled out a triple and one of the older boys, chiding Willie for his failure to come through in the pinch, said, "Why couldn't you do that?"

Willie, striking a moderately superior attitude, lisped, "My friend, I have always been suspicious of glory."

Rebecca shrieked when she saw her son's black eye at dinner.

23

WILLIE had just turned eleven when in August, 1926, the motion-picture industry found itself on the brink of a transition that eventually forced it out of its infancy and into adolescence. Immediately after having heard a few Warner Brothers' musical shorts in Hollywood, Moe called his staff together. This staff had in the space of five lucrative years grown considerably beyond the paltry five producers and one publicity director who originally constituted the nucleus of Miracle Pictures' Production Unit. There were now at least fifteen additional satellites, ranging from head title writer to chief cameraman, who were always included in important studio conferences. Therefore, Moe's office looked more like a political rally than an executive's retreat when he savagely announced from behind his desk, "Boys, we've had a lotta trouble with 'em before—but you ain't seen nothin' yet. . . . Now they've gone ahead and made the goddamn things TALK!"

And trouble it was! Stars upon whom studios had lavished millions of dollars' worth of publicity became a liability overnight. Directors who had never been inside a theater in their lives found a new medium completely beyond their comprehension. Hollywood's writers rose from their beds in daily sweats of fear. Technicians such as film cutters, set builders, cameramen, and electricians became for the first bewildering time conscious of the fact that the world had ears; and within a few months there was no more devastating description of a "has-been" than "he was a star in the silent days."

The conversion to sound was a slow process, accompanied by a great deal of fanfare and confusion. Every motion-picture company advertised its own particular brand of equipment as the best in the world. At first, the ballyhoo appealed successfully to the curiosity of moviegoers. It took a sort of courage to remain in the theater through pictures that started out as "good old silents" and suddenly began blasting away at the customers' eardrums. Eventually patrons began to resent the fact that they were being subjected to some of the weirdest shrieks that ever leaped from a silver screen. But despite these legitimate objections, movies with recorded music were still advertised as sound pictures and it was fully a year, or about four hundred fifty movies, before the vast picture audience was treated to its ultimate blessing, an all-dialogue feature.

The first one to hit the market was *The Lights of New York,* and what that production, plus the first part-dialogue film, *The Jazz Singer,* did to box-office records was enough to convince hesitant executives that the innovation was no plaything but a necessity.

Thereupon they organized talent departments and began scouring the legitimate stage for likely-looking actresses who could at least "say the words right," because many of the old Hollywood queens spoke gutter English or had foghorns that would empty a theater more quickly than a fire alarm. And when Moe suddenly realized that a voice could betray its owner, he paused to remark anent his female stars that between "deses and doses" he was going crazy. To which statement Richard Morse quietly replied, "It must be quite a strain."

In due time Morse, an old theater man, became Moe's prime consultant, supplanting even George Tilden, who nevertheless because of his contract remained the general studio manager. Morse, ever an idealist, suggested that it might be cheaper to teach the old stars English than to buy and publicize new ones. This plan seemed feasible enough until Arline Arden, playing an English noblewoman, turned to the director, Monte Cooper, in the middle of a scene in which she had been advised to use the long "a" wherever possible. She had followed instructions to the letter, but when she struck the word "elevator" and elaborately pronounced it "elevahtor," she felt she'd done enough for her art. So she just looked at the camera and suddenly announced, "We ain't gonna get far this way, brother!" And she was quite right. She was a bright girl and knew her limitations.

Arline Arden gave up her art and embarked on a new and more exciting career shortly after sound became a motion picture necessity.

A few weeks after she'd retired from the screen Louis entered Moe's new fifty-thousand-dollar Hollywood mansion in response to a wire requesting his immediate presence, and was considerably surprised to encounter his former star spread-eagled across the living-room divan and quite obviously mistress of the place. A beady-eyed Pomeranian leaped out of her lap and began yapping briskly at Louis's toes.

"You live here?" he inquired delicately.

Arline nodded coyly. "It's a secret, Louis," she said, "but you might as well know."

"Where's Moe?"

"If he's not at the stujio I'll beat the bejesus out of him."

The Pomeranian snuggled back into his mistress' lap. . . .

Louis nodded, pursed his lips, and fled.

He barged into Moe's office unannounced. Morse and George Tilden jumped up, ran toward him, pounded his back and pumped his arm enthusiastically.

"Just because he's the president ya don't hafta break him in half, boys," Moe interrupted, while he strode across the room to greet his brother-in-law.

"Welcome, old sonuvabitch!" he said, leading Louis toward the most comfortable chair.

"Don't you sonuvabitch me!" Louis snapped, jerking his elbow from Moe's grasp.

Morse and Tilden looked at each other and sensed that departure was the best form of diplomacy. Moe stopped them before they reached the door. "Don't go, boys!" he called. "Louis's got a complaint and we all work together in this joint. What's on ya mind, Louis?"

"It ain't business," Louis snarled.

"Is it about me?" queried Moe.

Louis nodded.

"They stay," said Moe. "They're muh pals."

"All right, you asked for it. What's that Arden dame doing in your house?"

"Oh, ya bin to the house awready!"

"Yeah."

"Louis, if you don't know what that Arden dame's doin' in my house ya ain't half the man I thought ya was."

"Yeah, I know all about that, Moe. But why Arden? Everybody knows what a tramp she is!"

"Oh, Mr. Levinson," Richard Morse interrupted, "Arline's not as bad as all that! You might say she's the studio's relict, but I wouldn't call her a tramp."

"Relic ain't the half of it, Morse," yelled Louis, thoroughly aroused. "That dame's an antique!"

"She may be ninety," Moe announced calmly, "but she's the best lay in town."

"And he knows!" Tilden added, opening the door and pushing Morse out ahead of him.

"Now that we're alone, Moe," Louis continued, "I must tell you that you ought to be ashamed of yourself."

"Louis, fa Chrissake! Wotsa madda with ya? Ya gone meshugga in kopf? Do I ask you how's with you and Becky, and how she is in bed, yet? Do I?"

"That's different, Moe," Louis replied indignantly.

"So what's different about it? I don't know what's got into ya. What the hell business is it of yours what I do? And who the hell are you to tell *me* what you think? You keep your schnozzola outta my affairs, Louis, and I mean *out*. O-U-T, with capitals! Get it?"

Louis lifted his eyes and spoke very quietly. "In that case, I'm afraid I can't stop at your house, Moe," he said.

Contrition suddenly struck Moe. He came over to Louis's chair and leaned forward. His voice was husky. "Listen, guy," he said, "I hate to say this, but watchu are ya owe to me. Nobody else on earth. And I got a real feelin' for ya. Nothin' should ever come between us, ya know that."

Louis nodded. He was near tears.

"Tell ya what I'll do," Moe continued. "I'll send Arline away while yer here. I'll get hell for it, but I'll do it. It'll gimme a chance ta get that mutt outta the house for a while. Now will ya stay with me?"

"Sure, Moe, I'll stay, and she can, too. But for God's sake don't tell Rebecca. She'd be out on the next train to rescue you and save me from the sinful life."

"Chris'!" Moe groaned. "My onney chance ta get ridda that goddamn Frou-Frou and you gotta turn it down!"

"Frou-Frou you call her?" Louis asked, and his eyes twinkled with amazement.

"Not her—the dawg."

"You don't like the dog?"

"You crazy? Yap, yap, yap, all night long! I should like that? He gimme the creeps!"

"Poor Moe," Louis sighed, his eyes twinkling with mock sympathy. "You can't have everything!"

"I'll get ridda that mutt wunna these days, if it's the las' thing I do. You'll see."

"I'm afraid if he goes, she goes too."

"To the *bathroom* they go together!" Moe bellowed, and both of them roared with laughter.

"Oh, Moisha," Louis finally sighed between chuckles, "I'm sorry I yelled like I did, but it was a pretty big shock seeing her there."

"Shock, hell! Get this through ya head, Louis, what I feel fa you comes from my heart. What I feel fa her . . ."

"Moe!" Louis interrupted, waggling a cautious finger. "Tell me what you got me out here for."

"The business ain't what it was, Louis. It ain't no fly-by-nighter's paradise no more. It's a industry. A great, big, wunnaful industry! It needs businessmen, and you're the businessman. There's enough punks like me. We need an accountin' deppommint, quick. Our own. We're payin' fat fees to a lotta outside pencil pushers and fa why, when we can get our own guys can make two and two come out five? You tell me! I think you're the guy to hannel this, anyway. You're

69

gonna be in contack with them from New Yawk alla time, you pick 'em.

"Another thing. We gotta set up a legal staff right here, onna lot. Nunna this runnin' downtown to a lawyer's office stuff. We need 'em under our schnozzles, now! Why, just the other day some dope sues Pathé fa half the profits on *The Life of Count Bernstein*. How should Pathé know the guy was alive? Or there was a Count Bernstein? Pathé makes pitchers, it ain't inna history business! The guy's family sued and *collected!* It takes brains ta perteck a studio these days, and you got 'em! Anyway, ya got that kinda brain. Thass why I called ya out here. Give ya a chance ta pick yaself a coupla shysters, hire some bookkeepers, and most important of all, I thoughtcha'd like ta see what's goin' on around here these days before ya go back. Tain't like it use ta be, Louis. We got new stars, new directors, new people ya oughta meet. So far their president's just a guy behind a desk in New Yawk and we gotta have closer contack."

Louis went up to the desk and poured himself a drink of water. "You're a great guy, Moe," he said after two long swallows. "I don't know what I'd do without you."

"I do," answered Moe. "You'd be sittin' behind a desk inna garment center doin' twice the work and gettin' half the dough. Le's go home."

At dinner they discussed plans for the new year. Arline sat at the head of the table and said very little.

24

WHEN MOE CONDUCTED his brother-in-law on a tour of the lot the next day, Louis was visibly impressed. Their little studio had grown up into a huge, sprawling plant. For two hundred fifty thousand dollars, the expenditure he had okayed in New York, Moe had built them a city with its own hospital, restaurant, and power generator. New buildings housing the stenographic, cutting, publicity, and property departments had sprung up overnight. Even the Administration Building had been renovated and Moe had insisted on electroplating the bust of Louis that crowned the studio's main gate.

"That's an extravagance, Moe," Louis protested as they walked around the lot together.

"Nothin's an extravagance till somebody tells ya about it," said Moe, with a grin.

"Thanks, anyway."

"It ain't much," Moe said, leading Louis to the climax of the survey.

Before them, giving an impression of Gibraltar-like solidity, stood the vast mass of concrete that was listed in the studio's inventory simply as "Sound Stages 7, 8, and 9."

Louis took a deep breath and touched Moe's sleeve. "It's wonderful!" he exclaimed.

The door to Stage 7 opened slowly in front of them.

"Le's go in. Price's shootin' *Twinkling Toes* in there," Moe said.

Louis looked up and laughed as they walked through the huge entrance into the Hangar of Art.

"What gives?" Moe asked.

"I was just thinking. It seems like only yesterday when the top of the stage was open and we hung muslin around to reflect the light."

"We come a long way since yestiddy."

"You bet!" Louis said, as he saw the veritable latticework of catwalks suspended from the ceiling. Men meandered slowly along these catwalks trimming arc lamps and changing their angles.

"Electricians," Moe said. "The lamps fit in grooves. They move 'em and turn 'em on and off. Fa that we gotta pay a fortune. Such a union!" He slapped the side of his face for emphasis. "They call a strike like it was a fire drill. Come on."

They walked past a hundred people lounging on boxes, stage furniture, and camp chairs. Some were smoking cigarettes, others chatted quietly in the gloomy shadows of the stage. When a glamorous-looking girl walked by and disappeared into her dressing room, not one of the extras turned to look at her. Theirs was the snobbery of unsuccessful people, and Louis never suspected that hatred and envy lay behind their indifference and contempt.

Nevertheless, he felt suddenly uncomfortable before them. He forgot momentarily that he was an executive and it embarrassed him to realize that he was the head of a business that treated human beings like cattle. Their listlessness filled him with a strange foreboding and he began to contemplate their futures with anxiety until he noticed that Moe was staring at him.

"Extras," Moe said quickly. "Five bucks a day. Seven-fifty in evening clothes. Twenny-five bucks if they speak a line. They register at Central Casting and are on call any time. Dopes, most of 'em."

Louis shook his head. "Moe," he said, "you're a mean guy."

"Sure. Ain't it swell? . . . Come on, there's the director. . . . Hey, Mel!"

Mel Price, who had been talking to his cameraman and assistant director, stopped abruptly in the middle of a sentence and turned toward the sound of Moe's voice. Catching a glimpse of the production chief through the haze, he waved and shouted, "Be right over, Moe!"

"A Harvid graduate," Moe explained to Louis while they waited. "Bright guy. Been makin' Westins. Made eight last year. Not a turkey inna bunch. Morse thinks he talked me inta givin' him a chance. But I tabbed him long ago. He come to me and says, 'Mr. Korn, I wanna do sump'm big. I hate cowboys.' So I says, 'Okay, Pricey, you're gonna do sump'm big. The biggest! *Twinklin' Toes.* Like the yearbook says, 'the most breathtakin' spectickle of song and dance and fun ever concocted!'

" 'I'm gonna do that, Mr. Korn!' he says, and the poor slob almost falls on his hands and knees thankin' me. . . . 'Sa crazy business, Louis."

"And you're not helping it any." Louis laughed.

Moe never even heard him. He was thinking what a crazy business it really was, and he was thinking out loud. "Yestiddy the guy's a nobody. Tidday he's a big shot. Awreddy he's got trouble talkin' ta himself. Nose inna air, a reglah A director. . . . Come on, Mel!" Moe shouted impatiently.

"Coming, sir, coming," Mel yelled. Then he concluded his instructions to the cameraman, forced a genial grin onto his face, and ambled over to Moe.

He regarded his boss's cheery greeting with increasing alarm until he heard the name, "Mr. Levinson." Then he smiled and shook Louis's hand. "You know, Mr. Levinson," he said, "I was just beginning to think you were a fictional character invented for the benefit of the stockholders."

Louis blushed uncomfortably till Moe came to his rescue.

"Don't mind him, Louis, he's just a hangover from Harvid. Listen, Mel, I gotta get back ta the office. Go on like Louis wasn't here, but show him the works. He ain't been on a movie set since sound was invented."

"With pleasure," said Price, guiding Louis toward the immense structure that towered above the forbidding gloom of smoke and emptiness that is a peculiarity of all "dead," or unoccupied and unlighted movie sets.

They were getting ready to shoot the big number.

"Okay, Joe?" Mel asked his chief cameraman, Joe March.

"Any second now, boss."

"Any second now," Mel muttered, half to himself and half to Louis. "The girls have been rehearsing their routines since nine this morning. Here it is three o'clock, we haven't shot a foot of film, and he says, 'Any second now, boss.' "

Mel Price suddenly nudged his cameraman. "This is Mr. Levinson, Joe," he said.

"I'll be goddamned!" Joe snorted. "The president himself!" Then he shouted to the electricians, "Hit 'em, boys!" and walked over to the camera.

Hissing sounds came from the catwalks and the set came to life in a flood of brilliantly diffused light.

An assistant director ran up to Price. "We're ready, sir," he announced.

"Okay. Let's take it."

"Places!" shouted the assistant.

The girls streamed out from the far corners of the set, climbed onto the tiers rising from the stage, and waited patiently.

Joe March shouted down to Price from his perch alongside the camera, "Okay, Toots! We're ready to roll."

"Excuse me, Mr. Levinson," said Mel, walking to the middle of the stage, accompanied by his assistant director. "Give 'em the whistle, Mortie." Silence descended on the set. All eyes focused on Mel Price.

"Girls," he said, "let's see if we can't wrap this one up in one take. Don't be nervous. You all know the routine. And if it doesn't pan out right, we can always do it again. But the cokes are on me if you hit it on the nose first time out. All set? Watch me and I'll cue you."

He stepped back toward the camera. "Mind if I ride with you, Joe?"

"Hop on," Joe said.

"You ready, kid?" he asked, as he climbed onto the seat in front of March.

"Yeah."

"Okay! . . . Roll 'em!" shouted Mel.

The slate boy stepped in front of the camera holding aloft a combination blackboard and clapper.

"Sound rolling!" yelled the man at the "mike."

"Start your music!" shouted Mel.

After a few introductory bars he nodded toward the star, Gladys Creighton, who took a deep breath, paused momentarily, then with professional accuracy timed and controlled her voice so that it blended in gently with the music. Gradually she increased the volume until the orchestra was a deftly shadowed overtone.

Then Price beckoned the girls. Down they leaped to surround the star. It was an altogether stunning effect, and Louis, who was at that time seeing something startlingly new, moved back a few feet in an attempt to capture the image that was being recorded on film. Now he was far enough behind the set to watch the mechanics of shooting a movie. Like little gnomish gargoyles, three men sat protruding from the side of the camera as it swung slowly forward like a huge gun finding the range of some far-distant target. All the menace of impending disaster seemed expressed in that relentless maneuver of the camera seeking out its prey. Louis watched, fascinated. These men were doing something interesting, exciting, something that was fun. While he sat in an office all day dealing impersonally with men and film alike, these boys were living all the glamor to be found in a great industry. Right now, he thought, I'd rather work on a set than be president, and then he remembered Rebecca and her unexpressed gratitude for luxury. He'd seen it in her eyes so often. Maybe it's better this way, he concluded, but someday I'm going to direct a picture. And in that conceit he expressed the longing of almost everyone connected with a studio. Directors yearn to be producers. Writers are often inhibited actors. Actors long to write, and producers fight each other year in, year out, in the vain hope that someday one of them may become president of the company.

Louis tiptoed forward again. The girls were concluding the number. Creighton sang at the top of her lungs. The orchestra blared triumphantly toward the finale. The camera, suspended in mid-air, seemed precariously close to toppling over and dumping its attendants into the middle of the arena, when suddenly Gladys Creighton stopped singing and walked off to one side of the set, where she stood with her arms folded across her chest, tapping one foot defiantly on the floor.

"Cut!" Price yelled quickly. "What's wrong, Gladys?"

75

Gladys's eyes narrowed. "Just how long do you expect me to hold that stinking note?" she demanded.

Silence enveloped the stage.

"The only stinking note around here," Mel said casually, "is the one you add. . . . Okay, boys, break it down for a close-up." He turned and shouted to the chorus, "The cokes are still on me, kids! You were swell!"

The boom brought the camera down. Mel stepped off. Louis walked up to him.

"She seemed to be singing very nicely. What made her do that, Mr. Price?"

"Don't you know, sir?" Mel asked earnestly.

"No, I don't."

"Well, it's all very simple. She just wants the number to end on her close-up. And she won't do another thing until she gets her way. Some people call it temperament. I call it selfishness. She's famous for that kind of thing. But she's been so nice for the past few weeks I'd forgotten about it. . . . Say, I've got an idea. She doesn't know you're here. I just want her to meet you. Stick around a second."

Louis wanted to flee. He didn't like the lady, and furthermore, if she'd carry on like that in public, there was no telling what she might say to his face. And he couldn't stand for that sort of thing. He turned to go and bumped into Mel and the star, who had come around behind him.

"Miss Creighton, I'd like you to meet Mr. Levinson, the president of Miracle Pictures, you know. He watched your last scene and thought you were particularly delightful."

"I did nothing of the sort," Louis blurted out. "I thought you were an extremely rude young lady."

Mel grinned broadly. Gladys Creighton looked bashfully toward the floor.

"I'm sorry, sir," she murmured.

Louis paid no attention to her. "I'm going to Moe's office, Mr.

Price," he said. "If he calls, tell him I'm on my way up, and thank you so much. You've really been very kind."

They shook hands. Louis walked toward the door.

As soon as he left the stage, Gladys whipped around to Mel.

"Nice guy!" she sneered.

"Served you right, Tootsie," he answered.

Gladys Creighton put her hands on her hips and hissed, "Now, listen here, baby, I been a nice girl till now. Do I get my close-up or don't I?"

She did.

25

IT WAS no mere accident that the Miracle Pictures' Conference Room approximated a feudal banquet hall. The décor had been suggested by Moe, who wanted "something big," and executed by George Tilden, who had the university graduate's instinctive reverence for Gothic architecture.

Fifteen men sat around a long oak table with ash trays and paper pads in front of them. The fifteen men were most uncomfortable because their hind ends, accustomed to plush upholstery, were parked in high-backed wooden chairs that were as uncompromising as the sixteen century clerics who had once sat in the originals. They welcomed the opportunity to rise to their feet when Moe and Louis entered the room.

It was a respectful gesture, accepted by both executives as a natural expression of esteem. They smiled briefly and sat down side by side at the head of the table, thereby starting the conference.

Mr. Korn rose, removed a cigar from his mouth, and leaning forward in the confidential manner adopted by professional executives, voiced the following sentiments to his audience: "Boys, this here's no reglah meetin'. This time the *president's* got sump'm on his chest. And I ain't gonna do my talkin' till he gets through. All of ya know him and mosta ya love him. If ya don't ya'd better. . . . Okay, Louis."

The telephone rang before Louis could get up. Moe answered it.

"She whaat!" he exploded, raising his hand for silence. His expression changed from surprise to anger. "A bonus she wants! I'll give her such a bonus she won't siddown fa a week! Who in hell does she think she is?" Long pause . . . then, impassively, "What *can* we do? She's got us. We're more'n halfway through the show. . . . Put her onna phone."

Moe looked around the room. The boys were watching him and some of them smiled nervously. Morse said, "Bet it's Creighton." Moe nodded at him.

"Gladys?" he said into the phone. "Ya know what happens to little girls who get their poppas mad at them?"

Another pause, then Moe suddenly shrieked, "Two hunerd more a week? Yer off ya nut!"

Tilden grinned at Morse.

"'Not a chance, babe! We got a contrack. . . . Ya don't care, eh? Okay, but yer agent will. You behave yaself, angel-puss, or ya'll never work in this town again. Never! . . . Ya'll take fifty bucks? You kill me! Ya'll take watcha get and ya'll get twenny-five and fa my part ya can shove it up—yeah, that's right! And fa Chrissake try actin' like a lady, ya tramp!"

He held the phone a foot away from his ear and winked as he turned it toward the boys. They began to snicker as Gladys ran through the ABC's of profanity. When she approached the fatal letter, Moe yelled, "G'bye, now!" and hung up. Then he leaned over and whispered in the president's ear, "Louis, fa Chrissake stop tellin' people watcha think of 'em. Out here that costs dough!"

Louis, who had been looking around the room, nodded impatiently. He hadn't seen most of these men for many years. The nucleus of his old company sat around the table, but he wondered if they would still respond to him. Moe had won their loyalty, or what loyalty you could expect in a cutthroat business, and Louis had no intention of encroaching on that feeling; only he did hope they might react favorably to his suggestion just this once. So much, he was certain, depended on it. He sincerely wanted his picture company to be an honest one. To live up to its promises. And when he heard Moe's voice saying, "Come on, Louis," he got up slowly and discovered he was trembling, and because he was nervous he dropped back into the idiom of the streets and the studio. He wasn't aware of it, but in this instance it was the clever thing to do. It made him one of the boys.

"Gentlemen," he said, "fa many years we been struggling together. Some longer'n others, but all of us have helped put Miracle onna map. And we put it onna map in black, not red."

The boys laughed and applauded.

Louis raised his hand. "How much credit belongs to the studio and how much to the New York awfice, we don't know. And it ain't terribly important. Natcherly, in Hollywood you boys think you're the reason for our success. And to a great extent I agree with you in that thought. But please to remember that many times—lotsa times," he added emphatically, "lousy pickchas have shown a nice profit through clever booking and finagling with the chains and innapennent theaters. And *we* made that money. In New York. You didn't. But that's not important. What I want to tell you is this: the possibilities of smart rental deals are getting less and less. And I tell you that sincerely. Remember it! There are too many good pickchas being made by other companies to force a man to play ALL of our product. So the man's gonna choose his pickchas, ain't he? And it's not gonna be long till theaters'll play just what their managers think is good for their neighborhood. And after all, ain't that the best plan? The local theater manager thinks he knows what his customers like better'n we do. Maybe he does, maybe he don't. But as far as we're concerned, whatsa use kidding ourselves there's any genius in this whole town can pick a winner every time. It can't be done. And because it can't be done we gotta make a better grade of pickcha. That's the answer, gentlemen. Better pickchas.

"Now last night I saw the yearbook advertising Miracle's future productions, and I must say if our features are as good as that book says they're gonna be, we got the best pickchas ever made."

The boys slapped their thighs on that one and Louis waited until their laughter died down.

He looked around the table and smiled. "Well, gentlemen," he said, "the joke's on you because they're gonna be that good or I'll know the reason why. I'm not gonna send my salesmen around the country lying to exhibitors who are our friends. And that's all I gotta say. I thank you."

Astonishment and panic seized the executives around the table as Louis sat down. They didn't applaud till Moe gave them the cue. Then they clapped discreetly and when Moe rose he didn't have to raise his hands for silence. They gave it to him quickly, like a hot roll that had burned their fingers.

Moe pursed his lips and shook his head at them. "Take it easy, boys," he said. "It's gonna be awright! Now, you all know that when a big shot comes out here from New Yawk, the local guys usually give him a big hand and the minute he leaves town they turn around and slip him the finger. But that ain't gonna be with us! We're gonna tell Louis why we can't do what he wants us ta do. And I'm gonna ask Dick Morse ta tell him why NO company in this town can make fifty-two GOOD pitchures a year."

Morse stood up and turned to Louis.

"The simple answer, Mr. Levinson—and I say this with all humility—is pressure. I say 'humility' because I, too, wish with all my heart that we could turn out only excellent pictures. But it can't be done, solely because of the problem of productive capacity. Unfortunately, there is no rest in this business. A director, writer, or actor barely finishes one job when, if they're any good at all, the wolves are at them for the next. And," he added, looking around the room, "by wolves I mean ourselves. And that's all cockeyed. A man

80

should have a chance to rest, to replenish his creative ability, before he does another picture. And it's not a question of money, either. No matter how much money you're prepared to sink into the production of fifty-two pictures, most of them will not be hits, simply because there isn't that much talent in Hollywood. You can buy *some* good pictures, Mr. Levinson, but not fifty-two."

Mr. Morse sat down. Mr. Korn beamed at Mr. Morse and looked at Louis.

"You see," Moe said, "it's as simple as that. Ya can't do it—so ya don't chuck ya dough away on it, specially when ya got a coupla B perducers who got brains. They don't need big dough fa their shows. Madda of fack, they don't want it."

He turned toward the boys. "And ya all know that although personally I think they're a coupla stinkers, they're about the best chiselers in town. And fa B pitchures ya gotta be from granite. Adelstcin ya know, Louis, from way back. Klein's a new face to ya. Stand up, Harry, and let the president get a good look atcha. And smile, fa Chrissake, ya don't wanna scare him to death!"

Louis knew what Klein was like long before they were introduced. He had been watching him from the beginning of the meeting. It was a new face, and by virtue of its formlessness, a fascinating one because it was impossible to hold it in one's memory. You had to keep looking back at it to make sure it was still there.

He quickly identified Mr. Klein as another refugee from cloaks and suits, but one who unlike himself would never for a moment recognize culture. He wondered what Klein thought of Tilden's production of *Hamlet*. Tilden had persuaded Moe to let Louis make the final decision on Miracle's first Shakespearean venture, and Louis had okayed it despite Moe's objections.

Long before Klein spoke, Louis knew how he'd speak, where he came from, and what he'd have to say. His lips were thick and sensual, and his mouth was as round as a button. But his eyes glinted sharply behind their tortoise-shell glasses. They were hard, quick, and contemptuous. And that was what Louis resented. The man's smugness.

Louis's pride in the heritage of his forefathers was a pride based on Jacob's concept of their fluid intellectual progress. And although Louis himself could never have Jacob's instinctive respect for learning, he had assimilated just enough to condone Moe, on the one hand, and to despise Klein, on the other. For Klein, he was positive, had never made any attempt to better himself, whereas Moe had pulled his whole family up to the level of prosperity they now enjoyed.

And Louis subconsciously knew that Jacob would have resented this man who found himself in the one business that involved at least a slight acquaintance with the arts, and who so obviously enjoyed making a mockery of them.

Klein was on his feet now, and there was a broad grin on Moe's face. An expansive, possessive grin. Louis suddenly realized that Moe was proud of his latest acquisition and he shook his head sadly.

"Tell him watcha know, Harry!" Moe yelled, pointing to Louis.

"Vot I know? . . . I know dese bestids hate mine gots! . . . Bahd de hell vid 'em. I make good pickchas. Vye? Because I know de pahblic taste. Vedder de prasident sess it ken or ken't be so, I know. End det's det! End foidermore, de reason I know it is because I ain't been edjicated like dem highbrow punks, Muss and Tilton. I godda make B's and dey make A's. So vot? So vodda dey got? Scrin stars sayink tinks like 'Oi, det dis too too sullied flash vould maalt, tor en' resulve itsalf into ado!' Because some lahnkhead writes a lodda crep a tousand yizz ago dey tink puttin' it inna pickcha makes it high-kless. Mebbe so. Bahd vot's Oshkosh care aboud 'de do'? Vell? I'm eskink. Sahmbody pleace to tell me?"

George Tilden frowned, thumped his fingers on the desk, and stood up.

" 'O that this too too solid flesh would melt, Thaw and resolve itself into a dew,' " he murmured quickly and with reverence; then he turned to Mr. Klein and said, "I'll tell you, Harry. It's not what you know in this business, it's what you forget that counts. After I finished college and came out here I had to begin all over again. To be a really *good* producer, a man must have a certain amount of background.

He must be acquainted not only with motion pictures, but in order to really *aim* at the public's taste, he should also have some knowledge of the theater, music, and finance, which knowledge he must be able to translate into the medium of the screen . . . and goddamn it, he ought to know how to speak English!"

"I AHBJECT!" screamed Adelstein, jumping to his feet.

"Siddown, ya dope!" Moe yelled. "Here I am tellin' Louis what a smart buncha guys ya are and whadda ya do? Ya make me look like a schlemiehl. Get the hell outta here, alla ya! Meetin's adjoined."

"Whad I do, fa Chrissake?" Adelstein kept asking, as the boys filed out of the conference room.

Moe heard him and looked at Louis. "By him," he said, "an earthquake even ain't his fault." Then he took a good look at his brother-in-law and frowned. "Wotsa madda, kid?" he asked.

"By me Klein's a goniff, Moe. A cheap, chiseling goniff."

"Yeah? . . . Well, let him alone. He makes about ten pitchures a year and all of 'em click."

"Don't I know? I screen 'em in New York, don't I? And every one of his pickchas, cheap as they are, are okay."

"Then whadda ya kickin' about?"

"Moe, a guy like that knows nothing. Absolutely nothing. How can he make a good pickcha?"

"Listen, Louis, Klein told ya, an edjication is a hannycap in this business. Looka me! I'm a iggeramus and I know it. But I'm head of the company and *you* know it. Sure, you're the president, and I put ya there. And there's nothin' inna world I wouldn't do ta keep ya there, but Klein's right. Thass a cinch ta see. Thass sense, experience, and ta us, money."

"Maybe you're right," Louis said. He got up and walked over to the window.

Moe watched him.

Louis turned and spoke very softly. "But someday I hope, and I think you do too, to see Willie in this business and I'd hate to see him give up an education to be a success. From what you say it might be a good idea to keep him on the—well, a little on the slow side. What do you think?"

"On the slow side he'll never be. What's on ya mind?"

"Sending him to school."

"He's goin' ta school, ain't he?"

"A good school, Moe."

"Ya mean where he'll learn sump'm?"

Louis nodded and quietly added, "I still don't agree with Klein, you know."

"I'm against it," Moe said. "Whadda ya wanna edjicate him for? It'll onney make him unhappy. And if he learns enough, someday he'll call ya a cheap kike and fa that ya gotta pay fifteen hunerd dollars a year ta some sour-puss collidge clunk? Wotsa sense in it? If ya edjicate him ya'll regret it fa the resta ya life. And don't let nobody else do it, either!

"Sure, if ya wanna keep him outta ya way for a few years send him ta collidge or some school if ya wanna, but beat the bejesus outta him if he learns anything. If that kid ever gets smart he's gonna be a stinker!"

Louis shook his head and smiled sadly. "When you say things like that I know you're just talking. I keep thinking of Jacob and the things he once told me—that an education is the most important thing in a man's life, the one thing that's his personal property forever. Nothing can take it away from him and nothing can help him more in his business or his daily life."

"In this business I tell ya it's a hannycap!" Moe insisted.

"I can't believe you," Louis said. "And you don't believe it yourself."

"Fa Willie, I do!" Moe answered, with such intense conviction that it almost crushed Louis's normal instincts and set him to wondering.

26

WHEN LOUIS RETURNED to New York, Rebecca met him at the train and greeted him to death. All the way up the ramp and into the car she kept on chirping about the family.

Momma and Jacob were going out evenings. They'd made friends with an elderly couple in the neighborhood. Sometimes they went to the movies together. Sometimes they went out separately. Jacob came home very late one night. In response to Momma's pointed inquiry as to where he'd been, he replied, "Listen, Sophie, married, we're not! Out, I was! And fun, I had!" To which Momma snorted, "De goil musta bin meshugga!"

The servants were fine and practically running the house themselves, but they still had a terrible time keeping Momma out of the kitchen.

Jacob still thought Louis was making too much money.

And William was rapidly growing up to be a "strong young man."

Louis listened with one ear and felt as though he'd been away a long time.

"I've been thinking," Rebecca concluded, watching Louis out of the corner of her eye, "that it might be a good idea to send him to a boys' camp this summer."

Louis didn't react at all.

"Did you hear what I said?" his wife demanded.

"No . . . what? I'm sorry, Becky." He had been thinking about how much he disliked Klein.

"I said I'd like to send William to camp this summer."

"Sure—sure!" Then he thought of what Moe had said and added cautiously, "Whadda ya mean, camp? . . . What'll he learn there?"

"Oh," Rebecca continued breathlessly, "he'll learn all about the woods and birds and how to make fires and things. The camp director told me all about it. He left a booklet describing the place. It looks beautiful! William'll meet nice boys and I think a summer in the open air will be good for him."

"They'll only teach him stuff about the birds, bees, and trees?"

"They also guarantee he'll learn to swim."

"Send him!" Louis chuckled.

27

MOE ARRIVED in town shortly after Willie returned from camp. He came east for the World Premières of Miracle's two most important pictures of the year, *Twinkling Toes*, the musical, and Tilden's *Hamlet*; and he brought a present for Willie. The present came in a wicker traveling basket. Its name was Frou-Frou.

When Willie heard a dog barking in the Levinson house, he ran down the stairs. Momma, Jacob, and Rebecca were already gathered around Moe, greeting him, helping him take his coat off, and sneaking quick, anxious looks at the basket on the floor.

Moe kissed each one of them and suddenly spied his nephew standing on the stairs.

"Willie," he said with a grin, "I brung ya a present."

"A dog?" Willie cried hopefully.

"A liddle duggie," Momma said, and she blinked both eyes at him and smiled.

Willie walked over to the basket and slowly settled on his knees beside it. Moe leaned over and unlatched the lid. Willie flung it open and looked down into the beady eyes of Frou-Frou. They stared at each other for a moment and Willie's spirits sagged visibly.

"Oh," he said, and he looked up at his uncle. "Thanks."

Frou-Frou licked his hand and Willie frowned. The dog followed him upstairs.

Late that night when Moe and Louis were finally alone, the first question Louis asked was, "How did ya ever do it?"

Moe smiled very wisely. "It was a cinch," he assured Louis, "a cinch. Day before I left she went shoppin'. I sneaked home, swiped the mutt, and had the express company take him down the station. I get home and she's off her nut, swears somebody stole him—so I puts an ad inna paper for her and makes out like I got a busted heart too. She eats it up, and tells me I really loved lil Frou-Frou too, onney I wouldn't admit it. So whadda I lose? Nothin'," he concluded with a shrug of his shoulders.

"Your gain is our loss," Louis laughed.

"Aw, ya'll like the mutt," Moe protested feebly. "He's awright . . . in New Yawk," he added as an afterthought.

Then they began a serious business conversation that lasted far beyond Louis's normal bedtime.

Moe's visit was in the nature of a double celebration. Not only were there going to be two gala openings, but Tilden's picture was also the first to be shown on the screen of Miracle's new Broadway theater, the Miracle Palace.

Moe had never even seen the place, but like most of the other large picture companies, Miracle had embarked on a vast theater-expansion program during the three years prior to 1929. And the Miracle Palace was the last, latest, and most lavish of them all. Into this, his pet project, Louis had poured two million dollars. And the president got his money's worth, even to the twin plaques of Moe and himself that adorned both ends of the mammoth foyer.

His New York publicity director, Tom Murphy, had talked him into hiring Philip Mamberstein, the most sensational and unpredictable of all theatrical showmen, to operate their "first-run" New York house. It was an era of stage shows, and "Mamba"—as Mamberstein insisted that his underlings call him—not only spent fortunes on his stage tableaux, but abruptly scotched all attempts at curtailing his budget. Whenever Louis cornered him and wailed about extravagance, Mamba would rattle off the box-office receipts of every theater he'd managed in the past ten years, leaving Louis flabbergasted and chuckling over the acquisition of an impresario who delicately described himself as "Mamba, the man who never muffs"! But Louis hadn't muffed much, either. In fact, he'd signed a theatrical wizard at the peak of his career and it was a salutary deal for both of them.

For the opening of *Hamlet* Mamba had arranged a most pretentious and lively stage tableau. Twittering chorus girls, pirouetting ballerinas, gyrating tap dancers, and soupy tenors paraded across the stage in gelatinous profusion.

But Mamba's pageant seemed interminably boring to Moe and Louis, who were sitting in the very best loge seats surrounded by the family. They felt the stage show might have been cut a little. The Melancholy Dane had been an expensive experiment and they were anxiously awaiting the critics' reaction to it.

Jacob had insisted that Louis give tickets to George and Fanny, who sat somewhere up in the balcony, but when they asked Willie if he'd like to go, he merely shook his head and said, "Yah, Shakespeare, who in hell wantsa see that?"

As a result of this criticism, which outraged Louis and gave Moe the giggles, Willie stayed home. But Rebecca, who was afraid to leave him alone, invited his former tentmate, Bob Levy, over for the night. The two boys had learned many things at camp besides Louis's birds, bees, and trees, and not the least of them concerned the fact that sugar added to grape juice ferments the latter with considerable rapidity. They had been too young to be included in the surreptitious and thoroughly innocuous drinking bouts staged by the older boys late at night in the woods; but the stories filtered down to them, and although they never learned that most of the boys pretended to be far more plastered than they ever were, they did manage to obtain and memorize the "secret" formula that transformed perfectly good grape juice into highly unpalatable wine.

While the family sat innocently in the theater, their youngster calmly broke the law of the land by concocting a brew in the Levinson kitchen that consisted of grape juice and sugar, to which Bob added potato skins, orange peels, and yeast, the whole of which they cooked for fifteen minutes in an oval wash boiler and then carefully poured back into the empty grape-juice bottles. They threw the metal caps away, pounded wine corks into the bottles, sealed the tops with wax, and lined the shelves of the cellar storeroom with their concoction.

Then they opened the windows, ladled the remaining scraps into Frou-Frou's dinner plate, washed the boiler, and went upstairs to bed.

Fifteen minutes later Frou-Frou scratched at the door. "Christ, let the pest in," Willie called to Bob from the bathroom. Frou-Frou staggered in and began to hiccup violently. "He's gonna be sick!" Bob said. Willie came to the door and looked at the dog. "Bring him in here," he said. Both boys held him over the toilet. Frou-Frou whimpered and hiccuped and finally let go.

"Jeez," Bob apologized, "the trouble is the stuff's not aged. When it's aged it oughta be okay. We followed the formula."

"Followed it, hell," Willie snorted. "We're way ahead of it. Let it set downstairs for a coupla weeks, then we'll try it."

"What if your family finds out?"

"They won't. They don't even know what goes on in this place."

The Levinsons thought the house smelled strange when they returned home, but brewing was an alien art to them and they agreed that the odors undoubtedly came from the street.

It had been a wonderful, exciting evening, and the morning papers were lavish in their praise of both the theater and the picture. *Hamlet* was hailed as a "laudable and audacious film" but most of the reviewers also expressed grave doubts concerning the advisability of bringing Shakespeare to the screen. "Movie fans crave the poetry of action, not of words," one critic hedged. And Louis, though well aware of the prestige Miracle had acquired through the film, found himself forced to agree with Moe as he watched the daily box-office reports roll rapidly downhill.

He had held out at first. "From here on in, Shakespeare's out!" Moe had said after the preview, and when Louis, still hoping the public would approve his judgment, suggested that they give it a chance, Moe had laughed at him and cracked, "Chris', ya kid calls 'em better'n you do! Wyncha give up?"

It was the last time Louis ever approved a story over Moe's objections.

By the end of the month plans had been completed for the première of *Twinkling Toes*. Gladys Creighton and Mel were both coming east for the opening, and Gladys would make the first personal appearance in the new theater. Opening prices were to be considerably lower than those for *Hamlet*, because Moe and Louis had long since learned that "turnover" paid off the mortgage faster than "class," and they wanted to popularize their first-run house. Miracle's two best shorts and a Fox Movietone News would round out the bill.

Tom Murphy had also convinced Louis that it would be shrewd publicity to invite the critics plus their wives or girl friends to the house after the show. Gladys and Mel were naturally included, and Murphy was beside himself with joy. He had stumbled across a new "gimmick," an informal press reception at the boss's home. No New York publicity director had ever pulled that one before and the "layout" looked terrific.

The preview went off without a hitch. And when the lights were turned on at the end of the feature, the audience rose to its feet and cheered. Rebecca reached over and squeezed Moe's hand. He smiled at her. "We ain't done bad, Sis," he shouted over the din.

"Thank God, after the last one," she laughed, grabbing her belongings and her son. "We'd better go," she said, and they rushed home to see that Fanny and George had arranged everything properly.

Willie was having a grand time. He was getting his first taste of importance, being pointed out as the Levinson heir. And since Tom Murphy was the one who had persuaded Rebecca to let him stay up late and attend the party, the two became fast friends—but not for long.

Tom had been in a quandary concerning liquor. Louis believed in obeying the law and said he would not serve it in his house. Whereupon the publicity director countered by suggesting that the critics be allowed to bring their own refreshments and he would personally reimburse them.

"I don't care what *you* do," Louis barked. "I will not have the law broken in my house!"

"It's not a question of the law, Mr. Levinson," Tom pleaded. "I want this party to be a success. For you!" he added.

"Not in my house," Louis repeated firmly.

Murphy knew when he was licked. "Have it your own way, sir," he said.

By twelve o'clock the guests in the Levinson living room had given up trying to smile at each other and sat back quietly waiting for something to happen. Moe had milked the critics dry of praise. *Twinkling Toes* was a success, but Tom's party began to look like visiting day at the morgue.

Tom had just asked George to pass the sandwiches for the fourth time in an hour when Willie came up to him and whispered, "Bum party."

"Jesus!" Tom muttered.

"I got a dart game downstairs."

"That's swell, Willie. You got a dart game downstairs. That's great. Go play with it."

"I was just trying to help."

"You're terrific, kid, terrific!" Tom said impatiently. He was beginning to sweat.

Louis joined them. "Do something!" he whispered.

A vacant look came into his publicity director's eyes. "What can

91

I do?" he muttered nervously. "Stand on my head? I told you before
—no liquor, no fun. I'm doing the best I can, Mr. Levinson. Your
family sits at one end of the room and your guests on the other.
They've got to mingle. Mr. Korn's the only one who's been any help."

"I'll see what I can do," Louis said, and he went up to Rebecca.
"Mingle," he said. She got up and crossed the room. "Mingle," he
said to Jacob, who nodded and joined Mel Price. "Mingle," he whis-
pered to Momma, who shrugged his shoulders and repeated, "Mingle?
Vich vun's Mingle? Vas a furrier vunce named Mingle. Hunerd
Feefty-fort Stritt, by'm Concourse."

"Mix with the guests, Momma," Louis explained patiently.

Tom watched the Levinsons cross the room one by one until he
felt someone tugging at his sleeve. He turned and looked down at
Willie.

"I heard what you said," Willie murmured.

"So what?"

"So you better come down and look at my dart game."

"Now, look, kid, I got no time for games."

"This one's different."

"Willie, for Chrissake stop bothering me! Go talk to the guests."

"They won't listen to me. Look, Mr. Murphy, I got what you
said you needed."

"You have, have you?" Tom muttered bitterly. "A case a gin in
your bedroom, I suppose?"

"Better'n that."

Murphy's eyebrows reached for the ceiling.

"Hey!" he exclaimed. Then he suddenly became suspicious and
snapped, "This better be on the level, kid!"

"Come with me," Willie said.

Tom followed him into the cellar.

"Grapejuice," Willie announced, indicating the bottles on the
shelves.

"Oh, great!" Murphy moaned. "Great!"

92

"Try it." Willie handed him a bottle.

"What the hell they sealed with wax for?" Tom asked, holding the bottle up to the light. "This stuff's cloudy. What makes you think it's grape juice?"

Willie handed him a penknife and grinned. "Break the seal, Mr. Murphy."

Murphy had his fingers around the cork when it suddenly shot out of the bottle and landed halfway across the cellar. Some of the stuff spattered on the floor. Murphy took a swig, gagged, swallowed, and broke into a long, low whistle. Suddenly he looked up at the ceiling and began to shake with laughter.

" 'There'll be no liquor in my house!' " he roared. "Set up your dart game, my boy! We're in business!" He patted Willie on the head.

"I want this to be the best party Pop ever had," Willie said, as the publicity director bounded up the steps. But Tom never heard him. He was already in the living room asking the critic of the *Globe* if he liked to play darts.

The critic shrugged his shoulders. "Not particularly," he answered.

"You will," Tom said quietly. "This is a very special game. Downstairs in the cellar. It's played with glasses. Be sure and take one with you."

The critic broke into a slow, grateful smile and left the room.

In twenty minutes, Willie was the hit of the party. Tom sent the guests down one by one, admonishing them to keep quiet and come back quickly. But most of them stayed downstairs, drinking Willie's wine and throwing darts.

Every fifteen minutes Tom would dash down to the cellar, grab five or six people, and shoo them upstairs, a procedure that had him panting for breath by one-thirty.

Somehow, by circulating among the guests and telling them Louis would die if he knew what was going on, he managed to keep the Levinsons from getting suspicious.

But Tom turned white around two o'clock when Louis looked around the room and asked him where everybody was. Luckily, one of the critics rescued him by saying, "Playing darts with your son. A fine boy, Mr. Levinson. A fine boy."

Louis beamed and Tom took off for the cellar. What he saw made him stop short at the bottom of the steps.

A woman was standing unsteadily in front of the target, trying to balance an apple on her head. "Quiet, everybody!" she yelled. "Me and the kid, we're gonna do another William Tell!"

Murphy looked around and saw Willie standing about ten feet away from the woman with a dart poised in his hand.

"Jesus!" he said, rushing up to the Levinson heir. "You done this before?"

"About five times," Willie said calmly.

"Kid, you crazy?" Murphy cried, snatching the dart away. "These things got points!"

"Go away," Willie said. "I got it rigged with the guy standing next to her. I make like I'm throwing it, he grabs the apple and sticks another dart in it. We've been doing it for ten minutes and she isn't wise yet. She's dopey."

"*She's* dopey!" Murphy exploded, looking around the cellar. "Get a load of this bunch!"

A drunk came up to him. "Hi, Murph," he said. "I'm going upstairs and tell the old man the kid throws a better party than he does."

"Nix, Charlie, nix!" Murphy pleaded.

"This is Mr. Webb," Willie said. "He's my friend. He's given me two drinks."

"Two drinks of his own liquor!" Mr. Webb roared.

"Charlie, for Chrissake, he's just a kid!" Murphy protested.

"Kid, hell! He's my pal, aren't you, Willie?"

Willie smiled—a little dazedly, Murphy thought, and he groaned, "Oh, my God." Then he said, "You all right, kid?"

"Sure." Willie grinned. "Sure."

The woman with the apple screamed, "Hey, you!"

She came over and pushed Webb to one side. "You gonna let us make like William Tell?" she demanded.

"Look, lady—"

"You gonna, yes? Or you gonna, no?"

"You better go home," Murphy said coldly.

"Me? Home?" The woman looked at him and giggled. "I'm going, upstairs and tell that Creighton dame who in hell she thinks she is!" She swayed and grabbed Webb's shoulder. "I am," she hiccuped.

"The hell you are," Murphy said.

"Then gimme the darts," she said, poking her outstretched fingers in his ribs.

Murphy backed away. "No more darts. No more drinks," he said.

"Look you—" the woman glared at him— "I know who you are. You're just a publicity punk. I'm a guest here! If I wanna drink, you *get* me a drink! Understand?"

Murphy frowned at Webb.

"Evans's girl. The *Gazette*," Webb explained briefly.

"Oh, God!" Murphy groaned. "A critic's dame."

"Yeah—and I wanna drink, *now!*" the woman said. She poked him again.

He brushed her hand away. "You've had enough already," he said, trying to placate her. "Besides, you wouldn't want Mr. Evans to see you this way."

"Mr. Evans's seen me every way. Gimme a drink."

"Sorry," Murphy said curtly, "there's not supposed to be *any* drinking on these premises."

"Thissa helluva time to tell me that!" She laughed. Then her eyes narrowed and her face assumed an expression of diabolical cunning. She had trapped her adversary. "You mean that guy upstairs, he don't know what's going on down here. That's what you mean, isn't it?"

"Well, not exactly."

"Maybe not exactly, honey. But exactly enough to get me a drink. Otherwise . . ." She pointed to the top of the stairs.

"Give her a drink, Willie," Murphy said.

Willie looked at Tom and shook his head. The party hadn't turned out the way he'd hoped it would. He'd wanted people to have a good time—but all they did was argue and fight. And they'd laugh so quickly, over things that weren't funny. And then the next moment they'd be mad again. Nothing doing, Willie thought, the shelf's empty and they can't see the six bottles Bob and I hid on top of the cupboard. He turned to the woman.

"It's all gone. See?" he said, pointing to the empty shelf.

"I see," she answered, and she came over to him and shook him violently.

The other guests rushed over to separate them. Tom Murphy grabbed her first and yelled, "Let go of him!"

She turned on Tom. "Take your hands off me!" she blazed. Then she quieted down and pointed toward the steps again. "Now, you gonna get me a drink nice and quiet-like or we gonna have trouble?" She stood very close to him, her jaw jutting out defiantly, and suddenly she kicked him in the shin.

"Jesus!" Tom yelled. And for the next second he stood face to face with his future. Blonde and a little blowzy, it was weaving back and forth in front of him, teetering between a year of lousy reviews on the *Gazette* and the loss of his job. He made his decision quickly and lunged for her. She struggled and slammed back against the cupboard.

One by one, six bottles rolled off the shelf, bouncing off the heads and shoulders of the guests and exploding when they hit the floor. The cellar was filled with flying glass and wine. Two women screamed. Drenched by home brew and speared by slivers of glass, Willie's customers made for the stairs in a body.

The Levinsons were on hand to greet them at the landing. Upstairs the explosions had sounded like gunshots.

96

Momma Levinsky took one look at what she thought was the first survivor and screamed, "BLAHD!"

Moe yelled to someone to take her upstairs. Rebecca stood in the middle of the hall and began to tremble.

The cause of the trouble rushed past the family and ran up to Evans. "They beat me, Jeff. They beat me!" she sobbed.

Jacob kept asking, "What is it? What is it?"

Frou-Frou came yapping down the stairs.

"Everybody in the living room!" Louis yelled above the uproar. "Everybody."

"Anybody else down there?" Moe called, peering down the stairwell.

"Nobody," Tom answered as he came up the stairs followed by Willie. "The cellar's a mess," he said as they passed Moe. "A hell of a mess."

They went up to the living room.

The survivors stood in the center of the room daubing each other with handkerchiefs, wiping the wine from their clothes, and in some cases trying to stem the flow of blood from minor cuts and gashes.

"Is anybody severely hurt? Does anybody feel sick?" Tom asked.

Most of them shook their heads and said, "No."

Rebecca stood in the doorway looking into the room. She suddenly felt very weak and leaned against the doorjamb for support. "All that blood," she murmured, "and on my rugs, too! . . . What's happened? What's happened?" Then she wondered about Willie and cried, "Where's William? Where's William?" She put her hand up to her forehead.

George touched her elbow. She turned to him. He smiled softly and led her into the living room. "Get some towels," she murmured. "Lotsa towels."

Louis and Gladys Creighton ran over and helped Rebecca into a chair. George went for the towels.

Rebecca kept moaning, "Blood."

"That's not blood, Mrs. Levinson," Gladys reassured her. "It smells like hooch."

Louis was so excited he never even heard her. "Willie's all right," he repeated three or four times as he rubbed the back of her neck. "He's in the room somewheres."

Moe brought a glass of water and made Rebecca sip it. "You okay, Sis?" he asked.

Rebecca nodded.

"Good," Moe said. " 'Cause ya husband's next."

"Me? Whatsa madda with me?" Louis demanded.

"Nothin' yet. Waid a minute." Moe turned and called to Mel Price. The director came over. "Tell him watcha told me," Moe said.

"Somebody's been making hooch in your house."

"Nonsense!" Louis protested.

"That stuff you think is blood is liquor," Gladys said quietly.

Rebecca gasped and turned paler than ever.

"I don't believe it," Louis said.

"There were bottles on the shelves and they exploded one by one. There's a small distillery in your home, Mr. Levinson." Mel laughed.

Louis glared at him. "Never!" he said sternly. "In my house, never!" He turned away and saw Tom Murphy wiping Willie's face with a towel. "Tom!" he called.

Murphy handed the towel to Willie and came over. "Yes, sir?"

"They say there was liquor in the cellar."

"Not exactly liquor, Mr. Levinson," Tom parried. "A sort of grape juice, I'd call it."

"Grape juice explodin' in bottles?" Moe asked.

"It fermented a little in the cellar."

"Nobody pushed it?" Moe asked acidly.

"Well, maybe," Tom hedged.

"Who?" Louis asked.

"Somebody."

Louis sucked his breath in sharply. "I asked you a simple question. Whose liquor?" he demanded.

Tom knew, without turning, that Willie was watching him anxiously. The kid had tried so earnestly to help. Tom sighed and faced his boss. "Mine," he lied.

Louis clapped his hands together and called, "Ladies and gentlemen! Quiet! Please!" The hubbub subsided and the guests gradually turned toward him. "I got an announcement. An apology to make. From me, to you," he began, his voice vibrant with sincerity. "A crime has been committed here. The law of my country has just been broken and some of you have been partners in that crime." He took a deep breath and said, "Liquor has been served in my house tonight."

The guests watched him with silent curiosity. He looked so serious and yet he couldn't be. No sane person could be that disturbed about violating the Eighteenth Amendment. It was incredible. They waited for the gag and one of the critics chuckled in anticipation.

Louis turned to him and shook his head. "Don't laugh," he said gently. "I feel it's a disgrace and I want you to know it was done without my knowledge or consent." Then he got angry again and added, "I wish I could say the same for my publicity director, Mr. Murphy. I wish it had never happened. Fortunately none of you are seriously hurt, but anybody feeling the need of medical services please send me the bill. On that I insist! That's all."

The guests looked at each other and realized the party was over.

They filed past Moe, Louis, and Tom, who were grouped around Rebecca, and paid their respects. Mel and Gladys left to get their coats.

Willie edged into the group holding the towel to his face.

"Pop," he said. But Louis was busy saying good night to his guests.

"Pop," Willie called again.

Tom looked at him and put his finger to his lips. Willie shook his head.

"Pop!" Willie cried impatiently. "I did it. It was my liquor."

Louis stopped in the middle of a handshake. "*Your* liquor!" he said, staring down at his son. "Your liquor!"

"Where'd *you* get liquor?" Moe snorted. He suspected Willie of trying to protect Tom.

"I made it."

"Out of what?"

"Grape juice."

"You did that in this house?" Louis asked sternly.

"Where else should he do it?" Moe muttered. "Inna street?"

"In the cellar, Pop," Willie confessed.

"Smart kid. Makes booze outta grape juice right under his old man's nose." Moe laughed.

"Quiet, you!" Rebecca interrupted. "This is serious with Louis. It's important."

"So watcha gonna do? Hang the kiddie?"

Momma had joined the group.

"You stay out of this," Louis snapped. "My son's broken a law. By breaking a law he injured my guests and damaged my reputation. He made a fool of me and he will be punished." He turned to Willie and said, "Go to your room."

Rebecca suddenly noticed the towel in Willie's hand. She jumped up and pulled it away. "He's been cut, Louis," she said. "Call Dr. Lansburgh."

Momma inspected the gash in Willie's face. "A bootlickka ya wanna be, huh, kiddie?" she said. "A hole inna face ya get fa makin' a bum fomm ya fadda."

"Levinson's liquor refinery." Jacob chuckled.

"It's no laughing matter! It's a disgrace!" Louis insisted angrily. Then he turned on his son. "I told you to get upstairs!" he shouted.

Mel and Gladys came in as Willie left the room. "Good night," they said.

"G'night," he muttered and trudged slowly up the stairs.

Louis and Moe told Tom to stick around and went down to the front door with Mel and Gladys.

"Well," Price said at the door, "this was more exciting than the preview."

"I'm glad you enjoyed yourself," Louis said coldly.

"Don't pay no attention to him," Moe said. "He's sore at the kid."

Gladys looked at Louis and winked. "Chip off the old block, huh?" She grinned. "You better keep an eye on him. Good night."

Her rich, low, throaty laugh floated back to them as they closed the front door.

Louis bounded up the steps to the living room. "Rebecca, where's William?" he shouted before he even entered.

"She's gone upstairs with him," Jacob said. "She's called Dr. Lansburgh. I'm going to bed, too." He said good night and left the room.

"Momma?" Moe called after him.

Jacob pointed upstairs without turning around.

"Well, Mr. Murphy," Louis said, "how did this happen?"

Tom shrugged his shoulders. "I just found the liquor downstairs," he said. "Willie told me about it."

"And you served it?"

Tom nodded.

"The kid's booze he served," Moe said. "A grown man takin' booze from a baby."

"I did try to take the rap for Willie," Tom pointed out.

"So yer a hero," Moe growled.

"Not a hero. It was the only decent thing to do."

"You're a fine one to talk about decency!" Louis snapped.

"Critics are critics, Mr. Levinson, and my job—for you—is to keep them happy."

"You think this made *me* happy?"

"I'm afraid not. But you've got to admit the party picked up," Tom said in self-defense.

"We got to admit nothing. Look at this place. Look at it!" Louis insisted.

"You look at it!" Tom said angrily, before he could stop himself.

"If you'da let me do what I wanted to do in the first place, this never woulda happened. Never!"

Louis and Moe looked at each other and Murphy knew he was through.

"Oh, well," he said hopefully, trying to change the subject, "maybe we shoulda had the party at the Astor."

"You should have thought of that before," Louis replied coldly. "Good night."

"Good night, Mr. Levinson," Tom said, and then he paused and looked anxiously at his boss. "Friday?" he asked tentatively.

"Friday," Louis repeated.

"Give him two weeks' salary," Moe said. "The punk tried."

"Thank you, sir," Tom nodded and he stalked out of the room.

Meanwhile, Rebecca and Willie were in the midst of their first serious argument. Rebecca, sick with embarrassment, lashed out at him furiously the moment they were alone.

"How could you do this to us?" she demanded.

Willie, who was too nervous and exhausted and too near tears to open his mouth, sat on the edge of his bed and slowly took his clothes off.

"Answer me!" Rebecca stormed. "At once!"

Willie bent over to untie his shoelace.

"You know these people are important to your father. Why don't you answer me?" she said between clenched teeth, and she leaned over and shook him sharply.

Willie straightened up and sighed. "I didn't mean it." And he kicked his shoe off.

Rebecca drew herself up indignantly. "You didn't mean it? Of course you didn't mean it. But you did it! You made fools of us in front of all those—those important people!" she wailed.

"Aw, leave me alone, Ma."

"I won't leave you alone until you tell me *why* you did it!"

"How the hell should I know!" he suddenly yelled, and Rebecca struck him instinctively. Then she began to cry and tried to put her arms around him, but he pushed her away sullenly.

"Whensa doctor coming?" he asked.

"Soon," Rebecca sobbed. "Soon. Get into bed." And she left the room.

Dr. Lansburgh put three stitches in Willie's cheek.

Louis and Rebecca decided it was high time to pack him off to prep school.

BOOK 2

WILLIAM LEVINSON

1

INCHCAPE PREPARATORY SCHOOL was situated on the banks of the Wallingford River in Connecticut, where its small cluster of gray, ivy-covered buildings had withstood the onslaughts of its pupils for many years.

Founded in 1840 by Thomas Inchcape, who had made his money in brewing and, at the behest of his socially snubbed wife, desired to perpetuate his name, the school had gradually flourished until it became the most select of all the academies that dot the New England landscape.

While many of its graduates attained national prominence, which was attributed by rival academics to the fact that most Inchcape boys came from rich and distinguished families, the school still—essentially because Tom Inchcape's grant insisted it do so—remained a liberal institution. It admitted two Jews a year. However, as a precautionary measure, the founder had ordained that all Jews must be personally recommended by graduates. The records of the class of 1910 show that it matriculated the first Inchcape Infidel, a man named Samuel Ahrens, who continued the academy's tradition by becoming an internationally famous painter. After Mr. Ahrens there were at least six or eight Jewish students at all times. And it must be said for the boys of Inchcape that they subjected all new lads, Jewish or otherwise, to identical patterns of probation, acceptance, and eventual friendship.

The question of racial differences was not important to them. At its worst it was a matter of occasional curiosity, but never prejudice. Whatever species of antisocial virus their parents might foster, it was in most cases dropped at the school gate and during the school

107

term it never attacked Tom Inchcape's basic concept of his institution, which was to accept only a select group of boys, and once that selection had been made, to admit of no further inequalities of background, birth, or breeding.

Occasionally a Jewish boy turned out to be a "drip," but he was never ostracized because of his religion. And the students were no more ruthless in their attitude toward him than they were toward the sociological sports within their own Christian sects.

For Willie, Inchcape was a far cry from Momma, Moe, and Louis. He and his friend Bob Levy had both been accepted on the recommendation of George Tilden, who was not only Inchcape's sole representative in the movie industry, but had been their star fullback in 1912.

The boys left New York together, with Jacob's parting injunction ringing in their ears.

"Remember," he had said upon the steps, as Rebecca and Mrs. Levy mothered their restless young into the car, "that in our growing up we often throw away the gifts we're born with. . . . Don't forget too much, boys. Please." There were tears in his eyes as he turned away and said, "God bless you." He knew that as Willie grew older their friendship would disappear, and he felt abjectly miserable.

But his misery was nothing compared to the bewilderment of Willie and Bob when they arrived at the school with the third busload of the day and fell into a vague semblance of order as John Chatsworth, the senior proctor, marched them across the threshold of the Administration Building.

They caught their first glimpse of the quadrangle through glass partitions at the end of the hall, but Chatsworth gravely steered them to the right before they came to the end of the corridor. They entered a large room with benches facing a counter that ran the length of the office to a door marked "Private." From behind that door, a fat little man with a cherubic countenance and no hair on his head waddled up to the counter. His one glance seemed to absorb the faces of all the boys lined up in front of the benches and then he nodded to

108

Chatsworth. The senior took a list from his pocket, called the roll, and told the boys to be seated.

"This," he concluded, nodding toward the roly-poly gentleman behind the desk, "is the school registrar, Mr. Everett Strickland. He has a few words to say to you."

"Stricky," as he was surreptitiously called by the older boys, leaned his elbows on the counter, surveyed his audience, and waited for silence.

"All right, boys," he finally said, "let's get this over as briefly as possible. There are one hundred and forty new students arriving by tomorrow and I'm getting tired of going through the same routine. So listen closely and when I get through *don't* ask any questions. Chatsworth knows all the answers. Ask him. To begin with, all new men will share rooms with older students. Secondly, you must feel free to ask your roommates any question concerning your classwork. Thirdly, Inchcape operates under an honor system, which you will learn more by absorption and contact than explanation, so I won't waste my time describing it. And fourthly, as John Chatsworth just told you, I'm in charge of your marks and as long as you keep your work above standard, you will find me a very charming person indeed. Fifthly, in a few moments, your future roommates will join us and you are to remain seated until you hear your name called, then you will rise briefly, until they see you, and then sit down again. When one of them comes up to you and taps you on the shoulder, walk out with him. Your belongings will be delivered to your rooms in due time.

"And, finally, there will be an assembly for all new men in the Chapel tomorrow afternoon. The headmaster, Dr. Louis F. Smith, will address you on 'Inchcape, Its Aims and Ideals'—and a very good address it is, too. I've heard it for many years."

The latter part of Stricky's speech was completely lost on the audience as they anxiously searched the faces of the older Inchcape men who trickled in by twos and threes.

"We will now call the roll."

Chatsworth stepped forward.

"Coates. Gordon. Green. Stand up!"

They stood, for what seemed an eternity. "Sit down," Chatsworth said.

Three upperclassmen detached themselves from the mob in the doorway and tapped the youngsters, who sprang up and followed them out of the room. This procedure was repeated four times before Bob and Willie's names were called. As soon as they rose, two husky boys stepped forward and tapped them. The registrar boomed, "Levinson, 207. Levy, 209!"

While they were walking down the hall the older boys introduced themselves.

"My name's Bill Rowse," said Willie's roommate.

"And mine's Jim Corlett," said Bob's.

They started across the quadrangle. Willie nudged Bob gleefully and whispered, "They're last year's freshman football stars!"

The football stars reached the middle of the Quad and noticing some of their classmates appeasing their curiosity by leering down from the windows, shouted up, "Hey, we got the Quota!"

"Better start them cramming for you right now!" Elliot Brumbaugh IV yelled down from the window sill, his elbows propped on an open volume of Ovid.

Corlett looked up and laughed. "Maybe we'll lend 'em to you, Squirter."

"Got our own book-monkeys, thank you," Squirter said. "Cute ones too. They're dust-busting the room already."

"Upperclassmen," Willie whispered proudly.

Bob's eyes were shining. "We're book-monkeys, I guess," he said slowly.

"For the whole first year," Bill Rowse added. "Let's go upstairs."

They turned off the walk and entered the building through a small Gothic archway. Rooms 207 and 209 were next to each other. The boys separated in the hall and Rowse took Willie into what was going to be his home for the next four years. In rapid succession

Willie was told where to keep his clothes, towels, books, and personal belongings.

The room was small but nicely furnished. The beds were day beds, and every morning after breakfast, new boys were expected to make up those belonging to their roommates as well as their own. Pennants and football pictures were tacked across the wall and a girl's picture occupied the place of honor on Bill's desk.

She wasn't really pretty, but Willie accepted her as the quintessence of beauty because he had completely absorbed the story-book axiom that the football hero's gal was the best-looker in captivity. Secretly he vowed that someday he'd have the picture of a gorgeous girl on his desk. And so did every other freshman in the school.

By dinnertime Bill had told so many stories of Inchcape, its past glories and memorable pranks, and had introduced so many new faces that Willie was fairly groggy with information.

They washed for dinner and walked across the Quad, through the Barn, as the boys called the building that housed and schooled them, toward the Dining Hall.

"The food's good," cautioned Bill, "for the first two weeks. Then you'd better start writing home for eats or God help you, you'll starve."

"Gee, Bill, that's a cinch! My mom'll send out all kindsa things! Lebkuchen, cookies, matzoths—anything!"

Bill looked blank for a second before he grinned. "Those matzoths'll get me all right!" Then he suddenly remembered their position and he scowled at his new roommate. "Listen, kid," he said, "I don't care what you call me in our room, but there's a rule here that all book-monkeys call their betters 'mister.' You call me Mr. Rowse. Jim's Mr. Corlett and so on. And don't forget it. And furthermore, if you're a crybaby and yell for home tonight, I'll whale the hell out of you."

It took Willie three months to assimilate the fact that, grand as Bill was in the privacy of their room, custom demanded that he treat Willie like a Dutch uncle as soon as they left that sanctuary.

111

And custom also dictated a rapid comprehension of the honor system. Inchcape students were immediately subjected to a code of ethics that extended far beyond the usual prep school rules governing petty thievery and cheating in a classroom.

Books, money, personal possessions could be left anywhere in perfect safety. Proctors never checked up to see that lights were out by ten. Students were expected to report their own infringements of any rules to the registrar's office, with only one exception—during examinations.

The boys of Inchcape were exposed to the ultimate temptation during this period, which was as much a test of their integrity as of their intelligence. No instructor stayed in a classroom during a written exam. Students could, if they wanted to, take their papers to their rooms, provided they left their doors open, and every Inchcape student was under oath to report not only his own violations, but also those of his classmates. Cheating was a disgraceful breach of the code, and it was followed by instant dismissal.

Malicious accusations were a more flagrant violation than cheating itself, and despite the intensity of some personal feuds, few Inchcape students ever preferred false charges against their schoolmates. Those who did were inevitably discovered and expelled.

Infringements of the code were punished with increasing severity as the pupils progressed from grade to grade, and Willie, like most of the other new boys, was flattered by the sense of responsibility the school had suddenly imposed upon him.

On Saturday nights, while sophomores and upperclassmen went to the movies in town, freshmen attended school rallies in the gymnasium, where Dr. Louis Flournoy Smith, called "Lefty Louie" by the student body, stressed with appalling regularity the importance of maintaining excellent grades. "The great punishment is *not* to be denied advancement at the end of the year," he reiterated, "but to look into the eyes of your parents and see the disappointment, hurt, and anguish written there."

112

At this point, young Coates, readily distinguishable as the class dunce, would sniffle audibly for the benefit of the doctor, and wink benignly at his classmates. Every time the doctor looked at Coates, he sighed. The prospect of listening to four more years of vain promises and false contrition was none too cheering. Dr. Smith was sixty-five now and would gladly have exchanged his exalted position as headmaster for a pension. But the trustees insisted on his staying in harness. Very well then, thought the doctor, adjourning the meeting, but why must each incoming class include one young man obviously sent by the Devil to plague me.

Lefty Louie, however, hadn't considered Willie's possibilities and within two semesters, the class of '32 included not only an obvious dunce but also a troubled one.

It was all Louis Levinson's fault.

Willie's first-year subjects were English, algebra, Latin, biology, and history. One hour a day at each, and an hour and a half every night studying for the next day's classes.

He was a busy little man, and to some extent enjoyed the independence granted him by a preparatory school that was run as much like a university as its trustees dared.

He made the Freshman basketball and ice-hockey teams and still managed to keep his marks above average. He received A's in biology and history, and passing grades in all his other subjects.

Louis Levinson was naturally proud of these accomplishments and expressed his gratitude by making a contribution to his son's education that was most certainly not included in the school's curriculum. A contribution that eventually resulted in Willie's being the most envied man on the campus.

Shortly before Christmas vacation began, Louis wrote and asked Willie what he would like for Christmas, and he gave him a choice of two gifts. Either something personal ranging in price up to a hundred dollars, or something that would be of value to others be-

113

sides himself, with no price limit attached, provided Louis approved of the idea.

Willie didn't hesitate a moment. He answered:

Dear Pop:—

For myself I'd want a lot of things, but I asked some of the other men what they'd want if they had a choice of something big like you said. They said, yachts and sailboats and cars, but you didn't mean stuff like that, did you? I think you meant something that would make a lot of fellows happy and I've got the answer, I think.

The main building's all chopped up with names like Brumbaugh Chemistry Hall—Squirter's father gave that one —and there are lots more—but they're all *school* buildings— and, Pop, what I'd like is to have a place where the men could have fun—like a theater for movies and stage plays and things.

Maybe it's a dream, but you asked me what I thought and that's what I thought.

Love to Ma and you and everybody and thanks. I'll be home soon.

Bill

Louis read the letter to the family. When he finished, he smiled and looked around the room.

Rebecca stood behind his chair and giggled with pride. "He's got big ideas for a little fellow. . . . 'I asked the other *men*,'" she repeated, and laughed possessively.

"Fa ten, tvenny tousand dollahs ya gotcha self a boggin!" Momma cried. "A teayter, von't bring a nickel revenoo!"

"Jacob, what do you think?" Louis asked.

"Revenue doesn't enter into it," Jacob said. "It's a moral question concerning a gift to an educational institution. I'm proud of my grandson. Proud and grateful that he's learning to be con-

114

siderate of others. If they teach him that, then it must be a good school and they deserve everything you can give them."

"I'll look into it," Louis nodded.

"Look into it!" Rebecca snorted. "For ten thousand dollars you don't have to do much looking. That kind of money you're not going to throw away if I have anything to say about it."

Louis looked up at his wife and winked. "It's deductible from income tax," he said.

"That's good, I suppose?"

"Better than your buying a thirty-five-dollar hat reduced to twenty-eight seventy-five when it's only worth ten." Louis laughed.

"Do what you want," she answered crossly. "I'm against it."

"I only said I was going to look into it, Rebecca," Louis chided her gently.

"Well, look good," Jacob interrupted, "and you'll find it's worth it."

Willie's exemplary behavior during his Christmas vacation helped to convince Louis that Inchcape was indeed a worthy recipient of his munificence. They spent a good deal of time together and Louis often took his son to luncheons at the Motion Picture Club, where he always introduced him as "my young man." The ease with which Willie conducted himself in the company of all the other important New York executives impressed Louis greatly. Willie was already sure of himself, and at an age which to his father had been one of bewildering doubts.

After a few weeks of negotiation, Louis donated twenty-five thousand dollars to Inchcape for a combined motion-picture theater and auditorium, to be called Levinson Memorial Hall. Why "Memorial" no one knew. But Louis had definitely specified that name in the contract. And the trustees never wiggled an eyebrow in accepting his offer.

It was rumored around Miracle, however, that when Louis had asked Howard Wile, Tom Murphy's successor in the publicity department, to suggest a dignified and appropriate title for his venture

115

into charity, Wile, a Yale graduate who was feeling slightly prankish, had suggested the name. Louis was supposed to have exclaimed, "Now, that's a name with class!" and accepted it on the spot.

At any rate, Inchcape got its own movie house, and Louis, who had poured twenty-five thousand into the project, found himself also saddled with the task of procuring pictures for it.

Naturally Miracle Pictures enjoyed a virtual monopoly on the screen of Levinson Memorial Hall. Outside shows that played the theater generally consisted of grade B opposition pictures used as "fillers" when there was no Miracle product available.

Louis chose his own features carefully. He wanted to build up Miracle's future reputation and at the same time give the boys only what he considered the best entertainment. Therefore, it was with no little bewilderment that he read the following letter from Willie about two months after the building had been completed:

Dear Pop:

The men here all want to thank you for the pictures. They think they're swell—in a way—and the Hall is crowded every Saturday night when they have the showings as you know.

I wish you'd come up and see one with us one of these days, so you could hear the fellows' comments. I think you should know about them so you can make changes in the pictures and improve them. And in the meantime, I thought I'd write and tell you what they say. I keep sticking up for them and always say—"If you think they're bad, look at the pictures Miracle doesn't make"—and when they see them— they sure agree with me.

Now, Pop, they got 4 general complaints. Here they are!

1. *Society Pictures*: The men say your stars don't:

    (1) look like society people.

    (2) act like society people.

    (3) talk like society people.

2. *All Pictures:*
   (1) My Eng. Professor says the grammar is bad.
3. The teachers seem to think more classics should be made. We're reading "Idylls of The King." Why don't you make a picture about King Arthur? He'd be great.
4. The boys whistle at the love scenes. WHY? Why so many love scenes?

As you can see the men *like* the pictures only that's what they say about them and I thought you'd like me to write and tell you what's going on. I want our pictures to be best and some of the men tell me they've seen other ones outside that are much better than ours. That's bad, isn't it?

Love to Ma,

Bill

Louis put the letter in his drawer unanswered. It was so outrageous he was afraid to answer it lest he lose his temper, and when Moe came into the New York office a few weeks later, Louis handed it to him without a word.

Moe read, quickly at first, then settled back in his chair and began to smile, a cold, mirthless smile. When he finished, he jerked a cigar out of his pocket and lit it.

"Well?" Louis asked.

Moe shrugged his shoulders. "Thassa good criticism," he said. "Expensive, too. Cost ya twenny-five thousand bucks—without overhead."

"What am I gonna do?"

"Thass your problem."

"Na, sure," Louis said, and he began to pace around the room, "na, sure it's my problem. I need *you* to tell me that? All the way from California you got to come to make such smart statements? You, my brother-in-law, on a family matter?"

"The kid makes sense, Louis, a lotta sense. Gladys Creighton, she don't look like no society woman. She looks like a tramp. She onney brings in a million bucks a year at the box office—but she *sure* looks like a tramp! . . . Thass point one.

"Point two." Moe took a long drag on the cigar. "WHO speaks good grammar? You know people speak grammar, Louis? You *like* them people? They got sump'm makes a heartthrob, maybe? What they got, mine Louis boy, we shouldn't have onna screen so long we live.

"Point three Classics we should make? Classics we made, my friend. Correction—YOU made . . . epis an epic. *Hamlet,* fa Chrissake. Should drop dead, the classics.

"Point four: love scenes. Why a love scene, the schlump wantsa know? You got a answer? I got no answer. Them kiddies don't know from the bees yet, thass why they don't like love scenes—ta them it's just a lotta schmoos and smootchin' onna screen. But we make pitchures with people, fa Chrissake, and people fall in love. So, we gotta have love scenes. So what's he want, the little fella, we should make movies with crocodiles, maybe? . . .

"You wanna know what to do? I told ya once, and ya never listened ta me! An edjication's poison fa that kid. He's gotta learn from life, not books. The more book crap he gets, the worse a stinker he'll be. Chris', he's been in that dump just long enough now ta start callin' us bums and, brother, he ain't wastin' no time! He's prolly the toppa his class, and you, ya dope, you're prouda that, I suppose.

"You gotta be firm, Louis. You gotta tell the kid ta have a good time and ta hell with bein' a goddamn perfessor. We're gonna need him inna business someday and you're startin' him off wrong, Louis, buhlee me. If I was you, I'd beat the bejesus outta him evvy time he comes home with a good report card.

"Buhlee me, if ya wanna keep his respeck, keep him dumb. He'll know more about pitchures. Thass an instinck, and edjication's got nothin' ta do with it."

Louis sighed. He didn't like to admit it, but the trend Moe had predicted was already showing up in Willie. He made up his mind

118

to take Moe's advice, and when Willie's report for the year showed A's in most of his subjects, he sat down and, though he hated to do it, wrote him a curt note, the substance of which was:

"I would prefer your NOT studying too hard as it might prove injurious to your health."

Willie read that line over four times. Even then he wasn't quite sure what his father meant. . . . And much as he wanted to believe the sentence as it stared up at him from the paper, he didn't dare take it as its face value—it might have been a mistake. So he wrote back that he was feeling fine and his father shouldn't worry about him. He also added that he didn't essentially enjoy his studies, but like most of the boys, he did just enough work to keep him out of the registrar's office. It was easier that way.

At this point Louis dictated a letter that rattled even his shock-proof secretary and made Louis Levinson the unwitting idol of four hundred fifty Inchcape boys.

Dear Willie:

You're fourteen now. When I was fourteen I worked very hard. Too hard. I got up at six o'clock every morning and worked in the fields till sundown so that your grandfather, whose earnings as a peddler hardly bought buttons for his two alpaca coats, could eat his beloved gefuelte fish on Saturday nights. I never got home till long after dark and for all this labor I received ten kopecks a week.

Those ten kopecks wouldn't keep you in chewing gum for two days, but I religiously turned that sum over to my parents and it helped them considerably.

Now, through a series of fortunate circumstances, I am in a position to make your life a comparatively easy one. I know that study and learning were never your favorite occupations and, very simply, I advise you not to worry about them. Marks and medals don't mean much. Be healthy, go out, exercise and have fun, that's more important. You don't

119

need an education in this world, much less in the movie business. What you need is the necessary stamina to shout down the next fellow. So don't waste your energies on book-learning. Have yourself a grand time, your memories will be richer for it.

Love,
Your Father

P.S. You see, I even have a secretary who corrects my mistakes and spells like a streak. Cost, $22.50 per week. So you should worry about bugs and French.

Willie's marks dropped rapidly down to C's and D's, and by the end of the term he barely skimmed into the next grade.

When the registrar wrote Louis about the abrupt decline in Master Levinson's work, he received a brief note from the Miracle Picture Company's president, stating, "That's your problem!" And shortly thereafter Willie paid regular Friday afternoon visits to the registrar's office, where he was cajoled, coaxed, and finally threatened with expulsion by Stricky.

The latter worried him. Willie liked Inchcape. So he wrote to Louis, who told him to do just enough to get by—no more, no less—and who in hell was the registrar to bother him about Willie's grades? He paid the school a fat sum every year to make a man of his son, not a bookworm.

Willie marched into Strickland's office and handed him the letter. The registrar read it and turned purple. He glared at Willie, then read the letter over again, and said, "Young man, we have standards here and you're going to abide by them."

"Yes, sir!" Willie replied. "But so long as I get a C average you can't expel me, can you?"

"We can do other things." The registrar frowned and retired to his office, where he promptly dictated a polite letter of protest to Mr. Levinson.

Louis merely took Strickland's complaint, clipped it to an itemized cost sheet of the building, film rental, and projectionist charges for Levinson Hall, and mailed it back.

The registrar took one look at the figures and gasped, "Oh, my God!"

He hoped Willie would maintain his C average.

2

SHORTLY AFTER WILLIE turned fourteen, an event of no particular significance to him burst upon a hitherto complacent America and smote its citizenry squarely on the pants. Stocks crashed, corporations failed, and a nation wailed its anguish to the skies.

In the forefront of those forced to attribute their annihilation to this financial riptide stood the motion-picture industry. And by 1931, when Willie was sixteen, it stood stripped. At this point there wasn't really much its administrators could do except, like any frightened babe, yell angrily for help.

And then, gradually, their pleas were answered by the few solvent bankers left in the land. Yes, they would supply money, but, in turn, they demanded stock. Of course they would take over the mortgages and loans strewn about in lusty profusion during the industrial expansion when, at exorbitant pre-crash prices, every theater and potential theatrical property in sight had been purchased, but . . . the movies must be put on a business basis and businessmen must run them. Furthermore, the banks would appoint those businessmen.

The boys were stuck. They had been caught in a financial juggernaut of their own creation and were expected to pay huge indemnities for letting it get away from them.

"Among those rumored considerably damaged in the current conflict with economic forces," euphemized one of the film trade papers, "is Louis Levinson. The president of Miracle Pictures cannot be reached to confirm or deny this rumor."

Louis hadn't been downtown for a month. Dr. Lansburgh insisted on his staying at home. No phones. No mail. No visitors. His nerves had begun to rebel against the periods of grueling depression to which they had been subjected by an overwrought mind. After two weeks Louis was finally permitted to sit up in bed. He stared vacantly into space. Then one afternoon Jacob heard him talking to himself.

"Next year we'da been outta the red. . . . Sixteen years' work wiped out. . . . It ain't fair! It's a crime!" he shouted unconsciously.

Jacob poked his head through the door.

"So what's a crime? So you're muchulla, broke, so what? You started a tailor—you wind up a tailor. But in between, for a short while, you were a success. What more can a man want?"

Louis glared at Jacob and for the moment hated him. He suddenly hated anybody who accepted things easily. He liked a person who'd fight back. That was it—fight. He said it out loud, "Fight!"

The sound of the word made him feel better.

3

JAMES BRANCH FITZHUGH'S English class dozed solemnly in their seats. They had been listening to Fitz's praises of his beloved Shakespeare for more than three months now.

Fitz droned on. The pupils jotted down occasional notes. Willie sneaked furtive glances at an unopened letter from his father. But every time he began tearing the envelope, the poetry seemed to concentrate in his vicinity. He finally gave up and put the letter back in his pocket. The class met from eleven to twelve, and after it was over he thought he'd get a chance to read it.

At twenty-five minutes after eleven the boys stirred. Wrist watches were consulted by the thirty pupils. Fitz's voice began to falter. As the time neared half past, all eyes turned toward young Coates. Fitz shuddered. He glanced hurriedly from the book to Coates and back again. Helplessly he stumbled through one of his favorite passages. At eleven-thirty on the dot, to the relief of the entire class and the professor, Master Coates belched long and loudly.

He was one of those anomalies of nature who could do so at any given moment. And he chose to belch every morning at the same time. Thus for the duration of ten seconds, Master Coates triumphed over Shakespeare.

The class maintained a respectful silence. They were no longer amused by Coates. They were merely interested in seeing if he'd be on time.

The lad was amazing, Fitz thought. And then, exactly as he'd done every day since the beginning of the term, Fitz cleared his throat, adjusted his glasses and continued the lecture. The class retaliated by relaxing into its traditional defiance of culture.

The twelve o'clock bell set Willie free and he rushed out of the classroom to read Louis's letter before lunch. He glanced quickly at the crumpled sheet of paper. It was the first time Louis hadn't written to him on office stationery. His father's longhand seemed strange. All the other letters had been typewritten and this one was a jumble of erasures, pen scratches, and crossed-out words. Willie sensed that something drastic had happened. He skipped the scratched-out opening sentences and toward the middle of the page discovered the simple paragraph that justified his fears.

I'm broke but not beaten. I've got to curtale all my expenses for the time being. And it hurts me to include you as an expense. But youre tuishion is O.K. The school was very nice. They said they'd give you a schollaship for the rest of your stay. So you better behave yourself—youre a free pupil now because of the Hall. And I arranged with Colombia to send you one picture a week—free, like we did. So the only thing I'll have to cut down on is your alowance.

You'll have to scrape along the best you can on 50c a week.

I'm sorry,

Pop.

Willie looked up slowly. The squat Gothic buildings and the trees had never penetrated his consciousness before. He'd merely accepted them, and acceptance dulls perception. Now he whimpered and sat down slowly on the dormitory steps. He wanted to cry, but Inchcape boys never cried. He wanted to help his father, but he knew that was an impossibility. He put his hand in his pocket and drew forth twenty-five cents in nickels and pennies. He looked at them blankly. Then gradually he realized what had happened. He began to weep quietly. He'd really been touched. They'd robbed his father, and through no fault of his, he too was penniless.

4

WILLIE FOUND it extremely embarrassing to be without his usual pocket money. This was his third year at Inchcape, and he had become one of the regulars making the weekly hegira to the metropolis of Wallingford on Saturday afternoons.

And now haircuts, cokes, magazines, all the million and one incidentals that clutter up prep-school life, were suddenly denied him. Fifty cents a week barely covered his school expenses. A month

124

went by. He no longer made vague excuses when the other boys asked him to join them on their jaunts to Main Street. He just sulked. His moodiness communicated itself to his roommate, Bill Rowse, in whom he ultimately confided.

"YOU'RE broke!" Bill exploded, after listening to Willie's tale. "What the hell do you think I am? My old man was a stockbroker! At least *you* know where your old man is. Mom and I haven't heard from mine for a year."

"What are you using for money, then?"

"Mom took a job selling real estate back home."

"That's a good business these days?" Willie asked doubtfully.

"Hell, no, but they're splitting up a lot of estates and Mom's friends have commissioned her to sell them. She sends me about ten bucks a month."

"You wanna jack that up?"

"Sure. How?"

"Anything in regulations about clubs?"

"No. Nothing I know of."

"Fraternities?"

"I haven't heard of any here."

"In that case, you're a president already."

"Of what?"

"The Friars."

"And what the hell is the Friars?"

"A way for us to make money. You, me, Bob, and Squirter."

"If I'm in, Corlett's in."

"Okay. Let's get 'em."

Bob, Squirter, and Jim Corlett filed into the room. They knew from the way Willie had corralled them that something momentous was up. They sat down warily. Willie stood in front of the window seat. Despite the fact that seniors were the only class allowed to smoke on the campus, and then only with the written consent of their parents, Willie grubbed a cigarette. It made him feel more manly.

"You guys okay for cash?" he asked.

"You kidding?" Corlett laughed.

"Nope. Gimme a light." He leaned forward, borrowed Corlett's cigarette, held it to his own, and took a few quick drags. Then he looked at Bob Levy.

"How're you heeled?" he asked.

"I'm in Corlett's class, and you know it."

"Squirter?"

"Okay. The oil business is still okay. I'm still getting my old allowance—but I'm strapped all the time. The whole joint seems to be sponging on me nowadays."

"You're interested in a few fast shekels, then?"

"Definitely."

"All of you?"

"Hell, yes!"

Willie walked over to the sink, wet his cigarette, and threw it in the basket. The boys waited patiently. Willie had become a campus character, a power in their cabals. Levinson Memorial Hall and his successful defiance of Stricky had contributed immeasurably to his reputation as a smooth operator. And he knew it. He took his time and smiled slowly.

"You guys are charter members in a secret fraternity called the Friars," he said. "And you're going to make a quarter apiece for every new member."

"What the hell are you talking about?" Bob Levy demanded. "There's a regulation against secret societies."

"There is not!" Squirter interrupted. "There's just never been one. But there's nothing in the regulations about them, and I know it!"

"Maybe not," Bob said doubtfully, "but how're you going to get guys to shell out good dough just because we're a secret society?"

"Because," Willie said, counting off the reasons on his fingers: "one, Bill's captain of the football team; two, Squirter's president of this year's cotillion; three, Jim's vice-president of his class, and four, you're the secretary of ours."

126

"We wouldn't want to trade on that, Willie," Jim said, "and you know it."

"You don't have to trade on it. The fact is you are, and that's enough. They'll come running, and besides, we'll give them something for their money. Each new guy pays two bucks. We take out a dollar and a quarter—that's twenty-five cents apiece. With the seventy-five cents left over, we buy hoods and gadgets for the initiation, give the guys a spread once a month, and when cotillion comes, the Friars' girls will all be given a special corsage, all alike, with an F made of flowers. That means a guy's girl is protected."

"From what?" Bob asked.

"How the hell do I know?" Willie suddenly shouted. "If you don't want to belong, you don't have to!"

"Sure. Sure, Bill, I do," Bob protested.

"Shut up, then."

"Okay."

"In that case I call the meeting to order. I move that we discuss rituals and procedures, elect officers, draw up a charter, and set the date for the next meeting. All those in favor?"

"Aye!" the five charter members shouted in unison.

"Uh-oh!" Bob Levy wailed very softly to himself.

5

WITHIN A WEEK, Inchcape's campus became an Occidental replica of a Tibetan lamasery.

The transition was gradual, the neophytes mysterious and silent, the professors bewildered and bug-eyed at the multitude of shaved heads that suddenly sprouted like mushrooms among the ordinary cabbageheads common to their classrooms. In all their experience with prep-school pranks, this epidemic of nude craniums proved the most trying. Their presence lent a startling checkerboard effect to every lecture. They were like ciphers intruding themselves on every sum. A sum, to be sure, not calculated to make neurotics of instructors, but one which, nevertheless, added up to the same thing.

Staff meetings, previously concerned with educational matters, began disintegrating into discussions of the best means of curtailing the school's tonsorial problem. A plan was finally arrived at. The teachers would first meet foolishness with ridicule. That was the best weapon, and after that—well, other measures would occur to them. But they found that lines like "the campus must have been swept by a high fever last night," merely provoked polite snickers without providing a remedy. So they tried personal interviews. But these, too, proved ineffective. The neophytes were violently non-committal. They fervently believed in the omnipotence of their new "order," and besides, they were pledged to secrecy.

In desperation, the teachers finally appealed to Dr. Smith, who by this time was well aware of the plague affecting his institution, but the good doctor, firmly convinced that this was merely another ephemeral fashion, did nothing, secure in the knowledge, drawn from his long experience, that this too was merely a passing fancy.

His conclusion was correct, however innocently arrived at. But his assumption that the campus had merely been invaded by a new fashion proved disastrously wrong.

Inchcape's first secret fraternity was in full bloom. And William Levinson had nurtured it to its first and only flowering on the campus.

The Friars' entrance requirements consisted of a shaved thatch, two dollars, and a masochistic appreciation of the beneficent kindness demonstrated by the Elders in condescending to admit one as a member. The rites were simple. "Applications for Membership" were automatically filed by prevailing upon a roommate or friend to shave one's head. "Official Recognition" of the application was

128

achieved by depositing two dollars with the organization's treasurer, William Levinson. In due time, the president, Bill Rowse, Vice-President Jim Corlett, and the Board of Elders met in solemn conclave to decide on the eligibility of each applicant. After acceptance, the novice received a slip of paper instructing him to sneak over to such and such a room at nine o'clock the following Wednesday. Failure to appear resulted in immediate dismissal and one blackball. Applications could be renewed by payment of an extra fifty cents. Three blackballs automatically barred one from membership, and young Coates had already acquired two when he finally arrived breathless and expectant at the door of room 209.

He knocked four times, two long and two short, as instructed, and slowly the door opened. A hand reached out of the utter darkness, grasped his and pulled him quickly into the room. A subdued voice warned, "Talk in whispers. Answer questions quickly, and whatever happens, don't scream. Friars are particularly famous for fortitude and you must demonstrate your capacity for enduring punishment. What's your name?"

"Coates, you dope. What's yours?"

"My name is Friar Brumbaugh, Novice Coates, and your insolence prompts me to doubt your qualifications for joining our order. . . . Baptize him, Friar Initiator!"

Willie upended a bucket of ice water over Coates's head.

"The Greeting!" Brumbaugh directed.

Whang!—A paddle thumped across Coates's rump and a hand covered his mouth. His scream of rage subsided into a blubber of struggling protest.

"The Blindfold!" Brumbaugh ordered.

Coates stopped struggling and began to tremble. Willie tied a handkerchief around his head.

"The Sacred Light!" boomed Brumbaugh.

Through the damp softness of his binding, Coates sensed a lone candle flickering in the room.

129

"On your knees!" came the next command.

"Yes, sir!" The shivering novice dropped to his knees on the wet rug.

"The Holy Oil!"

Coates's nostrils acquainted him with the fact that he was about to be anointed with oil of garlic. He shuddered involuntarily before he felt the liquid dripping on his bald scalp and trickling down his cheek.

"The Holy Food!"

Crack! An eggshell splintered across his skull.

"The Holy Fish!"

"Open your mouth!" Willie muttered in Coates's ear.

Coates did so. A thick mucous substance was tossed down his throat.

"Swallow!" commanded Brumbaugh.

He swallowed.

"The second one!"

Coates didn't wait for the command. He gulped it down, gagging a little.

"Novice Coates, two more things remain before you become a full-fledged Friar. First, do you swear never to reveal the members or secret ritual of this order?"

"I swear," replied Coates faintly.

"And secondly, do you grant us the right to inscribe an F in green paint on any part of your anatomy the Elders choose?"

"Whaaaat!" exploded the novice.

"Perhaps your hearing would improve if we greeted you a little more firmly."

"N-n-no, thanks. Go right ahead. . . ."

"Keep silent, Mr. Coates. . . . Elders," continued Brumbaugh, addressing the Friars, "where shall we place our insignia?"

"Last year, Friar Brumbaugh, Novice Coates was voted class dunce. I think that simplifies the question," announced Willie.

"The head, Friar Initiator?" queried Brumbaugh.

130

"The head," prescribed Friar President Rowse.

"Give, brothers!" said the Initiator, and he grabbed the paint-brush.

Whatever it is, it tickles, thought Coates.

"Remove the blindfold, Friars, and shake Friar Coates by the hand," concluded Brumbaugh.

Friar Coates blinked and looked around the room. Blankets had been tacked across the windows to insure secrecy. One by one the Friars marched up to him, shook his hand, and showed him their insignia. When Coates realized that all of them had F's daubed on their bodies in thick green paint, he became panicky and yammered for a mirror. When he saw that they'd decorated his entire scalp with their insignia, he turned ashen.

"You stinkers!" he shrieked, and for the first time in his life he suffered from an unpremeditated attack of gastritis.

Brumbaugh bowed low in mock courtesy. "Stinkers or not, Friar Coates, you're now privileged to join the Friars' Feast. Brothers, the victuals!"

The boys sat down to a banquet of sardines, peanut butter, saltines, bread, and jam. Friar Coates ate sparingly.

6

MASTER COATES'S distinctive appearance created quite a stir on the campus. Now that the ordeal was over, he was perversely proud of his decoration and doffed his hat at the slightest provocation. The reaction produced by this gesture invariably delighted his exhibitionist soul, but his enjoyment was short-lived. By noon of the next day, Master Coates was in the infirmary. Around ten he had begun to feel nauseous and to suffer from severe cramps. By eleven he was vomiting violently, his temperature was well above normal, and he felt extremely weak and tired.

The Friars were quickly apprised of their brother's condition and the Board of Elders, prompted by anxiety as well as courtesy, trooped over to the infirmary immediately after lunch to make polite inquiries concerning his health. They were not allowed to see him. Master Coates was quite ill.

By two o'clock the Board also learned that Dr. Smith had interviewed the new Friar before his confinement. They decided to hold a solemn conclave in room 209 as soon as classes were over.

Three of them were already in the room when Bob Levy ran up the stairs and almost tore the door off its hinges. Three heads whipped around and stared at him.

"You see the bulletin board?" he asked breathlessly.

Rowse, Corlett, and Willie shook their heads.

"I wrote it down," he said, taking a piece of paper from his pocket. "Here!"

IMPORTANT!

The men responsible for the organization of the secret society that initiated Henry Coates last night will report to Dr. Smith's office between the hours of 3 and 5 this afternoon.

They will appear singly or in a group.

Everett Strickland
Registrar

"Jesus!" Bill Rowse swore softly.

"I tried to tell you," Bob said with a gesture of helplessness, "but you wouldn't listen to me."

Corlett frowned at him. "Pipe down!" he snapped. "We're all in this together and we might as well face it together. Where's Squirter?"

132

"I don't know," Bob answered. "But don't get me wrong. No matter *what* I said before we started this, I'm in it to the finish."

"I knew you'd feel that way."

Bill Rowse turned from the window. "Squirter's coming up now," he said.

"I wonder how much Coates told Lefty Louie?" Willie asked.

Jim looked at him and moaned, "Would I like to know the answer to that one!"

"Look," Bill Rowse said thoughtfully, "I don't think the kid said so much. They'd know our names if he blabbed at all. And the notice didn't say anything about the *Friars,* did it? It just said secret society."

"And they weren't sure there was only one on the campus," Willie pointed out, "or they wouldn't have specifically mentioned the one that initiated Coates."

"In other words, they don't *know!*" Bob Levy trumpeted, and this realization pleased him so much he almost smiled.

Corlett brought him right back to earth. He shook his head and said, "So what? They'll know as soon as we get down there. We'll have to tell them."

"Hell," Bill said defensively, "we haven't done anything so God-awful!"

The other two looked at Rowse, and wished to heaven he were right.

Squirter opened the door and looked around the room. "How nice to see your smiling faces!" he grinned. "Cheer up! Coates'll be all right now. They just took him to the hospital in Wallingford."

"Close the door," Rowse groaned.

"They any idea what's wrong with him?" Bob asked.

"Ptomaine, I think. We kept those oysters too long. They should have been on ice."

"Oh, my God!" Jim said, and he sank onto the day bed. "It gets worse every minute."

"Hell," Squirter reassured them. "The Holy Fish stank a little bit, that's all. Two oysters couldn't kill anybody."

"But what they're doing to us!" Bill complained.

"If he's in the hospital, it's serious," said Willie gloomily.

"He'll be all right. We'll just lay low for a while. It'll blow over!"

"Blow over!"

The other boys looked at each other. Obviously Squirter hadn't seen the bulletin board.

"Give it to him, Willie," Bill said.

Willie handed the notice to Squirter, whose cockiness surged out of him in one long sigh. "Whew!" he whistled softly and sat down on the couch beside Jim.

"Well," Jim asked, "should we go down together or alone?"

"Together," most of them answered solemnly.

Bill Rowse shook his head. "No," he said. "Not together. One by one."

"Why, Bill?" Jim asked.

"They don't know how many are mixed up in this thing," Bill answered. "If we go down one every twenty minutes, the old boy'll have to talk to each one of us and we can talk back to him. If we go down in a bunch he'll just bawl us out and punish us on the spot. I'm for one by one. It'll wear him out. And the longer he waits, the easier the punishment will be. I'm for one at a time."

"He's got something there," Willie agreed.

"I don't think so," Bob said. "If we go down in a body, we take it together. We're all part of it, like Jim said."

"Squirter?" Jim asked.

"I never liked facing the old boy alone—"

"That's it, then," Jim interrupted. "Three to two—"

Willie listened intently. His natural desire to get it over with quickly was at odds with his subconscious instinct to delay the meeting as long as possible. He felt strangely weak and had to sit down.

Then he heard Squirter say, "Wait a minute! I said I didn't like

134

facing Lefty Louie alone, but this time Bill's right. If we all went down together we wouldn't have a chance to get a word in edgewise. He'd work himself into such a fit he'd be liable to fire all of us right the hell out of here."

"Bill's way," Willie said, "is best. Lefty Louie'll have to control himself till the last guy. That'll make it easier for all of us—except the last guy." He looked around the room at his friends and added, "I started this thing. I'm responsible. So I'll be last."

"Nothing doing, Willie," Squirter objected. "We all agreed with you, didn't we? So we're all responsible. Let's draw for it."

"Nix!" Willie protested. "I'm the guy and I go last."

"The hell you are!" Corlett said. "We'll draw. Me first."

Bob tore five strips of paper into varying lengths. "Longest goes last," he said, as Corlett reached for the first strip.

Willie got the longest one. "See," he said, experiencing an inexplicable wave of relief, "I told you I'd go last."

The boys left the room one by one in their appointed order. Bill, who was next to last, was the only one who returned.

"How was it?" Willie asked the moment the door opened.

"Christ awful," Bill replied. "He's sore as hell. Confined all of us to quarters, and we're not supposed to talk to each other."

"How do you know the others have been confined if you're not supposed to talk to them?"

"It's just a guess. If he did it to one, he did it to all. Well, you're next. We better go on silence when you come back—so, good luck."

"Thanks," Willie said and started for the door.

"You look green around the gills."

"Yeah," Willie said, "I feel lousy."

Bill shrugged his shoulders and winked at Willie. Willie tried to smile back but he couldn't make it, so he just looked at Bill a moment and opened the door.

"S'long," Bill said quietly.

"S'long," Willie muttered.

He walked slowly down the steps to the long corridor that led to Dr. Smith's office. He saw the Quad through the windows and suddenly he thought of his father, of the fact that he was a charity student, that Louis had asked him to behave and here he was mixed up in the worst mess of his life. The others were confined to quarters, sure. But what about him? What about Willie, the charity student? Coates had ptomaine and he had dropped the oysters down Coates's throat. Surely they could expel him for that. Jeez—what if they did?

What then? His father was broke and wouldn't want him around the house in New York. He would be an added expense. That's what had started the whole mess anyway—that added expense business. He'd so desperately wanted to earn his own way. Was that a crime? He was trying to make it easier for his father. That's what he'd tell Dr. Smith. He was just trying to earn his own way. But Louis would hear about it—and would be ashamed of him. He wanted his father to be proud of him and here he was making a damn fool of himself.

By the time he reached the bulletin board he was near tears. Dr. Smith's office was only fifteen feet away at the end of the corridor. He stopped to read the notice on the board, but he couldn't find it. The print seemed blurred. He shook his head. The board began to waver, then to spin. He told himself this was nonsense and tried to control himself, but his sense of balance left him and the whole corridor began to revolve so that he stood there weaving, trying to focus his attention on something that would stay still. He felt limp and knew that he had broken into a cold sweat. He tried to look at his watch to see how much time he had left before five, but he couldn't read the dial, and he suddenly realized he was going to throw up. He staggered back toward the bathroom near the other end of the corridor. Quickly, quickly, he told himself silently. He was vaguely conscious of a hand helping him, holding him by the elbow.

"You're sick," a voice said timidly.

Willie nodded. "Bathroom. Quick," he mumbled.

136

The lad propelled him down the hall and they stopped in front of the lavatory.

"It's the faculty john," the voice said hesitantly and Willie knew it belonged to one of the new boys.

"S'okay," Willie sighed, and leaned against the door. The lad helped him to the nearest washstand. Willie leaned over it, his hands gripping the outside of the basin with all their strength. He closed his eyes and felt a pounding in his temples, but he couldn't throw up. He stood there, his head weaving helplessly from side to side. He was bathed in perspiration and felt cold and clammy.

"I'll get somebody," the boy said.

Willie managed to mutter, "No. No. Be expelled. Keep quiet."

"Expelled?" the youngster repeated.

Willie was too weak even to nod.

"Okay, okay. I won't say anything. I know. You've been drinking. I won't tell. But I can't come back in here to see if you're all right. This is for faculty. Okay?"

The lad was embarrassed by Willie's silence.

"I'll leave you now. You're sure you're all right?" he asked again. His voice began to rise with excitement. "You sure?"

Willie couldn't answer him.

"Hey—listen! If you don't come by my room in an hour to tell me you're okay I gotta tell somebody! Understand?"

"What room?" Willie mumbled thickly.

"Three ninety-seven."

Willie nodded and then he heard the door close. Somehow it was wonderful to be alone. He staggered over to the toilet nearest the window and locked the door behind him. He unbuttoned his fly and suddenly the wall in front of his eyes jerked upward. He felt a wave of relief sweep over him. A faint tinkling sound reverberated dimly far in the back of his head. He saw his wrist watch now. In concentric circles the dial stretched toward infinity. The time? Three ninety-seven. Three ninety-seven. Three ninety-seven.

He opened his eyes slowly and sighed. He was too weak to move and he knew he'd fainted. But he couldn't figure out how his body became wedged between the bowl and the steel partition. It was as though he had folded himself straight down on his legs in an attempt to take up as little space as possible.

He heard the door to the lavatory open and recognized the voices of two instructors. Fitz was one of them, and the other was his math teacher, Mr. Bowles. "They got them," he heard Bowles say excitedly. "All four of them. There's going to be hell to pay."

"I hope they won't do anything drastic," Fitz said. "They're really nice kids. It's their nonsense that keeps me amused around here. What a dull job this would be if kids had no imagination."

Willie heard them pulling paper towels out of the dispenser. Then he remembered they'd said "four of them." There were five, and he was the fifth. He took a frantic look at his watch. It was five-fifteen. Fifteen minutes past the allotted time. Well, he'd wait till the instructors left the john, then he'd go to the office.

He had proof, anyway, that he'd been ill. The kid in 397. But what if he went out now? Fitz and Bowles would see him, and if he told them he had been sick, maybe they'd take him to the headmaster's office. Of course! That was the thing to do. But he heard the door close before he could struggle to his feet.

He lifted the latch and stepped out into the washroom. Then he washed his face and walked down the corridor to Dr. Smith's office. He felt weak, but in full possession of his faculties. It was as though he'd been cleansed of some horrible ailment, as though he were recuperating from an operation and all that was left was the pleasant sensation of changing the dressing.

He reached Dr. Smith's office as Miss Salter, the doctor's secretary, was leaving.

"The doctor in?" he asked.

She shook her head. "Dr. Smith just left. There's an important meeting tonight. What's troubling you?"

Willie shrugged his shoulders.

"Can it wait till tomorrow?"

"I suppose so."

"He'll be in after ten."

"Thank you," Willie said, and he turned slowly and started up the corridor to his room. After ten—that's too late, he thought. I'll be in classes till twelve and I won't be able to see him until lunchtime. Lunchtime *tomorrow*. He trembled slightly. Waiting was more of a punishment than punishment itself. Jesus, he thought for a frightening second, if only I didn't *have* to see him!

He walked up an extra flight and knocked at the door of 397. The boy who'd helped him opened the door.

"I'm okay," Willie said.

"Gee, I'm glad." The boy smiled. "My name's Hayes."

"That's good," Willie said curtly. "Thanks," and he turned away. He had quite a problem on his mind and he hadn't solved it when he returned to his room.

"Work out all right?" Bill wrote on a slip of paper.

"Yup," Willie said quietly. He was too ashamed of having been sick to confess that he hadn't even seen the doctor.

He stayed in his room when Bill went to dinner.

7

AT FIVE MINUTES past noon the next day as William Levinson crossed the Quad to Dr. Smith's office, the back door to the office swung on its hinges and Willie saw the headmaster emerge, jam his hat on his head, and hurry down the path toward the main gate. Willie broke into a trot and called the doctor's name. Dr. Smith paused momentarily, shook his head, and continued on his way.

Willie sprinted after him. Outside the gate, just as the doctor opened the door of his car, Willie caught up with him.

"Dr. Smith," he said breathlessly, "I've got to tell you something."

"Not now, William," the headmaster said, and he motioned the driver to go ahead.

"But—"

The doctor slammed the door and said, "Later, William."

The car started. Willie watched it turn down the gravel path and suddenly broke into a run. He chased it as far as the gate, but when it swung into the highway he gave up. His heart was pounding as he turned back slowly, walked up the gravel path, through the Barn, and into the Quad again.

He saw Stricky dash through the back door to Dr. Smith's office and he automatically followed the path that led past Miss Salter's window. It was a warm day and the window was open. He heard Stricky's voice in the headmaster's office. The registrar was breathing heavily. It was obvious he had just reached Miss Salter's desk.

"What's the matter?" he puffed.

"Coates. He's very bad."

"No!"

"It's serious. High fever."

"Oh, my God!"

"I've never seen the doctor so perturbed."

"I saw him from my window. He's never been in such a hurry. Never. I thought I'd better come over."

"There's nothing we can do but hope."

"Adolescents have amazing recuperative powers," Strickland said. "I think he'll get better."

"I hope so," Miss Salter said. "It would be such a blow to the doctor. Such a blow!"

Willie turned away from the window and walked silently down the path. "Please God," he prayed, "please God, he should get well."

140

8

TWO DAYS LATER Dr. Louis F. Smith called a special assembly in Levinson Memorial Hall. Special assemblies were rare indeed, and they presaged either very good or very bad news. Students regarded them with understandable apprehension and rumors concerning the purpose of this particular gathering flew fast and loose around the campus. But only one lad in the entire school came near the truth. As he trudged through the rain to the hall, Willie had a wild, frightening premonition that this meeting concerned him and he toyed with the idea of reporting to the headmaster. But, he argued with himself, what if I'm wrong? What if it has nothing to do with me? Why go down there now? Perhaps the whole thing will blow over. So he sat on the edge of his seat like all the other Inchcape students, and eyed Dr. Smith as he strode to the rostrum. By the end of the doctor's third sentence, Willie began to wish he were dead.

"Gentlemen," the headmaster began, "Inchcape knows its pupils are boys. It compliments them by treating them as men, but don't make the mistake of thinking we're not constantly aware of your adolescent predilection for pranks. In the past we've chosen to close one eye to them because they've been essentially harmless. But pranks are one thing and a betrayal of the faith the institution has placed in you is something else again. It has, most convincingly, been drawn to my attention that a certain group in this school has taken advantage of our good nature and behaved in the manner of hoodlums.

"These boys organized a secret society despite the fact that they *knew* there had never been one on the campus. And as a result of this despicable deed, this contemptible *trifling* with our code of honor, one of our students is now in the hospital."

141

The boys sat bolt upright in their seats. Most of them knew about Coates, but few had ever seen the doctor so indignant. They knew his vengeance would strike them, but where and how violently they had no idea. Nor had they any inkling of the fact that Inchcape history was in the making, that this assembly would become a legend through the years.

"Three days ago a notice was pinned on the bulletin board," the doctor continued, "requesting the ringleaders of this group to report to my office. Four boys did so. Four boys to whom Inchcape is a living thing, a symbol of decency and manliness. But—there were five boys responsible for this deed. Not four—FIVE! And I gave that last creature three days to present himself. Two days of grace! Two days to let our honor system seep through his miserable soul. Where is he now? . . . Where is that man who is a coward?"

The doctor stepped to the front of the platform and his eyes slowly surveyed the entire audience. From left to right he searched for the victim of his wrath, and William Levinson slowly lowered his head. He broke into a cold sweat and began to tremble violently. He heard the doctor only vaguely, knew he was pacing back and forth on the platform; half heard him bellow restlessly, "We do not know his name; but if necessary we can break precedent and *ask* the other four. This is his last and final chance! Will that fifth man *stand* UP!" the doctor roared.

Willie didn't even know he was on his feet. Only when he heard a grumble of dismay surge through his schoolmates did he realize that he'd reacted instinctively. He put his hands on the back of the seat in front of him to steady himself and faced the doctor.

Louis F. Smith stared at the culprit, and suddenly he too was almost sick with anguish.

"You? William Levinson!" he finally said, and his voice was low with bitterness and pity. "You? Here—in this hall your father gave—you did this thing?"

Willie opened his mouth, but no words came. He nodded and the tears ran down his cheeks.

"Sit down," the doctor said. "The only thing in your favor is the fact that the Inchcape honor system is so inculcated in you that it wasn't courage but instinct that made you stand up."

Willie remained on his feet.

"Dr. Smith," he said and his voice was barely audible, "I tried. That afternoon you—" He couldn't finish. He was conscious of his schoolmates. They were watching him, hoping he would disprove the doctor's accusation. But the words wouldn't come and he sat down slowly.

"Ah-ha! The afternoon I went to the hospital," the doctor said. "Yes, I remember that. It was the day *after* the notice had been posted."

Willie suddenly jumped to his feet and said, "I was sick, sir."

The headmaster looked at him contemptuously. "Not so sick as Coates," he said.

From the other end of the hall young Hayes stood up and blurted out, "He was quite sick, Dr. Smith. I saw him."

The doctor looked at Hayes. "Thank you, young man," he nodded. "But with all these extenuating circumstances, Master Levinson still had two days of grace."

He turned to Willie. "I will take your word for the fact that you were ill, and also that you tried to see me the next day. But what can you say for yourself concerning the two days between that attempt and this assembly?"

"Nothing, sir," Willie murmured, and he sat down.

The headmaster turned and faced his audience. "The four boys who gave themselves up will be confined to the campus for the rest of the term. There will be no further punishment for them. But as for you, William Levinson, the fact that you made a halfhearted attempt to see me will save you from expulsion. And there will be no confinement for you. Instead of confinement I will commend you to the tender mercies of your schoolmates, and heaven help your poor benighted soul."

Out of the corner of his eye Dr. Smith saw Strickland rush across the platform. He started to dismiss the boys, but stopped in the middle of his sentence. Strickland handed him a slip of paper. The headmaster read it. His face blanched. He read it again. Then he looked up slowly. He came to the front of the platform again and rested his elbows on the lectern.

"Gentlemen," he announced quietly, "Henry Coates is dead. He died of ptomaine poisoning and pneumonia in the Wallingford Hospital. This tragedy was the direct result of a schoolboy prank. You are dismissed."

The doctor glanced down at the floor, sighed, and walked abruptly off the platform. The boys sat motionless. Then one by one they got up and filed out. A few of them talked in astonished whispers.

Willie sat alone in the hall. A chill ran through his body. A sense of fear and utter desolation overwhelmed him. He began to think, quickly, disjointedly. He knew that henceforth no Inchcape boy would speak to him, that for the rest of his time at school he would be ostracized. Bill would move out of his room immediately, and every day, every hour of his life the other boys would go out of their way to avoid him. He would endure a living hell—and why? Why should it have happened to him? All because he'd tried to help his father. He had been done a great injustice. And now there was no turning back. This sense of innocence gave him new strength and he told himself it didn't matter what they'd do. He'd stand alone, against them all, if necessary. He'd stick it out and make them wish they'd never turned against him. That's what he'd do. He'd fight, by God!

And he screamed the last two words out loud. But they were swallowed up in emptiness and somehow the walls deflected his aloneness back to him.

He held his head in his hands and wished he could go home. If only he could write to them and tell them. But he couldn't. They'd never understand, and furthermore, they'd never even hear about it. Inchcape men never told on those they ostracized. It was part of the

144

code. Never tell an outsider. Why should he tell his folks? Why make them miserable?

There was nothing to do but stick it out. That's what he'd do. Stick it out—and he already hated everything about the school, its honor system, its teachers, its campus, and the men who'd been his friends.

And then he thought of Coates. He tried to reassure himself and muttered, "What the hell, you just die," but he hadn't realized it could happen so quickly and the phrase didn't give him the consolation he thought it would.

It was getting dark, and the sound of the rain, the gurgling rush of it as it sluiced down the drainpipes and splattered on the ground, increased his gloom. It was as though both he and the rain had spent themselves stupidly. In the morning the sun would come and there would be no more rain. In the morning the sun would come and there would be no more Henry Coates.

He began to miss Coates, but it was not until the following morning in Fitz's class that he became fully aware of a personality, a being, an individual removed from the sphere of his own immediate society.

Willie's first realization of death began to crystallize as the clock neared eleven-thirty. Several of the boys became grimly embarrassed as they caught themselves about to consult their watches. Fitz's voice began to falter. His hands shook noticeably. Finally he stopped talking and fingered his notes. He closed his book, tucked his papers methodically into his briefcase, and cleared his throat.

"It's a crime," he said, "that any youth, no matter how wretched within himself, must die. Class dismissed."

The boys rose slowly. Fitz walked over and opened a window.

Willie went up to him.

"Sir?" he said tentatively.

Fitz turned and looked at Willie, and walked away.

9

WILLIE STOOD outside the gymnasium. It was the night of the cotillion, and like the other boys who were inside dancing with their dates, he too was wearing a dinner jacket. The sounds of music and laughter drifting through the windows filled him with an aching loneliness beyond tears.

He ventured timidly toward the steps. It was nice just to sit there on the stone casing and watch the girls and their escorts strolling up and down the path that led to the gymnasium. Even though his schoolmates carefully looked the other way when they passed him, it was still nice. And some of the girls did smile. They were so pretty in their white fluffy dresses, and when they walked by, the odors of their chaste perfumes trailed after them and assailed his nostrils with a subtle invitation to inspect their innocence without availing himself of it.

It was a delicate challenge, flung with an air of naïveté. But it was there, nevertheless, for all its adolescence. And there was one girl who came out often, never with less than two young swains and often with more. She was an independent soul, obviously, flattering the boys and yet commanding them. And she wore black, in contrast to the other girls, who envied her for her poise, her manner, and her attractiveness to men.

Her black hair glistened in the light that flooded the entrance to the gym, and Willie found himself listening for her low laugh, waiting more and more anxiously for her frequent reappearances on the stone platform at the head of the stairs. From where he sat, he had to look up to see her at all, and even then it was difficult because of the lads invariably surrounding her.

"Janet," he heard them calling her—and he knew she smoked.

You could tell just by looking at her. She knew her way around.

And Willie wished desperately that she'd come out alone, just once, so he could talk to her. He knew just what he'd say—he'd carried on so many imaginary conversations with her in the past hour. She'd been inside now, for almost fifteen minutes; longer than any other time, he thought, looking at his watch.

And then she came out again with four young men in tow. They stood there laughing and talking and one of the seniors lit a cigarette. He looked around and handed it to Janet, who ducked behind his back, took a quick, deep drag and handed it back to him. Her eye caught Willie's as she exhaled. She stared at him for a moment, and suddenly began to talk to her admirers again. Then, just as abruptly, she stopped, broke through their circle, and came down the steps toward Willie.

He glanced sideways quickly to make sure there was no one else around him. He was quite alone and she was coming over to him. There was no doubt of it. His heart began thumping wildly. He never saw the look of shock on the faces of the four boys, never heard one of them call sharply, "Janet!" He just knew she was coming over to talk to him, and all the fine words he ever dreamed of saying to her fled; and she was standing there in front of him, smiling at him, a slightly defiant, taunting smile.

"You saw me?" she asked.

Willie nodded.

"Do you object to a girl smoking?"

"No," Willie said. "No. Of course not. I think it's fine."

"Well, light one for me, then."

Willie patted his pockets quickly. He knew he didn't have any with him. "I'm not a senior yet, so I don't smoke, miss," he apologized.

"Miss?" she laughed. "My name's Janet. Janet Mason."

And Willie laughed too. "Mine's Bill Levinson," he said.

"Well, you've been sitting here long enough. Come on inside and dance with me."

Panic suddenly surged into Willie's eyes. He looked at Janet Mason and shook his head.

"I can't," he said. "I'm sorry, I can't."

"Oh, come on," she urged, taking his hand, "don't be bashful. I'll lead you, if you're afraid," and she laughed that rich, throaty laugh he'd been fascinated by all evening. He tried to think quickly, squeezed her hand, then drew his own away.

"I wish I could," he said, "but I've got a bad leg."

She looked at him anxiously. The smile vanished from her face. She was quite serious now and embarrassed by her brashness. He knew she thought he was a cripple and he hastened to reassure her.

"It's nothing really serious," he said. "Just a slight injury. But enough to keep me from going inside with you. Don't worry about it."

But Janet wasn't put off easily. "In that case, I'll sit with you awhile," she said, and as she started up the steps to join him on the casing, he said, "No. Thanks, Janet, no. You'd better go back to your friends. They're getting sore, I think."

"Jealous, you mean," she laughed. "It's good for them. Keeps them interested," and she looked at them as she said it.

They were staring at her. One of them called, "Janet, come here."

"In a minute," she answered, and she turned back to Willie. "I'm sorry you're hurt."

"Janet!" the boys called her again.

"Right away!" she said over her shoulder.

"You'd better go," Willie murmured.

"I will. Good luck to you, Bill Levinson."

She turned and left him.

"Good luck to you, Janet Mason," Bill said. "And—thanks," he added softly to himself.

He heard one of the boys say, "You shouldn't have done that!" and Janet demand an explanation. Willie wanted to leave but he couldn't. He had to hear the answer. "You just shouldn't, that's all," another boy said.

148

"I want to know why," she insisted. "He's a perfectly nice boy."

"He isn't at all."

"That's your opinion."

"It's the school's opinion," the senior said flatly.

"Why?" Janet demanded again, and this time she stamped her foot.

There was a long, desperate, bewildered silence. Willie watched Janet's eyes question each one of her escorts.

"Come on, let's go inside and dance," one of the boys suggested.

"There must be a reason," Janet insisted, "and I'm not going anywhere until I know!"

"Because he's a Jew!" one of the boys snapped.

Willie shuddered involuntarily. Then he lowered himself slowly from the casing and walked down the steps. He knew her eyes were following him and he hobbled slightly as he crossed the campus to his room.

He never heard Janet say, "How foul of you, how foul!" And he never knew that the boy had said it less out of hate than out of desperation and bewilderment. So he sat on his bed and opened his tie slowly. "Because he's a Jew," he thought, and he couldn't help smiling bitterly to himself. That was it, then. That was the reason. . . .

He was a Jew. He and Bob Levy, both. What would have happened had another boy done the same thing? Would they have ostracized him too? Bob Levy, yes, but another boy, a Christian boy? Never. Punished him, yes, but not this way, which was worse than punishment. And the other boys had been just as guilty as he—only they took the easy way. They went downstairs and reported themselves. He, Willie, had done the really brave thing. He'd confessed his crime in front of the whole school. Sure, he'd cut the corners a bit, but he'd never really understood why the penalty had been so drastic. Now he knew.

He pulled off his trousers and stretched out on the bed in his underwear.

He'd be goddamned if he'd be a fall guy the rest of his life just because his parents happened to be Jews. Jesus, wouldn't it have been wonderful to have been born a gentile! Things were so easy for them. Think of the fun they had! He remembered their stories about yacht clubs and sailing on the Sound and weekend parties and the names of the clubs their parents belonged to. . . . He remembered all these things and *knew* they were wonderful, and he'd never be a part of them. Never.

"They belong!" he murmured. "They belong and I never will. Never."

And suddenly a wave of resentment surged over him, a wave of revulsion against his parents and his heritage, of hatred of the very gentiles he envied. And he thought back to the fun he'd had with them before he'd known or cared or even heard of any "difference." And he knew that from here on, for the rest of his life, consciously or unconsciously, he'd be fighting that "difference" because there was none and he was as good as they were, any day. And, furthermore, he'd prove it.

It would take time, though, and he'd never go through another scene like the one on the steps this evening, either. He'd never lay himself open to that sort of thing again. And over such a dizzy dame, too! All those dames were dizzy. Their air of virginity was such a professional one, anyway. That's what they were, professional virgins. They probably necked like hell in rumble seats, got guys all excited and then said "No!" because they were scared and frightened and had been taught never to "go the limit." Well, goddamn it, he'd find a girl who wasn't scared. All these guys playing around with a lot of finger-fiddling virgins—what a hell of a waste of time that was! And they never got anywhere . . . any of them. . . . Well, he'd find himself a *real* girl. A girl he could—"lay!" he said defiantly.

10

HER NAME was Annette Lejoux. She was the usherette at the Wallingford movie house. Far from pretty, she wore clothes calculated to set off her pudgy body with infinitely more allure than she could honestly lay claim to. Instinctively she understood that sex was a matter of scent, curiosity, and imagination. And she used that knowledge to the best of her ability. She had no uniform and her dresses were all cut on the bias from the navel up. They were invariably of rayon velvet or cheap satin. She never wore brassieres and in the lazy Connecticut summer she often forgot to put her legs through a pair of step-ins before she went to work. She lived with her family, but her weekend jaunts had been known to stretch for months. She held her job because the theater manager was a married man, and they had been on a hayride once. Her cheap perfume permeated the lobby, but it was better than the smells emerging from the rest rooms. Her attitude toward women customers was one of haughty indifference, but she bowed low when she showed male patrons to their seats and in the half-light they all imagined they had peered down her dress and seen the fullness of her breasts.

The first time Willie saw her she was standing in the lobby, her blondined hair and coyly colored cheeks, her red lips and curved breasts completing a veritable picture of sexual complacency. As she ushered him to his seat, she brushed against him and apologized softly in his ear. Willie sat down dumbly and determined to speak to her after the show. When he came out she had gone. It took two weeks to find out that she left work at nine in the evening. After that, he came to town every Saturday and spent most of his allowance at the movies.

He began to dream about her. They were strong sexual dreams in which she came to him and said she wanted him.

One afternoon he screwed up enough courage to mumble an invitation to dinner. She looked at him and laughed.

"What are you laughing at?" he demanded.

"Go away!" she said. "You're just a little boy."

"Mebbe so," he grumbled, "but I know what to do."

"What!" she exploded, staring at him defiantly.

He turned ashen. His heart pounded like a tom-tom. He bit his lip and fled quickly to the street.

When he returned the following Saturday, he saw three of his classmates standing in the lobby waiting for seats. He went straight to the men's room to avoid them, and waited there, combing his hair, until he felt certain they were in the theater. Then he came out and went over to the girl.

"I'm sorry," he said, "about last week."

She looked at him and laughed again, but this time it was a kindly laugh. "That's all right," she answered. "Don't let it upset you."

"It wasn't that," he stammered; "it's just that I should have known better than to treat a girl like you like that."

Her eyes widened defensively. Then she stared at him a long, long time. Exasperated, she finally turned and snapped, "Go on inside, will you?"

"Will you have dinner with me tonight?" he begged, and she took him by the arm and guided him toward the aisle. He felt her breast beside his elbow. "Please," he murmured as they entered the darkness of the auditorium.

"Ssh. I'll let you know later," she said and left him.

It was the first time he had ever been bored with a movie. He sat impatiently through the newsreel and feature until he could stand it no longer. In the middle of the comedy he left his seat abruptly and stalked up the aisle. When he got to the lobby she wasn't there.

He sat down on the couch and determined to wait. She couldn't have just left him like that. Not after what had happened—she'd held his arm so firmly on the way in.

The door to the ladies' room opened. She came out carrying a purse.

"Come on," she said, walking past him. He leaped up and marched obediently behind her.

She waited for him at the entrance and took his arm as they started to walk along the street.

"What's your name?" she asked.

"Bill Levinson."

"Mine's Annette. Annette Lejoux. I'm French-Canadian, a Canuck. You're a Jew, aren't you?"

"Yes," he answered hesitantly. "You like Jews?"

"Sure. Why not?"

He shrugged his shoulders.

"Where'll we eat?" she asked.

"Anywhere you want. I can't seem to think of a place now," he admitted ruefully.

"There's a quiet joint up the next block," she suggested.

The waiters seemed to know her and smiled as they entered. Willie pulled the table to one side and she sidled obliquely into the booth. He looked quickly down her dress and saw the inner contours of her breasts swaying forward as she struggled to her seat. He was too embarrassed to become excited.

During dinner she let their legs touch occasionally. They sat opposite each other and didn't talk much. She told Willie she liked the job at the theater. It didn't pay well, but the hours were easy. Two to nine in the evening and an hour off for dinner. It was too bad she had to rush so, but she had to be back by eight.

"I could call for you tomorrow night," he said.

"I thought you kids hadda stay in school. If you're caught out they fire you, don't they?"

"Sure," said Willie, "but I'll take that chance."

"For me?" she pursued.

"Uh-huh," he answered.

He sensed her hand reaching toward his beneath the table. Impulsively he grasped it and held it strongly, wrapping his fingers around hers, grateful for their hot stickiness. She put his hand on the bottom part of her thigh above the knee. Through the sheen of her skirt he felt the warmth of her leg. He became very tense.

"I like you," she murmured. "Lots. Meet me here at around ten after nine Monday night. I'll be outside."

Breathlessly Willie acquiesced and set about planning his evening's escapade as soon as he arrived back at school.

Although Inchcape instructors and proctors occasionally walked through the halls after 10:00 P.M., they never peered into rooms. Their pupils were on the honor system and no one ever suspected any of them of sneaking downtown. It was such a long trip, and besides, all the school gates were locked at night. But Monday afternoon Willie stole into the storeroom and pocketed an extra key from the janitor's shelf. He was safe as long as Buck didn't discover the loss. After dinner he sneaked out of school, walked about a mile, then thumbed a ride from a passing New York car. As soon as he got into town he went to a locksmith and had him make a duplicate of the pilfered key. Then he rushed over to the restaurant and arrived forty minutes ahead of time.

He paced aimlessly back and forth. He consulted his watch regularly. He read the gold letters on the store window until they'd impressed themselves indelibly into his memory. "Frank's Bon Ton Restaurant," they said. Down near the bottom a smaller sign announced, "Table d'hote" and "Ladies Served."

"Frank's Bon Ton Restaurant." 8:45. "Ladies Served." 8:46. "Table d'hote." 8:47. Gee, that was a car just like Fitz's. Wonder if Fitz'd turn me in if he saw me? Wonder if he goes out with girls? Nah, what fun's a professor? Jesus, time drags. But she smells so nice. Say, maybe she won't show up. That'd be nice. After me ducking out of school. 8:50. What a damned fool I'd be. She's got to come. Wish I could go around to the theater and pick her up. They all know me there, though. Hell, I'll wait. Hey, it's nine o'clock. Ten minutes and she'll be here. My Annette. Will she, though? She's got to come. Christ, my feet are getting tired. Here—look, it's 9:09, and she's not here yet. Aw, she'll come. Had to go to the ladies' room or something. Give her till nine-twenty anyway. Well, maybe nine-thirty.

A hand tapped him on the shoulder. "I got off early," she said. "Sneaked off like you did."

"Annette!" he cried, opening his arms to her. She looked around self-consciously. "Not here, silly. Not in the street!"

"Where'll we go?"

"Oh, let's walk a bit. Haven't you got a car?"

"A car? No, of course not."

"You could hire one from the U-Drive-It."

"I haven't got a license to drive."

"Not old enough to get one?"

"Sure I am," he lied. "Couldn't *you* borrow a car?"

"No, but there's an empty lot near my house. We could go there and talk. And I mean *talk*!" she added as an afterthought.

"Of course," Willie agreed, and they walked on in silence.

"Here it is," she said, stopping before a series of billboards advertising, among other things, the latest Miracle picture. "Ouch," Willie thought, snickering to himself as they squeezed between the billboards and an adjoining fence. She guided him up the rocky debris till they reached a grass-cushioned plateau.

"We can sit here," she said softly, folding her dress beneath her knees. He dropped down beside her. Then he put his hands on her shoulders and leaned forward to kiss her. She turned away adroitly. "You're a fast one, aren't you?" she laughed.

"What?" he asked, feeling unaccountably puzzled and ashamed.

155

She recognized the look and chided him. "Oh, don't take it so seriously."

"I want to kiss you so badly," he said.

She reached over and smacked his lips soundly with hers. "There! Now let's talk."

"Talk? Now?" he said joyously. "I've been waiting for this so long and now you want to talk! Oh, Annette—Annette. Kiss me again, please."

"How beautiful and far away the stars are," she said, remembering the line from a movie, and as she stretched out on the ground, she folded her arms behind her so they made a pillow for her head. She lay there looking up at the sky and for a moment felt just like the girl in the picture.

Willie leaned down beside her on his elbow. "Annette!"

She turned slowly toward him. He bent down. His lips touched hers. He felt quite safe in leaving them there. Her mouth opened imperceptibly. He opened his and breathed her breath. Her tongue caressed his lips. His brushed hers. His hand, on the outside of her dress, snaked up to her breasts. She held it there. Her hot breath beat against the down on his upper lip. He slid his fingers beneath her dress. She bolted upright and pushed him away.

"You better go now," she commanded hoarsely. "Go, for God's sake. I only wanted to play around with you. But you're so exciting. . . . Please. . . . Please! No. No, don't."

He took her hand. She pulled it away.

"Let me just kiss your breasts," he begged. "Just that, nothing more."

"No."

"Please. Please, Annette."

"Nothing more?"

He shook his head impatiently.

She unhooked the top of her dress and let it drop from her shoulders. Willie fairly tore it off for joy. He kissed her neck, the curve above her bosom, the rich, warm flesh of the breast itself.

156

She settled back on the ground again.

"Undress me," she whispered wildly. "Undress me and love me."

Willie never stopped to undress her.

11

DATE: May 31, 1931

NAME: Levinson, Wm..ADDRESS: 26 East 95th St..PHONE: Lenox 6230

AGE: 15..BORN: July 1915..HEIGHT: 5 ft. 7½ in...WEIGHT: 142 lbs.

PREVIOUS ILLNESS: Bronchial and lobar pneumonia..............

PRESENT AILMENT: Gonorrhea.................................

TREATMENT: Colloidal silvers, argyrol, rest, water................

NOTES: Contracted, according to patient, while playing in a field.

DR. LANSBURGH INSISTED that Willie stay in New York. Treatments, he told Rebecca, must be given regularly and to expose other boys to infection would be nothing short of criminal. To be sure, there were all kinds of quack cures, but only one that was infallible and would leave no residual effects, and that treatment took time. "Six months," he said. "Take him out of school and put him in my hands. His health is more important, and he'll learn more about life."

So Willie, who was a sick and angry lad, crawled back to the bosom of his family.

They tried to keep the news from Momma, but that excitable matriarch, her curiosity aroused by Willie's sudden return and

157

unusual churlishness, suspected something of a disgraceful nature. Her suspicions became confirmed the day Jacob told her never to use the boy's bathroom. So indefatigably did she pursue and question her daughter-in-law that Rebecca eventually broke down and confessed.

"He's got gone-or-rear," she explained carefully.

"Gohn-a, vot?" exploded Momma.

"Gonorrhea," Rebecca repeated sharply, hoping to avoid any further discussion.

"I knew it," Momma said. "I knew it!" Then she sucked in her breath and shook her head. "It hoits?" she asked.

"I'm not sure," Rebecca answered.

Momma frowned. "You his mudder en' you ain't sure?"

"I never had it," Rebecca snapped defiantly. "You see, it's a social disease."

Momma's eyes lit up quickly. "High-kless seekness? Dot's good!"

"It's not a high-class sickness. It's a nasty sickness."

Momma groaned at her daughter-in-law's stupidity. "So vot seekness is a nize seekness? Mizzles is nize? Or diptirria maybe? Or vooping cuff? Is by kiddies *any* seekness nize?"

"Momma," Rebecca hinted firmly, "this is no kiddies' disease. This is something that happens to a *man*. Something terrible. Something people don't talk about. Willie's a sick boy, believe me."

Momma put her hands on her hips and looked up at the ceiling. "By her," she complained, "is right avay tregedy. I ken't unnerstand it!" She turned on Rebecca belligerently and her arms drilled two exasperated arcs through the air before they slapped against her thighs. "He vukking around, ain' he?" she demanded. "On two lecks. Or is det ting going opstairs, downstairs ull day long, det's a ghost, mebbe, in long pents? Listen, Becky, by me a men's vukking around, he ain't seek. Stop vorrying!"

"Who's worrying?" Rebecca said petulantly. "I was trying to explain to you. You asked me what was wrong, remember?"

"Det's so. I did, dint I?" Momma murmured as she disappeared through the door. The problem no longer interested her. Whatever the secret was, she was a part of it now. And that satisfied her completely.

As the treatments progressed, the doctor initiated Willie into the technique of sexual prophylaxis, and Willie, to whom the very thought of women had become temporarily abhorrent, listened sullenly to Lansburgh's advice and answered his questions in surly monosyllables.

Despite this attitude, Lansburgh managed to persuade Willie to tell him the story of his experience at Inchcape, the impact of which, in the doctor's opinion, struck just this side of disaster. For Willie was neither willing nor able to face the fact of his own self-deception, and he met the doctor's oblique attempts to make him acknowledge his mistake with an air of belligerent neutrality.

Nevertheless, he had expressed his confidence in Lansburgh by unburdening himself, and although he resented the doctor's efforts to achieve a psychological catharsis, he pretended to be in polite agreement with him at all times.

On the day the treatments ended, Lansburgh suddenly said, "Willie, I know you've been bored stiff with me."

Willie sat up quickly, amazed that his feigned interest had been so transparent. "Not at all, doctor, not at all," he protested.

Lansburgh lit a cigarette. "Don't let's fool each other, Willie," he said. "I've come to know you in the past six months despite your reticence. Save your white lies for strangers and boobies, but keep your black ones from yourself. You're beginning to live one right now. You're ashamed of your family, aren't you?"

Willie swallowed hard. "Not of them—exactly," he answered after a long pause.

"Of what, then?"

"I don't know."

"You do, but you're afraid to tell me."

"I'm not afraid of anything!"

"You're afraid of being a Jew, for one thing."

"Afraid—hell!" Willie snapped.

"You resent it, then."

"Goddamn right I do!" Willie said vehemently.

"Why?"

"Why shouldn't I?"

"You're doing the most unintelligent thing a Jew can do, taking refuge behind the fact that you are one. You're seeing prejudice where you alone were responsible for what happened to you."

"Maybe."

"In this case, definitely. The boys who ostracized you were definitely not prejudiced, therefore it's unfair of you to accuse them of it. Lord knows there are enough prejudiced people as it is, and we've got to fight them, Willie—"

"Brother, am I going to do that!"

"How?"

"You wait and see."

"I've got plenty of time. It's the one thing we Jews have." The doctor smiled. "I'm glad you're going to fight—but I'm afraid in your present frame of mind you might easily use the wrong weapons, and betray your own people—"

"You think so?" Willie interrupted.

The doctor came over to the couch and sat down beside him. "Willie, there are Jews who might just as well be shooting other Jews in the back. Jews who are unconscious of their obligations, who fail to realize that their greatest weapon is their daily conduct with their fellow men. And this type of Jew who in his ignorance rides roughshod over people is as much a provoker of prejudice as the professional anti-Semite. And though, thank God, his tribe is in the minority, he is our enemy just as much as every decent-thinking Christian is our friend. The battle against prejudice transcends religious barriers, it ignores national boundaries, it must be fought to a finish somewhere in that strange, vast periphery that encompasses the conscience of the world.

"We're fighting ephemeral shapes like rumors and lies and

160

whisperings, the deep, dark, disembodied slime of centuries; and these things are best counterattacked not by denial, but by truth as exemplified in our daily living and our earnest desire to be good citizens. Being a good citizen is awfully important, Willie. It's part of being a good Jew. And I don't ever want you to be anything else."

Willie looked up at the doctor. At long last the words had begun to make sense. "Thank you, doctor," he said, quite sincerely.

Lansburgh took Willie's hand. "Listen, lad," he said, "you're the architect of your own future, and you're still—really—awfully young. Occasionally you sound like an adult, but for some time you're going to vacillate between being grown-up and being a child. Try to remember what I've told you about yourself and also about women. Keep yourself clean, and for heaven's sake be proud and use discrimination."

The doctor released Willie's hand and sat back quietly.

"You mean a lot to me, Willie, as a person, not a patient. And I've been talking to you like a father, not a doctor, so you need never even agree with me. But I do hope some of the things I've said will make sense to you someday, when you least expect and most need them. Because you're going to be in a position to do a great deal for yourself and your people. You're sixteen now, and you're going to Hollywood with your family in a few months."

"How do you know?"

"I'm their friend, Willie."

"But Pop's broke. What are we going out there for?"

"Your father was broke," the doctor explained, "but he didn't quit, Willie. He didn't believe the whole world was against him. He had confidence in himself—the way you will, in time. And when the bankers learned that it took more than businessmen to run a studio, they came to him and he made a deal transferring his shares in the Miracle Theater chain to them, in return for which they made a cash settlement and asked him to run the studio with your Uncle Moe, so they'd have some good pictures to show in their theaters. As for your Uncle Moe, I only know he went into voluntary bankruptcy. And it wouldn't surprise me if he made money on it, though your father assures me he doesn't think so. At any rate, he's kept his fingers in the studio, and he and your father are going to be together again making pictures."

"I've heard them talking about it around the house," Willie interrupted, "but I was afraid they'd leave me here and send me back to Inchcape."

The doctor shook his head. "No. You're going with them. They asked me what I thought and I said it would be best for you to live with them."

Willie stared at the floor and finally murmured, "I'm going to miss talking things over with you."

Dr. Lansburgh had to suppress a sudden impulse to hug Willie, but he had to respect the lad's desperate desire to be adult, so he merely said, "Three thousand miles is nothing, Willie. Call on me for anything at any time. I want to be your friend, and I'm afraid you'll need one as you grow older. Now, goodby, and good luck."

They stood up and shook hands.

"Thanks for everything," Willie said, and he walked toward the door.

"So long," the doctor called after him.

BOOK 3
THE GREAT PRODUCER

1

MOE MET THEM at the train. They spilled down the Pullman steps and surged across the intervening tracks, waving and jabbering affectionate nonsense as they came.

"I bought ya a house," Moe said simply, when they were all together.

Rebecca, who had her arms around him, drew back and said, "You crazy?"

"Nope." Moe grinned and started down the platform.

"Wait a minute!" Louis shouted. "I gotta find the porter."

They waited on the ramp leading down to the station. Louis found the porter, who gave him a check for their baggage, then he hurried back to the family and pushed Momma to one side so he could walk next to Moe. He took his hat off and ran a handkerchief around the inside of his hatband.

"A house!" he heaved breathlessly. "Right away you gotta make with a house!" He put his hat back on his head and they all moved down the ramp in a body. "You think I got money to burn?"

"H'estates ve got, awreddy," Momma snorted.

"Waste of money," amended Jacob.

Moe slapped his hands together. "Chris' Awmighty!" he groaned. "Two minutes off a Pullman car and awreddy they're grexin'! Nothin's good enough fer 'em. Nothin's right. . . . Go ahead, Becky. Putcha two cents in. You got a right ta squawk too. What's on ya mind? Ya can't afford it?"

Rebecca nodded.

"Dontcha think I know that? And because ya can't afford a home ya should live onna county maybe? Inna poorhouse?"

He waited for a comeback, but they were cowed into silence.

A man came up and Moe introduced him. "This here's Ira from the stujio transpitation deppommint. Give him ya trunk checks."

Ira smiled and said, "Glad to make your acquaintance, Mr. Levinson."

Momma sidled up to Louis and nudged him the moment Moe turned his back. "Da duggie," she whispered, "vere's da duggie?"

"I'll attend to him," Louis murmured. "They'll send him out with the trunks."

He riffled through his stubs, found the one he wanted, and handed it to Ira. "Make sure this item arrives tonight," he said, and reached for his wallet.

Moe saw him. "Ya don't hafta tip him!" he said.

"Quiet, you!" Louis barked, and he gave Ira a five-dollar bill. "Use it where it'll do the most good," he whispered. Then he turned back to Moe. "My money he throws away—but if I do it, he objects!"

"Jeesus!" Moe groaned. "Now listen to me! I done ya a favor. I bought the house with *my* money. It's a present. Ya can pay me back whenever yer ready. Any complaints?"

Rebecca looked at him suspiciously. "Where'd *you* get the money?" she asked, and by this time they were crowding each other into Moe's chauffeur-driven limousine.

"Arline kep' it fa me. I give it ta her ta put away."

"You gave money to *that* woman!"

"Yeah, I give it to her," Moe said sullenly. "Whadda *you* know about her?" And he suddenly looked at Louis, who flushed and turned away.

"I'd rather not say," Rebecca said.

"Oh, you'd rather not say. Well, lemme tell you sump'm. Arline's got more brains inna little pinkie than you got in ya whole behind!"

Louis leaned forward from the back seat and tapped Moe on the shoulder. "The boy," he said, pointing at Willie, who sat beside the driver.

"Wotta hell do I care!" Moe said impatiently.

Momma, who was sitting beside him on the other auxiliary seat, thumped his knee and put her finger to her lips.

Moe turned back to Rebecca. "Yer onney gettin' a house because Arline was smart enough ta put the dough in real estate. So it don't make no difference ta me *watcha* think of her. But fa Chrissake, she gimme the dough ta buy ya place! Arline. She says ta me, 'Where they gonna live?' I says, 'How'd I know?' She says, 'Here, take this an' make a down payment on a nice place fa them.' An' you sit there an' say she stinks."

"I didn't quite say that."

"Ya coulda. And lemme tell you she ain't a bad guy when ya get ta know her. Honest."

"I suppose not," Rebecca said dryly.

Willie turned halfway around in his seat. "Who'za dame, Unk?" he piped.

"Shut ya trap, squirt," Moe snarled at his nephew. Then, as a malicious afterthought, he muttered, "Sixteen years old an' got himself clapped up good awreddy. A reglah Levinson."

Momma's eyes opened wide. "Vaat!" she exploded. "So det's vot he's got! Vye dint sumvun tell me?"

She lunged forward. Her fat hand spun toward Willie's head and struck the side of his neck. Willie yowled, and in turning brought his nose within Momma's range. Smack! She scored a bull's-eye. "Hey, cut it out!" he whimpered, ducking. She followed his retreat, pummeling him angrily until his battered hat slid down over his ears.

"No-good! Loafer! Nafka-chaser!" She shrieked between clouts, and when exhaustion finally overcame her, she settled back in her seat and sighed, "My own grennson, too!"

"Welcome to Hollywood," Jacob said bitterly.

By the time they arrived at the house, the chauffeur had definitely decided to quit.

2

"THERE SHE IS!" Moe announced triumphantly.

The afternoon sun slanted against a two-story white stucco house, accentuating its size. Rebecca noticed and approved the high privet hedges, and smiled as they drove up the driveway flanked by a formal lawn that stretched for thirty yards from the street to the house itself.

The car stopped beneath a porte-cochere, and the elaborately carved imitation-oak door swung open to reveal a man and a woman servant bowing and beaming expectantly.

The Levinsons surged wearily out of the car. It had been a long, hard trip.

"Your servants," Moe said, introducing Max and Hilda. "They come witha house."

"Good afternoon," Rebecca and Louis mumbled in the apologetic tone one uses toward domestics who have inherited new masters in an old setting.

Max and Hilda bowed low until Momma's rasping voice suddenly interrupted: "Stup stennin' around! Get de becks in de house!"

The bags went into the house on the heels of the Levinsons, who were craning their necks as curiously as though they were traipsing through a wax museum. Their curiosity was natural. The 95th Street house had been imposing enough, but this was the first time anything had really been theirs—their own property, their own home, their own sanctuary. But because they had had nothing to do with its acquisition, their enthusiasm was tempered by suspicion—though not for long.

They passed through a wide hallway and stepped down a few steps into a tremendous living room. They stood there, silently surveying its feudal magnificence. The huge fireplace, the richly embroidered chairs, and the brocade draperies filled them with respectful pride. At the far end of the room, to the right, their eyes followed a wrought-iron staircase to a balcony.

"The liberry!" Moe giggled, pointing to the balcony. "Ya gotta read now, Louis. Scrips, anyway."

They pushed each other up the slender staircase to see the library. A carved mahogany desk stood in the center of an immense room lined with bookshelves. The Levinsons looked around silently and with reverence. It was a quiet room. A good room. A room for retreating from the world of reality. A room that only Jacob would use.

Willie shrugged his shoulders. "So where do I live?" he demanded, and like the sudden chirping of a sparrow at night, the sound of his own voice startled him. He winked guiltily at Momma. Momma scowled back. "Be glad ya got a roof ovahead, no-good!" she said.

"Stop pickin' onna boy!" Moe snapped. He turned to Willie. "We'll get around ta the bedrooms, and inna meantime stop hoppin' around like a nervous-jigger, will ya!"

"What's next, Moe?" Jacob asked.

"The dinin' room."

Rebecca paused on the balcony while the others followed Moe down the wrought-iron steps. "Goodness!" she exclaimed. "This living room's big enough for a ball!"

"Right away a poddy!" Moe grunted. But he was honestly pleased with himself, because he felt as though they were admiring his own masterpiece. "Come on down. Ya ain't seen nothin' yet!" he called.

They paraded across the foyer and entered the dining room, directly opposite the living room. Their smiles vanished slowly as their eyes focused on a huge mahogany banquet table. It was altogether too imposing to be comfortable, but Rebecca thought it enchanting.

"At this table," she thought, "I will now preside."

Momma caught the gleam in her eye and chuckled, "Looka her!" She nudged Jacob. "In sotch a place," she said to him, "ya gotta keep ya tie on, Jakie."

"You'd better buy him a new one," Willie muttered. "He collects soup stains and there's no more room on that one."

"Willie, why don't you go outside for a while?" Louis suggested.

"What's outside?"

"A swimmin' pool in backa the garden," Moe said.

Willie's rapid exit left the room in silence for a moment. A silence, completely shattered by Rebecca's next remark. "What," she asked bluntly, "are we going to call our new home?"

"Call it?" Moe asked. "Wotsa madda, ain't it got a number?"

"Oh, of course it has, Moe, but a residence like this . . ." Rebecca waved her hands in a gesture intended to convey an impression of magnificence. Then she smiled. A gentle, superior smile. "A residence like this," she repeated quickly, "must have a name!"

"So?" Momma said.

"Wyncha call it Louis's Place?" Moe growled.

"And sell beer," added Jacob.

"Prohibition ya never hoid of?" Momma asked indignantly.

"I got it!" yelled Louis. "Levinson Manor!"

"Phui!" Momma snorted.

"Why not?" Moe asked.

"Should be Levinsky Menna."

"Stop it, Momma," Rebecca said quietly. "I have the name. Miracle Manor."

"Hm! That's swell," Jacob said, putting his arm around Rebecca's shoulder. She looked at him curiously. "Fancy, too!" he added, with a grin.

"I wish I knew when you were kidding me," Rebecca said.

170

"Should be Meshuggina Flats," Momma grumbled, defiant even in defeat.

"Now the upstairs," Moe announced, jockeying the entourage toward the main staircase.

"Should be acceleraters," Momma puffed as she reached the top steps.

"Escalators, Momma," Rebecca said mechanically.

"Vatever dey are, should be!" the old lady snapped. "Vere's my room?"

"Try that one," Moe said, pointing down the hall.

They broke into groups of two and inspected the rooms Moe had assigned them. Louis and Rebecca rushed into the master's suite.

"It's wonderful!" Rebecca cried ecstatically. And in a sense it was, because it managed, though somewhat obliquely, to bring Louis XV to Hollywood.

The ceiling was stenciled with clusters of ruddy cherubs blithely clutching a pink veil that not only gave them continuity but also protected their more intimate parts from exposure. Cream-white wood panels covered the walls. The beds, of a size that indicated the previous owner's preoccupation with the libido, drew from Rebecca the housewifely observation, "Box springs, too!"

Louis smiled at her from beside the fireplace, and then led the way into the dressing room.

"This must be the bathroom," he said, tugging at the bronze knob on a full-length mirror. The door opened, revealing a magnificent display of black fixtures, gold tiles, and chrome-yellow walls.

"Louis," Rebecca exclaimed, "it's got a glass-enclosed shower for you."

"You know I like baths."

"Oh, but, Louis, you *look* so much better in a shower. You must try it."

"Nix."

"Please, Louis. For me," she pleaded. Then she looked at him and added coyly, "Then we could use the bathroom together."

171

"Rebecca!" he snapped, thoroughly outraged at her suggestion.

"Oh, dear, let's join the others," she said, wondering if all married couples turned prim at the thought of plumbing, and suspecting quite wistfully that they didn't.

Moe met them in the hall. "Like it?" he asked anxiously.

"It's grand, Moe. Thanks," Louis answered.

"Momma wants ya should see her room. It's downa hall. Come on, she's happy as hell."

"Such thick carpets!" Louis exclaimed as they stopped in front of Momma's bedroom.

"Up to ya hips," Moe said. "Ssh, don't talk. Le's surprise her."

They opened the door.

"Hello," Momma called from the bed across which she was sprawled in luxury.

"Solit comfit," she said. "A liddle late, but vunnaful. A bet like dis ya poppa never saw. . . . De tings ve slept on! Borts fomm vood, mit straw on 'em. Now, it giffs mettresses! Vid Poppa dead, *olav hasholem,* our own mettresses." She turned her face toward the window. "De tings ve did ven ve vas young!" she sighed. Then she looked at Louis. "Your poppa vas a mensch, mine Louis boy. Vid him I dint care vas straw or vood or rocks behind."

"Momma!" her son cried indignantly.

"So?" She raised her eyebrows. "So now is time fa sleep. In Keliphunya I find de best bets vomm my life en' is onney good fa sleep. . . . Is onney heff a pleasure, sleep."

Moe winked at Rebecca. "There's plennya gigolos in Hollywood, Momma. You're a cinch! Good-lookin' dame like you. With Louis's dough behind ya, ain't nothin' ya can't have."

"That's no way to talk, Moe," Louis said sharply from the window. "This is such a beautiful spot, it's a shame to carry on like that. Look at this view."

"All he vurries about is a few," Momma groaned. "Listen, Louis, I like Moe should tuk like det! Mecks me fill young. Mecks me leff. Mecks me heppy. So latt be!"

172

Moe changed the subject. "The foiniture's California-style—Monterey or sump'm, if anybody's innarested," he said.

"It looks very substantial, Moe," Rebecca answered, noticing the broad solidity of the beds and chest.

Jacob came in through the connecting bathroom. "In this room the furniture doesn't stand, it squats," he said.

"It's hokay vunce ya get into it," Momma replied possessively.

"I have the best place in the house," Jacob continued. "Sleeping porch, my own bookshelves, and, so help me, it's got a gabled ceiling like a church. Only one thing I don't like is sharing a bathroom with Momma. She spends hours in the tub and I'll have to bribe her to get in there at all."

"Det's wery nize, Mr. Doity-op-de-Sink," Momma snapped, rising from the bed in righteous wrath. "You got vid me drubbles, huh? But in *daytime* is drubbles. Me, I godda vurry about nighttime. Is all night lung Jacob going to de vorter closet. All night lung running in en' out like crazy. Hot nights, culd nights, is alla time Jacob stenning dere, shiffering in de dock en' flushing vorter closets. He should vurry!"

"Momma, in this house we got silent terlets. The latest miracle in plumbing fa Miracle Manor. Look!" Moe said, beckoning toward the bathroom. "See?" he said, pushing the plunger. "Not a sound."

"But how do you know if it works?" Jacob asked.

"Wotsa madda, ya blind?" Moe roared, his temper finally cracking under the strain.

"No. And I'm not deaf, either. If you were half as quiet as that contraption, I'd be a happier man," Jacob said, stalking off to the sanctity of his bedroom, followed by Louis and Rebecca.

"Hey, Momma," Moe asked, as soon as they were alone, "how'd you know Jake went ta the terlet all night?"

"In Ninety-feef Stritt house, he is vukking by mine room to de batroom. So going *to* de vorter closet his teet vud rettle, en' coming *beck* his bones vud kreck. Den ven he gets into bet again he's sighing so loud de house should fuhl down, en' you esk me how I should know? I vudda giffen heff my life not to know, en' sleep in peace!"

"Well, all right, then." Moe snickered. "A fella can't be too sure what's goin' on behind his back these days."

Momma smiled at him as he left the room.

A few seconds later the rafters shook in Jacob's room when Momma suddenly screamed, "You low-life, no-good momser!"

Louis and Rebecca jumped up. "Excuse us, Poppa," Rebecca said quickly. "It's been too much for her. We'd better put her to bed."

3

"WILLIE! Be ready for dinner in a few minutes! Wear your coat!" Rebecca called down the hallway.

Willie pushed Frou-Frou to one side and stood in front of a full-length mirror admiring his new suit. He liked his new room. It was "ultramodrin" in décor. Low, angular bookcases wrapped their tentacles around the corners of all the chairs, and the day bed, which practically spread its mattress on the floor, was bounded by a radio-lamp combination at one end and a built-in chest of drawers at the other. Indirect lighting and his own bathroom rounded out Willie's suite, which had a second entrance through an outdoor staircase that led down to the rear garden and the swimming pool.

He was indeed in festive spirits when he heard the sound of footsteps approaching his room. He walked across the rich maroon carpet and opened the door. Frou-Frou yapped at his heels.

"Hurry, Willie," Rebecca said. "Leave the dog."

"Okay, Ma. I'm ready." He put out the lights and nudged Frou-Frou back into the room with his foot as he closed the door.

The family had gathered in the hallway, and then descended the stairs together. Max met them in the foyer. They stared at his evening livery.

174

"Would madam prefer cocktails in the living room or the library?" he inquired.

"Cocktails?" repeated Louis incredulously. "Who said anything about . . ."

"Mr. Moe, sir," answered the butler.

"So?" Momma exclaimed. "Is inna house, Mr. Souse?"

"Mr. Moe went home some time ago, madam, but he said he'd be back for dinner."

Max turned to Rebecca. "In the library or the living room, Mrs. Levinson?" he asked again.

Rebecca darted an anxious look at her husband to see if he approved, but Louis only shrugged; after all, repeal was a certainty now.

"In the living room, Max," she said, reassured.

Max found a tense audience awaiting his cocktails. He passed slowly around the room, and each member of the family heard himself announced by Rebecca.

"One for Mrs. Levinsky," she said. "Take the napkin, Momma."

She followed Max to Jacob. "One for Father. Have a canape too, Jacob, dear."

"Louis."

"Myself. . . . None for Willie, Max."

"Vye not?" Momma spoke up. "He's a grunn-up mensch awreddy, our Villie. Got himself clepped op an' evvyting—von't hoit him de cucktails."

Max looked up sharply, unable to believe his ears.

"So?" Momma inquired, glaring at him.

Max retired swiftly from the room.

"*L'Chaim*, children!" said Louis, raising his cocktail.

"*L'Chaim!*" they chanted reverently over the brims of their glasses.

The sound of chimes suddenly consummated their ritual. A hush fell over the living room.

"What was that?" Louis asked nervously.

"Bells or something," Willie volunteered.

"Chust like in Schul," Momma beamed.

Max appeared in the hallway.

Rebecca called him. "What was that sound?" she asked.

"What sound, madam?"

"Like chimes."

"The doorbell, madam," he said, and walked on to answer it.

Willie gulped his drink and headed for the foyer. When he got there he opened his mouth to say hello, and stopped short. A woman was standing beside his uncle. He guessed who it was, and his eyes opened with astonishment.

Moe handed his hat to Max and beckoned to Willie with his free hand. The woman put her finger to her lips and Willie tiptoed up to them.

"They all in there?" Moe asked.

Willie nodded.

"Arline—Willie," his uncle said. They shook hands. Moe took her wrap.

"Jeez, Unk," Willie whispered, and his voice was husky with admiration, "you sure got guts!"

"Aw, shuddup!" Moe growled. "We wanna surprise 'em."

"You will," Willie answered, and he almost giggled with anticipation.

They walked to the living room and paused in the archway. Rebecca gasped. The family rose in unison as they came down the steps.

"This is Arline," Moe said calmly.

No one moved or said anything. Rebecca flushed and looked at Louis, who turned away. Jacob watched Arline's forced smile vanish slowly. Momma looked around at all of them; they were too surprised and shocked to speak. She fixed a cold eye on Arline and came to their rescue. "Good evening, nafka," she said.

Arline's lips tightened. She measured Momma deliberately and

176

knew this was the beginning of a feud. "Nafka, she calls me, the old bag," she said, and she almost grinned as she added, "How's by you, Momma?"

"You know me?" the old lady said, not without a touch of pride.

"By your size, dearie."

"That's no way to talk to my mother!" Rebecca snapped angrily.

"That's no way to talk to me! I know Yiddish. Nafka means a tramp, a tart. Right, Mosey?" Moe nodded. Arline turned back to Rebecca, "—and not the kind ya eat, either . . . unless yer like my baby here." She squeezed Moe's arm. "Besides," she said, nodding toward Momma, "she ain't yer mother. She's yer mother-in-law. And from what Mosey tells me, she's something."

"Denk ya, Muzzy," Momma said, by way of imitation.

"Quiet, you!" Moe snorted. He stood beside Arline and introduced her to the family. "Louis ya know, and Rebecca's my sister. Momma ya just met, and that's Pop. . . . Well, wyncha offer us a drink?"

"I just don't think we ought to," Rebecca snapped. She wished Jacob hadn't gone over to shake hands with that woman.

"Ya don't WHAT?" exploded Moe.

Jacob frowned and watched Moe and Rebecca staring at each other. They were standing very straight. Almost motionless. Then he heard his daughter say, "I don't think we ought to extend our hospitality to her kind of woman."

Jacob pursed his lips.

Moe took a deep breath and roared, "Well, I'm a sonuvabitch!"

"Ya don't stand a chance in this crowd, kid!" Arline said.

"Sez you!" Moe yelled, charging across the room to Rebecca. "Either she stays and has dinner with us, or we'll sella goddam house, and you with it! Don't ferget this joint's in my name!"

Momma belched. "Hmm! Ulla vay ta Keliphunya ve gotta go ta gat dispossassed!"

"Keep quiet, Momma. Let Rebecca handle this."

"She's botched it already," Willie blurted to his father.

"Upstairs, you!" Louis ordered curtly. He wasn't quite sure, but he thought his son had used foul language.

Willie, who hated to miss any part of the row, refused to move. Jacob looked at him and pointed up the stairs. As Willie left the room he heard Rebecca say, clearly and coldly, "That woman goes! Get her out of here! Immediately!"

"Aw, go—" Willie heard Moe growl, and he suddenly dashed up the stairs. He had devised a plan to get back into the room. . . .

Rebecca's face had turned white. She looked at Jacob. "Say something, Poppa!" she pleaded frantically.

Jacob nodded. "Very well, I will say something." He never raised his voice. "This girl's done a lot for you and she's made Moe happy. That ought to be enough for you. But I'm afraid you haven't the common decency to forget her past."

"How can we?" Rebecca asked coldly.

Jacob stared at the floor. "No matter what she was," he said, "your turning her away from here makes her better than you. And you ought to apologize, and apologize sincerely." He looked up suddenly and glared at his daughter. "If you don't, I won't sleep under the same roof with any of you!"

"But, Poppa!" Rebecca protested in wide-eyed confusion.

"Don't Poppa me!" Jacob stormed. "Can't you see I'm ashamed of you?"

"Ya oughta get kicked inna face, ya little snot!" Moe bellowed, backing up his father.

"Shut up, you!" Rebecca cried, slapping him in the face.

"So, kiddies, vot's gonna be?" Momma interrupted. "Ve gonna sit around ull night fightin'? By me is ull right culling it qvits. Giff de bitch a drink en meck her valcome."

"I don't guess there's much else to do," said Louis, screwing up his face into what he thought was a smile.

178

"If Poppa wants me to apologize, I apologize," Rebecca murmured.

"Now that you've all been so kind," Arline said, "I wanna tell you something. All of you, that is, except Moe's old man . . . Something I feel very deeply."

"What's that?" Rebecca asked, as sweetly as she could.

"Go to hell!" Arline thundered.

The family stood around and blinked, while Moe beamed triumphantly at his mistress.

There was a sudden commotion down the stairs. Frou-Frou dashed into the room pursued by Willie, who stopped short when he saw the horrified expression on his uncle's face. "He got away from me," Willie explained. Moe couldn't take his eyes off the animal. Like a man in a trance his gaze followed Frou-Frou around the room to Louis.

Louis came over and whispered, "I forgot to tell you. I'm really sorry."

Moe nodded blankly and they watched the dog run up to Arline, who fell on her knees in front of him. Frou-Frou barked happily as Arline gathered him up in her arms. She hugged him, rocking him back and forth like a baby, making little gurgling sounds and kissing him. Finally she murmured, "How'd you ever get here with these lugs?"

Moe thought quickly and dropped to his knees beside Arline.

"We found him yestiddy," he lied. "I thought ya'd like to have him . . . back," he added slowly.

They looked at each other for quite some time, silently. And then Arline shook her head. "Ya can't fool me," she said.

Moe's heart turned cold. Now she'd never forgive him or trust him again. For the first time in his life he was speechless. She took one hand away from the dog and touched Moe's knee. He was only half conscious of the gesture, and when she spoke, the words registered very slowly.

"It won't work," she said, "but you were sweet to try. It's the

179

nicest thing you've done for me. But this isn't Frou-Frou and I know it, Mosey. You can't fool me about my own dog. Frou-Frou would have run up to me and nipped my ankles. I know."

Moe rose to his feet and winked at Louis. A long, slow grin spread across his face.

Louis, unable to be a party to such deception, turned to her and very gently said, "It *is* your dog, Arline."

Moe shuddered. The family gaped at Louis, and he knew they thought he'd taken leave of his senses. Arline smiled and shook her head. She patted Frou-Frou and got up.

"Not in a million years," she said. "He's too fat, fa one thing, and I'd certinny know my own dog when I saw him."

Louis shrugged his shoulders.

"Well," Arline said, "if it's all the same to you, I'll eat my dinner home." She turned to Moe. "See you later."

As she started up the steps to the foyer, Frou-Frou ran after her and nipped her just above the heel. Arline stopped in her tracks and wheeled around. "Jesus!" she cried joyously. "Frou-Frou, it's you!" And she swept the dog to her bosom again. "Oh, Moe, he's come back to us! He's ours again! He's gonna live with us, not with these—" She stopped abruptly. Her eyes surveyed the entire room and her voice grew cold and hard. "These bastards stole my dog!" she blazed.

The Levinsons stared at each other incredulously. Momma looked at Arline and shook her head. "Gans meshugga!" she said, with a touch of pity.

Rebecca, summing up their resentment, indignantly protested, "We did nothing of the kind!"

"They sure did!" Moe said hurriedly, and he came up to Arline. "Take Frou-Frou home with ya and be back here in time ta greet the guests."

"Sure thing, honey," she said, and she stalked out of the house with the dog in her arms.

Moe came back into the living room. "I dunno how to thank ya fa that," he said caustically. Then he spotted Willie a few feet away. "You . . . you dope!" he yelled, and he swung at the lad with the back of his hand. Willie ducked easily and backed away.

"You said something about guests?" Louis asked.

"Yeah," Moe nodded.

"And may I ask who you invited over to our house?"

"Just somma the stujio crowd, Rebecca," Moe answered, "fa drinks—after dinner."

"How many?" Louis asked.

"Just a few," Moe hedged.

4

BY TEN-THIRTY that evening the Levinsons had not only become accustomed to the role of Hollywood royalty, but had begun to accept it as their inevitable heritage.

The living room looked like a theater lobby during intermission. A few haggard souls occupied chairs and couches but the majority just stood around in bunches and elbowed their way, drinks and all, from one group to another.

Rebecca sat on one end of the piano bench surrounded by song writers who plied her with liquor, cigarettes, and questions concerning the merit of their respective compositions. These they sought to recall to her by pushing each other away from the keyboard and ripping off elaborate arrangements of what they called their "smasheroos."

The competition was terrific, and Louis, talking to a few of his producers near the fireplace, eventually complained of the racket coming from the piano thumpers.

"Christ," said Tilden, "that goes on at every Hollywood party.

181

If you've got song writers and a piano the battle rages all night long. As a matter of fact, they travel around in droves and know exactly what the other guy's going to play. And they applaud out of anticipation for their own performance, rather than appreciation of each other's."

"Mr. Levinson?" a loud but plaintive voice interrupted.

Louis looked above the heads of those around him and recognized the bleary-eyed, broad-faced countenance of his top-notch buffoon, Harry Kelly. Mr. Kelly, wearing a wicked grin, staggered earnestly toward his boss.

"You Mr. Levinson?" he inquired again, flushed by his success at having reached the group at the fireplace.

Mr. Levinson nodded and extended his hand.

"Here y'are, sweetie!" Kelly giggled, planting two luscious kisses on Louis's cheeks.

The president of Miracle Pictures flushed with annoyance.

Mr. Kelly turned and shouted, "Adelstein! Ya owe me fifty bucks!"

Manny Adelstein appeared from nowhere to defend his interests. "Did he kiss him?" he asked breathlessly.

"He sure did!" George grinned.

"De bastid!" exclaimed Adelstein in genuine admiration. "Here ya' are, Harry. No. No, don't kiss me. Just go away."

Harry bowed and left.

"I'm afraid he's drunk," Louis said, trying to be generous.

"Drunk?" repeated Morse. "That guy could give himself an alcohol rub in his own perspiration."

"Is he always like that?"

"Pretty generally, and there's not much we can do about it. He's got a terrific draw."

"And knows it!" added Tilden. "Every time you call him about liquor or being late on the set he says, 'You're right, George. I'm wrong. But I sure pull 'em into the theaters, so what're you going to do about it?' And you don't do anything about it. Christ, every one of these guys has a screw loose somewhere. The bigger they are, the loonier they get. There's one now, the guy in the doorway. Recognize him?"

"Of course," said Louis. "Gilbert Whitney, the Englishman. Momma's crazy about him. Says he's a real gent. Whatsa matter with him?"

"Nothing. He's just serious, that's all," chuckled Morse. "Serves tea at four. Permits no visitors or interviews on the set. Won't allow people to talk to him between takes. Gets into the mood of his part weeks before the picture starts, and if he does feel like talking he'll take a half hour of your time explaining why the character he's playing always looks at a watch with his head cocked to one side. He knows he's a great actor, but the guy never lets up."

They turned to watch Mr. Whitney's brooding figure. Gradually the din began to subside and all heads, willing or not, veered toward the entrance. For a split second there was silence and in that second Mr. Whitney took his cue, unfolded his arms and said expansively, "Good evening, friends." Then, having devastated his audience with the magnificence of his presence, he walked slowly down the steps into the milling throng where Moe quickly captured him.

"Mr. Korn," the actor nodded.

"Hello, Gil. . . . Come and meet the president."

"With pleasure," Whitney said, and he strode across the room with Moe trundling along beside his elbow.

"Louis!" yelled Moe. "Meet the best actor in pitchures, Gilbert Whitney!"

"I'm very glad to meet you," Louis beamed.

"The pleasure's all mine, sir," answered Whitney, with a brusque smile and a bow.

"I wonder," said Louis, "if you'd do me a favor. You've been my mother's favorite actor for many years. She'd be so happy to meet you. Would you mind talking to her?"

"It would be a privilege, sir. A privilege!"

Louis led Whitney over to Momma, who was sedately settled in ᴜ large armchair. She had a handkerchief in her hand, with which from time to time she wiped beads of perspiration off her forehead and also signaled to innocent passers-by when she wanted attention. The latter feat was accomplished by something she'd seen in the movies. She dropped her handkerchief on the floor in front of her, and waited for a stray guest to notice it, pick it up, and hand it to her. After which she would smile politely, say "Denk you," and repeat the procedure as soon as her victim had moved away.

Right now, because the handkerchief had been on the floor a particularly long time, she took a stealthy look at the carpet and when she failed to see her bait before her she became frantic. She looked around anxiously and finally spotted it about four feet away beneath a young man's heel, where it had inadvertently been kicked.

"Hey, you!" she shouted angrily. "Aintcha got no menners? Stemping on a lady's henkachiff! Pick it op! I nid it!"

The young man, startled into automatic compliance, quickly bent down, rushed the handkerchief to Momma, saw Louis and Whitney approaching, and fled.

"Momma," said Louis, as his mother mopped her brow, "this is Gilbert Whitney, your favorite actor."

Momma looked up into the steel-blue eyes of her hero and became a temporary introvert. Louis returned to the fireplace.

"It's a pleasure," said Whitney, "to meet the mother of such a charming family."

"Vas nutting," answered Momma cautiously.

Whitney looked momentarily bewildered. "I beg your pardon?" he said.

"Vas nutting," Momma repeated.

"Vas nutting?" said the actor incredulously. "Vas nutting," he murmured again, searching the phrase for its mystic meaning. Then suddenly, never one to be caught off guard, he harumphed, "Yes! Yes, indeed! Ha-ha-ha, that's a good one! . . . Vas nutting!"

"Vot vas nutting?" Momma asked simply.

Whitney's laughter disappeared with the suddenness of a dime rolling down a subway grate. He felt as though someone had set off a skyrocket inside his head. The room reeled.

"Having fun, Mr. Whitney?" said Producer Tim Sullivan, slapping Gilbert on the back as he passed.

"Yes, yes, indeed!" the actor called after the receding shoulders of what he felt was his last friend.

"I say, Mrs. Levinson, do you mind if I get a drink?"

"De name's Levinsky," said Momma, "en' I dun't mind."

Mr. Whitney disappeared toward the bar. He felt quite shaken, almost as though he'd had an unearthly experience. "How curious!" he kept repeating to himself as he began sipping his whisky and soda. He was so distraught that he nodded to a fifty-dollar-a-week stock girl he'd snubbed for a year and a half. This unexpected courtesy unnerved her to such an extent that she turned to the young man next to her and shrieked, "My God, it moves!" Then she got an attack of the giggles.

"I'm terribly sorry," the young man apologized to Whitney. "I never saw her before in my life."

"It appears that neither did I," answered Whitney.

"Strange things are happening around here tonight."

Mr. Whitney suddenly became interested. "Have you noticed them too?"

"Sure, and the longer you stick around, the stranger they get."

"Too true! Too true! It's all pretty frightful, really."

"You said it!" the young man agreed.

"Shall we go somewhere else?" suggested the actor.

"Can't," answered the young man. "I live here. Name's Bill Levinson. What's yours?"

The actor put his drink down and gripped the bar firmly with both hands. Gradually he became conscious that Willie was waiting for an answer. "My name? What is mine," he declaimed cryptically, "is unimportant. What is yours, is, through an oversight of God, a plague! . . . Good night, sir!" And with that he strode out to get his hat and coat.

When he reached the steps leading from the living room to the foyer he bumped into Arline, who had just arrived.

"Stick around a minute, Gil," she whispered. "We're gonna have some fun."

"It's pretty terrible!" ventured Whitney.

"I know," she answered. "But stay for this. Excuse me, there's Moe. Moe!"

Moe, who had been avidly contemplating the deftly bolstered bust of Miracle's latest acquisition from the stage, Diana March, quickly returned to earth at the sound of his mistress' voice.

" 'Lo, Peaches!" he shouted blandly, even as he wondered if he'd ever get around to Miss March.

"I got them," Arline whispered after he'd kissed her.

"Where? Outside?"

"Yup. Any time you're ready."

"Well, here goes!" Moe said. He turned toward the guests and shouted, "Ladees and gennulmen, yer attention, please!"

The room quieted down reluctantly.

"The publicity deppommint of Miracle Pitchers has a little supprise fa our host." Then he turned toward the foyer and called, "Come on, boys!"

The boys responded quickly. Six of them trooped through the doorway bearing a long sign lettered with red paint on a huge piece of white oilcloth. They paused at attention like well-drilled theater ushers, and held up the sign so that not only Louis standing by the fireplace but everyone else in the room had an opportunity to be impressed by its sentiment.

"WELCOME TO HOLLYWOOD," it said, and "GOD BLESS OUR UNCLE LOUIS."

Louis flushed. He was aware that the guests were expecting a thank-you message. He knew if he looked up he'd see them all beaming at him and he resented their patronizing attitude; familiarity in any form embarrassed him. Suddenly he heard a voice shouting, "Three cheers for Uncle Louis! Hip! Hip! Go!"

186

"Uncle Looie! Uncle Looie! Uncle Looie!" roared the boys of the publicity department.

Uncle Looie looked up quickly and spotted the grinning face of Jock Merington, his broad-beamed genius of public relations. Anger swept over him.

"Now, look here!" he said coldly, and his words were audible throughout the room. "When I have so many relatives working on the studio lot that I don't want to embarrass those of you who aren't related to me, then I won't mind being called Uncle Louis. Until that time, kindly remember that my name is Levinson. *Mr.* Levinson. . . . I want to thank you, however, for your display of affection. It's too bad you couldn't have tempered that feeling with respect. Now, come on, boys, make yourselves at home."

The boys looked questioningly at each other, then broke and ran for the bar, disappearing into the crowd as quickly as they could.

"Nice people," said Whitney to Arline at the door. "Good night."

"Good night, Gil," she said, beginning to smile. "Guess he's gonna be pretty popular with the boys."

Whitney snickered as he stepped out into the cool night air.

"Arline!"

"Yes, Mosey?"

"You'd think Louis'd have more sense."

"Where is he?"

"Inside. Le's get him," said Moe, stalking into the midst of the melee, followed by Arline. "Louis!" Moe beckoned with his head.

Mr. Levinson left the fireplace and shoved his way across the room.

"Wotsa madda with ya?" Moe demanded. "First ya insult these guys, then ya tell 'em ta make themselves at home. Thass diplomacy, I s'pose. Thass bein' a big execkative!"

"I refuse to be Uncle Looied. That's the way I feel and I said so. But that's not important now. Take a look at your father."

Louis pointed toward a corner of the living room, where Jacob was surrounded by a cordon of what, in the old days, had been known

187

as Mack Sennett Bathing Beauties. These stock girls, as they were now called, seemed to be hanging not only on Jacob's every word, but also on every available portion of his anatomy. One was perched on his lap. Another stood behind his chair flicking imaginary flies off his bald head. A third sat draped around his feet playing with his ankles. A fourth kept adjusting his pocket handkerchief, and a fifth just stood around staring into his eyes. Poppa looked like a veritable pasha.

Moe grinned. "Not bad," he said, "fa an old guy sixty-five."

"Bad?" laughed Arline. "It's better'n you could do now!"

"They're scareda me. I'm the vice-president," Moe answered smugly. His evening tie had begun to sag. Arline reached out to straighten it.

"Scareda you?" she said, tightening the knot. "It's *me* they're scared of, baby." She gave the tie a final pat. "A regular Moe Brummel." She laughed approvingly.

"It doesn't matter who's scared of who," interrupted Louis, "I think something ought to be done about Jacob."

"What for?" Moe snorted. "Let him alone! He's havin' fun. And besides, he's safe. They're all kids. The younger they are, the better, around here. The older they get, the quicker they sue. Waddaya think I'm stickin' with Arline for?"

"You sonuvabitch!" Arline howled, and she made a grab for his tie.

Moe caught her wrists and held them. "No, honey, no," he begged, as her fingers came close to the bow.

"You gonna be a good boy?" she gasped, struggling and laughing at the same time.

"Yeah, honey, honest."

"Okay," she said, and as he let go, she stepped lightly on his toe. "Let that be a lesson to you," she added, and marched off for a drink.

"How long do these people hang around?" asked Louis. "It's twelve-thirty. We've had a long trip and we want to go to bed."

"Ya wanna go ta bed? Wyncha say so?" Moe said. "Watch! . . . Folks!" he shouted informally. "The poddy's over!"

There were a few regretful groans, but most of the guests quietly relinquished their drinks and filed toward the door, carefully thanking their host and hostess. It took twenty minutes for all of them to find their own hats and coats. As the last couple left, Louis and Rebecca closed the door and sighed with relief. They walked back to the living room. Momma was asleep in her chair, and Jacob was standing in the middle of the room with an air of utter detachment.

"Three of them look like they're going to spend the night," he announced. "Two under the piano and one behind the bar."

"Get Max," Moe said quickly.

Louis called the butler and asked him what was to be done.

"I'll call taxis, sir."

"Well, we'll leave it to you. Come on, Rebecca, let's go to bed."

"Don't you think we'd better wake Momma up?" asked Jacob.

He walked over to Momma's chair and shook her softly. Her head dropped slowly to one side. He shoved her more urgently. She groaned. Louis rushed across the room. "What's the matter, Momma?" he asked breathlessly.

"Ugh," she groaned, opening one listless eye. "Kips goin' round en' round, de room. Sotch a deeziness. Latt me sleep."

"Holy Jesus, the old girl's shikker!" Moe snickered to himself; then he yelled, "Come on, le's get her upstairs."

"I can handle her," said Rebecca. "Come on, Momma. Stand up. Put your arm around me. That's it. Come on. Ups-a-daisy. Here we go!"

"Vare ve going?" chuckled Momma, swaying across Rebecca's shoulder.

"To bed."

"Dough vanna go ta bet."

"Come on, Ma."

"Ull right."

They took one step forward. Momma indignantly pulled her arm from Rebecca's grasp and began to speak. "I vant air!" she said drowsily, and fell flat on her face.

Louis, Moe, and Jacob rushed to her rescue.

"Pick her up gently," cautioned Rebecca. "Remember she wants air."

"She wouldn't know what ta do with it," snorted Moe as they all grabbed hold of Momma, lifted her high above the floor, and carried her upstairs.

Rebecca thought she heard Jacob mutter something about "Brunhilde Levinsky," but she wasn't sure and she didn't know what he meant anyway.

"She'll be all right," Moe reassured her after they'd all come downstairs again. "Well, good night, kids. It was a swell poddy. Sleep good. Come on, Arline. We'll see ya tamorra. Saay, where's Willie?"

"Oh, he's probably gone upstairs to bed," answered Rebecca.

And that was precisely what he had done, with a blonde.

5

FRANCES WAS a well-proportioned, neurotic blonde and she had an apartment.

To Willie this latter fact was more alluring than black lace panties. It conjured up a vision of accessibility that was incredibly appealing. And to Willie, as to most young people, sex was a problem concerned more with convenience than with visual stimulation.

He had cornered Frances early in the evening. She had looked up at him archly from an armchair, which she occupied with all the oblique assurance of a Schubert chorus girl simulating familiarity with the purchasable luxuries of life, and informed him that she was "potentially the best bet Miracle ever put under contract." When Willie failed to utter the expected complimentary response she gave him a wan smile in self-defense. Then they went to the bar and the encounter with Gilbert Whitney separated them momentarily.

When they came together again, Frances was sure she was dallying with a virgin. The "virgin" was perched on the arm of her chair and had taken to surreptitiously pinching and exploring those parts of her anatomy that most vividly presented themselves for examination. Naturally she knew what he was up to, but the bungling timidity of his maneuvers threw her off the track. She knew how to handle the local Lotharios, but this was new to her. The casual strategy of Hollywood's successful Hall Room Boys, who merely transferred the tactics they had used in tenement hallways to swank roadsters, was old stuff to her; and she could give a riotous imitation of the technique employed by an enervated agent whose glands had just been "repossessed." But Willie's fumbling approach deployed under Frances' guard. She had forgotten her small-town romances, and subconsciously was quite amused by the fact that the kid was making a play for her. Besides, he was the president's son.

"What the hell!" she thought, while Willie summoned up his courage to ask the question that to him represented the consummation of a cleverly concealed campaign.

"How about it, babe?" he piped, and he was quite surprised by the shrillness of his voice, which he had hoped would sound professionally smooth.

"Where?" Frances asked, reverting to type out of sheer shock.

"Your place?" he suggested hopefully.

She shook her head and said, "Nope."

"Here?" Willie ventured timidly, hoping she'd turn him down.

"Okay, kid," she said with a smile, "here. I'd like to be laid in the boss's house."

The pit of Willie's stomach suddenly tore itself loose and in one wild leap surged up his esophagus to the back of his throat where it stuck, quivering rhythmically to the sickening throb of his pulse.

He gulped and grinned anemically at his ladylove. He looked anxiously around the room, hoping that someone would come along and take her away from him.

"Well?" she demanded.

"Follow me," he mumbled.

As she got up to join him, he turned and quickly muttered out of the side of his mouth, "No! . . . Wait till I get out of here. I'll meet you at the top of the stairs."

His heart pounding wildly, he waited for her on the landing. His hands shook. He found himself no longer wishing she wouldn't come, but wondering why she didn't. When she finally appeared at the bottom of the steps he beckoned excitedly for her to hurry up. But she took her time, so people would think she was going to the bathroom.

"Here," she whispered when she got to the top step, "I swiped this for us." And she handed him a bottle of whisky. He started down the hall. "Take it easy, kid," she said. He stopped. There was a frightened, bewildered look in his eye and it amused her. She put her arms around him, but she didn't kiss him. He tried to back away but she moved in with her hips and pinioned him against the wall. She held her head cocked to one side and watched him. He trembled. "You'll get there, kid," she laughed and she kissed him hard. He shied away and cried, "Not here, for Chrissake! Not here!"

"Well?" she asked.

"This way," he said, leading her to his room.

Once inside he heaved a sigh of nervousness and relief. It was his first curiosity-appeasing contact with sex and he kept the lights on well toward morning.

They got up at six-thirty and he sneaked her down the outdoor staircase. She paid her own taxi fare home.

Willie was too exhausted to be in the clouds, but by sunset when he'd recovered somewhat, he was in love.

He courted Frances ardently for three weeks, by which time she

192

became utterly bored with him and began breaking engagements. When he phoned one evening prior to calling for her she told him she was sick in bed and couldn't keep the date. Willie, still unaware that she was definitely avoiding him, went out and bought flowers, and just as he was about to enter the apartment house, looked at her ground-floor flat and noticed the lights were out. He walked over to see if she were sleeping and heard a man's voice coming from the open window. The man said, "Jesus, it's been a long time!" Willie's heart stopped. He looked angrily at the open window and instinctively heaved the flowers through it. Then he waited. A woman's hand reached up and pulled down the blinds. Willie turned away and walked home slowly, crying a little on the way.

6

WILLIE BROODED violently for the next few days. His troubles, however, were communicated to the rest of the family only by the fact that he'd lost his appetite. The moment they discovered he wasn't eating with his customary abandon, his problem became a matter of domestic concern. Rebecca worried and thought of writing Dr. Lansburgh. Momma suggested, "Mebbe de climate dun't agree vid him." Moe said, "It's this loafing around. It's enough to make anybody sick." Jacob, nearer the truth than any of them, said, "It might be his nerves."

They went so far as to prepare an evening meal consisting of his favorite dishes. The sacrifice failed. Willie's enzymes quailed before love.

All he wanted was another chance to see Frances. He tried various simple devices such as calling up and pretending to be another man just to hear her voice. He patrolled the corner opposite her apartment hoping to get a glimpse of her. And when he did see her, he succeeded only in adding fuel to his unhappiness because she invariably snubbed him. Finally in desperation he appealed to Jacob. He told his grandfather everything that had happened, omitting only the fact that Frances had spent a night under the same roof with the family.

"Tsk! tsk! tsk!" Jacob clucked in apathetic sympathy.

"She—she worries me." Willie concluded inadequately. And then, in a sudden burst of surly pride, he revealed how seriously his vanity had been wounded. "Someday," he said confidently, "she'll say she loves me."

"Don't worry," answered Jacob, "she'll never say it. Till the sun, the moon, and the stars fly out of their orbits, she won't say it. They either love you quick, decisive and sure, or not at all. . . . Laughter is the one thing that bowls them over. Laughter and power. The one you have at your finger tips and the other you will acquire when you love them the less. Power is just around the corner waiting for you. Why don't you go and see your father at the studio? Tell him you want a job. I think he'd rather you did that than waste another year in school. You seem to have got so little out of it."

"The studio!" thought Willie, ignoring Jacob's last remark. "My God, she works there!"

He ran downstairs to call a taxi. . . .

The man at the reception desk gave Willie a quizzical glance and reached for the phone. His hands were gnarled and cramped and he lifted his spectacles against his eyebrows so he could look down at the dial through his bifocal lenses. He called a number on the interoffice phone.

" 'Lo, Matilda?" he said to Miss Mayer, Louis's secretary. "Henry at the front desk. There's a young man down here says he's the old man's son." He winked at Willie without moving his lips from the mouthpiece. "Looks like an ortagraph pest to me. Whadda we do with him?"

194

"Why—why," Matilda sputtered, "he's an impostor! Mr. Levinson has no children."

Ten years at the front desk had made Henry cautious. He closed his eyes and sighed, "Take it easy, sister. Better make sure."

"Hold on," Matilda said, and she flicked a key on the dictograph board.

"Yes?" answered Louis.

"Sawry to bother you, Mr. Levinson, but there's a boy downstairs says he's your son."

"Send him up and let him wait," the boss commanded.

"Yes. Yes, sir! . . . Oh, my goodness," Matilda continued, all atwitter after Louis had hung up.

"Henry," she whispered into the phone, "it *is* his son! Send him up."

"Aw right. Don't get so flustered. We're just doing our jobs," Henry crabbed as he put the receiver back on the hook. Then he took a pencil and scribbled on a yellow slip. "Here's your pass, lad," he said to Willie. "Go right through the door, turn right, then up the stairs till you see a sign with Levinson on it and walk in. Glad to know ye, son. My name's Henry."

The boss's son shook hands with Henry, who kept smiling until the studio door closed behind Willie's back. Then he shook his head and muttered, "Christ! Another up-and-coming sonuvabitch to worry about!"

Willie sat on the couch in the anteroom of his father's office. Miss Mayer introduced herself and sat grinning maternally at the heir to Miracle Studios. The heir felt uncomfortable and after smiling back once or twice looked off into space.

"It won't be long," Matilda reassured him after a fifteen-minute wait.

"Thank you," he said loftily. At least to secretaries and gatemen, he was already a personage. And when Frances got wise to herself she'd think so too.

195

Two men finally came out of his father's office. The dictograph buzzed.

"You may go in now," Matilda beamed.

Willie nodded and went in.

"Well?" his father asked, fearing the worst.

"Look, Pop, I'm tired of loafing. I've been out of school almost a year now, and I want a job."

Louis was so astonished that he couldn't speak for a moment. Then he was so proud of his son and so afraid of revealing his pride that he took refuge in what he considered the proper attitude of an employer interviewing a prospective employee. "What can you do?" he asked abruptly.

"Anything," Willie answered vaguely.

"Anything?" Louis repeated. "Can you cut film?"

"No."

"Run a motion-picture camera?"

"No."

"Can you typewrite?"

"No."

"Write a story?"

"Sure—anybody can do that."

"Uh-huh," said Louis. "Wait a minute." He pushed Moe's button on the dictograph. "Moe," he yelled, unable to hide his elation any longer. "The kid's up here. He wants a job! Where'll we put him? . . . Cutting department? Okay. That's a good idea. See you at lunch."

"Willie," he continued, turning back to his son, "you're going to start carrying film in the cutting department and work your way up just like anybody else." Once again he turned to the dictograph. "Miss Mayer," he said, "tell Danny Gorlica he's got a new addition to his department. . . . Yes—my son. Thank you."

"I don't want to be a cutter!" snorted Willie. "I want to be a director!"

"What makes you think you're going to be a cutter? That takes years of experience. You start in the cutting department," Louis said, "and from there on, we'll see. Now, go out and tell Miss Mayer to take you down to Mr. Gorlica's office. Go on, I'm a busy man!"

"Yes, sir!" replied Willie, hoping to heaven Frances would never see him lugging film.

"One more thing," Louis called to his son, who was halfway through the door, "because you came to me and asked *me* for a job I'm going to increase your allowance to fifty dollars a week, and your salary will bring in another eighteen a week. Go out and buy yourself a little car to run around in."

"Gee! Thanks, Pop!" Willie yelled enthusiastically.

"Get to work!" the president ordered with mock severity.

Danny Gorlica, the head of the cutting department, sat behind his desk polishing his nails. He had certain peculiarities, but his boys loved him. Danny never shook hands with anybody but the bosses. He treasured his nails as Heifetz his Stradivarius and he drew a buffer across them with all the finesse and aplomb of a violin virtuoso rippling through a difficult cadenza. He blew softly across his cuticle and leaned back to examine his handiwork.

The dictograph buzzed.

"Yes?" said Danny.

"Matilda Mayer's here with the kid," said his secretary.

"What, already?" yelled Danny, tossing the buffer into his desk and slamming the drawer shut. He walked across the room and opened the door. "Come in," he said to Willie and Matilda.

"This is Mr. Levinson's son, William," Matilda giggled as soon as she crossed the threshold. "This is Mr. Gorlica. Nice fella, Mr. Gorlica. Well, I guess I'll leave you two alone." She looked at Willie. "If you want anything, let me know. G'by, boys."

" 'By," said Willie, extending his hand to Gorlica.

"Sit down, Bill," Danny answered, ignoring Willie's gesture. "Glad to meet you. Your pop just called. Said you wanted a job."

197

Willie sneaked his hand self-consciously back into his pocket and moaned, "Yeah, but I wanted to be a director."

"The best directors come out of the cutting room," Gorlica stated flatly as he sat down behind his desk.

"No!" said Willie, genuinely amazed.

"Yes. Besides, you'll find a swell gang of boys working down here. I don't drive 'em too hard because I believe in hiring guys who work without a whip. And I want to impress on you that discipline is self-imposed here by competition. . . . Know what I'm talking about?"

"No," Willie said honestly.

"I was afraid of that. Mind if I polish my nails? Well, promotions, which mean pay increases, are handled on a merit basis in this department and when a guy slacks we pass him by. Money means a lot to cutters. Most of them are married and supporting families. Now, if you're going to work for me, I want it understood that you're in no way to undermine that discipline. You'll get along best with me if you forget you're the president's son. Incidentally, your old man called and said I was to start you in as a film lugger, but I'm going to give you a chance to learn something besides. I'm going to assign you to the best and toughest cutter on the lot, Ace Luddigan. You'll be his assistant. Anything he says, you do, and don't complain. He's in Cutting Room 6 across the street. Tell him I sent you."

"Thank you, sir," said Willie, utterly cowed.

"You're welcome," Dan answered laconically.

The moment Willie was out of the room Dan reached over and pressed Moe Korn's key on the dictograph.

" 'Lo, M.K.? . . . I gave the kid the works. Scared the daylights out of him and assigned him to Ace. We'll make a motion-picture man of him if it's the last thing we do."

"Attaboy, Dan!" answered Moe. "Only remember that someday he's gonna be ya boss—if ya last that long. G'by." The buzzer clicked.

"G'by, indeed," Mr. Gorlica said to a closed connection. "G'by and nuts!"

Willie in the meantime found Cutting Room 6 and knocked timidly at the door.

"Come in!" a voice croaked. Willie ducked. The man's voice sounded like a chorus of frogs that had been weaned on whisky.

Willie knocked again.

The croak became a bellow. "Fa Chrissake, come in!" it roared. "Whadda ya think this is? The Ritz?"

Willie opened the door. At the other end of the small cutting room a squat, broad-shouldered man stood with his back toward Willie. He was winding a reel of film back and forth between two flanges. Occasionally he'd stop and examine the film over a light that seeped through an opaque glass fitted into the cutting-room table. Then he'd wind onto another section. Suddenly he stopped, looked up, and without turning, growled, "Goddamn it! Come in and close the door! Whadda ya want?"

"Danny Gorlica sent me."

"What the hell for?"

"I'm to be your assistant."

"Yer, whaaat?" Ace yelled, turning around to his victim. "I got one assistant and he gets in my hair. Whad am I gonna do with two?"

"That's for you to find out," Willie answered back.

"Oh. Wise guy! How the hell old are you? Looks tuh me like yer ears ain't set yet. What's yuh name?"

"Bill."

"Bill, what?"

"Levinson."

"Holy Jesus!" Ace groaned. "It's worse'n I thought! The old man's son, eh?"

"How'd you know he had a son?" asked Willie.

"I know everything," Ace answered with complete finality. "Hang yuh coat up and shut yuh mouth."

Willie took off his jacket and sat on a stool in the corner of the room. Ace looked to him like the toughest guy alive. The lines of dissipation around his eyes were more than offset by the bulge of muscles protruding from beneath his white shirt. Willie had a hunch Ace'd rather slug a man than talk to him.

"Here," said Ace. "Take these reels up tuh Room 5."

"Where is Room 5?" Willie asked fearfully.

"Find out! Don't bother me!" Ace snapped, grabbing his coat off a hook on the wall. "I'm going out for a smoke."

Willie gingerly picked up the three reels of film and followed Ace out of the cutting room. Luddigan disappeared around a corner, and Willie, being a bright lad, saw a sign "Room 5" right next door to their cubicle. He walked in. No one was around. He dropped his burden on the cutting-room table and returned to his own room. He sat on the stool and surveyed his first "office."

It was about twelve feet long and nine feet wide. The walls were painted a dark, dirty green. The windows looking onto the main street inside the studio were of opaque glass set in steel frames. The frames were embedded in concrete; they couldn't be opened. Ventilation was provided by an electric fan built into the frame itself. Steel film-storage cabinets lined the wall nearest the door. A Moviola machine stood in a corner. It was a boxlike contraption with two interlocking sections. On one side there was a photoelectric cell and a horn for reproducing sound, and on the other, a magnifying lens with a strong light behind it for viewing the picture. A cutter could run a scene and its sound track back and forth, and over and over again, without once going to the projection room to see if his cuts were okay. Willie had yet to learn that a good cutter regards his Moviola as a priceless fluoroscope through which he can diagnose the illness his patient has contracted on the set.

Two wooden stools, a broken-down canvas director's chair, and a number of small synchronizing machines, equipped to handle two or three separate rolls of film simultaneously, completed the equipment in the room. There were twelve similarly furnished cutting cubicles in the building. Willie thought it a particularly unexciting place and was glad to hear the door open.

"Did yuh get the stuff tuh 5?" asked Ace.

"Sure," Willie answered proudly.

Two seconds later the phone rang.

"Answer it!" Ace commanded.

"It's for you," said Willie, holding the receiver in his hand.

"Yeah?" Ace drawled, snatching it away from Willie.

"Mr. Morse's been waiting for ten minutes in Room 5," said Mr. Morse's secretary, "and the film isn't up there yet!"

"Okay, kid, don't get excited. It'll get there!" he said, hanging up and muttering, ". . . if I can ever find out where it went in the first place." He turned to Willie. "Well, Mr. Vice-President, where'd yuh take it?" he asked.

"Room 5."

"It ain't up there!" Ace shouted.

"Isn't Room 5 next door?" Willie asked innocently.

Ace got so mad he just looked down at the floor. He held his breath until the veins in his neck stood out like mountains on a relief map. Then he let go.

"Next door!" he screamed. "Yuh think I ain't got enough strength tuh cart me own film next door? Whatsa matta with yuh? Dontcha know *nothing*? Dontcha know Room 5 means *Perjection* Room 5? Where yuh been all yuh life?"

"New York," Willie ventured, sotto voce.

"Noo Yawk, eh? . . . Well, ain't that nice! . . . And furthermore, don't stand around here listening tuh me bawl yuh out. . . . Get the hell outta here, will yuh! And take 'at goddamn film UPSTAIRS tuh Perjection Room 5. Quick!"

Willie dashed out of the room to correct his error.

Ace mopped his brow. "Now why do I gotta go and get so mad about nothing?" he sighed to himself. Then he picked up the phone and called Danny Gorlica.

"Fine assistant you handed me," he said. "I tell him tuh take a coupla reels tuh Room 5 and he lugs 'em right next door. Drops 'em there, too! The sonuvabitch, he dunno when was last week! . . . Yeah. . . . Go easy on him? What the hell for? 'Cause he's the president's son. Listen, I can always get a job somewheres else. If he's gonna work fa me, he's gonna work! . . . I ain't hot under the collar! Goddamn it!" he said, and he slammed the phone on the concrete floor where it shattered into a thousand pieces.

7

WILLIE drove to the studio every morning with his father, and until he got his own car that was his last taste of luxury for the day. The moment he arrived in Ace's cutting room the grind began. Luddigan kept him hopping until six in the evening. Willie lugged film all over the lot, from cutting rooms to projection rooms, from projection rooms to the trick department, from the trick department to the film library, from the film library back to the cutting room. It was a vicious circle, with Ace in the middle of it, and it didn't take him anywhere near the sets where Frances was working.

But Willie was learning. Ace taught him how to put "lab" orders through. Lab orders are requests for the laboratory to develop or print certain pieces of film. Willie found it easy enough to make out the actual order, but each item had to be carefully checked with the "take" numbers as recorded on film or jotted down by the script girl. He learned that slate boys on each set held their slates in front of the camera just before a scene began. In this manner cutters and laboratory workers immediately knew the name of the cameraman and director, whether it was a day or a night scene, the production number of the picture, the scene number, and the "take" number revealing how many times the scene had been shot.

He sat in the dubbing room with Ace and watched the sound engineers re-record reel after reel of the picture Luddigan was editing. He found that each picture had a dialogue track on which the spoken lines of the players were recorded, a music track complied from the film library or actually scored on the music stage, and an "effects" track which cutters assembled from a stock library. "Effects" consisted of every sound from a door slam to an automobile crash. He discovered that dubbing was merely a system of blending many sound tracks into one, and Ace taught him how to "bloop" tracks preparatory to having them re-recorded.

"Yuh take this black paint," Ace had said, "and at every patch yuh cross the sound track with an arrow. That eliminates the click yuh hear when yuh run straight patches through a perjection machine and when yuh get up to the dubbing room everything sounds swell tuh *you* and lousy tuh the jerks at the dubbing board. Don't be afraid tuh paint the arrow good and black. The blacker it is the less light comes through. Less light, less noise. Savvy?"

Willie said, "Sure," and in a few days he became an expert "blooper."

Then, after dubbing, he followed Ace's picture through its three previews—two "sneaks" and one for the Hollywood press.

He also enjoyed the screenings, in which producers, directors, and cutters struggled with each other to get their pictures cut down to release footage without butchering them to the point of unintelligibility. It was during one of these nerve-racking sessions, consisting for the most part of running one reel over and over again, that Willie had his first taste of power and revenge.

The year before, notwithstanding the depression, Manny Adelstein had made a picture called *Detective Hammond's Crime,* which surprisingly enough made money. Because it was a B picture, a newcomer named Robert Todd was given a chance to play the detective. Mr. Todd, a tall, dark, handsome young man whose frank countenance was as deceptive as only frankness can be, set the girls on fire and the show clicked at the box office.

Unfortunately, Manny had been misled into accepting Archie Newbold's suggestion that Hammond be killed in the last scene.

"It gives ya dramma and a punch at the end," the director had said.

"I dun't care wotcha do wid it!" Manny answered, because he hadn't given a damn about the picture in the first place. "Shoot da sonuvabitch end wrep da show op fest!"

And that was exactly what Mr. Newbold did. Now their problem was to bring Hammond back to life again. Moe had taken one look at the box-office receipts and decided to make a series of Hammond pictures starring Todd. Reviving the corpse was their problem. He wanted Hammond on the screen again, and quick!

So Manny and Archie put their heads together and came up with the oldest turkey of them all. The new picture, *Detective Hammond Returns,* opened up with Hammond's funeral. As the coffin was being lowered into the grave, one of the mourners took another shot at it. This convinced Hammond's girl that her hero was still alive, so she ordered the coffin opened and Hammond stepped out, make-up and all, with another mystery on his hands.

Ace Luddigan had cut the film and under his deftly wielded scissors the picture had acquired a pace that caused the director to swell with pride at what he considered to be his own achievement. It was while the boys were screening the "rough cut," or first assembly of the entire picture, that thunder struck Willie.

Manny Adelstein, Moe, Danny Gorlica, and Archie Newbold were in the projection room. Frances Cord, Willie's unresponsive love, was with Archie. And what Willie didn't know was that Archie had been the man in her apartment the night she gave the Levinson heir back to the Indians. But Willie did know something, and that was a "cut" Ace had pointed out, which would not only speed up the picture but also virtually eliminate Frances Cord's part in it. Furthermore, Ace had confided to Willie that there was no use mentioning it at the screening because Newbold wouldn't stand for their making even "the teensiest, weensiest cut on his goddamn darling."

Around the middle of the third reel Willie leaned over to Ace and whispered, "Betcha they make the cut if you let me tell 'em about it."

"Five bucks!" snorted Ace, who should have known better.

As the reel finished the lights went on and the geniuses in the front row simultaneously shrieked their suggestions at each other. Then the racket subsided and they all sat back to digest and mull over their own particular morsels of strategy. During this lull Willie stood up.

"I got a swell cut," he ventured. "Drop that scene with the blonde. It's about two hundred feet long, and the two sequences around it tie in together perfectly."

The boys in the front row turned around to get a look at the intruder. Only Moe's face looked friendly. Manny's was a blank. Frances seethed, and Newbold looked as if he could have kicked Willie right in the teeth.

"Look, young man," the director growled, when he finally recovered his voice, "where I come from, assistant cutters keep their mouths shut!"

"Not that guy, he's a big shot!" Moe grinned, maliciously promoting the fracas.

"I don't care who he is, it's a lousy cut," Archie maintained.

"Anything that takes two hundred feet out of a picture ain't a lousy cut!" Willie replied, indignantly defending what had by this time become his own suggestion.

"The kid's got sump'm," Moe remarked judiciously.

"S'all right wid me. Megg de cot!" Adelstein agreed. "Naxt rill."

"Hold it, Manny," Moe said. "Before we go on, I'd like Archie ta know who he's arguin' with. Archie, meet Willie Levinson. Louis's boy."

"Louis's boy? Why the hell dincha say so? Chris', what guys!"

205

the director groaned, reaching over his seat to shake Willie's hand.

"And Frances Cord," Moe added.

"We've met," Willie mumbled.

"Didja hear that, Archie?" Moe asked blandly. "They've met!"

"At our party, Unk," Willie added quickly. He was really embarrassed now.

"Yes," Frances said, looking at Moe, "and a very interesting experience it was." She turned to Willie. "Wasn't it, Master Levinson?" The gang roared, and Willie's spirit suddenly sagged like a slice of raw bacon.

"Go ahead and laugh, you guys," Frances said. "The kid's gonna go far in this industry. He's gonna be a big shot, all right. And he'll break lots of hearts doing it. Including his own."

"Naxt rill, Ace," Manny said again.

The lights went out and the next reel began.

Willie shuddered in the darkness. He had no idea why he wasn't enjoying himself. He had wielded power and he felt miserable. Frances had really come off best. She'd robbed him, somehow. Well, at least he'd made five bucks out of it. He tapped Ace on the knee. "Gimme the five," he whispered.

"Aw, hold ya water," Ace grumbled. "You'll get it."

They had become friends.

8

BY THE TIME the negative of *Detective Hammond's Return* had been cut and the release prints made, Johnny Morelli, Ace's first assistant, was earning an extra five bucks a week. It was purely surreptitious income, and the raise, peculiarly enough, reduced his status to that of Willie's stooge. For Willie had suddenly discovered two things: first, that lugging film didn't essentially broaden one's knowledge of the picture business; second, that a slight but judicial dispensation of cash relieved him of that onerous duty. Ace greeted the deal with owl-eyed indifference. While he believed in putting Willie through his paces, he naturally realized the boy's connection with the cutting department was temporary. He could teach Willie more and eventually reap greater benefits for himself by keeping the kid at his side during the day. And besides, he could trust Johnny. Johnny was a good cutter already, which was something Willie would never be because he lacked the patience.

Accordingly, when Ace was assigned to edit *The Quest*, featuring Elena Maya, exploited by Miracle's publicity department as Europe's most seductive star, Willie was his constant companion, and since cutters spend much of their time on the set during the shooting of a picture, Willie found himself in a new world.

Ace introduced him to all the members of the cast, and very shortly Willie found out that Miss Maya, who was an extremely languid and exotic-looking wench, had been born Hazel Flynn in the Bronx. Every grip and electrician on the stage knew she'd climbed the ladder of fame the hard way—on her back—but not one of them disputed her right to assume the air of an innocent if somewhat petulant child. Her histrionic ability was for Miracle a questionable commodity. She had made two pictures and neither had been profitable. In her more aggrieved moments she claimed that only a European director could bring out her talents. Miracle had spent so much money launching her career that Moe decided to try just once more in the hope of realizing some return on their investment. The foreign office finally secured the services of Fritz Kornfeld, whose pictures had been smash hits in Europe and artistic successes in America.

As originally written, *The Quest* told the story of a woman torn between two loves, one poor but honest, simple and handsome, the other rich and evil. In the end, of course, the poor man won out.

207

Before signing the contract the great director read the story and made a request. Wires and cables were exchanged, and as a result the story was rewritten so that the rich man finally won the girl. Fritz knew women—sophisticated women, anyway.

The atmosphere on his sets was always electric, and when Willie first saw him he felt a queer shock. He couldn't analyze his feeling and comforted himself by murmuring, "The guy's nuts!" But what he'd really experienced was a unique sensation of subconscious respect.

Fritz Kornfeld spoke English with the German s, which is something between a soft hiss and a whistle. He was a combination of curious contrasts. A liberal who was emotionally a child. An egomaniac who was intrinsically a gentleman. A man who abhorred indulgence but allowed himself to be victimized by spasms of fury. A director who loathed yet pampered his players, whose most scathing denunciations were generally reserved for the more glamorous ladies of the screen, with whom, unfortunately, he had a predilection for having affairs. His pictures were famed for their finesse in the handling of love scenes, but it was doubtful whether Fritz had ever experienced that particular emotion himself. His search for love had been too intense and he demanded too much of it. Love, the thing itself, was afraid of him, and besides, he was inclined to be paunchy, for which disability he compensated by substituting many women for the elusive few. He was a miserable man and a sensitive one.

Willie was scared stiff of him.

The haphazard joviality of most sets disappeared before Fritz Kornfeld. Electricians, gaffers, or head electricians, assistant directors, and even the camera crew went about their work with an unaccustomed silent simplicity. The reasons were threefold: first, the man's presence awed everybody; second, Fritz's reputation had preceded him; third, they had to conserve their energy. Fritz was an exacting taskmaster. He made demands upon his men with the relentless impersonality of a time clock. He had a tremendous capacity for work. Twelve to fourteen hours of shooting tired him less than half an hour of social chitchat. In his complete concentration on even the slightest details he had no regard for the physical welfare of his crew. Though some of the boys cursed him, the majority found themselves less exhausted after twelve hours of Fritz Kornfeld than after six hours with any other director on the lot. He had a buoyant, vital, colorful spark that quickly communicated itself to his men and co-ordinated their work. On the set he always wore a monocle, tennis shoes, gray slacks, an old, dirty sweat shirt, and white gloves. However, the man's bearing was such that not even the ridiculous incongruity of his costume interfered with the Prussian discipline he imposed upon his underlings. He was also Germanic enough to enjoy power, not so much for its financial rewards as for the sheer outrageous fun it gave him. He admitted as much when he cracked, "Vunce on staitch, iss Kornfeld king, und all de blayers, buppets."

9

ELENA MAYA was determined to prove the fallacy of that statement. She didn't like Fritz. He was too overbearing. Elena had completely dominated her last two directors and her refusal to submit to direction had resulted in the failure of both pictures. Secretly she was contemptuous of anyone she could master, but she would rather alienate a man than subordinate herself to him. She had got where she was by compliance, but now that she had become a personality in the movie world she was determined that the very people toward whom she'd been more than acquiescent should become the valets of her ego. It was an understandable attitude, but one that Fritz Kornfeld had no intention of fostering.

The call sheet for the first day's shooting stated:

MIRACLE PICTURES Inc.

C A L L   S H E E T

DATE: April 29, 1933

DIRECTOR: Fritz Kornfeld

PRODUCTION NO: 542

TITLE: The Quest   COMPANY CALL: 9 A.M.

Name	Time	Location-Stage-Set-Costumes, etc.
MADE UP READY TO WORK	9 AM	INT ELENA'S APARTMENT
Elena Maya	"	Set 39—Stage 10
Gilbert Whitney	"	
Robert Todd	"	
STAND-INS		
Jean Connolly	8 AM	
Fred Maguire	"	NO VISITORS PLEASE
Walter Grant	"	
STAFF & CREW	9 AM	
Ready to Shoot	"	

George Tilden	Pete Mohr
Production Manager	Assistant Director

210

Elena purposely arrived an hour late and spent another thirty minutes fussing around in her stage dressing room. When she finally flounced onto the set, Fritz just sat and looked up at her from his canvas director's chair.

"I'm ready now," she announced, giving her evening dress a final breathless expectant fillip.

Fritz smiled at her. It was a smile born at the teeth and intended to penetrate to its victim's fingernails.

Elena smiled back at him. "Is something wrong?"

Fritz Kornfeld removed the monocle from his eye, carefully moistened it on both sides with his breath and with a silk handkerchief began, ever so slowly, to wipe it clean.

Elena stood it as long as she could. "Oh, you're angry with me!" she cried, like a pampered bride. "Is it because I'm late? Is it? I'm so sorry. I just had to get to the hairdresser's first. You understand."

"So?" Fritz hissed.

"I just wanted to look my best for such a distinguished European director."

Fritz pursed his lips and held his monocle up to the light.

"Then you forgive me?" she pursued with starry-eyed innocence.

"I vouldn't forgiff lateness in my crew," Fritz said, putting the monocle back in his eye. "Vye you?" he demanded, suddenly looking up at her.

"Oh, now, really!" she protested. "You certainly don't have to insult me just because I happen to be a few minutes late. I think it's downright bad manners and you ought to apologize to me."

Fritz took a deep breath and closed his eyes. Suddenly he bellowed, "She stinks, dis voman, she STINKS!"

Actors and technicians in the far corners of the stage heard him and stopped what they were doing. Then they stared at each other in amazement. A few of them smiled. Ace winked at Willie, who stood near the camera. There was no sound on the stage at all except for Miss Maya's voice.

"You know, I don't think we're going to get along very well," she said.

"Ve vill, if you come to verk on time. On zis I inzist." He smiled up at her, soft as a snake gliding over grass. "I zink ve go to verk now, yah?"

Elena shrugged her shoulders.

"Who's that bitch think she is?" Willie said within earshot of Fritz.

"Who do you zink *you* are?" said Fritz, turning on Willie, who blinked rapidly and said nothing.

"He's the boss's son," Ace volunteered after an awkward pause.

"Trow him out!" yelled the director.

"But—" Willie stammered.

"Out! Out!" Fritz roared. "I hate boss's sontz!"

Willie turned and walked out, grumbling "sonuvabitch" to everyone he passed.

10

A FEW MORNINGS LATER Fritz and Willie met accidentally at the studio gate. Willie turned away quickly. Fritz laughed and walked up to him. "Villie," he said, extending his hand, "I'm sorry about ze uzzer day. I abologized to your uncle about it. Forgiff me."

Willie burst into a broad, relieved grin. "Forgive *me*, sir!" he said, seizing the director's hand. "By the way, how are you and Elena Maya getting along?"

Fritz smiled. "Already she is submissiff to ze point uff boredom," he said. "You're coming on ze zet today?"

"I'd like to."

"Blease do, und stay near me. Maybe I'll teach you to become a director."

Willie felt like a bee with its nose near a flower. Fritz patted his arm paternally, turned away, and quite conscious of his charm, strode toward Stage 10, where later that day, under the guidance of Pete Mohr, Fritz's first assistant director, Willie learned something new about production.

"An assistant director's gotta work like hell," Pete told him. "And our job begins the day we get the first shooting script from the stenographic department. First we break the picture down into individual scenes, then we gotta figure out the number of sets and days the company's gonna be on location."

"Yeah, but every company doesn't go on location," Willie said, to impress Pete with the fact that he too knew something about the picture business.

"No, thank God!" Pete sighed. "We got enough troubles with them around here without digging up some more on a lousy desert."

"So you break the picture down—what else?" Willie asked, trying to minimize the work of an assistant director, because he had a hunch that Pete, with an eye to the future, was going to magnify its importance.

"Well, sometimes we suggest actors for minor roles—it depends what director you're working for; and then after the front office tells you who's gonna play what star part and featured-player roles, then your real headache begins and you start making out a shooting schedule. For this you gotta be a Houdini. 'Cause you not only gotta figure out the quickest, cheapest way of routing the unit through the sets, but you gotta estimate the time it's gonna take your director to wrap up each sequence—and, brother, do those guys vary!"

"If you know your director, that shouldn't be so tough," Willie said, still trying to deflate Pete's balloon before it really took off.

"Who ever knows a director?" Pete asked glumly. "Halfa them guys spend so mucha their lives telling other people what to do they ain't got time to know themselves! Besides, you got other problems, like washing up the free-lance players in the company.

There's always bits and minor roles cast from outside, and every wunna them people is added overhead to a production."

"But, Christ," Willie interrupted, "we got enough stars and featured players and stock jerks in this studio to cast a thousand pictures!"

"Not even thirty," Pete said. "Besides, the public gets tired of the same faces. At least, that's what they tell me. So they hire these guys by the week. Our job is to get ridda them as quickly as possible. But because you got a beautiful, tight, logical schedule, conserving sets and saving fifty times your salary every day, you got them goddamn free-lance players spread all over the map, working for four weeks instead of one. So what do *you* do? You go out and get stinking. Then you come back with a hangover, reshuffle the whole layout, and finally get it approved by the producer, director, production office, and studio executives. After this you gotta face a budget meeting."

"That's good?" Willie asked.

"That's where a lotta guys who should be earning buttons throw away millions to save a hundred bucks. They do this in very comfortable surroundings. They got a room for it. We call it the Broken Hearts Clubhouse. Producers and executives sit at a long table and each guy contributes his own idea for cutting production costs. And whatta you do? You pray, because it's taken you weeks to get the schedule completed and if they just increase or decrease that budget one goddamn buck, it's ten to one you gotta go to work again. And you got no friends in that room. The director's always asking for more dough and the other guys are beating him over the head. But you're the slob who catches it in the end, and, brother, you come outta that room knowing every boss is a bastard.

"Then when you're over that hump, your real work begins. They start production, and the assistant director becomes the unit's combination wet nurse and trouble shooter. All worries are his worries. The set's gotta meet the director's approval, the props gotta be right. You call the casting office every evening and tell them what actors you're gonna need the next day. You check with make-up and wardrobe and keep them posted on costume and make-up changes for each part. You gotta keep the director on schedule, bounce visitors off the stage, keep publicity men away from the star before an emotional scene, tell the company when to break for lunch, keep an eye on the clock so the laboring crews don't work a minute over the maximum allowed by the unions. And on toppa that, you not only hire extras for mob scenes, you usually gotta direct them. And for all this, the world, outside of Hollywood, thinks we're just a bunch of yes-men."

Willie, who by this time had really learned something, opened his mouth and muttered "Jeez" in open admiration.

"And that ain't all," Pete continued, now that he was wound up. "You should be on wunna them location trips. Your neck's in a sling there all the time. Whatever goes wrong, you did wrong. And, brother, you can't win! Studio cars, lunches, technical equipment, everything's gotta get there on time and you're responsible. And once you get them there, you gotta wet-nurse the hams, too. Generally, we don't care what they do so long as the townsfolk don't know about it. We do insist that they report to work on time in the morning, looking as though they'd just got outta bed instead of into one, but other than that they're on their own. We do all that," he concluded, "for a hundred and twenty-five bucks a week. And that's almost top money for an assistant. A coupla the guys at M-G-M and Paramount drag down a hundred and fifty, but the average pay throughout the studios is probably around eighty a week."

"When I get to be president," said Willie with a wink, "I'll fix that—we'll boost the pay down to sixty."

"You and your uncle musta come outta the same school!" Pete muttered blandly.

"My uncle never went to school," Willie answered. "He's a self-made slob."

Fritz strolled over to them. He was about to shoot the big seduction scene between Gilbert Whitney and Elena.

"Zis iss going to be *etwas*, boys," he said. "Villie, are you learning all about production?"

"Pete's told me a hell of a lot."

"You're going to see ze key scene uff ze picture made right now. Come und sit next to me."

Willie followed Fritz to his seat before the camera and perched himself on a small stool. The gaffer was bawling instructions to his crew on the catwalk. As each new lamp hissed and lit a portion of the set, Joe March peered through his camera and yelled, "It's too strong. . . . Swing it a little to the left. . . . Okay. . . . Douse the junior! . . . Let's try a baby spot in there."

Pete ambled up to Willie. "Cameramen!" he growled contemptuously. "They spend three hundred days a year lighting up sets and it still takes them an hour to change a setup."

"Yah," said Fritz, looking up, "but a good comeraman must haff ze patience uff a scientist."

"The guys that shoot B pictures don't take so long," Willie ventured.

"Right! Und zerefore zey shoot B pictures. Ve can hurry ven ve haff to. But remember zis, in zis bissness a man gets more money for ze time he vastes zen ze time he safes."

"I'll fix that too when I get to be president."

Fritz shot a long appraising glance at the heir to Miracle Pictures. "You'll cook your own goose!" he said quietly.

Willie frowned briefly. "Why?" he asked.

"Ze best vay to get good verk from ze big directors und players in zis bissness iss to let zem alone. Now, vere are ve?"

Fritz turned and looked at the set which Joe had finally lighted to his own satisfaction. The vast dimness had been transformed into a boudoir of satin splendor. A bed, fully six feet wide, topped by a resplendent white satin canopy, occupied the center of the stage. The bedspread was smooth as a piece of polished glass.

"Let's go!" Fritz called to Pete, who promptly yelled, "Miss Maya! Mr. Whitney!"

216

"Ahfter zey make a few good takes"—Fritz winked at Willie—
"ve got a great gak."

"A gag?" Willie repeated, amazed that such a great director
should indulge in horseplay.

"Sssh!" said Fritz. "Here zey come."

Elena slinked onto the set clothed in a silken negligee that
emphasized the voluptuousness of her figure. Mr. Whitney entered,
dressed so immaculately that his evening clothes heightened the impression that he was a lamb being led to slaughter.

"Zis, my children," said Fritz, "iss a scene uff rape. Und vile
I know Englishmen as a cheneral rule detest such maneuvers, you,
Mr. Vitney, must blay ze scene as zo you meant it. Zink uff ze voman
you possessed chust vunce—who vas all firc, but neffer came back
to you. Zink uff her . . . and vant her."

"How did you know?" Mr. Whitney grinned at Fritz.

"Ve all haff zem," the director snapped. "Now, Miss MacNeider,
ze notes I gave you."

Miss MacNeider leaned forward. She was a middle-aged American woman who had held script for Fritz on all his pictures. For
all her years in Europe she still dressed and looked like a small-
town schoolmarm. She took a sheet of paper out of the pocket attached to her canvas chair and cleared her throat.

"The picture depends on this scene," she read, without pausing.
"It must be played with sincerity. Miss Maya, your mood is one of
apprehensive curiosity. You are a virgin. You expect this moment.
After all, he has given you the apartment. But you haven't the lack
of curiosity that would permit you to run away from him. What you
have is every woman's normal curiosity to know what it is that men
have been talking about all these years. You struggle at first, then
you become passive, and then you discover you are indeed a very
naughty girl at heart." Miss MacNeider giggled slightly.

Fritz frowned and shook his head. "Ze scene description, blease,"
he said.

Miss MacNeider flushed and twirled her stop watch idly as she

217

chanted, "Miss Maya, you are in the middle of the room in front of the bed. You look to the door just before it is opened. You breathe quickly and walk over to the side of the bed, keeping your eyes on the door. Mr. Whitney, you come in, give her a polite smile, and walk over to the chair where you sit down and light a cigarette. Miss Maya watches you intently and listens to every word."

"Vit vide-open astonishment," Fritz interrupted. "Mr. Vitney, you vant ze girl, und vid vant goes—how do you say? *Listig.*"

"Cunning," Miss MacNeider suggested.

Fritz repeated the word blankly. "Cunning? Vot's dot?"

"Smart. Shrewd."

"Yah, right. Now, Miss Maya, you luff a poor man—"

"That's Mr. Todd." Miss MacNeider smiled.

Fritz ignored her. "—but you know luff enerwaits itself—"

"Enervates," Miss MacNeider explained.

"—and turns to drutchery," Fritz said, glaring over his shoulder at his script girl. "Drutchery," he repeated, to make it clear.

"I get it," Elena said. "Double talk and all."

"Good. Now let's dry it vunce."

"Quiet! Rehearsal!" yelled Pete.

Fritz nodded. Whitney came through the door and leered politely at his victim, whose expression vacillated between fear and yearning. He dropped into the chair, lit a cigarette, and said, "Sit down, my dear. No, over there on the edge of the bed where you'll be quite safe. You shouldn't be afraid of me, but you are. I can see it in your eyes. You're afraid because I've said nothing about marrying you. Why should I? Marriage is the poverty-stricken man's offering to love. I can give you more than that—"

"Quiet! Rehearsal!" Pete screamed for no particular reason.

"For Chrissake, keep qviet yourself, *du dummer esel!*" Fritz glared at his assistant, then turned back to the set and nodded at Whitney. "Go on," he said, "und Elena, at about zis boint begin coming toward him. He's fascinating you. Hitting you offer ze head vid verds. As he comps to ze end uff his speech slide into his lap . . .

und stay zere until he kisses you . . . zen get up horrified und retreat toward ze bed . . . zen leave ze rest to him. . . . Go on, Gilbert."

Gilbert lit another cigarette and continued his speech, "To an
intelligent person, marrying a mystery is utter insanity. And that's
why I've never brought the subject up. Nor will I, until we know
each other. . . ."

"Into his lap!" Fritz barked.

She climbed in. Gilbert put his arms around her. Held her. . . .

"To me," he whispered, "you will always be a mystery.
. . . Woman is wind crying in the nooks and crannies of caprice. . . ."
He kissed her. She struggled. Broke away. Ran toward the bed. He
pursued her slowly . . . smiling, sure of himself. His arms went
around her . . . and deftly supported her as she dropped timidly
onto the bed. . . . His lips found hers. . . . He fumbled at her
negligee. She opened her exotic eyes, looked into his, and half
trembling still shook her head in gentle reproach. He kissed her
again. She relaxed. Slowly her hands snaked around his shoulders
and held him close. . . .

"Cut!" yelled Fritz. He nodded to Whitney. "It's coming along,"
he said. "Elena, ven you glutch him, kiss his ears. . . . Vunce more,
blease."

They made thirty-two takes before Fritz was satisfied. And still
he asked for one more. Elena and Gilbert staggered back to bed
again. This time they were so exhausted they tore the scene to tatters.
Toward the end, while they were wrestling on the bed, Fritz nudged
Willie. "Komps now de gak!" he whispered. Joe March raised his
eyebrows and looked at Fritz. Fritz nodded. Joe pulled a wire. The
entire bed, canopy and all, collapsed on the lovers.

Fritz roared with laughter. The rest of the crew giggled more
with embarrassment than joy. In the center of the wreckage which
had settled down on them like a billowing tent Elena began to
tremble hysterically. Whitney raised himself on one elbow and
looked down at her.

"Don't Elena," he whispered. "He's not worth it."
Elena shook her head and fought back the tears.

11

WALTER MOFFAT was the Hays Office man usually assigned to censor the Miracle product. He regarded the movies as an experiment in sociology and this professorial attitude was complemented by his physical appearance. His predilection for conservative tweeds, a large pipe, and thick tortoise-shell-rimmed glasses, gave him a thoroughly studious look, which from the beginning had fascinated Willie. He knew the type well. Moffat could easily have played a dignified Inchcape English instructor if he were an actor, which Willie instinctively knew he was not. But Willie was also instinctively aware of the fact that Mr. Moffat was given to a more decadent personal vice. He wrote in secret.

Talking to him around the lot had given Willie a strong impression that Moffat was a thwarted littérateur, a man whose past was strewn with rejection slips and whose future was stifled beneath the weight of erudite, fusty manuscripts contrived in monastic splendor and embellished with the learning of the ancient monks. Willie had no use for scholars, but this one was different. He knew a clay pigeon when he saw one.

A pot shot in the dark when the censor screened the first rough-cut version of *The Quest* proved Mr. Moffat's undoing and became a factor in Willie's rapid rise.

Besides the representative assigned to review Fritz's picture, the projection room contained Willie, Pete Mohr, Ace Luddigan, Fritz, Moe, Louis, and George Tilden. Moffat's reaction was one of sheer stoicism until the later sequences in Elena's bedroom. These obviously aroused his interest to the point of consternation, and Willie, sensing Fritz's anxiety, reached over and patted the director's hand in the dark.

"Don't worry," he whispered, "with a little luck, I fix!"

A long, pregnant silence enveloped the room as the end title flashed off the screen and the lights went on.

"Well, boys," Walter Moffat finally said, "Gilbert's got to marry the girl in the end, or at least you've got to indicate his intentions of marrying her. And that boudoir scene comes out bodily. We won't pass a foot of that stuff!"

"But," wailed Fritz, "zat kills ze whole bremise uff ze story!"

Willie climbed out of his seat and took the floor. "Why are you nixing the boudoir scene, Mr. Moffat?"

"For one reason, it's dirty. And for another, it's a flagrant violation of the Code. Section A, Paragraph One," he quoted, "under the heading of Seduction and Rape, 'They should never be more than suggested and only when essential for the plot and then never shown by explicit method.'

"Furthermore, under the heading of Locations, Paragraph One, 'The treatment of bedrooms must be governed by good taste and delicacy.' Any rebuttals, gentlemen?"

"I will rebutt," Willie said. "Mr. Moffat, you read the original script and the Hays Office okayed it. No?"

Walter Moffat nodded.

"Why was it okayed?"

"There's a tremendous difference between typewritten words on a page and live figures on the screen. Mr. Kornfeld has allowed himself, shall I say, a great deal of license, let alone licentiousness."

"But you will admit the scene is essential to the plot."

"I will admit no more than that."

"Mr. Moffat, have you ever written a scenario?"

"Yes," the representative from the Hays Office admitted.

The Miracle board of strategy began to take an interest in the proceedings. Louis nudged Moe proudly, and turned back to watch his son.

"You have?" the son said, feigning amazement.

Moffat pursed his lips and nodded again.

"You done anything with 'em?"

"Not much."

Fritz, who sensed the tack Willie was taking, inquired, "You sold zem?"

"I'm not interested in selling them."

"Not innarested!" Moe snapped, and as Moffat turned toward him, Willie signaled violently to Fritz, who took the cue and said, "Ve'd like to see zem."

"I've seen too many great screen stories mangled at the hands of incompetents to be anxious to have mine maltreated."

"Would you call Mr. Kornfeld an incompetent?" Tilden asked.

Moffat blinked. "No. No. Not at all. If he wanted them."

"If he wanted them, what?" Moe asked.

"I might— No, I can't say it."

"Say what? You'd like to sell 'em?" Willie was back in the conversation again.

"Perhaps," Moffat hedged. He was getting leery. If the Hays Office ever found out, he would immediately be among the unemployed. And he valued his stipend. It gave him leisure and the opportunity to pursue his muse. He had better squelch the proposition and immediately.

"Gentlemen," he said sternly, "you're not really interested in my manuscripts, and therefore I suspect you of bribery!"

"Blease! Mr. Moffat!" Fritz pleaded, his voice dripping with righteous indignation.

"No. I couldn't think of it."

"One-fifty a story, Walt," Moe said, jumping into the breach. "How many you got?"

"Forty."

"Jesus!" Tilden groaned softly. He looked at Moe and they both grinned at each other. They were thinking the same thing. It would cost them a damn sight less than reshooting almost the entire picture.

"Fa six thousand dollars, ya cut yaself a nick of fame," Moe suggested slyly.

"I couldn't," Moffat protested. He was an extremely confused man and he wanted desperately to be convinced of their sincerity.

"Six thousand dollars," Moe repeated.

Willie shook his head. "Don't think about the money, Mr. Moffat. Fritz and I know your stories are good. You've seen so many pictures they *must* be good, and we really want them."

"Yah, dot's so," Fritz said.

"Overnight you'll be famous," Louis prodded their victim.

"Yes, but not under my own name," Moffat sighed. He was figuring. Six thousand a year. One-fifty a week for forty weeks, exactly twice his salary. And no agent's commission. The Hays Office be damned. It could be kept quiet. As a matter of fact, it might be rather amusing. To see your own story take shape on the screen. To censor it and not have anyone besides these few men know you had written it. . . .

"I have a pen name," he said suddenly.

Fritz looked puzzled. "A nom de plume?" he asked.

Moffat nodded.

"Good!" Fritz said. "Voltaire, Mark Tvain, great *schreibers*, too. *immer* a nom de plume. Vot's yours?"

"Gregory St. Malden."

Fritz ducked involuntarily.

"That's good!" Louis exclaimed. "Good. That's a high-class name."

Moffat smiled wryly.

"It's a deal," Moe said.

Moffat nodded. "Only under my pen name, of course. The Hays Office never heard of Gregory St. Malden . . . a regrettable but understandable oversight on their part." He smiled smugly. "But no publicity anyway, boys, and you'll still have to change the bedroom scene."

"Yah," Fritz agreed, "ve'll chaintch it. Make it symbolic."

"That's the idea," said Mr. Moffat, preparing to depart in the car the studio assigned to him. . . .

Listed among the scripts purchased sight unseen by Miracle Pictures was an unpublished novel titled *Cellini, the Magnificent,* by Gregory St. Malden. No one ever even bothered to make a synopsis of it.

12

MOE KORN was in bloom again. Sitting under a cloud of smoke, surrounded by his stooges and with Louis nodding him on, Moe was giving the boys grilling number four. The one with the stops out and the pain in the abdomen. Moe was hurt. The boys weren't treating him right. They were keeping their ideas to themselves. Miracle was paying their salaries and they were cheating Miracle. And he, Moe, was going to put a stop to it. Or else!— "Goddamn it!"

It was obvious to Helen Connally, typing in the outer office, that this was no ordinary meeting. The noise and fist-pounding reverberated with such gusto that the pictures on the wall shook constantly instead of periodically as they did during minor conferences.

When her dictograph buzzed, she muttered, "What chance has an earthquake?" and answered it.

"Get me Fritz Kornfeld up here!" Moe screamed at her.

"Okay."

While she was buzzing Fritz, Matilda Mayer sneaked through the door. "Is my boss in there, Helen?" she asked.

"If you hear a silence in all that racket, yes."

"Mr. Levinson doesn't talk much, does he?" Matilda said, by way of defending her employer.

"Those guys never give him a chance. . . . Excuse me. . . . Mr.

224

Kornfeld? Mr. Korn would like to see you right away. Yes. Thank you."

She reached over and flicked the dictograph key. "He'll be right up," she announced in the general direction of the mouthpiece.

"I told ya I dint wanna be disturbed!" Moe shouted, slamming the receiver back on the hook. Helen Connally remained imperturbable and pressed the key again. "Yeah?" Moe exploded. "You also told me to get Fritz Kornfeld," she said, and hung up.

Matilda shook her head at Helen. "I don't know how you keep a job," she said. "You're so fresh!"

"I keep my job because I both mind and know my business. . . . What's yours?"

"Mrs. Levinson called to tell Mr. Levinson something about a bill from Robinson's. Says she's charged for a dozen pairs of gloves she never bought and wants to know what to do about it."

"I'll tell him," Helen snapped. "In the meantime, why don't you check with the store? Then when your boss asks you about it, you might be able to answer him!"

Matilda snorted through her nostrils like an outraged hippopotamus and waddled back to her office to take Helen's advice.

Helen sighed, a superior sigh, and turned back to her typewriter. The door opened again. "What do you want?" she asked, without looking up.

"My uncle in there?" Willie asked.

"You show me a mass meeting on this lot without your uncle in the middle of it and I'll be a dead duck. What do you wanna see him for?"

"I just want to see him."

"Sit down and wait."

Willie sat. Fritz entered and said hello to him.

"Go right in, Mr. Kornfeld," Helen said. She tapped her lip and kept looking at Willie. Suddenly she had a hunch. Helen Connally was an Irish girl and she played her hunches to the hilt. "Willie," she asked archly, "how've ye been misbehaving?"

"The usual way." Willie grinned boastfully.

"Know many girls?"

"Sure."

"About a dozen?"

"Yeah. How'd you know?"

"Ever buy gloves for them?"

A look of petrified surprise hit Willie's face with the suddenness of a bird swooping into the radiator of a car doing sixty miles an hour. Helen smiled and clucked reprovingly. "You better go down to Robinson's and fix it up," she said. "Your mother's checking her bills this month."

Willie leaped from the couch and ran over to kiss her gratefully on the brow.

"Get away, you whore's delight!" she snapped, pushing him aside.

"Thanks, Helen," he said, and dashed out of the office.

The moment he was out of sight the buzzer rang again. "Get Willie!" Moe ordered. Helen rushed to the door, caught him halfway down the hall, and brought him back.

"Go right in, Mr. Levinson," she said tartly.

"And God help you, you poor slob," she added, after the door to Moe's sanctum had closed.

Suddenly a strange silence descended upon the room. She frowned and moved her chair near the connecting door. Noise meant nothing to Helen Connally. It was a healthy sound. Full of fury, signifying progress. But silence was a sickness, a banshee, the solemn symbol of disaster, and she listened closely. She heard Fritz's voice alone.

"So, chentlemen, I inwited Villie here. I see no reason vye he should not be here too! You exbect me to discuss my bissness in front of you, but you vill be disappointed. You are executiffs. Pig shots. Villie's a nobody. I like Villie. He listens. Pig shots chust talk. So you, Mr. Klein, and you, Mr. Adelstein, and you, Mr. Morse, and you, Mr. Sullivan, vill be so kind to go, yah?"

"Now, Fritz," Moe laughed, out of respect for any man who'd take command of a given situation, "ya can't kick our whole perduction staff around like that!"

"Moe Korn, my contrekt cess I can—and ven you call me into a room full uf stootches to explain my story chaintches, I vill kick zem out und qvick! . . . To you and Mr. Levinson I talk, and Villie maybe, but ze rest, glear out!"

"Scram, boys!" Moe said.

The boys scrammed.

"You asked zem for sutchestions behind my back?" Fritz inquired accusingly.

"Sure. What've we got 'em around for? And besides, we still dunno watcha gonna do with the bedroom sequence."

Fritz sighed and looked at Willie. Moe looked at Willie. "Scram, kid!" he barked.

"No, he should stay," Fritz said.

"I don't want to stay. I got some place to go. Be back in an hour."

"Meet me in my office, zen," Fritz said, smiling.

"Sure thing. S'long."

Willie left and tore down to Robinson's to pay the bill and hush up the store's credit manager. He could have paid for the gloves originally, but it was more fun to see what he could get away with, and Matilda, in the meantime, her patience exhausted, had given up trying to trace the bill on the phone.

"Now," said Moe, "what about this symbolic business?"

"At heart, Mr. Korn, I am a realist, but somedimes, ze symbolic iss more realistic zan ze actual. You understand me?"

Moe nodded impatiently and asked Louis, "Get it?"

"Sure." Louis smiled vaguely. "But what about that bedroom sequence?"

"I am going to place my comera like so"—Fritz demonstrated—"behind Vitney's head. Elena sits on ze bed. Vitney crosses ze room—comera behind him, remember. Zen, ven he comps glose to her, ve zoom past his head to Elena's ice. In a great pig glose-up her ice express ze emotions uff fear, supprice, indignance, resignation, und joy, in zat continuity. Zen comps ze trick. Ve pan over to a bowl uff turtles at ze side uff ze room. Ve haff established zease turtles in an earlier scene as Elena's pets. Zen, after ve pan to ze turtles, ve cut to an insert showing zem getting togezzer. You know, vun jumping to ze side uff ze udder? . . ." Fritz suddenly felt the need of reassurance, and paused.

He looked at Moe. Moe looked like a man whose eyes had just been replaced with raisins. Fritz became desperate despite himself.

"Look," he explained. "Zey are side by side. Togezzer. Glose. Intimate. Like ze people, see?"

Moe turned to Louis.

"You like it?" Fritz asked.

"It stinks," Moe answered.

"I dunno, Moe," Louis said, "I've found lotsa things stink on paper and look satisfactory on the screen. Fritz is a good director. The rest of the picture was very good. Let him try it."

"Try it!" Fritz said. "My contrekt giffs me ze right to do as I blease wiz my pictures. You forget I don't haff to tell you anyzing! I'm being nice because I vant to ask a favor uff you."

"Wotsat?" Moe asked cautiously.

"I vant Villie to be my assistant."

The lords of Miracle Pictures sat up as though their thrones had become electric chairs. They turned toward each other and shook their heads incredulously.

"You crazy?" Moe demanded. "He's just a kid!"

Fritz looked at Louis. The president was breaking into a slow, proud smile. He had a chuckle in his voice as he asked, "Why Willie? He's got plenty of time. There are others. Natcherly I'm pleased you want him. But I think you're trying to schmeichle us."

"No, chentlemen," Fritz remonstrated, "I'm not trying to schmeichle you. As a matter uff fact you should schmeichle me. I come to you in friendship. Simple friendship. Kornfeld needs no favors. I vant your Villie because he knows how to handle people.

228

Zensors, buplicity men—all ze zings I haff no time for. He's a smart boy. Zat vass a good idea he had viz ze zensor."

"Yes. But now that we bought the stuff, what are we gonna do with it?" Louis asked.

"Ferget it," Moe' said. "Moffat's a cinch fa us from here till Tombsday. If the Hays gang ever finds out what he's been up to, they'll tie a can to him quicker'n he can say, 'It's censable!' Inna meantime we get away with murder. He's gonna be our personal patsy."

"I'm nod interested in ze zensor," Fritz interrupted. "I am interested in your Villie. I vant him. Okay?"

"Why dontcha make him ya perducer?" Moe snickered.

Fritz ignored the crack. "Chentlemen, say yes und let me tell him."

"It's okay with us," said Moe. "Le's get the retakes over with."

"Ve go to verk in sree days," Fritz said, closing the conference. . . .

As soon as Willie returned he went to Fritz's office. "Sit down, boy," the Herr Direktor said. "How vould you like to be my assistant?"

Willie, immediately suspicious, didn't jump up and greet the idea so effusively as Fritz expected. Instead, he looked knowingly at Fritz and said, "Whatsa catch?"

"Catch? Zere iss no catch. You know vot's going on in ze studio. I like ze vay you deal vis outsiders, und besites, all you haff to do iss keep your ice und ears open at ze dinner table. Zat vay I zink ve shall go far togezzer."

"If we understand each other," Willie parried, "we will go far. If we don't, I won't work for you."

"Exblain, blease," Fritz demanded.

"Naturally, Fritz, I know the ropes around here. And anything I hear that will benefit me I'm going to use for myself, because someday I wouldn't be surprised if I turned out to be the head of this company and I don't want to be too old to enjoy it. If you're willing

229

to string along with me, we will, as you said, 'go far togezzer.' Now, you've got no official producer behind your pictures. You shoot 'em and make 'em. George Tilden's running your unit. But how do you know that someday Moe and pop won't stick a Manny Adelstein or a Harry Klein on your neck. Your contract says no interference but it don't say no producer. Figure it out. Make me your producer— I'd work out better for you than any of them other guys. What can you lose? And besides, you'd have somebody plugging for you right in the boss's house. Think it over. All I want is a credit line on the picture saying 'Produced by Willian Levinson.' As far as the actual work is concerned I'll most gladly be your assistant."

Audacity appealed to Fritz. He grinned. "So you vant to be a producer," he said. "You know nuzzing about making a picture, but you vant to get ze credit. Vell, you're a smart boy, Villie. Vot you hear around ze house you don't haff to tell me, so long you giff me your promise zat anyzing uff a detrimental nature to us you vill com und tell me about. Zen ve make a deal!"

"What kind of deal?" Willie asked.

"Vis your kind permission I vill allow myself to be my own producer, but, if you like, ve might arrange it so you get picture credits as associate producer. But you must verk for my interests and I vill verk for yours."

"What do you want, Fritz? I thought you were satisfied with your contract."

"Someday I vill vant a percentage on ze receipts uff my pictures besites a salary."

"Someday you'll get it. It's a deal."

They shook hands solemnly. Finally Fritz smiled and scratched his nostrils. "You're a sonuvabitch," he said, "but an honest vun. Vunce you learn how to blay tricks you'll go far."

After they had taken the close-up reaction shots of Elena in the rape scene, Fritz told Willie that he wanted him on hand for the insert of the turtles. He also instructed the lad to take charge of getting the props: two small turtles, a large glass bowl and enough sand and pebbles to perch one turtle high and dry above his mate floating in the water. "I vant you should be in charge uff all ze inserts in my pictures—und zis iss a good time for you to begin. Make ze necessary arraintchments for our comera crew, electricians, und I imagine ve'll use ze old Staitch 1," he concluded.

"No sound crew?" Willie cracked.

"If you can find talking turtles I vill be only too glad to hire a sound crew."

"Why, Fritz, do you want me to do all these things when we've got an insert department on the lot? It isn't because I don't want to do them, I just want to know why . . ."

"Because I don't trust outsiders with my verk, und secondly, during ze next picture you might be making ze necessary inserts yourself vile I am shooting on ze sets. Now go. I vant to begin early tomorrow morning. It vill not be so easy a chob as you zink."

Fritz was more than right. In the first place, it took an hour to line up the shot with an angle that satisfied him. Then they discovered that the silence during shooting confused the turtles, who pulled in their heads the moment the racket of setting up the scene subsided. Fritz overcame this by making the boys shout to each other the moment the cameras began to turn over. Next they found that when the turtles kept their heads out of their shells they had a tendency to flip out of position. One of the men finally solved this by taping a string to the underside of the mate in the water and gluing the other end of the cord to the bottom of the bowl with waterproof cement. Their next problem was to get the male on the shore to plop into the pond beside his lady friend. This they did by propping a spring beneath him, which Fritz controlled by a wire strung through a hole drilled in the topside of the bowl.

By the time they had settled all these difficulties it was past noon and not a usable foot of film had been photographed. Fritz called one ill-fated rehearsal just before lunch. Everything went well until he released the catch on the spring. Unfortunately the tension was of such force that the turtle suddenly catapulted head

231

over tail past his mate, out of the bowl and onto the floor, at which point he drew in his head for keeps.

"Let's eat," said Fritz. "Und, Villie, get anuzzer turtle."

Willie went on his errand and joined Fritz in the commissary at the executives' table.

"I got it," he said, as he sat down beside his boss.

"Got what?" asked Louis, who had overheard the remark from his place at the head of the table.

"A new turtle," Willie answered.

"Trouble, Fritz?" asked Moe.

"Yah. Can't get zem to move ven und vere I vant 'em."

"Wyncha use prop turtles?" Moe suggested.

"Fishke pitchers ve're makin'," sniggered Harry Klein.

"Fishke pictures you're making!" Fritz retorted. "Real zings I alvays like to use. In zis bissness everyzing iss phony. Sets! People! Situations! Dialok! I prefer taking a little more time if I can only giff ze imbression uff reality to vun little scene. So don't begrutch me my turtles, blease."

"What the hell are you using turtles for?" Dick Morse asked.

"A love scene," Willie answered.

"Christ," Morse snorted, "any guy directing turtles in a love scene ought to be left strictly alone!"

After lunch the boys ambled out of the commissary and back to their offices. By three in the afternoon Fritz had perfected his apparatus so that he got four shots of the turtle clambering aboard its mate. Just as they were about to leave the set Willie got the happy inspiration of calling Moe and Louis. "Come on down the set," he said, by way of boasting about his boss's directorial magnetism. "We got a turtle that jumps on cue."

"A what?" Moe exploded, answering the phone in Louis's office. "We'll be right down." He hung up. "A coupla meshuggina cowboys! . . . They got a turtle jumps on cue!" he explained to Louis. "We gotta see this."

"You think we're kidding?" Willie shouted, as he spotted his

232

relatives striding across the stage. "Come over here and look."

They gathered around the bowl.

Fritz, who had concealed the wire by running it up inside his trousers through a hole in his pocket, pointed toward the inside of the bowl with his free hand. "Vatch," he said, "ven I giff ze verd, he vill jump into ze vater beside his mate. . . . Back up now! It von't verk if you stand so glose."

"Turtles don't jump, do they?" Louis asked hesitantly.

"This one does, Pop." Willie perked up. "Any bets?"

"No," Louis said mistrustfully.

"Five bucks," offered Moe.

"You're on," Willie snapped.

"Okay, boys? Here ve go." Fritz's fingers closed over the release plunger in his pocket. "Ven I giff ze verd, he chumps. Ready? Chump!"

The turtle flipped into the pond.

"I'll be goddamned!" Moe yelled. "Do it again."

"Villie," Fritz asked softly, "vould you be so kind as to reblace ze turtle?"

Willie did as bid. "Another five?" he asked Moe.

"Nix. Onc's cnough."

"Ready? Vun. Two. Three. Chump."

Once again the turtle plopped onto its mate who, certain by this time that the idiot had taken leave of his senses, pulled in her head and sank indignantly to the bottom of the bowl.

"Fritz, ya wunnaful," Moe laughed. "How'd ya do it?"

"Telepathy," Fritz murmured humbly.

13

AFTER FRITZ had managed with superb modesty to struggle through interminable congratulations at innumerable previews, and after the publicity department had duly exploited and planted the trade-paper raves they considered reviews, the picture negative was finally shipped to New York for release printing, beyond which point *The Quest* was definitely on its own.

Within a few weeks everyone in the studio realized the trade and the local newspaper critics had undershot their mark. The picture piled up magnificent grosses wherever it played. One superior drama defender on a metropolitan daily captioned his review with the headline "THE MOVIES COME OF AGE." Other picture critics throughout the country hailed Fritz's deft handling of the rape scene as "a piece of consummate artistry." The nation's billboards proclaimed *The Quest* as "The Masterpiece of a Master Director!" Fritz's monocle became virtually a symbol of imperious superiority, and Miracle Pictures' questionable asset, Elena Maya, woke up to find herself a screen celebrity. People became interested in her clothes, her food, her sleeping habits, and her lovers. This phenomenal curiosity concluded with her agents' pounding at Moe's door demanding a new contract for "more dough."

Fritz had kept his word and wangled an Associate Producer credit from Louis and Moe, and Willie, now endowed with the outward manifestations of genius, promptly traded on his fame to collect a new stable of women.

He was convinced that his debauches were justifiable explorations into the realm of what he called "experience." And now that

234

his name was coupled with that of a celebrated director he had little trouble rounding up as varied an assortment of ornery mares as ever nipped a bottle of gin.

By 1934 Hollywood had become the paradise of parasites, the mecca of a million inland tourists. Slick, toothpick-sucking promoters stood around street corners concocting tight-lipped plans to fleece the established gentry, who they knew would surrender their last dollar to defend what little respectability they had managed to glean from 'a grudging world.

There were, as there always have been on the fringes of every theatrical enterprise, the inevitable gentlemen who led with the libido. An exposed libido made a fine target for these shakedown artists, who backed their schemes with choice selections of extra girls who had failed to make the grade and would-be stars who wound up washing dishes. The girls satisfied a craving and the boys grabbed off the cash. However, when the depression had hit Hollywood, most of the gentlemen returned to their wives, leaving the Hall Room Boys with an oversupply of wenches on their hands.

Willie, never one to impede progress with modesty, allowed rumors of his exalted position to precede his descent into the market place. In no time at all the girls became aware of the fact that a young man who was the heir to Miracle Pictures and a producer in his own right was trying to corner the available supply of what Hollywood refers to as "talent." Since *The Quest* his opinions had taken on a vast amount of local importance. His bright sayings were printed in the daily trade papers, and people who had merely seen his pictures in the rotogravure (captioned "Youngest Associate Producer in the World") nodded to him on the streets.

Now, one of the peculiarities of Hollywood is that the minute anybody becomes important, he finds himself surrounded by satellites who hang on every word and run errands for him. Joey Finney, who was twenty-eight, a louse, and a graduate of New York City's reform schools, became Willie's private satellite. He also became

Willie's personal secretary and for the first time in his life earned a steady salary. His services consisted largely of hiring an apartment and procuring innumerable women for his patron, who believed in the trial-and-error method of selecting those worthy of his attentions.

"Dere ain't nuttin' like a movie-struck daughter fomm a respectable family," Joey advised.

Since to him any girl came from a respectable family if her father and mother remembered each other's given names, this definition gave Willie quite a field.

There was Claire, who had a trim, boyish figure and bounced, as Willie put it, "like a mechanical rabbit," and Helen, a rather large and dull extra girl, who never spoke in the presence of strange men, but surveyed them blankly, focusing her vapid, cowlike eyes on their hands. But Willie's most harrowing experience was with an Irish girl named Rena. Rena was married and, being a true voluptuary, was blessed with a sense of sin. She hated being unfaithful.

It took Willie two dates to get her up to the apartment. Once there, she writhed and struggled and alternately touched his trousers and pulled herself away shaking her head and moaning soft, staccato sobs of anguish through her conscience-troubled lips. When she finally gave in she was so passionate and eager to satisfy herself that she got hysterical and began to maul Willie with such fury that he felt as if he were being attacked by an unleashed vacuum cleaner, and all he cared about was getting rid of her before she annihilated him.

To compensate for this shattering mishap, Joey introduced Willie to Louise. Louise was six feet two. She was admirably proportioned and her long legs were strong and beautiful. Willie thought she was pretty swell. "Just like walking through an open stepladder, only it's not bad luck!" he confided to Joey the next day.

He also became acquainted with the town's leading Lesbians, Daphne and Boo-Boo. Daphne was a cheery, cigarette-smoking heavyweight whose instincts were originally bisexual, but she was one of those unfortunate women men drink with and never love. And in a few short years time had withered and custom staled her natural emotions. As for Boo-Boo, she was a wee slip of a girl whose first love affair had ended in an abortion. They made a lovely couple.

One night Willie and Joey took the girls on a drinking tour of the various night spots. The girls and Joey got pretty stewed, but Willie, who preferred sex to alcohol, kept his head. When all of them returned to the apartment, the boys prevailed upon Daphne and Boo-Boo to spend the night. They agreed only when they were promised the bedroom. Joey poured another round of drinks. Willie prepared the day bed in the living room and undressed. The girls looked bored. A few more slugs and Boo-Boo was sitting on Daphne's lap. After a while they stumbled into the bedroom. Willie followed them. They were too drunk to notice him. His natural prejudice prompted him to flee, but curiosity conquered his revulsion and he attempted to join them. Daphne pushed him away, mumbling, "No! No!"

When he advanced again she straightened up on the bed, pushed a stray lock of hair out of her face and cocked a tipsy eye on Willie. "Is zat a way to act just because a lady's naked?" she demanded.

Willie stood his ground.

"She's mine, you sonuvabitch!" Daphne screamed hysterically. "Stay away from her! She's mine—mine—mine!"

Boo-Boo looked up from the pillow and winked at Willie.

"Okay, Tarzan," he snorted, and left the room to join Joey on the day bed.

"Couple of deadheads," he grumbled, turning out the lights.

After three months of this revelry, Willie began to find individual girls boring, and began throwing orgies with three of four women in his bedroom. The weaker his responses became, the wilder the parties. Eventually the landlady had to throw him out of the apartment, at which point Louis and Rebecca entered the picture.

Willie had refused to pay his last month's rent. The landlady threatened to sue him. Willie sent Joey around to tell her that since he was under age there was nothing much she could do about it. This little bit of information cost Willie a pretty penny, for the landlady promptly threatened to sue his father. Whereupon Willie paid his rent with considerable alacrity. Shortly thereafter he got a bill for a hundred dollars. When he sent the bill back demanding an explanation it was returned to him with the word "furniture" scrawled across it. A few weeks later he got one marked "plumbing." He paid them both quickly and began to lose weight. At this point the landlady sent him a curt note thanking him for his prompt payments and he began to breathe easier, but he had reckoned without Joey, who knew a sure thing when he saw it and suddenly demanded a fifty-dollar-a-week raise.

"You gone nuts?" Willie yelled. "You—my pal? They won't go for it and you know it."

"They won't, but *you* will—and you know it," Joey said very coldly.

"You think so, huh? You think I'm gonna sit right here and be shaken down by a bum like you? You think so, huh? Well, I'm not gonna be. . . . I'm tired and fed up with this whole business. I haven't had a night's sleep since this damn thing started. . . . Now you get the hell outta here—and quick!"

"Okay, hot shot. So I'm fired, but I'm walking upstairs before I'm walking outta here. I'm gonna see your old man!"

"Go ahead—see him!" Willie snapped. "And he'll fire you outta here so fast your hand won't even touch the doorknob."

Joey looked at him and mumbled, "Maybe so, maybe you're right." And Willie felt quite safe, which was exactly how Joey wanted him to feel, because he didn't want Willie to keep him out of Louis's office—and Louis was the sucker he had wanted to play in the first place.

On the following morning Joe Finney spilled the whole story to Louis, who listened incredulously at first. When he realized that Joey was trying to blackmail him, he reared up and said there was nothing a person like Joey could do to injure a name or a reputation, and he promptly ordered Mr. Finney heaved off the lot. But he had learned enough to become sickeningly angry, and he was so distrustful of his own emotions that he called Rebecca down to the studio to help him face his son.

Willie admitted everything.

"How do you think your mother and I feel about all this?" Louis asked.

"I don't know."

"You dunno! Our flesh and blood beds down with whores and you dunno how we feel? We feel as though God had punished us for some horrible crime. That's how we feel!"

"We're ashamed of you, Willie—and ourselves. We feel somehow it must have been our fault," Rebecca sobbed.

"Aw, for Chrissake what's all the hullabaloo about?" he snapped. "I was just getting experience."

"Experience?" Rebecca wailed. "For what?"

"Just experience."

"Supposing I had come to your mother from the arms of whores, do you think she'd have married me?"

"Maybe I'da been better off if she hadn't," Willie replied.

Louis Levinson rose from his chair and walked slowly over to his son. When he was about two feet away from him he let go with a punch that caught Willie flush on the mouth and sent him spinning into a corner of the office.

Willie yelled. All his sophistication vanished. He sat cringing on the floor. He was a baby again and looked helplessly at his mother. Rebecca, heaving frantic, anguished sobs, stumbled blindly toward her boy. Louis caught her before she reached him. "Don't touch the swine!" he ordered.

Willie got up slowly.

"You get out of here," Louis continued, "and don't ever let me see you again."

"Where'll I go?" Willie wailed.

"Go to your sluts! See if they'll take you. Show them how much money you've spent on them and see if they'll give you so much as a glass of milk. Go anywhere, but get out of my sight!"

"No, Louis," Rebecca cried. "Don't send him away. Punish him, but don't send him away."

"Mom's right," Willie pleaded. "Give a guy a chance."

"A chance? Show me anyone that's had your chances! And what've you done with them? Well, answer me! What?"

"Let me take him home, Louis," Rebecca begged. "The boy's shaking."

"All right, Momma." Louis sighed and turned away. "Take him home."

14

THE LEVINSON HOUSEHOLD became an armed camp. Nobody spoke to Willie, and his appearance inevitably produced an awkward silence. Dinner became an embarrassed siege. What conversation there was was limited to trivialities, and every time they approached a moment of levity, the sight of Willie frantically hoping that the next word would end his ordeal sufficed to terminate their pleasure.

It was a most effective punishment. Willie was tormented by the possibility of an eventual truce, or at least a sudden explosion, and he suffered agonies as each day passed without any indication that the family had relented.

His behavior during this period of excommunication was singularly circumspect. He refused all communication with his former friends. Telephone calls, letters, even two telegrams, went unanswered. And although he found himself leering at the maid one evening, he firmly believed his virtue would bring him a just reward. When, after three and a half weeks of deliberation, Louis suddenly pronounced judgment, his son was taken completely by surprise.

240

"Your mother and I have decided," Louis intoned, leaning across the dinner table, "that we were wrong about your schooling. Jacob has convinced us of that."

Jacob saw the look of bewilderment flare up in his grandson's eye. "Listen to me, Willie, and listen closely," he broke in. "This is for your own good."

"You sure, Grandpop?" Willie asked earnestly.

"I'm sure," Jacob answered.

Willie listened.

"Sometimes people do things that seem smart and right at the time . . . things they regret later because they're done without any consideration for a person's future . . . and that's exactly what happened to you. It isn't really your fault that you ran around with a lot of whores. It's ours. Your father went against his natural instincts when he agreed with Moe that you didn't need an education. Now he knows you did, and he's sorry about it. Sorry, because without an education you had no chance to develop a sense of pride in yourself or your heritage . . . let alone a sense of proportion or discrimination concerning women. Someday you will want to get married and there isn't a decent girl alive who won't resent your association with those women . . . particularly if she's a Jewish girl. . . ."

"And if she's a gentile?" Willie snapped. There was a challenge in his voice and they accepted it in shocked silence.

The look of scorn on Momma's face stabbed Willie clear across the table. Louis stared at Rebecca and Jacob lowered his head.

Rebecca finally said, "It wouldn't surprise me if you would," and her voice was cold with fury.

"If I loved her, sure I would," Willie said defiantly.

Jacob looked up at his grandson and shook his head. "Willie, the first obligation of a Jew is to marry his own kind. His happiness comes easier that way. It would take a great deal of love on your part to make a gentile girl happy with us. Being a pariah by choice is no better than being one by birth. So think twice before you inflict us on a gentile girl . . . and if you do think twice, you'll probably marry a Jewish girl, because she understands our troubles, our mistakes, our devotion to our faith and our families."

"You got in dis femily devushion?" Momma asked caustically.

"Look, Jacob," Willie said, ignoring her, "if I do marry a gentile girl she'll be a swell guy—you can be sure of that."

"I am sure of it," his grandfather smiled, "but I don't think you will—and in the meantime you've got a lot of work to do."

"That's what I want to hear—when do I go back to the studio?" he asked his father.

"You're going back to school," Louis said firmly.

"School?" Willie wailed, his eyes popping with indignation. "What do I want to go back to school for?"

"So you can learn how to behave yourself."

"I'll behave myself. Honest I will. Look at how I been behaving the past few weeks!"

"We have ALL decided you're going back to school," Louis concluded with absolute finality.

Willie's gorge rose. "And if I don't want to, who's gonna make me?"

"You'll go back, all right."

"Aw, now, Pa, look, please!" Willie pleaded desperately. "Give me a chance!"

"You've had your chances."

Willie looked helplessly around the table. Momma nodded with pursed lips, Jacob avoided his eyes, Rebecca looked at Louis. "Aw, Christ!" he cried, tears choking his voice as he jumped up and ran out of the room.

"Where are you going?" Louis called after him sternly.

"Gonna get the hell out of here!" he stormed over his shoulder.

Rebecca rose to follow her son.

"Let him go," Louis said quietly.

"More strudel, blease," Momma said, passing her plate to the head of the table for the first time in three and a half weeks.

242

15

WILLIE TUCKED a toothbrush, a comb, and twenty dollars into his pockets before slamming the back door behind him. He paused breathlessly by the swimming pool, half hoping someone would call. He knew what he'd do. He'd tell them he'd never come back. He was leaving for good. If they didn't appreciate him he'd go where he *was* appreciated. He'd show them!

But nobody came out after him and he began to whimper inwardly; if they *had* called he'd have rushed back into the house blindly, quickly, gratefully. After a while he shrugged his shoulders and trudged down the lawn. The soft tropical night closed in on him. He became aware of its beauties as only those in anguish become aware of nature. The smells of honeysuckle, magnolia, and jasmine found their way into his heart which, he assured himself, was closed forever to his family.

Just wait until he became president of Miracle! Until now, he thought, it might have happened pleasantly, with the passing of time. But after this, never! It would be a bitter struggle and they'd come around someday, but then it would be too late.

Anger gave way to resentment as he walked and plotted his revenge. The mental picture of their plight cushioned his hurt and unconsciously he plodded in the direction of Moe's house. By the time he reached the corner of Sunset Boulevard and Laurel Avenue he began to think of Rebecca and Jacob. A sudden surge of remorse prompted him to turn into a drugstore and call up the house. Max's voice reassured him. "Let me talk to the old man," Willie mumbled.

"Oh, yes, Mr. William!" Max responded joyously. "Just a moment."

"Yes?" Louis barked into the phone.

"Pop, it's me!" Willie said.

"Are you sorry?" Louis asked bluntly.

"Sure I am, Pop."

"Are you ready to go back to school?"

"Aw, for Chrissake, NO, Pop! Gimme a chance! I want to work. Honest I do."

"Come on home."

"Do I have to go to school?"

"You certainly do."

"Aw, nuts!" Willie cried, and hung up.

He came out of the phone booth slowly, took another nickel, slipped it into a pinball machine and pushed the release trigger. Ten iron balls rattled down the board. As he pulled the plunger back someone said, "Hello, Mr. Levinson." Willie looked up at a man with slick black hair and a girl in a sweater and skirt. "My girl friend here recognized you from your photographs. She said if I asked you you'd give us your John Hancock."

Willie broke into a smile. "Sure," he said. "Got a pencil?" The man plunged into his coat pocket for pencil and paper. He had neither. Willie glanced at the girl. "Hm. Big ones," he mused. Then he thought quickly of his home and his troubles and the fact that he wouldn't be a producer any more. Terror leaped through his eyes and communicated itself to the girl. Willie turned abruptly and fled from the store just as the man came back with paper and pencil.

"Well, I'll be goddamned!" the man said. "Another genius!"

"He seemed unhappy," the girl answered vaguely.

"I'd be unhappy too—at that salary," her companion snorted.

Willie stood on the corner. A bus passed. It gave him an idea. He'd go to Moe's house. It was six miles away in Cold Water Canyon. He hailed a taxi and told the driver to hurry. He had a hunch Moe would back him up and he had felt curiously attached to Arline from the very first moment they'd met.

After he rang the doorbell he had a moment of misgiving and wanted to run away again. But he stood his ground until Arline opened the door. Because of the soft amber light cast by the hall chandelier she wasn't quite sure she'd seen correctly. A Levinson at her doorstep! She switched on the entrance lamp and began to smile.

Frou-Frou barked happily. Willie bent down to pet him.

"Mosey," Arline shouted into the depths of the house. "The boy wonder's here and he's been bawling. Come in, Willie," she beamed, taking his hat. "Your uncle's in the den. What's the matter with you?"

Willie looked up at his uncle's mistress. "Everything," he answered abjectly. He felt her arm circling his shoulder as she led him toward the den. Moe rushed into the hall and met them in his shirt sleeves.

"Wotsa madda, kid?" he asked breathlessly.

"It's the people he lives with!" Arline snorted.

"Oh, quiet!" Moe snickered. "Come in, Willie. Into the den. Now, siddown. Gee, it's nice ta see ya. Here, I mean. Wanna cigarette? Sure, ya can have one. Here, I'll light it for ya m'self. Close the door, Arline, and throw the mutt out. Wanna drink? No? Well, I do. How about you, honey? Okay, make it two."

Willie opened his mouth once or twice to stem Moe's expansive greeting. When the opening finally came, he heard himself say, "Well, I will have one." Then he added quickly, "If you won't snitch on me."

"Snitch? Don't be silly," Moe said.

Willie felt much better.

"Scotch and soda?" asked Arline.

Willie nodded.

"We drink gin," Arline said. "Your uncle's the only gin-drinking Jew in Hollywood."

"Get Booker ta make the drinks, will ya!" Moe complained impatiently.

"Boss in the office and louse in the house," Arline said, stalking off with Frou-Frou.

"Gee, Unk, you're not at all like you are at the studio."

"Watcha mean, kid?"

"Well," Willie hesitated, "you're nice. I like it here."

"Ya mean I ain't yellin' my head off like I do at the office?" Moe pursued.

"Yeah."

"I'll letcha in on a secret."

"What, Unk?"

"Arline won't let me. She's the boss here—and I love it!"

"You're happy, aren't you?"

"Damn happy—and so would you be if ya got yaself a nice girl."

"Ma don't think Arline's a nice girl."

"Ma's a bitch."

"I don't think so, Unk. I think she's just a dope. And my old man's a pious old bastard."

"Ya got sump'm there!" Moe said. Arline knocked on the door. "Come in, dearie," he called, "this is strickly a family party."

"Booker'll be right in," she said, sinking into a comfortable armchair.

"Let's have a fire when he does," Moe suggested.

"It's all ready for you. All you gotta do, Mosey, is strike a match and put it in the fireplace."

Moe got up and shrugged his shoulders at Willie. "Ya see what I mean?" he smiled.

Pretty soon the logs crackled sharply in the fireplace. They sat looking at the flames. Booker, Moe's Negro servant, eased into the room with the drinks. "Put the lights out," Moe said after they'd taken their glasses.

"Yes, sir!" Booker nodded.

"Gee, it's nice here," Willie said again.

246

"Ya said that," Moe cracked. "Now, wotsa madda?"

"Aw, they got mad at me and my dames."

"Ya can't diddle 'em all, ya know." Moe grinned.

"Your uncle tried, before I got ahold of him—but he's settled down now," Arline announced with the utmost satisfaction.

"That's a fine thing ta tell a kid," Moe protested meekly. "Well, what else?"

"Well, they wouldn't speak to me for three and a half weeks."

"You dunno when you're well off!" Arline said.

"Goddamn it—will you shut up!"

"Jeez, Unk," Willie blurted out, "I thought you were happy!"

"Sure I am. I'm happy 'cause I can say what I please around here. She don't hafta listen ta me—so long as I can get it off my chest. So go on with ya story."

"So they want me to go back to school."

"And you dowanna."

"Nope."

"Why not?"

"I just don't want to!" Willie parried.

"What'd Jacob say?" Arline asked.

Willie shrugged his shoulders.

"You musta been wrong, then," Moe said quietly.

"It ain't a question of right or wrong!" interrupted Arline. "It's a question of being human. And they ain't! They're like a pack of wolves when it comes to morals. They dunno how to forgive anything. They ain't got a Christian virtue!"

"You and ya Christian voiture! Every time she gets mad," Moe explained to Willie, "she makes with her Christian voiture! She dunno a thing about it."

"That may be, but your family stinks anyhow," she cried, throwing her drink, glass and all, into the fireplace.

"Saay, when'd you start drinkin' tidday?" Moe asked suspiciously.

"Aw, that's not it, Moe. I'm sore! They got no right to treat a kid like that. I'll bet he ran out on them tonight. Ya did, didntcha?"

"Yes," Willie confessed. "I did. And I wanted to go back again but they wouldn't let me unless I said I'd go to school."

"Whad I tell ya!" Arline said smugly.

"Whadda ya wanna do?" asked Moe.

"Look, Unk, I'll make a bargain with you. Let me produce one more picture and if it's no good, I'll go back to school. No kidding."

"Whadda ya mean one more pitchure? You ain't perduced nothin' yet. Fritz did the last one. Who ya tryin' ta kid besides yaself? Me?"

"No, Unk, no. But I gotta have another chance."

"Didja tell yer old man that?"

"He said, 'Nuts!' "

"Well, he's right, Willie. Between you and me, he's right. Ya got no business futzin' around with pitchures."

"Futzing around with pictures! Listen, Unk, *you* put me in 'em! *You* made me a kid star when I was a baby. And something happens to you in this business—"

"Sure," Arline snapped, "overnight you're a bum."

"Naw—naw, Arline—" Willie laughed nervously—"it's not that. It gets inside your blood. You—you're a part of it before you know it—and, Unk, you're my last chance!"

Moe sat back and blew a smoke ring at the ceiling. "Scared, aintcha, kid?" he said. "Scared stiff ya ain't gonna see a dame fa six months. Nah—don't gimme that look. I know ya think it's 'cause yer goin' back ta school again—but it ain't. It's dames."

"Unk, I want to stay in pictures," Willie said flatly.

Moe looked long and hard at his nephew. Then his eyes narrowed and he suddenly asked, "How good ya really think ya are?"

"Plenny good," Willie said, trying to sound as tough as Moe.

"Ya gotta be, fa the job I got in mind for ya. Would ya be willin' ta try one alone, on yer own—without Fritz?"

"Jeez, yes!" Willie exclaimed, sensing the way the wind blew.

"And if it's no good ya go back to school and no kicks?"

248

"Word of honor."

How much ya gettin' now?"

"Eighty-five bucks a week. I'm getting producer credits and an assistant director's salary."

"We'll give ya more. Go on home. I'll see Louis inna mornin'."

They shook hands. Arline told Booker to get the car and waited with Willie at the entrance. Moe went back to the script he was reading.

As Booker drove up, Arline took Willie to one side. "How'd ya like the act I put on?" she whispered. "I used to be pretty good in the old days, but yer uncle couldn't see me for dust!"

"Gee!" Willie said, and just before he got into the car, he turned and kissed her quickly on the cheek.

"So long, kid," she whispered huskily as the tires crunched down the gravel driveway. "And if I was you," she added as an afterthought, "I wouldn't trust your uncle too far."

16

WHEN LOUIS ARRIVED at his office the next morning, he found Moe waiting for him.

"What's up?" he asked.

"Ya kid was at my house last night."

"Hm!" Louis commented, hanging up his hat.

"He's gonna do one more show," Moe said.

"He'll do nothing of the sort!" Louis snapped.

"Now, Louis, listen. The kid's all broke up. He wants one more chance and we'll give it to him."

"Willie belongs in school, not in the pickcha business."

"But I got an idea . . ."

"I don't care what you've got," Louis interrupted. "With me, my family comes first!"

"And with me is business first, last, and in between!"

"Nothing doing," Louis said curtly.

"Waid a minute, will ya!" Moe shrieked. "Lemme tell ya what's gonna happen!"

Louis sat down.

"The kid promised me if the show's a louse he'll go back ta school and forget about the pitchure business. Besides, he's gonna make it by himself. No Fritz Kornfeld behind him this time. Now there's two people on this lot I wanna get rid of. They got with temperment and nothin' else. You can't *give* 'em away ta other studios. With a bonus they can't see 'em even. Metro said, 'We got our own schlep-alongs, ya think we wanna borrow yours?' So I wanna get out from under their contracks. They been here fa years and they just been overhead the last two. Their options don't come up fa another eight months, we've used up their layoff period, and we ain't gonna pay 'em salaries fa kickin' around doin' nothin'. See what I'm aimin' at? No? No, you wouldn't.

"Well, we'll give 'em both ta Willie and let him pick his own story. The kid's sure ta pick a stinker. I don't think he ever read a scrip in his life. So we get another pitchure outta them punks and when their agents come around I tell 'em their clients screwed up the show. See? Gladys Creighton's one of 'em and she never showed up on a set on time since the day she got in pitchures. The later she answers her calls this time, the better I'll like it. The other one's that Harvid bastid, Mel Price. That low-life's looked down his nose so long he can't see the handwritin' fa the wall."

Louis couldn't help agreeing with his brother-in-law. "But why Willie?" he asked.

" 'Cause there ain't another perducer on this lot'll make a show with either of them guys!"

"All right," said Louis, "but it better be bad!"

Moe made a leave-it-to-me gesture and went out to call Willie.

"Ya gettin' five hunerd a week," he said over the phone. "Get ta work and pick a story. Mel Price is ya director. Creighton's za star. And stop arguin'! We ain't payin' ya that much dough just ta hear a lotta sass!"

Willie hung up slowly.

17

WILLIE RUSHED into Fritz's office. "Oh," he said, noticing a languid young man draped in the armchair, "you're busy!"

Fritz looked up from a sheaf of sketches.

"No, Villie, I'm not so bissy. Zis iss Raoul, our new costume designer. Mr. Levinson."

Raoul jumped to his feet. "Mr. Levinson, I'm very glad to know you. I've heard so much about you."

"He's ze son, nod ze fazzer," Fritz advised, curtailing Raoul's enthusiasm.

"Oh, dear," Raoul groaned, dropping gently back into his chair. "I didn't *think* so tender a bud could manage such a ruthless business."

"Raoul's been here two days from New York," Fritz explained. "Hates it. Chust let me look over his drawings, Villie, und I'll be right vis you. Sit down."

While the director buried his nose behind the sketches Willie and Raoul fidgeted. A great man was concentrating, and in Hollywood when important people concentrate, silence is the shadow cast by their thought. To relieve the tension both Raoul and Willie simultaneously leaned out of their chairs and reached for the lone trade paper on Fritz's desk. This synchronized gesture embarrassed them and they subsided into a diligent inspection of the wallpaper.

Fritz finally put down the sketches and cleared his throat. "You zink zese are fashionable?" he queried.

"They're the latest thing in chic, smartness, and style," Raoul assured him.

"I don't vant my vimmen dressed up too much. In pictures it iss smart to be sparing vis materials. Ze audience should *feel* ze body vissin ze dress."

"That is the essential purpose behind designing clothes for younger women."

"Good. Zen make some more sketches for Elena's costumes. Und remember she neets a build-up somezing awful."

"You mean an uplift?"

"Brezicely—but make it sexy."

"I thought this was to be a sophisticated story."

"Vell?"

"Sophisticated women don't emphasize sex in their gowns, Mr. Kornfeld."

"Zey do in *my* pictures," Fritz said abruptly.

"Very well, Mr. Kornfeld, if you prefer, I'll dress your people like houris."

"You don't haff to be insulting, Raoul; remember I got you zis chob. Zat vill be all."

The costume designer picked up his sketches and left the office.

"Now, Villie, vot are you doing here? I thought you vere going to school or somezing."

"Nope. I'm gonna do a picture."

"Good! Vis me?"

"No. Alone."

"Ach, Gott!" Fritz sighed, unable to keep a deprecating tone from creeping into his exclamation.

"You gotta help me, Fritz. Listen," Willie said, "they want me to make a bust so's I'll have to go back to school. They gimme Creighton as a star and Price as a director and I should pick a story. What the hell do I know about stories? You got any?"

252

"Only *Fascinating Lady*, my new script. But maybe I could giff you an idea."

"Giff, Fritz, will you!"

"Vell, ze trouble vis Miss Creighton and Mr. Brice iss zat for ze past two years zey've been making nuzzing but musicals. I think ze public has tired of her singing pictures. Ze minute zey see ze name Creighton, zey know vot's going to happen. She falls in love und she sings. He leafs her und she sings again. She sighs und she sings. He comes back to her und chust as he iss about to kiss her she sings again. End title. I'm getting tired chust talking about her. Now, to ze public, Miss Creighton isn't an actress, she's a voice. I happen to zink she's got more zan zat; und' unless people are extremely versatile zey cannot expect to get by permanently vis a personal act. Fanny Brice? Yah. Beatrice Lillie? Yah. Gladys Creighton?" Fritz shook his head sadly. "No."

"Look, Mr. Director," Willie interrupted. "I *know* what's wrong with the Creighton dame. I want to know something that'll make her right!"

"Vait, boy. I zink I haff it. Ze lady in all her personal contacts iss a bad-tempered bitch. She iss also a dark-haired cutie. In America ve haff had a straintch, and to me, very interesting phenomenon—highvaymen on an organized bissness scale, you call zem gangsters. Vye not make Gladys ze evil influence behint a gangster's murderous misdeeds? In zat vay you vill have an action picture—und zey need only to be moderately good to click at ze box office. You vill giff Gladys a natural role in vich she ought to be good. Und Mel Brice vill be so grateful for a different kind of picture, he'll do a great chob for you."

Willie began to beam. "Fritz," he said. "I don't know what I'd do without you."

"You'd be going back to school. Und, Villie," he called after the departing figure of his former assistant, "don't forget vat I told Raoul—make it sexy!"

18

WILLIE'S FINGERS drummed impatiently on the ultramodern glass-top desk in his new office.

"My voice is in great shape," Gladys assured him, as she scooped inside her bag and rummaged around till she came up with a bejeweled cigarette lighter.

"And we've figured out some swell routines," Mel Price added automatically from the corner.

The producer looked apathetic. "How long did it take you to figure out those routines, Mr. Price?" he asked abruptly.

"Three months."

"Well, forget 'em. And you, Miss Creighton, how long have you been training your voice?"

"Since I was a baby," Miss Creighton cooed proudly, adjusting her silver foxes with an eye to keeping them from fraternizing with the floor.

"Well, you're not going to use it except to talk with," Willie snapped.

The director and his star suddenly became conscious of an alien spirit in their midst. They looked at Willie sharply.

"I called you in here to tell you two things," he went on. "First, as you know, you're going to do a picture for me—"

"How nice!" Gladys gushed with relief. "I remember meeting you when you were a little boy in New York—"

"Swell!" The director beamed.

"And second," Willie continued, ignoring their enthusiasm, "to tell you what everyone else thinks and nobody's told you. You're through—both of you. Your pictures stink and audiences—"

254

He got no further. Gladys Creighton sprang from her chair, yanked her silver foxes off her neck, clutched them fiercely in her left hand and by way of emphasizing each irate word, shook them violently in front of Willie's face.

"You snip!" she cried, as Willie retreated before the flying fur. "You lousy little two-bit snip! You telling ME I'm through! I like that! I'll be going on when you finally grow out of diapers. Why, goddamn it, who are you to tell me a thing like that? A producer?"

Willie tried frantically to brush the fur to one side. Every time he succeeded, Gladys thrust it right back at his face where it shuddered in angry ecstasy. This wasn't at all what he'd expected. It was his first real meeting with his own "people" and he'd wanted to be so dignified. And instead, he was confronted with a raving dame and an agitated furpiece that danced the Charleston in front of his nose. Well, there was nothing to do but settle back and let her wear herself out.

"You're not even dry behind the ears yet—and talking like that to a great actress. A *great* actress, understand? You little twirp. You couldn't understand! Why, I—*goddamn* you!" she suddenly shrieked, snatching the cut-glass inkwell off Willie's desk.

Mel Price lunged forward to grab Gladys's upraised arm. His fingers closed over her wrist just as she was about to heave the inkwell at her new producer's head. Instantly all three of them ducked a deluge of ink. It spattered on the walls, ruined Mel's suit, traced idiotic designs on Gladys's hat, and dyed Willie's hair. Gladys began to cry. Willie came up from behind the desk, a very hurt and horrified look in his eye. Mel picked up a blotter and began working on his jacket.

"Jeez!" Willie said. "Ain't you something!"

Gladys looked at him and groaned. She hurled her hat defiantly on the floor and strode back and forth sobbing furiously.

"I knew it! I knew it!" she commiserated with herself. "Oh, why did I ever get into this business? What's it ever given me? Anguish and despair and no privacy!"

"And a lotta dough," Willie muttered.

"Yes," she sighed, sinking into a chair, "a lotta dough."

She sat looking blankly at the wall. Willie suddenly remembered he was an executive.

"Listen, you guys," he snorted, "you ain't really through! And I'll tell you why. I've got to make a good picture with you, or I'm through too! So we're all in the same boat and here's my plan. America's full of a lotta burglars on an organized scale. You call 'em—I mean, we call 'em gangsters. My idea is to have you play a gangster moll."

"Me?" yowled Gladys. "Play one of them frowsy trollops! Good God!"

"Give him a chance, will you!" Mel shouted, sensing a new locale for their repertoire.

"You're the *queen* of the gangster molls, Gladys. You're hitched up with the biggest big shot of them all!"

"Al Capone?" they asked in unison.

"Yeah. Al Capone. Only it ain't Al Capone. Naturally we can't use his name. But that's the idea."

Mel and Gladys smiled at each other.

"It'll be a swell dramatic part for you," Willie continued.

"Hey, that's a great thought, Bill. A great thought," Mel repeated appraisingly.

"Sure it is. But we all gotta work like hell. We're gonna do the best gangster film that's ever been made. And kids, we gotta pull together. And don't tell anybody I told you that the front office expects us to make another song-and-dance flopperoo."

Out of the corner of his eye, Willie noticed Gladys coming toward him. Instinctively he retreated. She laughed and extended her hand. "Come here, Mel," she said. "We three are gonna work together and put one over on the guys up front."

"What's our budget, Bill?" Mel asked.

"I don't know yet."

"Oh, let's shake anyway," Gladys suggested magnanimously.

256

All three of them solemnly took the pledge.

"Not a word!" Willie cautioned as they started for the door.

"Don't worry," Gladys said.

"Any songs?" Mel asked.

"No songs."

"Hoopla!" the director shouted, slamming the door behind him.

Willie sank back into his chair. "All I gotta do now," he sighed, "is get a script and some writers!"

19

THE NEWS got around that Willie had been upped to a producer's berth and the trade papers published the following squib:

LEVINSON LAD LEAPS

William Levinson promoted from Associate
to Producer rank by Miracle Front Office
is readying "Gangster Moll" for cameras.
Grind starts in 6 weeks. Gladys Creighton
set as star. Mel Price wields megaphone.

In a few days Willie's office was swamped with agents. By the end of the week two writers were struggling to create a script for *Gangster Moll*. Willie had picked neither of them.

The studio had assigned Maxwell Aaronberg, a contract writer, to the picture, and Paul Kersey, the author of an analytical best seller, *The Rivalries of Gangdom,* was "sold" to Willie by Meyer Schwartz, Inc., the best and most cordially detested agents in the business. They were feared because they had the majority of Hollywood's best brains and beauty on their list of clients, because they practically dictated their own terms in deals with studios, and finally because they honestly fought for the interests of "their people."

Allan Colby, Meyer Schwartz's personal representative on the Miracle lot, had clinched the deal by stating the obvious truism that Kersey knew as much about gangsters as Aaronberg did about the technique of motion pictures. The cost? A mere seven hundred fifty dollars a week and a four-week guarantee. Miracle would also please pay the transportation—round trip from New York.

When Paul Kersey arrived Willie discovered he'd hired himself a society guy. This shocked him. He had expected a tough, hard-boiled expert on gangster lore and wound up with a gentleman—or at least what his experience at Inchcape had taught him to accept as one. The Kerseys traced their family history back to the Middle Ages. Paul's forebears were of Huguenot stock. Their original name had been de Coeurcy, but succeeding generations had whittled it down to Courcy, and eventually to Kersey.

His collaborator, Maxwell Aaronberg, came from the Bronx.

Maxwell's father had worked hard and eked a respectable up-town income out of the shirt business. Little Max became stage-struck at the age of six when his mother took him downtown on his birth-day to see Fred Stone in *The Wizard of Oz*. He grew up with a devotion to Broadway that unfortunately exceeded his talents as a play-wright. His was one of those gnarled minds that can master only the things it holds in contempt. It was this contradiction that eventually led to his success in motion pictures, a medium of entertainment he thoroughly despised.

But when Willie brought these two opposing forces together, Maxwell hadn't as yet climbed out of the hack-writer class. Paul immediately respected Max for his complete and quickly absorbed knowledge of the picture business. Max in turn envied and admired Paul's self-confidence, his craftsmanship, his sense of proportion, and his familiarity with gangsters, their jargon and their reactions. The combination was rare among Hollywood collaborators, in that they actually had something to contribute to each other's work.

258

The very first time all three of them were together, Willie explained the circumstances connected with their predicament. Max, familiar with the peculiarities of studio politics, took the information in his stride. Paul, apparently dismayed by the tawdriness of Moe's scheme, lit a cigarette, drew a long breath and announced, "Bill, if I may call you that, this sort of thing really annoys me. Gangsters have a higher code of ethics than that. They'll shoot you from behind your back without giving you a chance. It's short and sweet and finis. The only advantage to the deal you're getting, which, naturally, at this point involves us, is that there is a way out. But I'm not sure it's worth the effort. I think your basic idea about Miss Creighton is correct. And I also think we can whip up a pretty good script, but it's entirely dependent upon one thing."

"What's that?" Willie asked, anxious to agree to anything that would save his neck.

"You stay out of it completely until we're ready to show it to you."

Willie swallowed hard. "I'll tell you something, Mr. Kersey," he confessed, "I don't know a goddamn thing about a script and I won't bother you guys until you ask me to."

Kersey smiled as he rose from his chair, and extended his hand to Willie for the first time. "I like honesty," he said.

It was such a bald statement that Maxwell found himself staring at his collaborator. Somehow the phrase reminded him of a politician patting a baby on the head.

"He likes honesty," Maxwell repeated. "Who doesn't? But who expects to find it in this business?" He smiled at Willie and started for the door. "Come on, Paul, let's knock this thing out."

"Don't forget, guys," Willie called after them, "a hundred and seventy thousand budget!"

At the end of three weeks Paul and Max came in with the script. Although Willie didn't know the difference, it was at that time a definitely novel treatment and theme for the screen. The underworld epics previous to *Gangster Moll*, with the exception of *Scarface*, had

259

been pretty tame stuff. The script written by Paul and Max was a vicious story about vicious people. Its humor was rough and bawdy, its language that of the gutter. It was an exciting script because it was a moderately honest one. And machine guns are always good movie fodder.

The story opened in a crowded tenement district on a hot summer afternoon in 1904. Some kids had opened up a fire hydrant and were bathing in the street.

"Then," Max explained, "a cop comes along and turns off the water. At that time the city didn't have any shower arrangements to give kids a bath—at least, that's what Paul says."

Willie nodded.

"At any rate, this is their first contact with the law, and naturally they hate it. The cop's a tough guy and they begin to play tricks to outwit him. Eventually they begin to steal. At this time one of the kids takes the lead in organizing all their raids and activities. This same kid is crazy about a little dark-haired Italian girl who calls him 'Nasty Face' and slaps him when he says he loves her. Nasty Face grows up to be our hero. We dissolve to 1925. The gangs of 'Slats' McGonigle and 'Twitch' Klein are shooting it out for control of the city. Twitch's gang wins. They have a banquet in honor of his victory. In the middle of the banquet Twitch, who gets his name because the side of his face jerks convulsively every time he kills a guy, gets up to make a speech. As he starts talking the lights go out. The camera zooms up to the balcony and in the half-light of the hall we see the ugly puss of our hero, Tony Mandetti, now known as 'Trigger.' 'Don't move!' he yells. 'Yer all covered! And yer all trew! Twitch, I'm taking over. Let 'em have it, boys!' Then the room goes crazy. Trigger's boys keep pumping their tommy guns from the balcony till Twitch's gang is butchered to the last man. As the last guy alive flips a fin where his arm once was and falls to the ground, we zoom up to Tony on the balcony again. He leers and says—" Max stopped short. "Gimme the scrip, Paul."

Paul handed him the script.

Max thumbed quickly to the page. "Trigger's the boss now!" he emoted. "Trigger Mandetti. Lil Tony. And he's no small-time pertater. When Trigger kills, he kills like a general. Wipe 'em out! That's Trigger! Slaughter 'em! Fill their bellies fulla lead so they know who the big shot is.

"He laughs," Max continued dramatically, "as we fade to a night club."

"A beautiful girl is singing, Lilly Biano—that's Gladys Creighton. . . . ." Kersey added.

"Couldn't you cut out the song?" Willie interrupted hopefully.

"Naw—it's in character," Max snapped. "Trigger and his boys call her over to their table. 'Ya slapped me wunst,' he says, 'but ya wouldn't dare do it again!'

"'Nasty Face!' she answers, surprised and even happy to see him. After all, twenty years have elapsed and she's forgotten their childhood quarrel.

"'He ain't Nasty Face,' one of the yeggs growls. 'He's Trigger Mandetti.'

"She leaps to her feet and turns on Tony. 'Murderer!' she says and slaps him again. One of Tony's boys starts after her. Tony says, 'Nix, she's got spunk. I like 'em rough. Bring her to my apartment tonight.' He leaves.

"That's as far as we got so far. Whadda ya think?"

Willie took a long breath. "Jeez!" he said, bursting with pride. "It's swell!"

Two weeks later the script was finished.

"It ends like *Hamlet,*" Max said. "Everybody kills everybody else off—like the St. Valentine's Day massacre, only it ain't in a garage, it's in a warehouse."

20

FRANK GALLARDI, Miracle's casting director, eased his tall, thin
body into Willie's most comfortable armchair. There was ample
space for him to tuck his player lists and the latest *Academy Talent
Directory* on the cushion beside him.

"There isn't a guy under contract to us who can play the male
lead," he groaned. "Harry Kelly is available for Looie, the comedy
relief, and we've got all the minor parts cast, but Berkley's too old,
Todd's too handsome, and Whitney's too English to be Tony Mandetti. So what do we do? Eddie Robinson would be swell, but Warner's won't let him go. Metro's got all the best people in the business
tied up and they won't talk a deal unless we give them Elena Maya.
That's impossible, of course. She's our biggest draw at the moment
and M.K. would die at the thought of it. Universal can have the lugs
they got. Fox's got a guy named 'Tracy, but he hasn't done much.
Warner's is planning another film with Paul Muni and Paramount's
players you can have. So what are we going to do?"

There was an awkward silence.

"You're the casting director, ain't you?" Willie finally growled,
holding his head in his hands. "Why don't you do something?"

"I'm thinking," Frank said mechanically, "thinking."

"I got it!" Willie shrieked suddenly. "Miss Holmby," he called to
his new secretary, a nervous, efficiency-plagued maid of forty, "get
me Moe Korn!" Then he snickered, "The guy'll die!" as he waited for
the connection. "Helen? Lemme speak to Moe. Yeah, it's Willie. . . .
I haven't got a dictograph! Okay, put one in."

Helen put the call through. " 'Lo, Moe?" Willie said, "You remember the script I sent you on *Gangster Moll?* What do you think of

it? ALL RIGHT? It's gonna be the best picture this company's made! Listen, Moe, how'd you like to be an actor? No fooling. You'd make a swell Tony Mandetti. Wait a minute! Moe? . . . Hello? . . . He said no!" Willie chuckled.

"Hang up, I got an idea myself," Frank said.

"What now?"

"Barton Keller."

"Never heard of him."

"Stage actor. New York. Specializes in tough parts. The guy's great!"

"Yeah, but he hasn't got a name west of the Bronx."

"Oh, no? He's played the subway circuit and all the key cities in the country."

"He's still a punk. Listen," Willie said, thrusting his index finger toward Gallardi's nose, "if we gotta use a guy without a name I got one around here that's just perfect. All the time I was hearing the script I kept thinking of him."

"Who's that?"

"Ace Luddigan."

"You mean the cutter?"

"Sure."

For a moment Frank was too shocked to conceal his dismay. He sat up slowly and scratched his ear. Then he shrugged his shoulders and agreed that Luddigan looked the part. "But," he asked cautiously, "can he act?"

"Act? He don't have to act. The guy *is* Mandetti. He's a natural!"

Frank looked dubious.

"I'm not saying he's gonna play it," Willie continued, "I'm just suggesting he might. Think it over."

"I'll give you a list of the players we ought to try to get anyway," Frank parried. "It'll be ready in the morning."

"Take it up with Mr. Korn first. He'll have to okay the deal in the end," Willie ordered, terminating the interview.

Frank picked up his papers and scooted right up to Moe's office.

There is a general and correct impression in the motion-picture business that unless the boss knows what a man's doing, there's no sense in doing it. Frank had had his own preferences for the part throughout the discussion, but he saw no reason to inform Willie about them. After all, he could take the matter up with M. K. himself.

"Here," he said, thrusting his list of male leads for *Gangster Moll* under Moe's nose, "are the actors we might use."

The Master picked up his pencil and gave the sheet a cursory jiggle. Then he dropped it back onto the desk and drew unerring lines straight through the names of Cagney, Robinson, Raft, Carrillo. "No deal," he said. "They cost too much."

"But, M. K.!" Frank protested.

"I know," Moe interrupted reassuringly, "sure we wanna make good pitchures, but not at them prices." He looked up and smiled knowingly at his casting director. "What did Willie say?"

Rumors of a family feud had permeated the lot and accordingly Frank figured he had nothing to lose by advancing himself at Willie's expense.

"Well, M. K.," he stammered, "you asked for it! He suggested that a cutter play the part."

"A what?"

"A cutter. Ace Luddigan. Now, I ask you!" Frank concluded, superiority oozing out of every syllable.

"Ace Luddigan? Well, well, well!" Moe purred with rising gratitude. Willie was exceeding his fondest expectations.

He swung his swivel chair around and faced Gallardi. Frank shuddered involuntarily. Shrewd employees have a nose for danger. Fully aware of the menace in M. K.'s eye, he flinched while his boss swung into action.

"Well, wotsa madda with Luddigan?" Moe demanded icily. "Who could fit the part better? Ya know anybody? Yer the castin' director! So, cast! Who else shouldn't cost us a thousand a week? Ya got no answer? Five million actors in Hollywood and my nephew's gotta get the onney bright idea onna lot in months. Why, Ace could play that part in his sleep!"

"Maybe it would be better that way, sir," Frank agreed hastily.

"Ya think he can't do it?"

"I didn't say that, sir. Only I don't think he can act."

"Act? Who said anything about acting? Name me a dozen movie punks can act! Come on, quick! Just a dozen!"

Frank shook from head to foot. His mind was blank.

Moe, bored with the abject terror in his employee's eyes, grudgingly calmed down. "Now, look, Frank, let the director worry about the actin'. Ace Luddigan plays the part. And ya'll have a helluva time gettin' him ta do it. Now go ahead an' make the necessary arrangements. And wipe that sour look off ya puss!" he concluded with obvious disgust.

21

THEY FOUND LUDDIGAN in his cutting room. Willie, Frank, and Mel Price trooped through the door and crowded into the cubicle.

"Christ! It's a convention!" Ace exclaimed, looking up from his magazine.

"We wanna talk to you, Ace," Willie said, like the chairman of the Monongahela Ward Heelers' Club.

"Shoot!" grinned the cutter, leaning back and slinging his left arm around the post of his canvas-back chair.

The boys paused warily.

"Yuh look goddamn impressive!" Ace reassured them.

"How'd you like to be an actor?" Frank finally asked.

"An actor?" Ace laughed. "I got enough half-assed directors hanging around here telling me what tuh do. I should go up on a stage and let 'em make a monkey outta me in public? Nuts!"

"I won't make a monkey out of you, Ace."

"You couldn't, Mel!"

"Well, we want you to play the lead in *Gangster Moll*," Willie blurted out.

Ace rose slowly from his chair. "Listen," he said, his voice cracking with excitement, "I'm doing awright where I am, see? I'm knocking off three hunerd a week cutting film and it comes in every week on the nose. If I'm gonna be an actor I wanna know what's in it for me. Steady, I mean. I don't wanna be one of those fifteen hunerd dollar a week guys working five weeks a year. Thass the shits."

"Ace," Willie interrupted quietly, "we're not gonna pay you any fifteen hundred a week. Get that out of your head. But the point is this: you're the highest paid cutter on the lot and I happen to know you're not in line for any raises. But if you'll play this part, we'll hike your salary to five hundred a week and that goes for the year. If at the end of that time they don't use you in any more shows you go back to three hundred. So what have you got to lose?"

"Nothing."

"Will you do it?"

"I dunno."

"Come on, Ace—just for me."

"Okay. On one proviso."

"What's that?" Gallardi interrupted.

"I cut the show, too."

"Why do you want to do that?" Mel asked in utter astonishment.

" 'Cause, yuh punk, if yuh can't make an actor outta me, you ain't gonna see me at all, and if I'm good, yuh ain't gonna see nobody else. Catch?"

"Yeah," said Willie, "I catch. Okay. It's a deal. You act and cut the picture, but under Mel's supervision and mine."

"Whadda you gonna supervise, yuh junior-genius?"

"That's no way to talk to your producer!" Willie snapped.

Ace turned to Mel. "Who's yuh crew?" he asked.

"My usual staff. Fred MacGowan's the assistant director. Minetta

Irving's the script girl. Gladys has her customary make-up man, Harry Abbott. Dick Hemet's recording. Johnny Allbright's handling the camera, and you, my friend, are the co-star."

"With Gladys Creighton, huh?" Ace rubbed his hands together. "Boy, I been waiting fer a chance tuh knock that dame down. Am I gonna nail her! Four years she's been giving me the brush-off and onna fifth, the Lord created Luddigan! When do we start?"

"Two weeks from Monday," Frank Gallardi said. "And we've got to give you a new name."

"Fer why?"

"Fer because 'Ace Luddigan' stinks. What's your real name?"

"Leroy, and I'll smack the guy what giggles."

There were no takers, and Ace continued. "Whyncha call me Louis Levinson and make me the president?"

"Oh, don't worry, we'll get you a name," Frank said. "Something nice and romantic, like Geoffrey Twippet."

"Okay, be funny! Now scram outta here and get me a script so's I can—er—study my part. Hey! Hey!"

He did an "off-to-Buffalo" out of the room, leaving the three of them completely satisfied and chuckling over their good fortune.

"Jeez, Mel," Willie said, "I'm getting a leading man for two hundred a week! That's buttons! And we'd have to pay any decent cutter at least a hundred and fifty a week. Now we got one of the best in town, thrown in!"

"Yes," Frank agreed bitterly, "but what kind of actor have you got?"

"This show's gotta make money," Willie said firmly, "and the less production costs we got, the better our chances of bringing in a winner. Now let's get going!"

22

THE *GANGSTER MOLL* COMPANY had been shooting six days when Willie, hurrying down to the set in response to a call from Mel Price, felt someone tugging at his elbow. It was Fritz. He had seen Willie's rushes the day before and was bursting with news.

"You got zem all vorried," he said, grinning. "Moe got all egzited yesterday. After ze screening he stood up und shouted, 'Vad are ve going to do vis zat kid? He's shooting ze only good show on ze lot!' Six films zey got before ze comeras und yours iss ze best. I'm so glad for you, Villie."

Willie grasped the director's hand. "Thanks, Fritz," he said, a little embarrassed. "I won't forget what you've done for me."

"Good luck, boy," Fritz said, and walked off.

Willie smiled to himself and headed for Stage 9. When he got there he was greeted by a sight that gives producers nightmares. The company was idle. Extras were lolling around the corners of the set smoking cigarettes. Technicians lounged on their equipment and talked about the races. In the center of the ring formed by these apathetic spectators, Mel Price was arguing violently with a man who was a stranger to Willie.

"This is an outrage!" he heard Mel shout, and he rushed over to join them as the stranger shrugged his shoulders.

"What's the matter, Mel?" Willie asked.

"We called you because this guy wants Ace Luddigan to have a star dressing room, shorter hours, a stand-in, top billing, and more pay."

"Is that all? My, oh, my! And who is the sonuvabitch?"

"His agent."

"Agent!" Willie shrieked, his eyes wide with astonishment.

"Permit me to give ya my card, Mr. Levinson," the gentleman said, sliding a plain white pasteboard slip out of his wallet. Willie slapped it out of his hand. "We ain't got around to having 'em printed yet," the stranger continued blandly, "but when we do, they'll read Brennan and Guilfoyle, Agents. I'm Brennan, Luddigan's agent and brother-in-law."

"Brother-in-law, huh?" Willie snorted. "Where's Ace?"

"Here I am," Ace said, quietly easing himself out of the crowd surrounding the battle.

"What have *you* got to say to all this?"

"He's me manager now, Mr. Levinson. Yuh'll have tuh take it up with him."

"What the hell are you talking about? Your contract says—"

"There ain't no contract, Mr. Levinson," Brennan corrected firmly.

"Jeez!" Willie admitted ruefully. "He's right! Call Gallardi down here right away."

Mel turned and shouted, "Freddie! MacGowan! Call Gallardi right away!"

"Doing it, Mr. Price," the assistant director answered from a corner of the stage.

The contestants parted, mumbling vague threats at each other. Willie occasionally burst out with the admonition to "Get another clunk to play the part!"

Gallardi finally arrived and after hectic explanations asked, "How much more do they want?"

Nobody had taken the trouble to ask.

Brennan walked over to the casting director, looked him right in the eye, and said, "Fifty dollars a week!"

"Fifty a week!" Mel and Willie chorused in amazement at being hijacked for such a piddling sum.

"Holding a company up for fifty a week!" Gallardi protested scornfully.

"Make it twenty-five," Willie suggested quickly.

"Twenty-five and top billing," Brennan countered.

"Gladys would walk out on us," Mel cautioned.

"Make it fifty and no top billing."

"It's a deal!" Brennan snapped.

"Draw up a contract right away!" Willie barked at Gallardi.

"Well, that takes care of my commission, Ace. Ten per cent of five hundred." Brennan smiled triumphantly at Luddigan.

"Yeah, but what about the dressing room and stand-ins?"

Brennan raised his eyebrows at Mel and Willie.

"Throw it in!" Willie ordered sullenly.

"I'm beginning tuh like this racket," Ace chuckled.

23

WILLIE STROLLED back toward his office. As he passed the various cutting, writers', and office buildings he nodded curtly to those who smiled or said hello to him. When he felt right he smiled and asked about their families. But like all executives, he retained the privilege of scowling at them when things went wrong. He knew they'd understand. They had to.

He opened the door to his secretary's office and found Raoul, the designer, waiting for him with a batch of sketches spread across his lap. "Mr. Levinson, I've some designs I want you to see for Gladys's cabaret costume."

"Just a moment, Mr. Levinson," Miss Holmby interrupted, "Mr. Korn called. Wanted you to come up immediately. Said it was very important."

Willie shrugged his shoulders. "Wait for me, Raoul, I won't be long."

He bounded up the stairs and met Helen Connally on the landing. "Where are you going?" he asked.

"Lunch," she answered. "It's almost twelve o'clock. Go right in. They're waiting for you."

If they're waiting for me, Willie thought, entering Moe's suite of offices, then it *is* important and they'll lie about it.

He knocked on Moe's door.

"Come in, Willie!" his uncle called.

Willie walked into the room and saw his father, hands clasped behind him, staring out the window overlooking the lot. Moe lit a cigar. No one spoke, or moved, or turned. For a full minute, while Willie chose the most comfortable chair in the room, they ignored him. It was as though a ghost had entered the room. Willie looked at the averted heads of his father and his uncle and smiled.

"I hate to disturb you boys," he finally said, "but one of you called me."

"I did," Moe admitted, exhaling smoke and surveying the lighted end of his cigar.

"So?" Willie asked.

"I hate sayin' this, but somebody's gotta do it and it might as well be me. We ain't satisfied with ya work."

"You what!" Willie exploded magnificently.

"Now, don't get excited, Willie," Louis wheedled, turning from the window. "Wait till Moe gets through."

"He's said all I want to hear already!"

"Now, Willie," Moe continued, exuding unctuous disappointment, "You know I always believe in fair play."

"Since when?"

"Since always. So whadda ya grinnin' about? Ya got sump'm ta grin about? You, with your rushes this mornin'?"

"Yeah, me with my rushes. I got something to grin about."

"What?"

"You."

"Me!" Moe complained indignantly.

271

"My stuff was terrific this morning and you know it."

"Not terrific, Willie," Louis said judiciously. "Good, but not terrific."

"Nuts! It's better'n any other show on the lot. That's almost a quote, isn't it, Uncle Moe?" Willie smiled blandly at the vice-president.

"Now, Willie," Moe said quickly, "don't get me wrong. If I didn't think ya pitchure had a chance, I'd fold it up tamorra. So ya rushes were okay tidday. So what? One day's shootin' don't alter the fack we still think ya show's gonna be a stinker. We got a feelin' maybe ya need a little more money. We wanna give ya an even break, kid. We don't wantcha goin' back ta school sayin' we didn't give ya a chance. Fack is, we might even up ya budget if ya ast fer it."

"You're gonna give me more dough because I'm making a stinking show, is that it?"

"Exackly."

"Moe Korn, you're a lying sonuvabitch."

"Willie! That's no way to talk to your uncle," Louis snapped.

"In this crowd, anything goes. Lemme tell you guys something. I've been onto you from the first day you gave me this assignment. You musta thought I was an awful dummox, handing me Creighton and Price and keeping a straight face. But I was onto you right then and there. You thought I'd make a louse, didn't you? But I double-crossed you. So now, as a big favor, you're gonna give me more dough. Well, don't throw me no crumbs! . . . I'm good. My picture's good. And you're both bums!"

Louis looked helplessly at his brother-in-law.

Moe sighed and shrugged his shoulders. "It's all up," he said glumly. "The kid's right. We tried takin' him fer a ride and we got took. So what? So we win anyway." He turned to Willie. "I wanna tell ya sump'm, kid, yer the first mistake I ever made in pitchures. I had ya all wrong. Ya makin' a good show. Better'n I figgered ya would."

272

"What do you mean, better?" Willie snorted. "I'm making the best one on the lot!"

Louis walked over to his son and stooped down to touch his arm as he spoke. "William, my son, we're proud of you," he said, in a sudden outburst of paternal fervor. "You won't have to go back to school."

Willie leaped indignantly out of his chair and screeched, "Back to school! Goddamn it, I want a raise!"

"You'll get it!" Moe promised, waving his hands in a gesture that was half annoyance, half conciliation. "Only keep ya father happy and lay offa the broads."

"What's women got to do with it?" Willie demanded defiantly.

"Nothin'! Just lay off, that's all!" Moe yelled with an emphasis born of exasperation.

Willie changed the subject. "I just hadda raise Luddigan fifty bucks a week."

"We heard all about it," Louis said. "The contract'll fix that up. But, please, Willie, promise me you won't get mixed up with fast women again, will you?"

"Listen, Pop, I'm making a good picture and I'm gonna make more of 'em; but my personal life doesn't enter into it, see? You heard Moe, he just admitted he never guessed wrong in his life until he figured me out as a stumble-bum. Now, you let me run my own life and *you* won't make any mistakes. If I'm old enough to run a unit, I'm old enough to take care of myself. I won't get you into trouble. Anything else?"

"Just this," Moe drawled, "if ya need more money fa ya show, or extra time on some sequence, take it. We've upped ya budget!"

"To hell with that. How much have you upped *me*?" Willie demanded.

"Twenny-five a week."

"Make it a hundred and it's a deal!"

"Sevenny-five and get outta here!"

"Thanks, boys," Willie said, giving them a mock salute as he closed the door behind him.

He returned to his office. At my age, he mused with satisfaction as he sank into his own chair, I'm already earning five hundred and seventy-five bucks a week. "Not bad!" he chortled out loud, picking up Raoul's drawings.

"Thank you, sir," the dress designer beamed.

"Not you—me." Willie frowned. "Try the green one," he said curtly, flicking the key on the new dictograph. "Miss Holmby, have 'em send the day's rushes up to Room 5. I want to say thank you to a lotta hams who'll never hear me."

"Very well, sir." She had already learned to accept Willie's enigmatic explanations at their face value.

24

A FEW DAYS later Willie trudged across the studio to the back lot where Mel was shooting the warehouse killing, already ballyhooed by the publicity department as "The Most Sensational Finale since the Birth of a Nation."

It was one of those sweltering midsummer afternoons in which tempers become sultry and actors walk away from each other without indulging in the casual chatter that usually marks the completion of a take.

Willie dropped into a chair beside Ace's dressing table. "How in hell do you manage to find time to get the film together?" he asked his cutter and co-star.

"I ain't cutting any more. Johnny Morelli's handling the film. Me, I just supervise," Ace grumbled into his mirror.

"The rushes look swell!"

"Yuh can't tell a pitcher by rushes!" Ace said, nodding curtly

274

to the make-up man who stood hesitantly behind him. "Catch the nose, Harry," he ordered without pausing. "Yuh gotta wait till it's in rough cut and still yuh dunno."

The make-up man propped his kit on the table, opened it and pulled out a frayed powder puff the color of yellow clay. "Yuh run it in a perjection room," Ace continued, "and yuh think it's great. Yuh take it out on a sneak preview and yuh house tells yuh it's lousy." Harry hovered around them like a bird, judiciously patting powder wherever beads of perspiration glistened on the star's face. "Yuh work over it again," Ace said, looking straight ahead while Harry stood aside to survey his handiwork, "and at the press preview them punks that think they're critics give yuh wunnerful write-ups. Then it goes out tuh the country and that's the last yuh hear of it till the bankers come around and wanta know who double-crossed 'em."

"Think this one will be okay?"

"I just told yuh, yuh can't tell!" Ace shouted, pushing the make-up man to one side and leaping up to answer a "Places, please!" call from Fred MacGowan.

Willie sighed and automatically followed Ace up to the cameras where he perched beside Mel while the director shot sixteen takes of Tony and his gang biting the dust. The stagnant air was acrid with the smell of blanks. At the end of the sixteenth take, Gladys Creighton stayed where she fell, an exhausted, grime-caked lump of flesh. They carried her into a car and took her to the studio hospital.

"She's surprised even me," Mel said after the commotion subsided. "Worked like a trouper. No complaints. No temperament. Just hard work. It's no wonder she fainted. We ought to finish in three days."

"In that case, maybe we'll sneak in two weeks," Willie answered. "I think we got a hit on our hands."

"So do I. Now, scram, will you—so I can shoot some close-ups while Gladys is getting patched up."

"You think she'll be all right?"

"She'll be back in a half hour. Now go away. Every time Ace sees you he gets an apoplectic stroke."

"What've I done?"

"Nothing. You just draw down more pay than he does."

"What's the crime in that?"

"He's money-nuts. Spends it like crazy and his palms itch all the time. Now, go!" Mel pleaded.

Willie went, and didn't appreciate Mel's statement until the night of the first sneak in Glendale.

Staged by an industry that adores secrecy, sneak previews are planned in an atmosphere of laborious deception calculated to keep those most interested in the picture from entering the theater. The exclusion of these various groups of agents, minor employees, and critics gives the production an air of such importance that all of them begin scurrying around for inside information concerning the spot chosen for the debut. They seldom find out; and, as a general rule, executives and cutters are the only ones who learn the name of the house before the preview. They are the chosen few. And even though they belong, they stand around the lobby of the theater, eying each other furtively as though each mistrusts the other's right to be there.

The evening of the preview Willie, surrounded by a group of these suspicious executives and department heads, missed the significance of Ace's last-minute arrival at the theater.

Along about the middle of the picture Willie began to realize that he had been betrayed. Ace had secretly turned the sixth reel into a thousand-foot close-up of himself performing against a background of off-stage voices.

He was a ham at last.

The preview cards proved it. Some people liked the action, but almost all objected to the "long" scenes of the gangster.

When they got back to the studio Willie and Mel chased Ace out of the cutting room and went to work with Johnny Morelli.

276

They stayed up all night eliminating the unnecessary close-ups and cutting the film for action. The picture had to be redubbed, and all in all, a week passed before they sneaked it again. This time the audience reaction was favorable. But they wanted a smash hit, not an acceptable movie. Mel called the cast together and shot retakes of scenes that slowed up the picture's pace. The music department scored the entire feature. They held a final sneak and the only adverse criticism they received was one card stating, "Its theme is too vicious."

The reviewers at the press preview labeled it "a courageous step forward in the progress of the industry." And Willie, never hampered by modesty, took more than his share of bows.

He had finally become a Hollywood Producer.

25

THREE WEEKS after the release of *Gangster Moll* the boys at Miracle knew they had a hit on their hands.

Moe and Louis casually congratulated Willie, but purposely failed to tell him that they'd received a wire from the New York bankers who controlled the company, advising them that "SUCH A FORTUNATE COMBINATION OF TALENT AS LEVINSON AND PRICE SHOULD NOT BE BROKEN UP. IF THEY CAN MAKE A GOOD FILM OUT OF A LOW-BUDGET PICTURE WHY NOT TRY THEM ON SOME A'S? REGARDS, CASE AND OGILVIE."

"If we show it ta him," Moe told Louis, "he gets a swell head. If we just give him another pitchure, he knows everything's jake, and he ain't gonna bother us fa more dough."

Louis agreed and Moe pulled an old property out of the story files called *The Nebraskan.* It was an epic of frontier days that had often been revised but never actually brought before the cameras. It meant location, a six hundred thousand dollar budget, and stars.

Mel and Willie picked their own cast. Diana March, the dark, glistening-eyed dramatic star from the New York stage. John Berkley, the character actor, as her father. Robert Todd as the dashing, romantic frontiersman.

Mel didn't want to direct it because the word "Western" in connection with a "quickie" or an "epic" made him shudder. So he suggested T. Monte Cooper for the job. Cooper was an old hand at Spectacle and he could do it while Mel worked on a new script for Gladys. Kersey and Aaronberg would be busy with revisions for the Western anyway.

"Okay," Willie said. "And we'd better notify Paul and Max that they're on the Western as of now."

When they heard about their new assignment, Kersey and Aaronberg dropped into Willie's office to receive suggestions from the fountainhead of their success. The only advice Willie gave them was to keep it moving, a motion-picture axiom he had gleaned from *Gangster Moll*.

Paul lingered a moment to ask Willie if he'd care to drop by the house that evening, as he was having a party to celebrate the signing of his new contract—with options.

Willie glowed inwardly. This was what he'd been striving for, ever since Inchcape—to meet what he considered socially important people on their own ground, to be invited to their parties, not because they went to the same school or had a common background, but because he had earned his right to mingle with them.

He had a mental picture of fashionable women in very soigné evening gowns, women full of chitchat and high spirits, attending a salon presided over by Paul Kersey. There was no connection in his mind between the little girls he'd seen at Inchcape dances and his idea of society. For the latter was a sort of collage of pretty advertisements of station wagons, estates, dogs, minks, and immaculate stables, the whole pasted together with pictures of people currycombed like

278

horses, against a background of bright sayings by gossip columnists and the chi-chi of fashion editors.

And now at last there was a place for William Levinson in that picture. For one completely satisfying moment he saw himself dominating the world of fashion by the sheer magnificence of his wit and the magnetism of his presence. He smiled at Paul, but he was shrewd enough not to betray his enthusiasm by appearing over-anxious.

"I'd love to come," he said, trying to sound offhand, "if I don't get tied up down here."

Willie told his secretary to cancel all appointments after four-thirty. He planned to go home early to rest up for his initial appearance as the young Hollywood producer who took society by storm.

He was about to leave his office when Helen Connally called and told him Moe wanted to see him. He grabbed his hat and dashed upstairs, prepared to duck out as soon as Moe had relieved himself of his latest brainstorm. But Moe kept him waiting in the outer office till six o'clock. When he finally emerged and apologized by saying, "I thought I'd go home with ya," Willie stood up indignantly.

"You sonuvabitch," he yelled. "I've been waiting two hours for you. Two hours!" And he waggled an angry finger before Moe's nose.

"Helen musta made a mistake and called ya early," Moe said, winking at his secretary.

"But I've got my own car here!" Willie protested, sensing a further delay at the parking lot.

"That's okay. I'm goin' ta yer place. I'll ride with you and Booker can pick mine up."

They drove home in silence.

When they opened the front door of Miracle Manor, the whole family swarmed over them, shrieking, "Surprise! Surprise!" Willie, who instinctively stepped back to escape the greeting, felt Moe's flat hands pushing him forward into the bosom of his family. They pounced all over him, pummeling him with a fervor generally reserved for such occasions as the completion of an ocean liner's maiden voyage. They dragged him into the living room, plunked him into a chair, and told him to close his eyes. He complied automatically, and when he opened his eyes again Max was standing before him holding a huge cake topped with a legend: "To Our Boy Who Made Good—The Family."

"Jeez!" Willie stammered, overcome with gratitude. "Jeez, thanks!"

He began to laugh and they all crowded around him, smothering him with attention.

Momma put her arm around him. "By dem you're a suggcess, baht dun't led it bodder you, by me you're still a nix-noots. Gimme a kiss. . . . So!" she puckered her mouth so all could see.

"You'd better go upstairs and wash, Willie," Rebecca interrupted, pulling Momma aside. "We've got a big evening planned for you."

Willie tore himself away and flew up the staris. In the bathroom he suddenly recalled Paul Kersey's invitation. His excitement subsided with alarming rapidity.

"They *would* pick tonight!" he groaned. "How am I gonna get out of here?"

When he came downstairs he saw Arline in the house for the second visit of her life and it gave him an inspiration.

"Arline," he asked, "if you were invited to two parties in one night, what would do you?"

"I'd go to both of them," Arline smiled.

"That's what I'm gonna do," Willie announced.

The family's exuberance skidded to a silent stop.

"Willie!" Rebecca cried reproachfully. She walked over and stood before her son. "We've planned this for a week now. The other party can't be so important."

"But it is!" Willie pleaded, anxious to please everybody, including himself. "I gotta go. It's business."

"Where?" Louis asked.

"Paul Kersey's."

"Oh, high-class people," Moe snorted.

"Ride avay, he makes suggcess, he gats fency-schmency, heh?" Momma said.

"If he wants to go, let him," Jacob said. "He's only young once."

"Once is enough," Arline cracked, thinking of her own misspent youth. "I wouldn't go to ritzy parties if I was you, Willie. In the first place, you don't belong. In the second place, they're never fun and besides, it must be an extra-special day when the family asks me over!"

"Let's forget all about that, Arline, please! You're one of us now," Rebecca begged.

"That's no compliment," Arline snickered.

Rebecca shook her head and Moe turned on Arline.

"No madda watchu say it's always the wrong thing," he snapped.

"I was only kidding," Arline protested.

"Goddamn it!" Moe continued. "It's high time we all got along around here!"

"Who's fightin' who around here?" Momma demanded. "You fightin' Arline? Arline fightin' us? Or ve tryin' to gaht dis loafer to stay home fa vunce."

"Personally—" Jacob began.

"Nobuddy esked you. Poissonally, or oddervise," Momma interrupted. "Now, votcha gonna do, kiddie? You gonna stay by us fa dinner, or you going out vid de crowt?" She leaned forward sardonically to indicate her complete contempt of such a smart-set word as "crowd."

"I'll eat with you—then scram," Willie compromised.

"Dun't do us no favors!" Momma snapped.

"Let's eat. I want to go."

"Go!" Momma commanded angrily. "Ve vanna eat!"

"Aw, Jeez, Ma," Willie pleaded.

Rebecca turned her back to him.

"Go ahead, Willie," Jacob said, "some of us understand."

Willie walked out to get his hat and came back to the living room. He wanted to apologize, to say something, but his eyes filled with tears. He turned and ran out of the house.

26

HE WALKED down the corridor and paused before Paul Kersey's door, listening. Out here he was still alone, detached, apart from the murmur of voices, the occasional burst of laughter, the sound of ice tinkling in a cocktail shaker. For a frightening moment he experienced the exquisite loneliness of an artist studying his subject objectively. Then he recalled Arline's warning that he'd never belong, and he became defiant. What the hell did she know? He could go anywhere, be accepted by anyone, and besides, he firmly believed that Paradise lay in wait for him on the other side of that door.

He rang the bell. A strange man peered out at him.

"Hello," Willie said. "Paul Kersey in?"

"Sure. You're Levinson, aren't you?"

"Yeah," Willie grunted, standing timidly inside the door while the man shouted, "Paul! Your boss is here!"

Kersey rushed up, freeing one hand from the napkin swaddling the cocktail shaker.

"Glad you came, Bill. Drop your hat and come on around. And don't be surprised at anything you see. I only know half the guests myself, but they all seem to be having a good time."

Willie followed his host into the room. A girl came up to him and thrust a highball into his hand. Paul put his arm around her waist.

"This is Marian Stoddard, Mr. Levinson," he said. "Maybe you recognize her, Willie. She spends her weekends in the rotogravure."

"Oh, sure. Hello," Willie said.

They moved on. Willie was introduced to a man who had one of those names that make people wonder if they've heard correctly.

"I beg your pardon?" Willie said.

"Armand Erp," the man volunteered.

"The photographer. Undresses women and makes them glamorous," Paul said.

"Glad to know you."

They shook hands. Paul excused himself to greet more guests. Willie smiled wanly at Mr. Erp. And then he saw a girl. She was sitting quiet in a corner chatting with a man who sat Buddha-like on the floor in front of her. She was obviously a stranger too, because she would lean forward, whisper something in the man's ear, and wait for him to identify whoever it was that had aroused her curiosity.

Willie watched her for some time before he asked Erp, "Who's that girl?"

"Which one?"

"Over there, in front of the bookcase. The blonde with the red coat."

Mr. Erp took a look. "The ash blonde in that exquisite mandarin coat?"

"Mandarin coat!" Willie snorted. "The one in the Chink outfit with the gray eyes—"

"And the deep-red mouth?"

"Yes!" Willie said anxiously. "That's the one!"

"Interesting-looking."

"Sure, sure, but what's her name?" Willie said impatiently.

"I haven't the slightest idea."

"Oh," Willie groaned.

"But there's Paul," Mr. Erp suggested. "Perhaps he knows. Let's call him."

"Paul!" they both shouted in unison.

"Coming!" Kersey called, and he plunged through the crowd holding the cocktail shaker out in front of him, guarding it tenderly as though its silver shell contained the secret of his popularity. "Which one of you?" he asked, looking for their glasses.

Mr. Erp and Mr. Levinson declined with thanks.

"Not drinking?" Paul asked reproachfully.

"That isn't what we wanted to ask you," Willie said, putting his glass down on a convenient end table.

"How can you come to a thing like this and not drink?" Paul asked aggressively.

Mr. Erp detected a harshness in Paul's voice. A defiant harshness as though he detested his own party and, above all, his own guests.

"You're plastered," Mr. Erp said.

"Quite," Paul admitted. "And why not? There are only two things you can be sure of at a cocktail party. Liquor, and the kind of conversation that goes in one woman and out the other. So I get plastered."

Mr. Erp shrugged his shoulders.

"We want to meet someone," Willie said.

"Good!" Paul laughed. "Where is she?"

"The one over there with the lovely face."

"Where?"

"Over there!" Armand Erp pointed. "And he wants to meet her."

"Oh!" Paul exclaimed. "He does, does he? Why?"

"I like the way she carries her head," Willie said quietly. "High, proud, and moderately superior."

"I had a hunch you'd find her," Paul said warmly. "Her name's Lucy Strawbridge. But, Willie, before you meet her I want to warn you. She doesn't quite belong out here. She's different from the other girls in this town and you'll have to treat her differently. She's gone to school for one thing, the best schools . . ."

"She breathes, doesn't she?" Willie snapped.

"Sure."

284

"Well, then, stop giving me the Emily Post routine. So long as they breathe I can handle them."

"That's just it. You don't handle this kind of girl, Willie."

Willie suddenly glared at his host. "Why don't you pipe down? I know how to behave."

Paul handed the cocktail shaker to Mr. Erp. "Of course you do, Willie," he said. "I'm sorry. I'm drunk, that's all. Forgive me?"

"Okay."

"Come on over, and good luck."

They elbowed their way through the crowd. And suddenly Willie was standing in front of her. He heard Paul say, "Miss Strawbridge, this is Mr. Levinson, the producer. He wanted to meet you." Willie was too nervous to do more than smile mechanically.

He took a good look at her. There was something singularly aggravating about her attractiveness. He saw the pinpoints of her breasts through her jacket, and he became obsessed with a desire to touch them. It would have been a reverent gesture rather than a curious one, but no one would have understood it. No one but himself—and, he hoped, Miss Strawbridge.

Gradually he became aware of her voice. It was warm, mellow, and comforting, like the luxury of one's bed at the end of day. It would be a lovely voice to hear in the dark when, aside from the flesh, one had so few reassurances.

What was she saying? He raised his eyes to hers. She wasn't saying anything. She was just looking at him. Waiting for him to answer her. And he couldn't. You just can't answer a question you haven't heard, can you? he asked himself. He shrugged his shoulders aimlessly. She broke into a slow smile.

"I asked you if you'd like to sit down, Mr. Levinson," she said, indicating a place on the floor in front of her. "Move over, Oggie. This is Ogden Hubbard, Mr. Levinson."

"Oggie's coming with me," Paul said, yanking Oggie to his feet. "I need him at the bar."

"Let's go soon," Oggie murmured to Miss Strawbridge as he left.

Miss Strawbridge nodded and watched him follow Paul to the far end of the room.

"Now," she said, turning back to Willie, "why did you want to meet me?"

"How did you know I did?"

"Don't you remember? Paul told me."

"Oh." Willie just sat at her feet and stared at her. She raised her eyebrows. "I—I really couldn't tell you," he stammered.

Miss Strawbridge waited. Willie's eyes devoured her and she became uncomfortable. "You're in the movies, aren't you?" she finally asked.

He nodded impatiently. He hadn't come to talk about the movies. "Do you like it?"

"It's all right," he said vaguely, following every little motion of her lips.

Lucy Strawbridge sat back and frowned. This was really embarrassing. He hadn't said anything or done anything annoying. It was just the way he looked at her. And yet it wasn't just a look. It was more—more of a pounce. That was it! He was sitting in front of her like a tiger, tight in his haunches, all set to spring and stifle the life out of her. Well—not this time. She smiled to herself. If you were smart or brittle or witty, I'd know how to handle you. But this—this naked, brutal, insatiable curiosity stuff—that's not for me.

Where's Oggie? He *would* disappear. The trouble with all homos is that they're like dew. They wet the flowers a little bit but nothing grows. But this thing at my feet. Now there's a cloudburst for you! She was quite shocked, amused, and just a touch embarrassed by her thoughts. And suddenly she laughed out loud.

"Did I do something?" Willie asked shyly.

"No." She smiled reassuringly. "Not a thing."

"I wish I had. I'd like to make you laugh."

"Would you?"

286

"Yes. You're beautiful when you laugh."

"Almost everybody is."

"That's true, isn't it?" he agreed reflectively.

She nodded and leaned forward. "You're a very intense young man, Mr. Levinson."

"Not always."

She shook her head. "I don't believe that," she said. "For another five years at least."

"For another five years at least, what?"

"You'll be intense. You're searching for something. But you don't know what. Whatever it is, though, I hope you find it. I've got to go now."

Willie was on his feet by the time she was halfway out of her chair. "You can't go—please," he said, and his hand instinctively reached for her elbow.

She drew back and looked at him inquiringly.

"Talk to me some more. You talk wonderful."

She sat down and shook her head. "I talk too much," she confessed.

"No, you don't."

"Yes, I do. I like to talk. The sound of my voice fills me with security."

And suddenly Willie found himself stammering, "I don't know what I'd do if I didn't hear your voice again."

Lucy Strawbridge lit a cigarette and inhaled deeply. "Now, look, Mr. Levinson," she said, and her voice was gentle, "you're in the motion-picture business. I'm not. Your craft consists of a writer's tools, some film, a player's talents, and a prayer. As for me, I'm one of those very fortunate souls who can absorb and reflect culture without creating it. It's too bad we haven't more in common. If we had, believe me, I'd say yes to you."

"Yes, what?"

"Yes, we could see more of each other."

"I didn't ask you that, did I?"

No, damn it, Lucy admitted to herself, you didn't. But you would. Given half a chance, God knows what you'd ask!

This was a different kind of rudeness from anything she'd ever encountered before. It was native, not studied, and its very bluntness shocked her into taking refuge behind a fatuous compliment.

"You movie people say the most amazing things."

Willie shuddered. "I'm not movie people," he protested. "I mean what I say."

He sensed that she was appraising him and he detected an overtone of disapproval. His confidence fled abruptly and he mumbled, "I *was* going to ask if I could see you again. But now, I'm afraid—"

Miss Strawbridge took the unasked question in her stride and leaned forward again. "Good heavens, what is there to be afraid of? It's very simple. You want to see me again. All right. You will. I promise."

But her kindness came more from her desire to be rid of the young man than from any emotional response.

She looked around the room impatiently. Oggie was still in hiding—behind the wallpaper, she suspected. There was a slight pressure on her knee. She glanced down. Mr. Levinson's hand held her attention. He withdrew it slowly as though he'd been caught in some despicable crime.

"You've made me very happy," he said.

"So quickly?" she asked. She couldn't help teasing him. He was so serious.

"So quickly," he answered.

Lucy Strawbridge felt strangely inadequate and unsure of herself. She put her hand on his shoulder and smiled at him. "I can't understand why you should want to see me again," she murmured.

"I do, though," Willie whispered and he felt a promissory chill run up and down his spine.

"I thank you for that," she said softly.

She patted his shoulder and with her other hand crushed her

cigarette in an ash tray. Then she closed her cigarette case and tucked it in her handbag.

"There he is," she said.

Her bag fell to the floor when she stood up, and Willie retrieved it for her with what amounted to gracious pride.

His eyes followed her across the room to Oggie. He never looked away until he saw her hat disappear in the doorway. He had experienced nothing when he saw Paul kiss her cheek, but when the door closed behind her he suddenly became aware of the babbling voices around him and he felt miserably alone.

He left shortly afterward and forgot to say goodby to Paul.

He drove to Santa Monica and parked the car on a cliff overlooking the ocean. The stars were out and the moon peered into other cars lined up at the side of the road. Cars with two faces in them looking out to sea.

Willie began to cry again. This time with ecstasy and joy, not anger.

27

WILLIE DROVE the car into the garage, doused the lights, shut off the motor, and quietly closed the door. He tiptoed across the driveway, hoping to deaden the sound of his own footsteps, crunching across the gravel. He wanted to get up to his room without being seen. He had no sense of guilt—it was just that he had fallen in love and wanted desperately to be alone.

He crossed the moonlit lawn beside the pool and as he approached the back stairs leading to his room, he looked up and noticed that the house was ablaze with light. Normally the sight of such extravagance would have aroused his curiosity. But Willie was in love and he heard no other sound, saw no other face, felt no other presence but that of Lucy.

He stood on the balcony and lit a cigarette. The moon caressed his face and he shuddered ecstatically. He called her name softly, "Lucy. Lucy!" and the winds wrapped it up and thrust it back to his lips again.

He went into the bedroom and undressed without turning on the lights. He was grateful for the enveloping comfort of darkness and only vaguely aware of his surroundings.

Strange cries drifted up from below and while he was brushing his teeth he heard a knock on the bathroom door. It was Jacob.

"Yes?" Willie gurgled through the bristle and foam of his toothbrush.

Jacob came in and sat on the edge of the bathtub. "I came up to warn you," he said. "Your grandmother's very sick. You'd better come down and get it over with."

Willie spat into the basin and turned defiantly. "Get what over with? What have I done now?" he demanded.

"Nothing, really. But they're excited and when people are excited they don't think. So they're blaming you."

"Goddamn it!" Willie yelled, grabbing his bathrobe. "We'll see about this!"

He dashed down the hall, his bathrobe billowing behind him like the spinnaker of a scudding schooner. Jacob's slippers paddled rapidly astern and the old man, puffing hard, caught up with his grandson at the door to Momma's room.

"Easy, boy, easy!" he pleaded breathlessly.

"Okay, okay," Willie grumbled.

He opened the door. Momma was stretched out groaning on the bed. Rebecca held her hand. Louis, sitting beside his mother, kept shaking his head with grief. Moe was talking to Dr. Einstein, the studio M.D., in one corner of the room, and Arline, impervious to the tragedy before her, had pushed her chair into the corner nearest the door, where she sat idly flicking the pages of a magazine while she kept an impatient eye on Moe.

"It's all right, Mr. Korn!" Dr. Einstein piped in a high, squeaky voice. "It's just indigestion from overeating."

"You feeling better, Momma?" Louis asked timidly.

Momma groaned and shook her head. Little rivulets of perspiration ran down the clefts of her double chin. "It's turrible," she rasped. "Turrible. Fife apfel domplings should give me indichastion! Never before. Ai, sotch cremps!" She rolled from side to side.

"Oh, Momma," Rebecca said tearfully, "you'll be all right. Dr. Einstein gave us a prescription. Max just went down to the drugstore with it."

"Latt be! Latt be!" the old lady groaned.

Willie, standing unnoticed in the doorway, shrugged his shoulders at Jacob and whispered, "So where do I come in?"

Jacob didn't answer and Louis, turning slowly, finally saw his son. "You're gonna be the death of your gramma yet, young man," he said sternly.

"What the hell are you talking about?" Willie demanded, his voice cracking with resentment.

"If you'd have remained home with us," Rebecca said indignantly, "this wouldn't have happened."

"You mean there wouldn't have been five apple dumplings left so's the old lady could make a pig of herself?"

"Let's go home, Mosey!" Arline pleaded, slamming her magazine to the floor.

"Waid a minute, cantcha?" Moe snapped.

Louis lunged for his son. He grabbed the lapels of Willie's bathrobe with one hand and shook them violently.

"Listen, you!" he said hoarsely. "You may have no respect for your parents, but I love my mother and if anything happens to her, so help me, I'll kill you!" He relaxed his grip. "Now, go to bed!"

291

Willie stumbled out of the room, angrily slamming the door behind him. He stood for a moment in the hall and heard his father say, "Moe, you better call Dr. Lansburgh. Tell him to come out on the next plane. My expense."

Willie turned and trudged toward his bedroom, away from the jumble of voices. He felt no anger now, just emptiness. He kept his hands in the pockets of his robe and kicked open the door, then he kicked it shut again and pressed his back firmly against it, as though weight alone could bar the entrance to his family. He stood there a long time, staring at the patch of moonlight on the floor. And still Louis's words tormented him. If they called Lansburgh, he thought, it's serious. Maybe I should have stayed home. What if she dies?

"Oh, Christ, what can I do?" he cried out loud, looking toward the ceiling where God might have been suspended from a convenient two-by-four. "Why should they hate me so? Why is everything my fault? Why? Why? Why?"

And then he paused and looked down and removed his hands from his pockets. Slowly he brought them up in the conventional clasp of prayer. And then he knelt and pleaded, "Dear God, please. Please make the old girl well."

He rose to his feet greatly relieved and went over to the bed. He sighed, kicked off his slippers, and threw himself on the quilt. He put his hands up to his troubled head and rolled it wearily from side to side. "Oh, Lucy!" he murmured. "Lucy, my darling!"

There was a knock on the door.

"Please!" Willie cried. "Please don't come in!"

He heard Jacob's footsteps plodding down the hall.

28

MOST VISITING MOTORISTS leave California convinced that Los Angeles is the one town in the world where the first driver through an intersection is the only one out alive. Certainly there is some justification behind the malicious rumor that the streets of Los Angeles are paved with glass—broken glass blown out of headlights, windshields, tail lamps—and the brains of the most idiotic drivers east of the Pacific.

And Willie, who was the owner of a rather tired Ford roadster, was by no means exempt from this classification.

"It gets me around," he always said when people remarked that his car looked slightly frayed around the edges. However, on this night of all nights, when he was about to have his first date with Lucy, the chance remark of a passing motorist made him acutely aware of his jalopy's shortcomings.

Driving out Sunset Boulevard, immersed in thoughts of Miss Strawbridge, he reacted somewhat more slowly than usual to a stop signal and wound up with his bumper wedged beneath that of a large sedan in front of him. The driver of the other car, jostled to the point of exasperation, stalked angrily up to Willie and snapped, "They oughtn't allow junk heaps like that on the road!"

It took them fifteen minutes to unhitch bumpers and after they'd exchanged license numbers, both of them drove off indignantly.

Lucy had said, "Pick me up at seven." That was three days ago, and after circling the block twice looking for the number, Willie felt as though he had spent all the intervening time hunting for her house.

He rattled around the block again, cursing the fact that no two houses ever exhibited their identifying numerals in the same place. Some people had number plates on their front lawns, others painted them on the sidewalks or stone walls; some tacked them up on front porches or fences, and the rest, doubtless seeking privacy, seemed to keep theirs carefully buried in the back yard. By a process of deduction rather than discovery, he finally pulled up in front of a trim English cottage.

This must be it. At least he would get out and ask. This sort of thing could go on all night. He rang the bell. A maid appeared and scanned him through a peephole.

"Could you tell me where the Strawbridges live?" he asked, and he tried very hard to make his voice sound casually refined.

"Come right in," the maid said, opening the door.

"I'm Mr. Levinson."

"Go right in. Miss Lucy will be down shortly."

Willie stood in the doorway of the dropped living room. There was a large mirror over the fireplace. Two love seats separated by a coffee table stood face to face before the hearth. Willie squeezed past them to get at the mirror, where he adjusted his tie and smoothed his hair. He failed to notice that Mrs. Strawbridge was watching him.

"Mr. Levinson?" she said from the doorway.

Willie turned awkwardly. "Yes'm," he answered in a slightly startled voice.

"I'm Lucy's mother." She came forward. "Won't you sit down?"

"Thanks," he said, plucking at the knees of his trousers to save the crease as he settled on the edge of the love seat.

"Shall we have cocktails before Lucy comes down? She's always an hour late, you know."

Willie looked apprehensive.

"Well, twenty minutes, anyway."

Willie smiled. Mrs. Strawbridge rang the service bell.

"You're in the picture business?"

294

"Yes. I am."

"It must be exciting."

"Sometimes."

The maid reappeared.

"Three old-fashioneds," Mrs. Strawbridge said briefly. Then she turned back to Willie. "Lucy and Paul have told me quite a lot about you. You're quite young to be making such a name for yourself."

Willie shrugged his shoulders.

"I'm jes' a perducer now," he said, automatically lapsing into studio jargon at the mere mention of the motion-picture industry.

"I know, but isn't that an important position?"

"Nothing to what I'm going to be."

"How nice!"

He wished Lucy would come downstairs. He wasn't interested in Mrs. Strawbridge or the picture business or anything. His heart was pounding with expectation, anxiety, and happiness, and this woman kept rapping at his eardrums, demanding his attention.

"I like young men who know—or think they know—what they're going to be. Only, sometimes the fates aren't quite so decided as the young men, are they?"

"It's in the cards, Mrs. Strawbridge," Willie reassured her impatiently. "It's in the cards."

They heard the sound of footsteps on the stairs.

"I'm so sorry," Lucy said, before she got down to the bottom step.

"Someday, Lucy," her mother advised, "you're going to say that to an empty room."

Willie kept his eyes on the entrance. She was standing there in a gray sports suit, swinging a blue beret back and forth on the end of her little finger. A small cloth bag was tucked securely under her arm.

"Hello," she said to Willie, and she came down the steps and dropped her bag and beret on the nearest chair.

Willie stood up and gulped, "Hello."

"Mother's such a punctual person," she explained as she crossed the room. "She always feels there's something shameful about being late. But there isn't, really. I don't do it on purpose. Do sit down."

Lucy sat down on the seat beside her mother, facing Willie.

"I'm still waiting to see your expression the day you come downstairs and say 'I'm sorry' to an empty room."

Lucy smiled at her mother. "You'll have a long wait, I'm afraid. I've never missed yet."

"I'm not so sure," Millicent Strawbridge said, and Lucy flushed slightly. She hoped Willie hadn't realized the remark was aimed at him. But Willie was so flustered and so concerned with making a good impression that he obviously couldn't concentrate beyond the shadow of his own nose. And Lucy was extremely grateful for his confusion. It protected him from a woman whose tongue was occasionally sharper than her wits.

"Where would you like to eat?" Willie asked.

"Anywhere you suggest," Lucy answered gently.

"Dear me!" Mrs. Strawbridge said, in a tone that somehow managed to convey a feeling of guilt and relief. "Perhaps we should have asked Mr. Levinson to dine with us."

"Thank you very much." Willie smiled. "But I don't mind eating out. I'm tired of home cooking."

Mrs. Strawbridge raised her eyebrows.

The maid brought the cocktails. Mrs. Strawbridge lit her cigarette. Willie began to break into a cold sweat. This was a hell of a beginning. That woman tied him up so! Besides, he'd hoped to find Lucy alone.

"Good drink," he said, over the rim of his glass.

Mrs. Strawbridge gave him the kind of smile that dropped another ice cube into his old-fashioned. Lucy suddenly realized they had to get out of the house—and quickly.

"What was the name of that place you mentioned?" The question was a plea, plaintively and desperately delivered.

"What place? I didn't mention any place," Willie answered blankly.

Lucy shrugged her shoulders and gave up.

"Why don't you decide what you're going to do later in the evening and let the restaurant take care of itself?" Millicent Strawbridge asked.

"Good idea," Willie said. "What'll we do?"

That floored everybody and there was a long silence. Mrs. Strawbridge sat back and enjoyed herself. She looked from one to the other and when she finally saw how completely baffled they were, she took pity on them and reluctantly suggested, "You *could* stay here."

"God forbid!" Willie heard himself scream, and he felt his face grow crimson with embarrassment.

Mrs. Strawbridge giggled in spite of herself. "Do you like music?" she asked.

"Sure," Willie said, thinking how nice it would be to hold Lucy in his arms while they were dancing.

"I have some tickets for the Bowl you could use tonight."

"Aren't you going to use them?" Lucy asked.

"No. Take them. They're on my desk, in the bedroom."

Lucy ran up the stairs.

Willie and Mrs. Strawbridge sat looking at each other with polite exasperation until Lucy came down again.

29

HE FOLLOWED her down the path to the curb. She waited for him to open the car door. This rattled him considerably for he had begun to confuse manners with servility. Subconsciously she recognized his resentment for what it was—rebellion against the stylized conventions of society. She was used to the polite amenities, but what the hell? She opened the door herself and he ran around to get in the other side.

"Where'll we eat?" he asked again.

"Indecision," she laughed, "if it does nothing else, drives me crazy. How about the Gotham?"

"Why, that's just a Yiddisha delicatessen!"

"I like Jewish food, and besides, it's on the way to the Bowl."

Willie suddenly felt unaccountably proud of himself. "Swell! he agreed, stepping on the starter. The car snorted and backfired. Willie giggled self-consciously. He jammed the accelerator to the floor and they tore off toward Sunset Boulevard.

The soft night air swirled around the windshield post and caressed Willie with the delicate fragrance of Lucy's perfume. He adjusted the rear-vision mirror so he could catch an occasional glimpse of her face.

"Gee, you smell nice!" he shouted above the roar of the motor.

"Thanks. L'Arpège, Lanvin," she confided.

"No," he answered gallantly. "It's you."

Aha, she thought, this is one of those young blades who can never dissociate women from their scents. He will expect me to taste like some exotic, ethereal concoction of the gods because he is an idealist and therefore a dope.

"Bill," she said suddenly, "you mustn't take Mother seriously. She's a good scout, but it takes a while to get used to her."

"I liked her," he lied.

"She liked you too," she said, crossing her fingers and looking up at the smallest star in the sky.

They arrived at the parking lot, where an attendant took the car. Willie took her arm for the first time and they walked up the street together. She stopped and turned toward the restaurant window. It was stocked with an elaborate display of patés from Strasbourg, sardines from Norway, English jellies, Russian caviar; she felt like a child looking at a shop window full of gaudy toys.

"Where, Bill, but in a Jewish delicatessen would you find delicacies like that?"

It was only after she'd asked the question that she remembered

Charles & Company in New York, Fortnum and Mason in London, Potin's in Paris. All memories of her youth. Memories that involved stretching on her tiptoes to peer into the wonderful glass showcases.

Willie yanked her back to Hollywood.

"Do you really like Jewish things?" he asked, hoping very earnestly that she did.

"How could I help it? They're as rich as the people themselves. And Jews are rich, here," she said, pointing to her heart, "like the Filipinos."

The comparison baffled Willie completely. She looked at him curiously and hesitated a moment.

"Go ahead," he nodded. "You've got something to say. Say it!"

"I will," she answered, "and hope you'll understand. There are only two classes of Jews I dislike, and that's not because they're Jews."

"Meaning?"

"I've met those in the dress-goods business and I've been warned against those in the movies."

"Oh," Willie exhaled. He had a vague feeling he had suddenly lost caste through no fault of his own.

"I didn't mean it that way." She smiled. "Let's eat."

"She likes me!" Willie thought, breaking into a grateful grin.

Two hours later, after the inevitable traffic jam and frantic scramble up Pepper Tree Lane, they were in their seats, puffing but victorious. They'd made it in time to hear the overture. However, the fact that they were completely out of breath contributed somewhat to their apathy toward the music.

By the middle of the overture they had recovered both their composure and their wind.

"What's the name of the piece?" Willie whispered.

"Beethoven's Leonore Overture," Lucy informed him. "The third."

"Ssh!" somebody hissed indignantly from the next box.

Willie sank down in his chair and scowled. It would be fun, he thought, if they suddenly swiped the orchestra off the stage and let the conductor beat his arms around all alone. Jeez, he'd look silly. Silly as an actor in the silent days.

The overture concluded in a surge of glory and applause. The floodlights went on. Latecomers swarmed down the aisles searching for good seats. A few lordly box holders wandered leisurely into their pews and, once settled, disdainfully surveyed the culture-conscious rabble above and below them.

"It's really a lovely spot," Lucy said, looking around at the stars, the trees, the immense expanse of seats behind them, and the symmetrical simplicity of the orchestra shell. "If only the orchestra were better."

"They're no good?" Willie asked.

"What do you think?"

"I wouldn't know."

"You don't like music?"

"It's my first time," Willie confessed.

"Your first—?" she repeated. Then her voice broke with incredulity and amazement. "You've never been to a concert before?"

"Never had time," Willie answered, taking refuge behind Hollywood's stock excuse for ignorance.

"Oh, Bill, what a shame! You've missed so much, and through no fault of your own, I'm sure."

She couldn't help herself. She hardly knew this man and already she was profoundly concerned over him. He was so young and success had come to him so quickly. He really had no actual awareness of the world outside his own private little circle. There were so many things for him to discover. Things that would make him happy later on. Things that would help mature him now. She felt strangely maternal toward him and curious about his past.

"Tell me, Bill, what have you been doing with yourself in the evenings?" she asked.

Willie looked at her intently. "Waiting for you," he said.

She couldn't help smiling to herself. He was trying so desperately to be gallant and grown-up.

"What a horrible occupation," she said. "And such patience, too!"

"Huh?" Willie frowned.

"Don't mind me, Bill. I say some very foolish things. Things you're not supposed to understand, but that happen to amuse me. Pay no attention to them. They're going to play the César Franck symphony next and I'm glad you're getting a chance to hear it at your first concert because it was the first symphony I really liked. I was a little girl then, about twelve. And Mother packed me off to the children's concerts at Carnegie Hall every Saturday morning. I was in love then." She paused reflectively, and couldn't help noticing Willie's sudden hurt, envious expression. "He was a man of thirty-five," she reassured him. "A friend of Father's. And every time they played this symphony it tore my heart out. It's old-hat now to a lot of people, but it's an old friend to me and I hope you'll like it."

"If you did, I will," Willie said. Come what may, he'd love the damned thing.

Suddenly the floodlights were turned off. The drone of conversation gradually diminished. An aura of hushed expectancy filled the Bowl and latecomers scurried to their seats. It was dark again and Willie sneaked a quick look at the white outline of Lucy's gloved hand. It lay, enticing in repose, upon her lap.

The conductor strode rapidly across the stage, mounted the podium and turned to acknowledge the ripple of applause with a peremptory bow. He tapped his baton quickly on the light stand and raised both hands high above his head. *Eins, zwei, drei*—and the boys were off.

The long, slow lament of the first movement began to conquer Willie. Subconsciously he recognized the repetitions of the main theme and it began to stir him. By the time the orchestra swept triumphantly into the last chords of the movement, Willie found

301

himself enthralled. Concentration on music in the presence of one's beloved brings its own reward.

Willie sighed.

Lucy, not knowing whether to interpret this as a sign of emotion or of relief, interrogated him with her eyes. He smiled, the heart-warming smile of a person sharing a secret in a crowded room, and nodded emphatically. She leaned over and took his hand in both of hers.

"I'm so glad," she murmured.

However, when Willie sought to capitalize on his advantage by maneuvering closer to her, she shot him a quick, apprehensive glance and withdrew to her corner of the box.

At the end of the last movement the Bowl rocked with applause and the floods were turned on again for the intermission. People stood up and looked around at their neighbors. A thousand Hollywoodites told a thousand tourists that a pin dropped on the stage could be heard in the farthermost reaches of the Bowl. The inevitable movie queens began their inevitable fashion parade in and around the boxes.

Elena Maya, swathed in furs and followed by photographers, spied Willie and rushed up to him.

"Why, Mr. Levinson," she gurgled, "I didn't know you were interested in music!"

"Just feeding my soul," Willie apologized, in the tone of a country boy saying "Aw, shucks!"

Lucy looked straight ahead and frowned slightly.

"Shake hands with him, Miss Maya!" one of the photographers shouted from behind his view finder.

"That's Elena Maya!" the seat holders in the next five rows murmured, standing up to get a better look. Autograph hounds appeared from nowhere and attacked the box.

"Yer ortagraph, Miss Maya! Yer ortagraph!" they chanted.

"Jesus Christ!" a photographer swore. "Wait till we get our pictures!"

302

"Hold it. . . . Thanks. One more please."

"How about one of you, Mr. Levinson, with the lady?"

The boys were busy replacing their used flashbulbs. Willie protested feebly.

"It'll take just a moment."

Lucy, who was an eastern girl, was getting her first taste of the limelight and she loved it.

"A little closer to him, please," one of the photographers said. "That's it!"

They took three or four poses. Lucy couldn't tell how many. She was blind for twenty seconds after the first flash.

"What's the lady's name, Mr. Levinson?" she heard a man ask.

"Now, boys!"

"You wouldn't want us to label her 'Unidentified Blonde'—she's too pretty for that!"

Willie swelled with pride and looked at Lucy.

"Lucy Strawbridge," she said.

"Thanks. Thanks a lot. Swell music. Good night."

They were alone again and Lucy shook her head. "Sometimes this place is beyond my wildest dreams but maybe that's what makes it fun to be here."

"You been here long?"

"This is my first trip."

"I thought you lived here."

"I shall, for another six months or so."

"Oh!"

"I come and go as I please. Mother and I have an apartment in New York. Last year we sublet it and went south. But this year I wanted to come out here and Mother thought it might be fun."

"You like it so far?"

"It's certainly been interesting."

"I hope you'll stay a long time."

"Thanks," she laughed, accepting the compliment gaily. "We might."

303

"You must!" he said very firmly, and he looked straight ahead at the orchestra shell. Something in his voice startled her and she looked at him curiously.

"You're serious, aren't you?" she asked.

He nodded.

"Oh, don't be, Bill, please. Not that serious, I mean."

"Why not? I want you to stay here." He turned around in his chair and rested his chin in his hand. "What's wrong with that?" he asked softly.

"Nothing, Bill. Nothing—but please don't be serious with me."

"Afraid?" he asked confidently. And there was such adolescent insolence in the question that Lucy had a difficult time suppressing her laughter.

Willie saw the twinkle in her eyes, and her independence infuriated him. The color ran out of his cheeks and he turned away again. A wave of self-pity sent a shiver up and down his spine. This girl, this dream of his, didn't really like him. He knew that now. It was all in his mind, this vision of a perfect evening. And she had shattered it so quickly. He wasn't angry, he told himself, just hurt, but he turned on her abruptly.

"If you feel that way about me, why did you go out with me?" he demanded.

She was still smiling at him, gently by this time, apologetically. He ignored the apology.

"Why?" he demanded harshly.

"I don't know why," she hesitated.

"That's no answer."

And his persistence suddenly began to annoy her. "You couldn't take my answer," she said coldly.

"No?"

"No."

"That's where you're wrong."

She looked at him quietly for a moment and then said, "Very well, I think it was curiosity, if you must know. Although I didn't tell Paul, I *had* heard about you. I do read the papers, you know. Theatrical section, and all. And I was curious to see what you were like, that's all."

Willie suddenly looked like a sucked grape and his anger melted quickly into misery. "That's not very much, is it?" he murmured slowly. "You see, I'd hoped you might like me for myself."

"No, I'm afraid it isn't," Lucy admitted, searching for something else to tell him. He was waiting so anxiously to be told that she liked him, and there was really so little to say. She didn't even know him, when it came right down to it, and probably never would; besides, at this point she certainly wanted their relationship to be impersonal.

"Look, Bill," she said suddenly, "you're an awfully nice person, you really are! You're not at all the sort of menace one expects a Hollywood producer to be. You're a nice, sweet guy and I respect you for it. If I didn't, I wouldn't talk to you like this. It's no trick for a girl to be coy, you know. I think we can be friends. But you must give me time." She knew that he was going to say that was exactly what he wanted with her—time—so she hurriedly asked him how old he was, hoping to change the course of the conversation because she felt, quite definitely, that she wouldn't see him again.

"Twenty-four," he lied.

It worked, she thought. "Twenty-four, and you don't even know a note of music."

"I know every band in the country! Whiteman! Duchin! Ellington!" Willie said defiantly.

"Who's Toscanini?"

"An Eyetalian band leader."

"Right, by God! What band?"

"The New York Philharmonic. Got you there, didn't I?"

"You certainly did. You amaze me, Bill, really. You know, in a way, someday I may be very proud of having known you. I hope so. You've a great future ahead of you."

"What about you?"

"What do you mean, what about me?"

"What about *your* future? You think I can't help you?"

"Can you?"

"Sure I can. You're prissy."

She pursed her lips and looked down at the floor. She knew she'd been pretty hellish.

"And besides," Willie continued, now that he'd got started, "nobody ever talked to me like that before!"

"I'm sorry, Bill," she said. But she was still confused. He was so strong at times and childlike at others. He made her say things she didn't mean, or that didn't sound right when she did mean them.

"Okay," he sulked. "Just let me hold your hand through the rest of this damned thing."

She shook her head in amazement, and when the lights went out she took his hand in hers and held it till the concert ended.

They drove home in silence. When they parked in front of her house, Willie, somewhat chastened but still an optimist, put his arm around her and tried to kiss her good night. She backed away and put her hand over his lips.

"No. No, Bill," she said softly. "Your wanting to kiss me isn't important, but when the time comes and I want to kiss you—look out! Good night."

"Good night," he said, kissing her hand. She got out and turned toward him. "Don't bother coming to the door."

"When'll I see you?"

"Call me."

"Good night."

"Good night."

As Willie drove home he experienced alternate waves of exaltation and depression. He felt vaguely that he had been shortchanged, but he didn't know how. . . .

"Did you have a nice time, dear?" Millicent Strawbridge called down to her daughter the moment she heard the front door close.

306

"Certainly!" Lucy shouted back, a bit defiantly.

"Come on up."

Lucy walked slowly up the stairs and into her mother's room.

"That was a strange young man."

"Oh, he's nice enough."

"Personally, I suspect he'd rape his grandmother's iron antelope if he got the chance, and if she had one."

Lucy looked blankly past the bed and out the window at infinity.

"Oh, Lucy! I didn't mean to upset you. You're brooding about something. What is it?"

"I'm afraid I've been a bitch," Lucy said, closing the door quietly behind her.

30

"IT'S NOTHING SERIOUS," Willie heard a familiar voice reassuring his family in the living room, "but she's got to be careful about her diet."

Willie dropped his hat, adjusted his tie, and marched in to join the family.

"I can't understand it, doctor," Rebecca protested, as Willie, beaming with anticipation, watched Dr. Lansburgh from the doorway. "We've always given her the best food money can buy."

The doctor nodded and shot a wry smile at Rebecca. "Well, from here on in, the best food will buy a one-way ticket to the grave," he said.

"Hello, Doc!" Willie called cheerfully.

"Willie!" Lansburgh cried, rushing forward to greet his former patient. "How's my boy?" He put his arm around Willie's shoulder and turned toward the family. "You know, deep down I've always expected great things of this lad. How's he been behaving?"

This rhetorical question embarrassed the Levinsons, who were essentially literal-minded folk. They squirmed awkwardly and smirked. "As good as could be expected," Rebecca said.

"There's been a quarrel?" the doctor guessed.

"Yes," Jacob replied, looking up from his newspaper.

"No!" Louis shouted defiantly. "He's just been busy. And besides, Jacob, you've been about as interested in Momma's sickness as—well, I dunno what!"

Jacob slapped his paper against his knees. "Now, let me tell you something, Mr. Son-in-Law, I don't need fancy specialists from New York—begging your pardon, doctor—to tell me what's wrong with Momma. I know what's wrong with her!"

"And just what do you mean by that?" Louis inquired icily.

"She's got a Yiddisha stomach," Jacob answered, going back to his paper.

"Excellent diagnosis, Mr. Korn," Dr. Lansburgh laughed, "excellent!"

"So! Fomm Noo Yawk ya godda get expoits yet to tell Jakie vot a smott mensch he is!"

They all looked at the doorway and gasped. There was Momma, a mound of flesh tied together by a bathrobe.

"Momma!" Rebecca shrieked, rushing over to her. "What are you doing on your feet?"

"Stending on 'em. Vodda ya do vid yours?"

"Momma, go to bed!" Louis ordered, striding across the room.

"Is downstairs de duktah, is opstairs no Momma!" The old girl grinned.

Louis shrugged his shoulders helplessly. "You see? We can't do a thing with her."

"I'll tell you what we'll do, Momma," Lansburgh suggested, "you get into bed and we'll come upstairs to keep you company."

"Det's vot I need," Momma said. "Company, opstairs, in bet. Comm vid me."

308

The family marched up the stairs behind her. She threw off her bathrobe, climbed into bed, and sat up smiling.

"Villie," she said, assuming the role of matriarch, "how's ya schicksa?"

"What schicksa? I don't know what you're talking about," Willie lied, hoping to avoid an open discussion.

Momma appealed to her physician. "Duktah, ven a boy breaks avay fomm a femily poddy in his honor, he's got a schicksa. A Joosh goil vooden allow sotch a ting!"

"Have you, Willie?" Lansburgh asked gently.

Willie hung his head. "She's a lady," he growled. "Not a schicksa."

"Phui!" his grandmother ejaculated.

"She could be, you know," Rebecca said magnanimously.

"Jantile *ladies* dun't go vid liddle Yiddisha boys," Momma snapped. "No good comms fomm sotch tings."

"What's her name?" Jacob asked, rubbing his beard.

Willie, smarting under their taunts and proud of his Lucy to the point of defiance, snorted, "It wouldn't mean a thing to any of you!"

"I wouldn't be so sure about that," the doctor cautioned.

"Well, maybe *you* know her," Willie conceded, "but not this bunch!" Then he lowered his head and muttered to the doctor, "Her name's Lucy Strawbridge."

"Strawbridge—now, let me see!" the doctor mused. "Strawbridge. From Baltimore?"

"Wrong!" Willie crowed. "They're from New York."

"They were from Baltimore before they were from New York. Millicent Strawbridge was Dr. Whitman's daughter and very rich. I studied under Whitman at Johns Hopkins. And I know young Lucy, a bright and extremely attractive girl. Her father became head of some big gas company. Died many years ago. They've been traveling ever since."

"Sa-ay," Willie ejaculated, "maybe you can help me."

"I'd be glad to. Strawbridge was a patient of mine."

Momma coughed.

"—long before he died, Momma Levinsky," Lansburgh hastened to reassure her. "And Mrs. Strawbridge, who's a very gay soul, has been a transient patient and friend ever since."

"Let's make a double date with the old lady some night," Willie suggested.

"All right. But I might take the daughter away from you. I don't betray my years, you know."

"Aw, Doc, you wouldn't do that!"

"I suppose not. When it comes to women I agree with Ovid—— 'No new wine for me.'"

"It's a date, then."

"You set it."

"I'll let you know," Willie said, leaving the room.

"Dese goyim," Momma wailed, "dey got no shame! Foist dey take our kiddies, den dey steal our duktahs fomm us!"

"Now, Momma, you've got nothing to worry about. And, besides, Willie's going out with the best people."

"I always knew he'd make it," Rebecca giggled, sticking her tongue out at Louis, who frowned and asked dourly, "Would you like him to marry her?"

"God fahbid!" Momma shrieked, tossing her hands heavenward.

"She'll still be fighting on her deathbed," the doctor chuckled.

"Good night, Momma," Louis said, adjusting her covers.

She slid beneath them and sighed, "Sleep vell."

They filed out of the room, the doctor lingering behind to douse the lights. "You feel fine, you battle-ax," he whispered.

"Sure," she laughed, "baht unly you en' me know dat!"

He grinned and closed the door behind him.

31

WILLIE ARRIVED at the studio early the following morning. Only by keeping himself constantly occupied, running down to *The Nebraskan* set and up to rushes, did he manage to restrain himself from calling Lucy too early. Precisely at the stroke of eleven, he seated himself at his desk and dialed her number. The maid answered the phone.

"Miss Lucy there?" Willie asked. "Mr. Levinson calling."

"Mr. Levinson? Just one moment please, I'll see."

He waited an interminable two minutes before the maid returned to say, "I'm sorry, she's not in."

"Do you expect her back?"

"I don't know."

"Oh."

"Any message?"

"Tell her to call me before twelve-thirty," he said, hanging up brusquely.

He felt frustrated. She *must* have been at home, else the maid wouldn't have taken that long to tell him about it. Besides, where would she go that early in the morning? Another man's apartment? If he could only get in right with the old lady, he'd know more about the daughter's movements. She wouldn't go to another man's apartment. Probably wasn't that kind of girl. Couldn't be. He couldn't take her up the back stairs to his room, either. She was definitely a front-door girl if he ever saw one. Maybe it would be a good idea if he did have an apartment . . . and a new car. But what about the money he was saving to buy Miracle preferred stock secretly, in small quantities, so that on his twenty-first birthday, when the family gave him his annual present of the same number of shares as his age multiplied by fifty, he'd have enough interest in the company to be able to tell Moe and Louis to go to hell? What about that? Well, for twenty-five hundred dollars you could pick up a swell car—and jeez, that was less than a month's salary. He buzzed Miss Holmby.

"Get me the Packard agency," he ordered.

"There's a call for you, Mr. Levinson," she answered.

"Put it through!" he cried impatiently.

It was Lucy. He knew it. He cleared his throat as he swung around and picked up the phone. It would be best to sound busy.

"Hello, sweetheart!" he cried gaily.

"Sweetheart, yourself!" T. Monte Cooper snorted into the phone. "Come on down. We got a great gag figured out."

"Can't. Got an important call coming through at twelve."

"Switch it down here."

"Nope."

"Come on. She'll call back."

"This ain't a woman! It's a business deal!" Willie lied indignantly.

"She'll call back anyway," Monte persisted. "Come on down."

"Okay."

He left instructions with Miss Holmby to call him the moment a Miss Strawbridge phoned and went down to 11.

"What is it?" he asked Cooper.

"Two bad men come into town at the same time. They've sworn to kill each other on sight. They see each other from opposite ends of the main street. Then they get off their horses and start marching toward the middle of town. Neither man draws first, each figuring himself to be the better shot. It's a code, you know. Then when they're only twenty paces apart, each man reaches for his gun. But they don't go off. Their guns ain't loaded. They been out duckhunting."

Willie took a good look at Cooper. "You shot that yet?" he asked.

"No."

"Good. You're fired. No wonder you ain't producing here no longer. No wonder no other studio'll even give you a directing job.

"You're through, mister. You need a rest, so's you can catch up with the parade that's passed you by. Mel Price'll finish the show. We'll pay your salary and when you come back we'll make a new deal. . . . Company's dismissed for the day!"

Willie stalked out and back to his office, where he arranged to have Mel take over the picture.

Cooper also left the stage, through ranks of extras who looked the other way when he passed because they pitied him. Only one man broke the silence, an electrician who had been with the great director many years. "I'm sorry it had to happen this way, Mr. Cooper," he murmured. Cooper put his hand on the man's shoulder. "It had to happen sometime, Joe," he said. His eyes clouded with tears and he closed the stage door behind him. . . .

Willie drummed impatiently on his glass-topped desk. It was almost twelve now and still Lucy hadn't called. He couldn't resist the urge any longer. He dialed her number. She answered the phone.

"For heaven's sake!" Willie cried sarcastically. "Imagine actually finding you in!"

"Why, hello, Bill. I just got your message. I went out to get my hair done. How are you? Did you sleep well? I thought of you long after you left last night."

Willie was completely disarmed. "Nice things?" he murmured.

"Not all of them."

Willie's ego rose to almost implausible heights. "Well!" he chuckled pointedly. "Well! Well!"

"I decided that although I'd behaved very badly, you'd be kind enough to forgive me."

"For what? Course I do!"

"You'd forgive me almost anything, wouldn't you, Bill?"

"You bet!"

"Then try to understand this. You're a darling, but I think we'd better not see each other again."

"Oh." Willie exhaled sharply, like a pricked balloon.

"In the first place—and I do hate to say this—you're younger than I am; in the second place, I think you're much too nice for me. Now, wait, Bill," she cried as he tried to protest, "let me finish. You see, I also can't help thinking that your family wouldn't approve of me. So don't make it difficult—just let me say goodby, and bless you."

He heard the phone click, but he sat there still holding the receiver in his hand. Momma's prophetic words flashed through his mind. "Jantile *ladies* dun't go vid liddle Yiddisha boys." He resented Momma almost as much as he impetuously resented Lucy. He didn't realize that she was trying to let him down easy. That she had shouldered the blame for everything herself.

He just sat there brooding and wondering how he could get her back, and why, when he'd finally met a real girl, everything had to go wrong. And suddenly he hit upon a bright idea. He called Dr. Lansburgh and explained the situation.

Yes, the doctor said. He would call the Strawbridges, make a date, and tell them he was bringing a young man for Lucy. No, no names.

Willie heaved a panic-stricken sigh of relief.

32

ON THE WAY to the Strawbridges' Willie drove his new Packard convertible sedan, and kept his eyes glued to the mist-blurred road to hide his nervousness.

"Look, Doc," he said, after several minutes of silence, "you've known her all her life. What about her?"

"What do you mean, Willie?"

"I mean, what's she like? What's she been up to?"

Lansburgh leaned back against the leather cushions. "Let's see," he said slowly. "A good school, summers in Europe, Vassar, a year at the Sorbonne, back to New York, then a short-lived little literary magazine—she was an assistant editor there, and had her own apartment in Gramercy Square."

"She did?" Willie exclaimed, swinging the car abruptly around a sharp turn.

"I went there for a few parties," the doctor continued. "Very pleasant—a literary crowd."

A slow, satisfied grin spread over Willie's face. Her own apartment, eh? That was something to know.

"Yeah, but what about—you know, the men, the guys?"

Willie felt, rather than saw, Lansburgh glance at him sharply, but he kept his eyes straight ahead.

"Now, Willie," the doctor said quietly.

"Aw, come on, Doc. This is important."

"I'm not sure I can tell you much. She was engaged once—I know that. It was after she came back from Europe, and I suspect it was more of her mother's doing than Lucy's. Nothing came of it. After that—well, young poets who write for small literary magazines don't usually make good husbands."

Willie could hardly keep from laughing out loud. The field was clear, and whatever had happened before hadn't been anything to worry about.

But when he started up the walk beside the doctor his optimism began to wane. He tugged nervously at the sleeves of his dinner jacket and for a moment wanted to bolt and run. He paused just beyond the circle of light cast by the lamp over the front door. The fog had crept in from the sea and a hazy spray settled softly on his face, filling him with loneliness.

"Okay, kid?" the doctor asked, turning around.

"Okay! Okay!" Willie lied nervously.

Lansburgh smiled and rang the bell. "Keep your chin up," he cautioned as the maid opened the door.

"Dr. Lansburgh—and a friend," Lansburgh announced on the threshold.

The maid beckoned them in and betrayed her astonishment at seeing Willie again by dropping his hat.

"Good evening," she said. "Perhaps you'd like to wait in the living room."

"You wait in the living room," Lansburgh muttered to Willie. "I'll prepare things out here."

Willie nodded and left his friend in the foyer.

Suddenly there was a great deal of commotion and feminine squealing at the head of the stairs. Willie, seated by the fireplace, heard both Strawbridges bounding down the steps.

"Oh, Richard," Mrs. Strawbridge gushed, "it *is* nice to see you again!"

Willie snorted. He heard the rustle of silk in gay embrace and Lucy chattering, "Sir Galahad, Sir Galahad, kiss Cinderella too."

There was the sound of a rich, enthusiastic kiss. And Willie shuddered involuntarily.

"Richard, you haven't changed a bit."

"Why should he, Lucy? He's the perennial Romeo!"

"Gadfly is more like it," Lansburgh laughed.

"I knew that," Lucy teased, "but I didn't know you cared to admit it."

Mrs. Strawbridge smiled at Richard and said, "Where's your young man?"

"Inside."

"Oh."

They lowered their voices. But Willie, enveloped in the silence of the living room, still heard them.

"What's he like?" That was Lucy.

316

"He's horrible-looking, nasty-tempered, fat, middle-aged, and sullen, but he has the soul of an unborn artist."

"My God," Lucy groaned, "I can hardly wait to see him."

"Come on!"

They were coming now, Willie thought. And panic seized him. His heart thumped like a wheezing naphtha engine. For a sickening moment he wished he had fled. But he was imprisoned as effectively as though he had been slapped into jail, and he knew it. Lucy was looking at him from the doorway. For a frightened, resentful second he met her glance and then the thought flashed through his mind that she might just turn on her heels and leave.

But even as he misjudged her she was thinking how definitely she had underrated him. This lad whom she had dismissed as just a youngster was resourceful and ruthless. He played the game without rules. As a matter of fact, he wasn't even playing a game. There was no shame about this, nor any sham either. He had simply moved heaven and earth, in his own way, to see her again. This observation simultaneously fascinated and frightened her. She stood in the doorway and heard herself cry, "Bill!"

He dropped his glance quickly. It had seemed an eternity before she spoke.

He heard Mrs. Strawbridge gasp to Richard, "I didn't know you knew each other," and he looked away as she and Lucy crossed the room to join him.

He felt someone grasp his arm and he turned his head slowly. Mrs. Strawbridge offered her hand. "Forgive us, and welcome!" she said. "A friend of Richard's is a friend of ours."

Willie heaved a sigh of relief and then he laughed for the first time in five days.

"He's my favorite patient and private prodigy," the doctor said, "and I see you've met before."

Lucy stood behind her mother and looked down at Willie sitting on the opposite couch. "Bill, would you do something for me?" she asked.

Willie smiled and nodded.

"Come with me a moment?"

"Sure!" he said fervently, leaping out of the love seat.

"We'll be right back," Lucy reassured her mother.

"I'll call you when the cocktails are ready."

"Don't get lost," Richard called after them as they walked across the living room.

"Don't worry." Lucy smiled back. She shut the patio door behind them.

The garden smelled of gardenias and jasmine and bouvardia. The heavy, sickly sweet odors of romance hung like a mist around the stark white blossoms of gardenias glistening in the light of floodlamps shining from beneath the eaves. It was quiet and cool and a little damp.

Lucy shivered slightly.

"Cold?" he asked.

"Not cold," she smiled, and swung around so that she stood in front of him. "Bill," she said softly, "you engineered this whole evening, didn't you?"

He didn't answer. He just looked down at her and wanted to kiss her. But he didn't dare. He had been told to wait. Her body wasn't close to him, yet he felt her warmth—or thought he did. She was smiling at him and her eyes were soft. Her hands reached up and grasped him lightly behind the ears. Slowly she lowered his face to hers and suddenly, so quickly that he hardly had time to prepare for it, her lips closed over his.

It wasn't a passionate kiss, rather it was a friendly one, but it took Bill completely by surprise. She drew back and looked at him.

"There," she said, "I told you I'd kiss you first."

She smiled at him with the poised patience of a woman expecting a clever answer. She never got it. He grabbed her instead. And slowly, quite against her will, her lips were forced open. He was kissing her now, with the cruel, hard lust of a skeptical conqueror, resentful of the past and frightened of the future. She quivered

318

slightly and arched her body against his. He felt her loins pressed close against his thighs. And for the first time, his own passion began to embarrass him. Slowly, as though their frenzy had exhausted them, they parted.

He looked at her and her eyes were still closed. She shook her head.

"Good God, Bill!" she murmured.

He put his arms around her and hugged her to him. "Lucy," he whispered in her ear, "I know I'm only a kid to you. But, so help me, I love you. Please, please play square with me!"

There was such terror in his voice that her eyes filled with tears and she could only nod her head over his shoulder. She broke away from him and grabbed the handkerchief out of his pocket to dab at her eyes.

"Forgive me," she pleaded.

"Oh, Lucy!" he cried, hugging her again in grateful ecstasy.

"Cocktails, children!" Mrs. Strawbridge called from the living room.

"Cocktails," he repeated with the gaiety of a gravedigger.

Lucy smoothed her hair and took Bill's arm. They walked into the house together, each of them radiating the serene indifference that shrouds young lovers from the rest of the world.

They got over it quickly. At least, Lucy did. Mrs. Strawbridge took one look at her daughter and remarked acidly, "Your lipstick's slipped, Miss Strawbridge!"

Lucy looked at the floor and turned crimson. "Goddamn!" she cried, stamping her foot.

"My God, they're actually embarrassed!" Mrs. Strawbridge said. "I'm sorry, children. Really I am. But you can't go in to dinner looking like that. Come here, Bill."

Bill crossed the room obediently. She took his handkerchief and scrubbed his face with it. Lucy excused herself and ran upstairs.

Lansburgh put a drink into Willie's hand and whispered, "Okay now?"

Willie cried "Okay!" with such fervor that Mrs. Strawbridge instinctively sank into the most convenient chair. She was one of those women who preferred to face enthusiasm sitting down. It gave one an air of immobility, which had always been her best weapon against Lucy's chronic exuberances. She wasn't quite sure about this young man. A kiss in the garden was one thing. But they had both had that horrible light in their eyes when they came into the room. The kind of light that looked like rape wrapped up in tinsel. Well, Lucy was no fool. Or was she? The girl had given up a man of good family for a series of half-baked poets. But this young man had that same mercurial quality that always seemed to attract Lucy . . . but certainly her sense of humor would come to her rescue and make her see the ridiculousness of such an alliance. I don't mind his being a Jew, Mrs. Strawbridge thought, but a *young* Jew—that's preposterous!

She forced herself to smile calmly. "The doctor told me about your grandmother. I hope she's better."

The doctor poured himself another cocktail.

"She's all right," Willie answered shortly.

Lucy stood in the doorway a moment, then crossed the room. There was a long, uneloquent pause and the maid came in to announce dinner. They gulped their drinks and filed into the dining room.

"Richard," Mrs. Strawbridge asked, "how long do you think you'll be here?"

"Another week or so. At least till my patient's able to relish her strudel again."

"Our dream girl," Willie muttered.

"Now, Bill," Lucy said, laughing, "you're prejudiced. You have to live with her."

"That's just it, I don't! I'm going to have my own apartment soon."

He sat back proudly in his chair and devoured Lucy with a long, intimate look. She turned helplessly toward Lansburgh and shook her head. She wasn't used to being menaced by a passion that surged across the family dinner table. She didn't know how to cope with it.

"I said," Willie persisted, "I'm going to have an apartment!"

Lucy looked up at him and frowned. It was quite obvious that he was wrapping an apartment around her, trapping her there alone.

Millicent Strawbridge resented the exhibition wholeheartedly. She didn't want to be rude. Yet something had to be done, and she too turned to the doctor.

Lansburgh was so annoyed at his protégé that he pounced on him without warning. "Willie," he said sharply, "stop making the word apartment sound like 'love nest'!"

Willie gaped at Dr. Lansburgh, but for the first time in his life he saw no friendship in his face.

"I'm—I'm sorry," he mumbled, mostly to Lucy.

The doctor made himself smile at Willie. "Chances are the family wouldn't let you take an apartment anyway, Bill."

"No. I guess not," Willie admitted. "But I want a place where I can lead my own life and invite my own friends."

"Richard," Lucy said, ignoring Willie, "you're the honored guest. What would you like to do after dinner?"

"Anything."

"There's a new night club called the Trocadero," Willie suggested timidly.

Mrs. Strawbridge inhaled deeply. Willie wanted to duck. She'd been so nice all evening that he fully expected her to turn on him.

"I hear all the stars go there," she said surprisingly. "I've been here two and a half weeks and all I've seen is one producer." She nodded pleasantly at Willie.

"That," he yipped, "is what you might call getting in at the top."

Mrs. Strawbridge blinked and couldn't help smiling. "Shall we go?"

"Let's," Richard agreed.

33

THEY DROVE DOWN in Willie's new car, which the Strawbridges immediately assumed was Lansburgh's. It commanded considerable attention at the entrance to the night club, where only the slickest of sleek conveyances were deemed worthy of an admiring nod by the doorman. Parking attendants swarmed around the doors and graciously assisted the occupants across the sidewalk.

"Super, superservice!" Richard murmured as they strode up the steps to the café.

"I'll bet if the President of the United States drove up here in a tired old Ford, they'd spit in his eye."

"You're wrong, Lucy," Willie laughed. "They'd ask him if he was an agent and if he said no they wouldn't let him in."

"Quite an establishment!" Mrs. Strawbridge commented as the man at the entrance looked them over coldly and asked if they had any reservations.

Richard shook his head.

"I'm sorry," the man said.

"I'm William Levinson," Willie announced, stepping forward.

"Oh, this way, sir! A reservation for four?"

He led them through the lobby, which was papered with photographic reproductions of Paris blown up to four times the normal size.

"A front table," Willie ordered.

Lucy poked him and whispered, "He's the kind of gent who frisks your clothes off when he looks at you."

"Now, Lucy!" Willie laughed.

She winked at him but her heart wasn't in it.

322

They were seated at a ringside table. The dance floor was jammed with overdressed women and dapper men. Occasionally the broad shoulders and well-tailored physique of a celebrated leading man hove into view propelling his true love of the moment. The women wore evening dresses, sports suits, tea gowns; the men, business suits, well padded at the shoulders. All the girls who were dressed informally topped off their costumes with hats and furs. Many of the men sported diamond stickpins and opal rings. The nails of both sexes were manicured to a fare-thee-well, and somehow the swarthy, sun-tanned complexions of the men, the pallid, exquisitely made-up faces of the women were just perfect enough to convince no one that they had graduated from the country club set back home.

Lansburgh looked around the room and sighed. "In all my life I've never seen so much grease poured into evening clothes."

"You're wrong, Richard," Willie said, calling him by his given name for the first time. "Aside from us, the only guys in evening clothes are out-of-towners, strictly here for a look-see."

"What about the girls?"

"Oh," said Willie, who could see nothing wrong with the girls, "I guess they're not so hot."

A waiter hovered around them.

"Highballs?" Richard yelled over the blare of the band. They all nodded.

"Nothing to eat?" the waiter asked.

"No."

He looked at them contemptuously and stalked off to fill their orders.

"Dance?" Willie asked Mrs. Strawbridge, who glanced at Richard in utter amazement at the young man's sudden spurt of manners.

"Why don't you dance with Lucy?" she said, with a smile.

"Nope. Come on."

"All right."

Mrs. Strawbridge clambered around the maze of chairs and joined Willie on the dance floor.

"What do you really think of him?" Richard asked Lucy as soon as they were alone.

"That's not fair, Dick," she countered.

"Yes, it is. I'm asking as a doctor and whatever you say is purely confidential."

"You're asking as a curious old lecher," Lucy teased, looking him right in the eye, "but I'll tell you. Just for a moment this evening he—well, I was dreadfully attracted to him. But when I think about it . . ." She shook her head slowly and spread her hands in an attitude of hopelessness.

"Why?" the doctor pursued.

"Oh, Dick, he's a child!"

"I'll grant you that. But on the other hand, you've known *men*. How many of them have or ever will have what that boy's got now? Young as he is, his word is almost law. The things most men spend lifetimes looking for—career, money, fame—they're all his now!"

"If that's what he wants, it's swell for him. Let's let it go at that."

"Lucy, that lad's got something."

"I know what he has and what he hasn't got. I'm interested in him to a certain extent, naturally. He's got power and an intense feeling for it that makes him a vital human being. And I must say he hasn't done any bragging about it to me, either. But he will, Richard, he will!"

The doctor lit a cigarette and smiled at Lucy. "So he will. So what? Now, what's really wrong between you?"

"Very simply, when he kissed me tonight I reacted as I haven't in a long, long time. And that's dangerous. It's not too late to get out now."

"It is, for him."

"Nothing to what it will be."

324

"You couldn't hurt him, Lucy. No matter what you do, just knowing you would be good for him."

"What makes you say that?"

"The apartment business. There was something quite pathetic about it. Although he thinks you're the motivation behind it, you aren't, really. Subconsciously Willie's trying to break away from his family. He's been taught independence at school and run spang into a patriarchal setup at home. He must be persuaded not to attempt an open break. That sort of thing can become quite vicious."

"Not necessarily."

"No, not in your case. You've got Millicent well under your thumb and you've done it without antagonizing her. But some young people through whom the impulse for independence runs like a prairie fire come up against a concomitant measure of parental tyranny. Then you get fireworks. Just let them sense that Willie wants to be physically free of them and they'll have him spinning around like a Fourth of July pinwheel before they get through. They'll fight back so hard he'll be groggy. I'm afraid he'll win, once he starts, but he may have to burn the house down doing it. And that's the sad thing about it. He can win his independence within the pattern of the family, as you've done. Only someone's got to show him how. Someone who's here, near him. The lad's got a great deal of strength and a firm conviction about himself and his career—"

"More than that, Richard," Lucy interrupted. "There's a strange hardness about him at times. You think you've got him well in hand and suddenly he strikes like a cobra. And when he does that, you want to run away."

"He's just a kid, Lucy—a baby, picturing himself as an extremely urbane and important man. He's not sure of himself at all. He knows his family's got where they are by being tough and hard. So he tries to be tougher and harder, when all he needs to be is just a little more intelligent. He wants to do daring things, but he's got power confused with boldness, and boldness, in any business, is based on one's receptivity to new ideas. Willie's receptivity is nil. He's growing a shell around his mind before it's reached maturity. But there's still a little opening there. A chink in the armor. And someone's got to help him keep it open, to help him develop his soft, sympathetic impulses, which at this moment, I'm afraid, are virtually dormant. And you're the kind of person who can do that."

"Me?" Lucy exploded. "Nonsense! You're much better at that sort of thing."

"I've tried, Lucy. For six long months, back in New York, I tried and I failed to get through to him. But, you see, he wasn't in love with me. He's in love with you—now—so you're the only one who can do it."

Richard stopped talking and smiled at Willie and Mrs. Strawbridge, who were trying to attract their attention as they shuffled up to the table.

"He's fun," Millicent stage-whispered. Little beads of perspiration had formed on her upper lip. She leaned over Willie's arm and touched Lucy's shoulder. "And a good dancer, too!" she added.

"Your mom's okay!" Willie said enthusiastically, as the crowd on the floor forced them away from the table.

Lucy smiled wryly. Then she heard Richard say, "I think you should know his family would resent you," and she knew he was deliberately challenging her.

She shook her head. "It won't work," she said. But before she could stop herself, she added, "Why wouldn't they like me?"

"Have you ever seen a Jewish family whose son loved a goy?"

"Have you?"

"Of course."

"Whose?"

"Mine."

"Yours!" Lucy sat stunned for a moment and shook her head. "What did you do?" she asked gently.

"Nothing."

326

She took his hand impulsively and asked, "Couldn't you have married her?"

"She died."

"Oh, I'm sorry, Richard—really sorry."

She sat back and picked up her glass. He had briefly opened up a whole private world of his own misery and she realized it was something he wasn't capable of doing lightly. She leaned forward abruptly and looked into his eyes. "Richard," she said, "it never occurred to me that being a Jew could be a problem for you."

"That was the only time. It's never interfered with my life otherwise."

"Not even in your practice? Grandfather once told me that Jewish doctors have a hell of a time."

"Competition makes them better," the doctor said. And then he smiled. "We like to think so, at least."

"What about your patients? Do they know you're Jewish? You don't look it, you know."

"Some know it. Some don't. It doesn't seem to matter. When I was a little boy, my father used to tell me, 'Neither wear your creed upon your sleeve, nor bear it as a cross.'"

He stopped talking momentarily and looked across the years at his youth. Then he shook his head. "That's one of the things Willie's losing sight of," he said slowly: "pride of himself and of the accomplishments of his people. You don't boast about them. But you're aware of them, way down deep in your loins. And Willie's going to need that feeling badly. It's a shield he can wear against the cruelties he's going to have to face as he grows older. And if he doesn't have someone to help him, someone he loves, he may become quite cruel himself. And the day he does . . . is the day he dies— to himself—forever."

Lucy sighed and stared at the ash tray. She was idly turning it clockwise on the tablecloth. She looked up slowly. "All right, Dick," she said, "I'll try it—for a while. Now let's finish our drinks and get out of here. I want to go home."

34

GRADUALLY Willie became aware of the fact that a second obses-sion had crept into his life. One that seriously threatened the first, which was still to thwart the family's determination to dominate his life—an end which he believed could best be achieved by taking their business away from them. This second obsession would, he hoped, in no way interfere with his first. Lucy might, as a matter of fact, be turned into a very enthusiastic disciple. If only he could feel sure of her.

Morning, noon, and night he thought only of Lucy. He found his mind wandering enthusiastically away from details that needed his immediate attention. If only she could spend the entire day be-side him! What fun it would be to wake in the morning, drive to the studio, answer the morning's mail, and see the rushes together. They could walk importantly onto the sets and in the privacy of their office, search for the next script. And it would be *their* office. He could share things with her. It was only his family that he feared.

How she would enjoy watching *The Nebraskan* take form in celluloid under his guidance! He was making his own decisions now, firmly and surely. There was no more need for trickery or the as-sistance of better minds. He knew *The Nebraskan* was good, and he knew that he was adding immeasurably to its success. But Lucy was coming between him and his work. It was necessary, therefore, either to eliminate this new obsession or weave it into the existing pattern of his ultimate objective. He chose the latter, and by the time Lans-burgh left for New York, Willie had embarked on a spectacular if somewhat hectic courtship.

Lucy found herself on a merry-go-round of previews, night clubs, and moonlight rides in the new automobile. It was while they were parked in the Hollywood Hills one night that she remarked casually that previews and night clubs were not exactly her idea of a good time. Willie, momentarily baffled, sulked before suggesting that the reason they were in such a constant whirl of activity was because she didn't have enough sense to give in to him.

She looked at him long and hard before she answered, "That isn't what I mean, Bill. . . . I want to share things with you. To share your work, to live your life, and let you share mine. The kind of life I think we both want to live. You don't really enjoy all this gadding about, do you?"

"I did."

"Oh! Well, there's so much more to do than that, really, Bill. Books to read, music to hear. A whole point of view to change." That was a silly slip, she thought, and she hoped he hadn't noticed it.

"Lucy," he said, after what seemed to her an interminable period of deliberation, "do you really want to share my work? Because I'd honestly like to have you around."

"If I knew what your daily problems were I'd be able to help you, and I want to do that more than anything else in the world."

"Come for lunch tomorrow?"

"It's a date."

Willie smiled. He wanted so badly to get her interested in the studio and here she was begging for a chance. He'd have her working with him in no time! But Lucy smiled too. She had a duty to perform and the first wedge had just been hammered home.

Willie took her hand in his and kissed it. He turned the palm toward his lips and licked it like a cat finishing a bowl of milk. Lucy looked out over the lights of the city spread below them and sighed ever so slightly.

"Oh, Bill, look below, at the lights," she said. "They're like so many distant magic lanterns rustling in the wind. Look, Bill!"

Bill looked for a second, then he lunged for her. She struggled instinctively—cried "No!" softly, without anger but with determination. His arms were around her, drawing her closer. She became frantic. If only she could avoid being kissed. He had no right to be so exciting.

"Goddamn it!" Willie swore. There were tears in his voice, tears of frustration and resentment. "Please! Please, Lucy, darling, please, just a kiss."

She shook her head and shuddered in ecstatic self-denial.

"Oh, Christ, Lucy. You don't care for me a bit."

"I do, Bill."

"You can't! Jesus! I want to be near you so badly! To feel your body against mine! You kissed me once. You felt the same way I did then. What's happened?"

"Nothing, Bill, nothing—except that I'm afraid, afraid to death of loving you."

"You love *me*?" Willie's voice went treble with excitement.

"I don't know, Bill," she answered. "I suppose if fear is love, I do."

He lunged for her again. She pushed him away.

"It doesn't make sense!" he stormed. "Love with a fence around it. . . . Just once, show me you love me! Prove it to me!"

"We'd better go now, Bill. . . . Please!"

He knew he had hurt her, but he didn't know how and he didn't know why. He wanted to say something, but he didn't dare. They drove home silently and she said goodby as she got out of the car.

Willie had a terrible night.

35

THE MORNING MAIL lay unopened on the desk before him. Miss Holmby had been told not to interrupt him and he had been moping self-indulgently since nine o'clock. He sat drumming a pencil against his finger tips, brooding gloriously on the injustices in the feminine ego. He was angry and scared. His plans had gone cockeyed and his Lucy would never show up for lunch.

It was just eleven now and Miss Holmby was in a quandary. Flowers had just arrived and the card was addressed in a feminine hand; perhaps that was the trouble and if it was, better to take a chance and cheer up the foul brat than to suffer a day's misery at the hands of a desolate producer. She pressed the buzzer.

"Sorry to bother you, but some flowers just came."

"Flowers?" Willie asked incredulously. "Send 'em in."

Miss Holmby entered, opening the box as she crossed the room. "Iris," she said.

"Any card?"

She handed it to him and slowly the scowl on his face subsided. His hands trembled slightly. "Lemme alone," he growled.

Miss Holmby bowed, a bit too obsequiously. Willie never even saw her. He heard the door close and yanked impatiently at the envelope. He read the card:

Dear Bill,

Please don't expect too much of me.

The iris are for last night and the things I couldn't say. They're much more eloquent than I could be under the circumstances, anyway.

See you at twelve.

Lucy

She was coming, then.

The simple dissolution of his doubts left him curiously depleted. Building up an immunity against a disappointment that didn't materialize had strained his nerves to the snapping point. Like Buddha, a little weary at having attained Nirvana, he sat there contemplating the walls with a smile of utter relaxation. Vaguely he remembered there were things to do. He called the set and told Mel, "I got a visitor coming for lunch. Someone I want to impress. If you see me anywhere put it on a little bit, will you?"

"What's she like, kid?" Mel laughed. "Come on down and I'll start bowing the minute you enter the stage!"

"Funny guy," Willie groused and hung up.

Then he spent an hour fidgeting around the office, adjusting his tie, opening mail and rereading letters that didn't make sense even after the fourth try. Miss Holmby had never seen him so jittery or known him to run out to the bathroom so often. She sensed a festive event in the offing and it filled her with vicarious joy.

When Lucy came in at twelve Miss Holmby realized that Willie had really found something to be despondent about. This was a charming person, and a lady—not a Hollywood trollop. Miss Holmby knew the difference. She had been in the business long enough to know that a lady was someone who didn't sit on the desk, chew gum, and say "Hi-ya, baby." A lady also could wear a small string of pearls and look as though she'd been born in them. And as for furs—well, ladies wore them with suits, not slacks. And their suits were smart, not like the Kampus-Kut tailored exaggerations worn by the sisters of Bernhardt whose art had degenerated into memorizing four lines and fluttering an eyelid.

Miss Holmby liked Miss Strawbridge. Liked her the way a shut-in enjoys a breath of fresh air. Her voice said as much when she announced "Miss Strawbridge to see you!" over the dictograph.

Willie betrayed his impatience by flinging the door open before his secretary reached the buzzer that unlocked it.

"Lucy!" he cried. "Come in. Come in."

Lucy beamed and entered.

"And to think I thought you wouldn't come. . . ."

"I was thinking about it myself," she confessed. "But we've had enough of this undependability of mine. You can count on me from now on! Did you get my flowers?"

"Uh-huh. Thanks. And I think I know what you meant."

"What, Bill?" she asked, looking at him as she sat down.

332

"Well," he hesitated, "I shouldn't ask for proof any more. Just sorta accept you. Right?"

"Right, Bill. Just as I am. You do understand that, don't you?"

"Sure. No passes, no horsing around."

Lucy nodded. "We've got so much more than that, Bill, already. And I don't want anything to ruin it. Really I don't. And if you're honest with yourself you'll see that that sort of thing might very well do it."

Willie didn't see it at all, but he had been so desperately afraid he'd never see her again that he was ready to accept anything.

"It's a bargain," he said. They shook hands.

"You want to eat or look at my rushes first?"

She shrugged her shoulders.

"Let's look at rushes."

He pressed the dictograph key. "Miss Holmby, see if the company's in the projection room yet. . . . Miss Strawbridge would like to see her dailies."

He turned away from the dictograph. "How'd you like to be a producer, Lucy?"

"Lesser brains than mine have made it."

"It don't take brains," he confided. "It takes a touch. The magic touch. Pulse-a-the-public, that's what you gotta have."

"Bill, you amaze me sometimes."

The buzzer sounded. "They're going upstairs any minute now, Mr. Levinson," Miss Holmby announced.

"Thanks. Come on, Lucy. We'll wait up there for them."

"You're going into the executive projection room," he said as they traipsed up the stairs arm in arm. "Mine and Moe's and the old man's."

"How exciting," she said, unimpressed.

They sat down in the big leather chairs, grooved for comfort by the impressions of many well-fed executives.

"You'll meet Mel Price, the director; Diana March, John Berkley and Bob Todd, the actors; Johnny Allbright, the cameraman;

and the cutter, Ace Luddigan, who used to be an actor, but he's back cutting now. There'll also be a coupla script girls and lots of assistants."

"Who are the script girls and assistants?"

"I don't know their names."

"And they're working on your picture?"

"Sure."

"Amazing."

"Listen, Lucy, this is a business, not a country club."

Lucy smiled. Bill was living up to her worst expectations.

"Swell room, isn't it?" he asked proudly.

She looked around at the silver- and gold-plated gargoyles leering down from the walls, at the plush seats done in what might be called baroque moderne, at the Greek caryatids supporting the screen, and although it almost killed her, she agreed.

"A little bit 'modrin,'" she said, "but swell."

"Knew you'd like it," Bill chortled. Just breathing the fire of her presence filled him with an exuberance that bordered on the reckless.

The door opened and *The Nebraskan* company filed in, gabbling about the horse races, football games, and the week's radio programs. Mel Price was the first to see Willie and immediately turned on his noisy troupe.

"Quiet!" he shouted. "Mr. Levinson is here."

Now, the average motion-picture unit is so accustomed to informality that a sudden and sternly delivered command exacts a shocked if somewhat resentful obedience. The more outrageous the order, the more quickly complied with. And Mel's request that the boys "pipe down" in Willie's presence was unprecedented enough to electrify them into silence.

So when Mel apologized to Willie for the unseemly noise and begged that he excuse the company because they didn't expect him to be in the projection room so early, the crew took their cue and murmuring awesomely, "Good morning, Mr. Levinson," shuffled past

334

him to their seats. Only Ace Luddigan spoiled the performance. Ace, who invariably came in last, walked right past Willie just as the projectionist doused the lights and started the running. Before anyone could warn him he growled, " 'Lo, lug."

Willie shot out of his chair and barked, "That's no way to talk to me!"

"Who're you, yuh pip-squeak?"

"Who'm I? I'll show ya, who'm I! You're fired!"

"Aw, screw!" Ace bellowed, grappling for the arm of the seat beside Mel.

"Sssh!" someone hissed from the back row.

"And stop shushing me!" Ace growled, focusing his attention on the screen, where one horseman raced past the camera and dragged another to the ground. "See! . . . Just like I told yuh. The scene stinks!"

"You're fired!" Willie shrieked, still on his feet.

"Aw, fa Chrissake, we gotta go through that again?" Ace growled in the same tone of exasperation he would have used to complain about a persistent fly.

"Get out of here!"

Ace turned in his seat. "Listen, you! Moe hired me and Moe's the only guy's firing me, see! And besides, yuh lil punk, all you know about this business yuh owe tuh me, and don't fa . . . *gell* . . . *ill*!" Mel Price had reached around and clasped a firm hand over his mouth.

"Ouch! You sonuvabitch!" Mel suddenly screamed into the darkness.

"That'll teach yuh tuh stick yuh fingers in my teeth!" Ace laughed. "What are we doing here, having a fight or looking at rushes?"

Mel leaned over and whispered in Ace's ear.

"Ooh, Jesus!" Ace giggled.

Somebody pressed a button. The picture stopped and the lights went on.

Ace turned to his glaring adversary. "Jeez," he murmured abjectly, "I dint know it was you, Mr. Levinson. Honest, I dint. Would I talk tuh you like that, Mr. Levinson? Oh, please, sir, can I have my job back?"

"Of course, Ace," Bill said magnanimously. "Let's go on with the show."

The troupe turned its attention back to the screen. Ace snickered softly in the dark.

"The jerk!" he whispered in Mel's ear. Mel shook him away.

Lucy dabbed at her eyes. The tears were running down her cheeks. She'd tried so hard not to laugh that she'd begun to cry.

"Very good," Willie pronounced pontifically as the running ended. "Bring in another day's work like that and we'll be in the bag. We wind up tomorrow, don't we, Mel?"

"Yes, sir," Mel answered as the crew began to file out of the room. "We'll be on 10 later this afternoon. You coming by?"

Willie nodded.

"Be glad to see you—and your young lady. She ought to be in pictures."

"That's what I think. Miss Strawbridge, Mel Price the director. Walk over to the café with us, Mel?"

"Sure thing."

They strolled out of the room and crossed the lot to the commissary, where Mel left them to join Ace and Bob Todd at the cigar stand.

"Ace, you're a panic," Price said quietly, as he tossed a coin on the counter for some cigarettes.

"You ain't suh bad yaself."

"What gets me," Bob Todd mused, "is what makes a guy like that show off for a dame?"

"And just when he's really getting so's he almost knows what he's talking about," Ace added.

"That's high praise, coming from you," Todd said.

336

When Willie and Lucy walked into the restaurant, the head-waiter rushed over and attempted to lead them over to the executives' table.

"No, we'll sit here," Willie grunted, picking a table for two.

"Sorry, sir, I thought you always sat at the executives' table."

"Not today, Henry. Just give us some menus. We're in a hurry."

"Yes, sir. Yes, sir!" the man said, waving his arms at all the waitresses, and shouting, "A menu for Mr. Levinson! A menu for Mr. Levinson!"

"Take it easy, Henry!" one of the waitresses said. She came over to the table slowly and smiled. "Good afternoon, Mr. Levinson."

"Hello, Betty."

"What'll it be? Eggs again?"

"Yeah."

"Does everybody treat the headwaiter like that?" Lucy asked.

"Sure. He's just a nuisance. We keep him around here to impress visitors."

"You don't give him much of a chance."

"You're not a visitor. I feel as though you're working here already. I wish you would, you know."

"Why, Bill! That's sweet. But why?"

"I like having you around."

"What'll ye have, miss?" Betty asked impatiently. "The eggs is good, but I wouldn't recommend nothing else. 'Cepting a salad, maybe."

"I'll take the salad, Betty," Lucy said with a smile.

Betty picked up the menus and trudged toward the kitchen.

"She's a fixture here. Been around five years. Mothers everybody. Tells 'em what to eat and brings 'em what she thinks best, no matter what they order."

"The homey touch."

"Yeah. That's it."

The restaurant was crowded with extras in period clothes, stock girls in slacks, featured players in furs, and a few gaping visitors. Although most of the stars ate in their dressing rooms, one or two of them sat at the executives' table each day. But it was only twelve-thirty, and the moguls seldom appeared until after all the small fry were seated.

Richard Morse came in a little before schedule, sucking his pipe. In rapid succession Fritz Kornfeld, Manny Adelstein, Tim Sullivan, Archie Newbold, and Mel Price paused imperiously in the door-way and strolled over to the large table. Each one with the exception of Price, smirked slightly as they noticed Willie, and in passing dropped their jaws in an elongated grimace of approval. Willie smiled back self-consciously. Lucy pretended indifference.

At one-fifteen Moe came in, with George Tilden, Frank Gallardi, and Jock Merington, the publicity director, jogging obediently at his heels.

Lucy, amused, asked, "Who's that?"

"My Uncle Moe."

"Oh. The man in the saddle . . . and his saddle-ites."

"My old man's *supposed* to be the boss."

"Will he be here too?"

"Sure."

Willie watched Moe take his place beside the chair at the head of the table permanently reserved for Louis. The boys were strangely silent.

"Wotsa madda round here? Somebody die?" Moe asked.

Fritz pursed his mouth and nodded surreptitiously at Willie's table. Willie turned away quickly.

Moe looked and shrugged his shoulders. "A man's gotta eat some time!" he laughed, picking up his menu.

"With a schicksa?" Archie prodded quietly, pursuing a tack that might lead to some amusement.

"If she's good-lookin', why not? Whadda ya tryin' ta do? Get a rise outta me? Yer pickin' onna wrong guy, Archie. Arline don't look

338

like no Frozen Puss from the Frozen People ta me! Waid'll Louis comes in. Onney let him fine out fa himself. No cracks from youse guys. Here he comes now."

Louis walked briskly into the restaurant, nodded to the boys, and sat down. They watched him silently. He stared right back at them, and recognizing the silence as the prelude to a gag, leaned over to Moe to forestall it.

"What's the matter?" he stage-whispered. "We in bankruptcy again?"

The boys laughed uproariously.

Louis always suspected his jokes weren't entitled to the audience reaction they received. Moe, on the other hand, accepted all tributes from his employees as a mark of respect for his position. He was always sure of himself. Louis, never. And occasionally Moe greatly enjoyed deviling his brother-in-law.

"Louis," he said, "dontcha notice anything strange around here?"

Louis shook his head.

"Dontcha miss nobody?"

"Not yet. Where's Willie?"

The question was purely rhetorical. He always asked for Willie, even if the lad happened to be sitting beside him. It was simply a habit. Therefore it surprised him to see Moe turn to the gang at the table and inquire like the end man in a minstrel show, "Has anybody here seen Willie?"

The straight men shook their heads morosely.

"Tsk! tsk! tsk!" Moe clucked. "That looks like him over there! . . . But it couldn't be! With a schicksa?"

Louis turned white. He clutched Moe's arm. "It's her. It's that girl! Come with me!" he said hoarsely.

Moe winked as he left the table and followed Louis out of the commissary. They stood on the sidewalk.

"We gotta do something!" Louis cried.

"Well, wadda ya wanna do? Meet her or get rid of her?"

"She's the girl that caused the trouble the night Momma got sick! The first girl he's ever taken out to lunch, too. It must be serious. We gotta proceed delicately."

"Come on up ta my awfice," Moe growled. "And fa Chrissake stop shakin' like a leaf. Where the hell's ya sensayuma?"

Not for himself, but because he feared they might make a scene, Willie quaked inwardly when he saw his father and uncle rush out of the restaurant. It would be the end of Lucy. He knew that. If only she'd hurry with her salad. Then they could rush over to the stage. But she was enjoying herself and obviously in no hurry. He smiled nervously. She winked at him. A glad, gay wink, and asked, "Are we in a hurry?"

"Oh, no. No. Take your time." He sighed.

And then he saw Dick Morse walking over to the cashier's counter. If only he'd come over to the table, Willie thought, then Moe and his father would behave themselves. Toward Morse, with whom Willie had had little contact, Moe and Louis showed the innate respect of all movie magnates for those who have been identified with the theater.

"Dick!" Willie yelled, beckoning Morse to their table.

Morse took the pipe out of his mouth and came over to join them.

"This is Mr. Morse. Miss Strawbridge. Sit down, Dick. Mr. Morse used to be connected with the stage."

Lucy smiled. "And what do you think of the picture business?"

"It's not a business, Miss Strawbridge, it's a three-ring circus with the stockholders left holding a peanut bag. The bag is usually empty."

"It must be fun making your own pictures, though."

"Sure it's fun. It's the most exciting way I know of to make a living. The most exciting and the most dangerous."

"For stunt men, he means," Willie explained.

"No, for you and me, Willie. Think of what this business has done to people you know. People who were nice guys and wound up bums. From the farm or college kid to the immigrants and the guys from the streets of New York—all of them came out here to make money, and a lot of them lost a good deal of themselves doing it. Maybe that's why they pay them such high salaries. Maybe subconsciously they know what they're doing to decent people and decent families. The very idea of uprooting any number of kids from good homes and bringing them out here just because they won a beauty contest or a dance prize—giving them a glimpse of glamor, training them, making a minor fuss over them, and then suddenly turning them loose, equipped to do nothing whatsoever for the rest of their lives but hang around this God-forsaken burg looking for jobs—the whole damn thing's abhorrent to me."

Lucy suddenly smiled at Mr. Morse. She felt she'd known him for a long time and liked him.

"Nothing's happened to *you*, though," she said. "And there's no reason why it must happen to everybody."

"There's no reason for it to happen at all. But it does. Maybe not everybody. The little people, the underpaid ones, are safe— secretaries, writers, and technical workers—but the stars, top directors, and executives have a hell of a time keeping themselves above and beyond the horrible pettinesses of a business that somehow, despite itself, manages to put some really wonderful pictures on the screen."

"It isn't really despite itself," Lucy said. "It can't be. And there will always be others like you in the business," she added, looking at Willie.

But Willie never heard her. Out of the corner of his eye he saw Moe and Louis come charging through the café doors. He yawned nervously and bounced to his feet as they stopped beside the table. Morse looked up and rose also.

"Is this Miss Strawbridge?" Louis asked, smiling graciously.

Willie swallowed hard and nodded in amazement.

"I'm very glad to know you," Louis continued. "Sit down, please,

Dick. You too, Willie. This is Willie's Uncle Moe. Mind if we have a seat for a moment?"

Lucy broke into a warm, generous smile. "Please do. I knew right away you were Bill's father."

"And I knew who you were. Dr. Lansburgh spoke so well of you."

Sounds as though it were over my corpse, Lucy thought, but she said, "He's a born flatterer."

"G'wan, he knows what he's talkin' about. You're a lulu!" Moe rasped.

Willie shuddered.

Lucy laughed. "You're not so bad at flattery yourself."

"See!" Moe said to Willie. "She's za first dame ya ever kep' company with that I'd give a plugged nickel for!"

"Keep your plugged nickels for the company," Louis interposed. "Miss Strawbridge, if there's anything I can do to make your visit here more pleasant, please call me. My office will be open to you at all times. Well, we must be going. Willie, you bring the young lady out to the house some night. Goodby."

"Come on, Morse. Stop hangin' around!" Moe winked at the producer as they got up to go.

"You see what I mean?" Dick laughed. He stuffed the pipe in his pocket and followed the moguls out of the commissary.

"Your father's awfully nice, Bill," Lucy said.

"I'll be goddamned!" Willie exploded.

"Why, Bill, what's the matter?"

"Let's get outta here and I'll tell you as we walk."

She picked up her bag and furs and as they walked toward Stage 10 Willie said, "They never asked me to bring anybody up to the house before. And you a gentile girl! . . . You shoulda heard the fuss they made about Moe."

"Your uncle?"

"Yeah. He got all tied up with Arline Arden, the old actress. She's practically my aunt now. Maybe they got over their old prejudice, but I don't think so. I think they're up to something. And I'd

342

like to know what. Why don't you come up some evening? I'll arrange everything, and let's see what it's all about? Huh?"

"Sure, Bill. I'd love to if you think it's all right."

"Oh, boy! What a gang you're gonna meet!"

36

SIX WEEKS LATER *The Nebraskan* was released and Willie had another hit on his hands.

Moe, beaming with a personal pride that almost transcended Louis's, suggested that the lad be given his own unit and complete charge of the studio's A productions. After all, the kid hadn't missed once. And besides, the contract could be so worded that Moe and Louis would still, in the final analysis, retain their ultimate authority. Louis rejected the idea. "It's too quick, and he's too young," he said. Moe nevertheless submitted the plan to Case and Ogilvie, the bankers, and it was only after their approval had been received that Moe's enthusiasm, too, simmered down to caution.

"You were right," he admitted to Louis. "We better wait for the next one."

Willie meanwhile went on a story hunt. He appealed to Lucy, who brought him a stack of books, mostly biographies.

"Whad I do with these?" he demanded, pointing to the pile.

"Read them."

"All of 'em?"

"Surely!"

"Whyncha make me out a synopsis on 'em? It'll take me a coupla years to plow through that stuff."

"Don't you read your own stories?"

"Nope. I skip through 'em like the other boys. A coupla pages here and there and I can tell immediately what it's gonna be like."

"Well, you can't do that with these books."

He looked at the titles. "Beethoven, Sherman, Byron, Cellini, Poe. . . . A lotta deadheads," he said. "Whyncha bring books about wild, exciting people like—well, like Jesse James, or Caesar, or one of them reckless guys?"

"Ever read *The Autobiography of Benvenuto Cellini,* Bill?"

"Who ever heard of him? He's an artist, ain't he? You can't make a picture out of a guy that paints."

"That's nonsense, Bill. Read it, will you? Just promise me you'll read it!"

There was such enthusiasm in her voice that it startled Willie and he looked up quickly and murmured, "Sure. Sure, if it means that much to you."

"It does," she said, and she went home and sat down in front of her typewriter. She had to convince him that this was the sort of picture he himself wanted to do. Not the routine Westerns and gangster epics that made money. Something better than that. Something that would make him a bigger man, a man with vision. She stared at the keys on her typewriter and suddenly realized that she wanted this for him—that she had never felt so keenly about a man's career, or become so rapidly involved in his future. The future of *her* man, she almost thought, and she stopped short and lit a cigarette. This was incredible! The power of the man, the whole relationship—everything had happened so abruptly there had been little time to think.

She realized that keeping him at arm's length had been a purely protective move on her part. Absurdity or age had had nothing to do with it. She'd done it to preserve their relationship because she was afraid she would lose her ability to influence him before she'd had a chance to exert it.

That was it, wasn't it? It wasn't because she was afraid of losing him. Not for a minute. She wanted to help him, that was all. To have him prove to her that she could be of importance to herself as well

344

as to him in the shaping of his own career. And this was her first chance. This was what she had been waiting for.

She inhaled deeply and because she wanted so desperately to convince him, to lift his imagination above and beyond that of the average motion-picture producer, she became excited and suddenly the words came, easily, quickly, rolling over one another, tumbling onto paper in a pattern of solemn conviction.

"Cellini wasn't just a painter, Bill," she wrote. "He was also a swashbuckling fighter, a wencher, a liar, and a quick-tempered braggart with a dagger in one hand and a mallet in the other. He slept with the ladies of the court and caroused through the streets with the rabble of Florence. He consorted with popes and dukes and harlots alike. Why, Bill, imagine, just imagine doing the story of this man against the backdrop of his time! Henry the Eighth marrying his wives and lusting for power. Luther preaching a new religion to the world. Ponce de Leon discovering Florida. Columbus still voyaging across the sea. . . .

"Those were the days when the world was stretching itself and waking up. When, for the first time, Man dared to raise his voice against authority, to demand his right to think, think freely, beyond the bonds of superstition, to shed light on his forbidden dream of Truth.

"And men were killed for thinking then. Just thinking, Bill. Nothing more . . . and you, you had the nerve to sit there and tell me you wanted a reckless guy like Jesse James! Read Cellini, my boy, then let me know what you think. And furthermore, I won't see you till you've finished it. . . ."

"Jeez!" Bill sighed in bewildered admiration. "Jeez!" He put the letter down, picked up Cellini and went to work.

Three days later the publicity department announced *The Life and Loves of Cellini* as the next picture to be produced by William Levinson.

345

And the very same afternoon Moe called Willie into his office. "Willie," he said, before his nephew got past the threshold, "I gotta hand it ta ya."

"What now?" Willie asked suspiciously, easing himself into a chair.

"Fa two days this Moffat guy's been botherin' me. Ain't we never gonna make his stories? He didn't sell 'em to us fa the money. He wants 'em onna screen. 'They got a message,' he says. 'They gotta be perduced.' So I brushes him off, deaf-like, and now, you gotta do it!"

"Deft-like, with a *t*," Willie said automatically. He wanted to ask, "Do what?" but he also wanted to appear aware of whatever it was he had done, so he just waited and said nothing.

"You dunno, do ya?" Moe asked.

Willie had to confess he didn't.

"Well, I'll tell ya. This morning I gets another call. It's Moffat. 'Mr. Korn,' he says, 'I can't thank ya enough fa watcha done fa me. I know it'll be a great success, but there's onney one little thing: the word "love" inna title lacks dignity,' he says. 'Wooden it be better just callin' it *Cellini, the Magnificent,* which was my original title?' . . . How ya feelin', kiddie?" Moe roared at his nephew.

"I'll be goddamned!" Willie grinned. "You mean to tell me he's got a Cellini story in that crap we bought?"

"Yup. And that ain't the half of it."

"Give it to me, Moe. I'm dying. He wants to act in it, or something?"

"Worse."

"What could be worse?" Willie laughed, shrugging his shoulders.

"He wantsa adopt the screen play."

"Across my dead body."

"He's the censor, ya know. He can butcher the goddamn thing when ya get through with it."

"The hell he can. He can't open his mouth. He's scared stiff we'll squeal on him. And if he ain't, we'll fix it so he is. We got nothing to

346

lose. And if you wanna keep him happy, we can give him screen credit for the original. Okay?"

"Okay," Moe said. "Onney, fa Chrissake keep him outta my hair!"

"Outta your hair!" Willie exploded. "You think I want him hanging around me? You tell him we'll give him screen credit only if he doesn't interfere. Tell him we got a wonderful idea based on his story and if he opens his yap just once, we won't make it. Wait a minute," he said, as Moe reached for the phone. "I'll do it. You'll get it all bitched up . . . on purpose," he added as he started for the door, "just to see me squirm."

"Willie!" Moe protested indignantly.

"Stop looking like a sick moose!" Willie laughed. "I'll attend to that guy!" And he did.

Moffat signed a special contract giving him screen credit and an extra hundred dollars for agreeing to all the provisos stipulated therein by the legal department.

By the end of the week, Willie had hired two of the most expensive writers in Hollywood, Norman Schwarzkopf and Jack Dale. He assigned Bob Todd to the leading role and chose John Dodge, who had graduated from Westerns to become the best director of men in the business, to shoot the picture. Dodge was bound to make an exciting, romantic figure of Cellini, if he stayed sober long enough to get it in the can. And Willie had promised to fire him at the first offense. In ten weeks the picture was under way.

It had been four months now since Louis had asked Willie to bring Lucy to the house. Nothing further had been said. But Rebecca's birthday was just a few days away and Louis was planning to give her a surprise party.

When Willie asked if he could bring Lucy, Louis said, "I sort of thought we'd keep it strickly family, but if you think she'll enjoy herself, bring her along."

The afternoon of the party Moe took Arline and his sister to the races to get them out of the house while Louis, Momma, and Jacob transformed it into a Dennison paradise. Paper lanterns, hats, favors for the table, all the silly little things associated with parties from childhood days, waited expectantly at the proper places. Gifts were piled beside the fireplace. Even Willie was touched as he came down the stairs on his way to pick up Lucy. "Jeez, it looks swell, Pop," he said.

"Ya gonna wear tuxedo?" Louis asked.

"Why not, Pop? Makes it look important."

"Jacob?" Louis asked.

"All right with me. Let's!" said the old man.

Willie even kissed Momma just before he dashed out of the house.

"Bring on your schicksa," the old girl laughed after him.

37

"THEY'RE IN THE LIVING ROOM, Mr. William," Max whispered as he opened the door.

"Ma back yet?" Willie asked apprehensively.

"Oh, no, sir. Not yet."

Unconsciously Willie and Lucy fell into the mood of conspiracy that surged from the living room where breathless voices were babbling last-minute instructions. They tiptoed across the room.

"Hello," Willie called quietly as they sidled through the portieres.

The family turned from the pile of presents beside the fireplace and gaped. Momma sank into a chair. Louis smiled gallantly and strode across the room. He took Lucy by the hand and led her down the steps.

"It's a pleasure," he nodded. "I'll introduce you to the folks."

She followed hesitantly behind him and felt a vague loneliness, a fear born of Lansburgh's statement that they'd resent her presence. After all, this was distinctly a family affair and she wouldn't have come. Only Willie had been so insistent . . .

This, then, was Jacob, bless his heart. Such a kindly face. His hand felt friendly.

"Welcome!" he said. She smiled at him.

Louis touched her arm. "I want you to meet my mother," he said.

Lucy turned and looked down into a fat, shrewd face with a mouth that drooped at the corners as though the years had visited only anguish and bitterness upon it. It was a thin mouth, thin with age, and capable, Lucy realized instinctively, of malice. But the eyes sparkled. Like mirrors, they reflected all the old woman's natural gaiety, and much against her will, betrayed it to the world. Lucy decided to play to the eyes.

"I'm so glad to meet you," she said pleasantly.

Momma acknowledged the greeting with a grunt.

"Lucy's the girl Dr. Lansburgh spoke about," Louis explained, hoping the doctor's magic name would transfuse Momma with a modicum of warmth.

The old girl leaned back in her chair and looked up at Louis. "Yah," she sighed, waving her hand in a gesture of utter futility, "the schicksa."

"I know what that means, Mrs. Levinson," Lucy replied, forcing a smile.

"De name's Levinsky," Momma snorted.

Willie charged angrily into the impasse. "Now, goddamn it, Momma!" he shouted. "Behave yourself! When I left the house you yelled, 'Bring on your schicksa,' and you laughed when you said it. You were prepared to like her then. So what are you griping about now?"

"So?" his grandmother quibbled. "Vot fun iss liking people ride avay? Should foist eenspect, be keffil, mebbe *not* like! So in ent, comms frandship mit supprice, iss fife times welluble. You vant I should like her ride avay? So, ull ride, I'll like her. Baht if she tinks I dun't like her, she'll like me batter ven I do. Unnerstand?"

Lucy leaned forward and touched Momma's arm reassuringly.

"En' dun't gaht familiar too qvick, eider!" the old lady snapped.

Lucy retreated slowly, as though she'd patted a snake by mistake. Willie took her to one side and Jacob joined them.

"Don't mind her," he said. "She's just an old turtle. Snaps a lot but has no teeth. You'll find her a lot of fun after a while. I do."

"Ssh!" Louis hissed suddenly. "They're coming. Get over here and turn the lights out!"

They rushed to the fireplace. Jacob flicked the switch and they waited in breathless silence.

A car door slammed in the driveway and footsteps crunched across the gravel. It seemed an eternity before the doorbell rang. Lucy found someone's hand holding hers. She squeezed it and the pressure was returned.

Jacob mumbled, "S'not them. They'd be talking."

"Ssh!" Louis warned.

Willie giggled.

Max opened the door and closed it. There were no voices. Louis groped his way across the room. "Max," he called hoarsely, "who was it?"

"Oh, I'm sorry, sir. It was the caterers."

Louis sighed and turned on the lights. Lucy looked around. Momma was standing next to her. The old lady turned on her heel and walked to the sofa. Lucy's eyes followed her across the room. Momma sat down.

"So vot?" she said.

"So, shame on you!" Lucy laughed.

The faintest flicker of amusement flashed across Momma's face.

350

Then she recovered herself. "How long ve godda sit here vaitin'?" she complained. "I hate vaitin'!"

Three sharp blasts of an auto horn interrupted her complaint. "The lights!" Louis whispered frantically.

They all rushed to the fireplace again. The same sounds were repeated outside. But this time when Max opened the door they heard Rebecca say, "Thanks so much, Moe. Come on in for a second. Maybe Arline would like a drink. Don't go."

Then Arline chirped, "How's about it, Mosey? Let's!"

"What the hell for?"

"Come on," Rebecca urged.

Their footsteps neared the living room. The curtains parted. Louis whispered, "One. Two. Three!"

"Surprise!" They all shouted at the top of their lungs.

Jacob flicked the switch and Rebecca stood there blinking incredulously till Moe and Arline pushed her down the steps and into the room.

She was completely stunned. Her head swung back and forth as aimlessly as a captive bear's searching for a familiar face in the crowd outside his cage. Then her lips trembled and she fought to stem the tears. She opened her mouth to speak but something snapped inside her and she closed it again.

"It's us, Mom!" Willie laughed, breaking the silence.

Rebecca suddenly recognized Louis and rushed across the room. He put his arms around her and murmured, "It's all right, Becky. It's all right!"

The family formed a semicircle in front of the fireplace, reassuring her with words of comfort. Rebecca alternately smiled and stared at them until she finally succumbed to the hysteria born of her initial shock.

"Get her a drink, Moe," Arline snapped. "A stiff one, before she wets her pants."

Willie glared at Arline. Didn't she realize there was a lady

351

present? Arline caught the look on Willie's face. "Fa Chrissake, what's the matter with you?" she asked. "A ghost hitcha?" Then she followed Willie's horrified gaze across the group to Lucy, who was standing on the fringe of the family circle trying to look as sympathetic as possible.

"My God!" Arline groaned. "A foreigner! A white woman! Welcome! Say, what the hell are you doing to that kid? Look at him! The virtue's pouring out of his eyes like somebody crowned him with a halo. Little St. Anthony, the big producer!" She grinned confidentially at Willie, who shuddered and sighed, "This is Arline Arden, Lucy."

Louis heard him and suddenly remembered he was the host. "Meet Willie's lady friend!" he shouted across the room.

Arline was the only one who paid any attention to him. She went over to Lucy. Moe pressed forward, carrying a tray of cocktails with Max right behind him bearing a resplendent platter of hors d'oeuvres which they distributed to the assembled guests. Moe tried to get Rebecca to take a drink, but the others had surrounded her and were raining affectionate congratulations on their birthday girl.

"Lady friend, eh?" Arline repeated, looking much too wise.

"Not exactly," Lucy protested. "You're Arline Arden the actress, aren't you?"

Arline began to smile. She had found a friend. "Boy, what a memory you got!" she said as she took Lucy's arm and led her off to a corner of the room.

"You don't really think so," Lucy said.

"Nope. I don't," Arline admitted. "I think Willie told you just before you got here."

"Before that."

"Primed you, didn't he?"

"It helps to know."

Arline drew back and looked at Lucy. "I wonder if it does?" she asked quite seriously. "In this case, I wonder if it does?"

"You didn't, did you?"

"Kid, I came into this outfit greener than a raw tomato!"

"It's all right now, though?" Lucy asked earnestly.

Arline pursed her lips and appraised Lucy slowly. Then she looked toward the family and asked. "What do you think?"

"I don't know," Lucy said; then she thought about herself and added, "I think it will be all right."

Arline nodded. She noticed Lucy's finely chiseled features and the pride in her eyes, and she murmured, "I hope so, but I wonder."

At the other end of the room Rebecca finally managed to free herself from the embraces of her family and sank into a chair. Moe thrust a cocktail into her hand.

"Now, how did you do it?" she demanded. "I never knew a thing about it. Not a thing! . . . And all the fancy decorations! Goodness, it just shows you, you never know what's going on in your own house. . . . Louis, darling, I'm so happy."

She began to whimper a bit. Louis bent down and kissed her.

"Ve got prasints," Momma said. "Big end liddle. Heppiness in evvy peckedge." She dropped hers into Rebecca's lap.

Before his mother could open it Willie leaned forward. "Mom," he began. She cut him short. "Come here, Willie. Just come here and keep quiet." She put up her mouth to be kissed, and then patted his hand. "Willie, my boy, on this my birthday I wish you everything in the world. Everything. And let's have a peaceful time of it this year."

Willie withdrew and Rebecca began untying her present. "Ugh," she sighed, shaking her head, "I'm exhausted. And you, Moe, you Smart-Meyer! Takes me to the races and says, 'Maybe we'll run a picture at the studio tonight' . . . and me wondering if anyone remembered my birthday. Well, the horses did. I won thirty dollars."

"Arline won a hunerd." Moe laughed boastfully.

"Yeah, but you lost three hundred! As a picker, my darling brother's a louse!"

She plunged through the tissue paper and came up with a blue knitted afghan. Rebecca held it up for all to see. They smiled and felt it respectfully.

"Mate vit mine own hents!" Momma said. "Kip it on ya bet nights . . . in case det loafer ya merried ken't kip ya varm any more. He's gattin' uld, ya know."

Rebecca laughed and got up to kiss her mother-in-law. "Don't you worry about that!" she whispered. Momma snickered.

"Quiet, you two!" Louis smiled. "There's more presents over here."

"Mom?"

"Yes, Willie?"

"Ugh!" Momma groaned. "The schicksa."

"Schicksa?"

"Miss Drawbritch," the old lady drawled, mimicking Willie's rather formal introductions.

"Oh, Willie, I'm sorry," Rebecca apologized. "But you must forgive me. I was so excited I hardly recognized anybody when I came in—you know that."

"She's with Arline."

"Well, bring her over."

"Lucy!" Willie called. She crossed the room. "This is my mother."

"Hello, Lucy," Rebecca said, extending her hand graciously. "I'm glad you're with us."

"I'm glad to meet you, and happy birthday. Oh, my goodness! I almost forgot. Excuse me!" Lucy exclaimed. She turned and fled past the family into the foyer.

Rebecca nodded to her son. "Nice girl."

Willie beamed.

"Here!" Moe interrupted, thrusting another gift at his sister.

"Couldn't be worth as much as you lost at the races, I hope," Rebecca grinned. She shook the package. "I'll bet it's perfume."

"Open it and see," Moe said.

Rebecca read the card out loud before she pried the ribbons

loose. "To Moe's Sister and My Friend—With Best Wishes, Arline."

"How kind of you!" Rebecca murmured. It was perfume. A magnum bottle of Shalimar. Rebecca, grateful to the point of helplessness, shook her head.

"Don't thank us. Just use it in good health," Arline said.

The two women looked at each other and smiled.

"From me," Louis said, handing her another package.

Rebecca read the card to herself. Then she turned and kissed her husband. A long, earnest, almost embarrassing kiss. "I know what it is," she said quietly, her voice choking with emotion. She unwrapped the package and lifted a mink coat out of the box. She handed it to Louis while the family ohed and ahed ecstatically. Louis held it for her and she slipped into it.

"Not bad!" Jacob said.

"Nifty!" Moe seconded.

"High-kless," Momma approved.

"And this is from me," said Jacob, "for your soul."

"Mine fadder," Rebecca smiled, pirouetting happily around the room in her new coat, "*immer etwas für die* soul."

"It's a book, *Jean-Christophe* by Rolland. I loved it," Jacob said. "I think you will."

Rebecca reluctantly unfurled the coat and dropped it in a chair. "Thanks, darling," she said, taking the present and kissing her father.

"From me, Mom," Willie said, stepping forward to hand her his offering.

"Ya better put it in water foist," Moe suggested.

"Vye vorter?" Momma asked, but nobody paid any attention to her. They were watching Rebecca. "Vye vorter?" Momma persisted.

"It might be a bomb," Jacob snapped impatiently.

"I dun't gat it." Momma shrugged her shoulders.

Rebecca laughed and suddenly shouted, "Why, Willie, they're stunning!"

"Lucy helped me pick them out."

"Well, now, isn't that nice? I knew *you* couldn't have such exquisite taste."

"Let's see," Louis said.

Rebecca sat down and handed her husband a pair of smartly tailored pearl-gray lounging pajamas.

"Mmm!" Arline said to Willie. "You're learning!"

Lucy came rushing back into the room. "This isn't much, Mrs. Levinson," she said, "but with it go my very, very best wishes."

Rebecca looked into an open florist's box. In it was one camellia. A Pink Perfection.

"It's for your hair," Lucy advised.

"My hair?"

"Yes. Wear it in your hair."

"I never heard of such a thing."

"Won't you try it?" Lucy said.

"Vine leaves, like Hedda Gabler." Jacob grinned.

Rebecca perched the flower awkwardly on her head. Lucy caught it as it fell. "Let me pin it," she said.

"Why, why, it's lovely," Arline cooed.

Momma snorted, "Bevare uf Gricks."

"Where'd you learn that?" Lucy laughed.

"In dis femily," Momma sighed, "ya loin lotsa tings!"

Max parted the draperies.

"Dinner?" Rebecca asked.

"Yes, madam," he bowed, holding the curtains to one side as the Levinsons and their guests trooped toward the dining room in leisurely pairs.

Louis took his accustomed place at the head of the table and waited patiently behind his chair while the rest of the party skirmished around the room looking for their place cards. He cleared his throat.

"Willie, say grace!" he said,

356

"Our Father Who art in heaven . . ."

"*Bo-ruch, atto, Adonoy.* . . ," Jacob, Louis and Momma chanted in unison.

"We thank thee for these and all thy blessings . . ."

"*Elohenu, melech, ohohlum.*"

"Amen."

"*Leolom voed.*"

Chairs were drawn back from the table. There was a faint rustle of silk and taffeta as the women settled into their seats. Napkins were unfolded and draped across laps. Spoons clinked against the rest of the cutlery and the family plunged into the first course, which consisted of baked grapefruit.

Later on, there was noodle soup with matzoth balls, followed by turkey with all the trimmings, and when Max brought a bottle of Chablis to the table, Willie got up to propose a toast.

"To all of us!" he said. "Good luck on the occasion of my mother's birthday."

The family rose self-consciously and drank its health.

Then all but Louis sat down again. "To my wife!" he said, "The best of health and all my love." Rebecca blushed while they drained their glasses once more.

"Alzo, now can ve eat?" Momma inquired blandly.

"You better be careful, Momma," Jacob grinned. "Remember the doctor's advice!"

"Good advice costs money, Momma," Moe admonished. "When ya get it fa nothin' ya gotta pay fer it somehow." Then he turned and nodded to Louis, who cleared his throat and said pointedly, "That reminds me, Lucy. I understand you suggested the Cellini story to Willie. The rushes are exceptionally good, especially the sequence where the Pope's castle is defended by Benvenuto."

Lucy smiled modestly and looked down at her plate.

"Young lady," Louis continued momentously, "maybe you ought to be working for Miracle Pictures!"

Willie smelled a rat.

"If ya got talents, we want 'em!" Moe added. "Ya can work as Willie's assistant."

"Don't trust 'em!" Arline called across the table.

Louis ignored her. "In an advisory capacity, picking stories or something," he continued.

"And then ya can see him evvy day!" Moe leaned forward and grinned at Lucy, an intimate, salacious grin on his face. "That would be nice, wooden it?"

"Well, it's kind of you to think of me," Lucy hedged, "but may I have some time to think it over?"

"Sure!" Louis said. "Take your time."

Willie could have sworn he saw Moe nudge the president beneath the table. So that was their plan. To throw them together so much they'd get sick of each other. Well, Willie thought, it won't work with me, though I'm not so sure about Lucy. He looked at her. She smiled across the table. He smiled back and took a deep breath. Suddenly he began to laugh—a long, loud, relieved burst of laughter. Rebecca looked at him in astonishment. Willie raised his glass to her and sang:

"Happy birthday to you. Happy birthday to you. Happy birthday, dear Mother, happy birthday to you."

On the second chorus the whole family joined in.

38

HELEN CONNALLY simultaneously pressed the buzzer beneath her desk and with her free hand reached over to push the unlatched door to Moe's private office. Then she walked in.

"Yeah?" Moe growled, without looking up from the stack of papers that surrounded him. His secretary closed the door behind her.

"There's a dame outside. Classy looker, too. Says you'll be glad to see her. Thought I'd better come in and check first."

"Wotsa name?" he asked.

"Lucy Strawbridge."

Moe's eyes opened wide and he broke into a slow, satisfied smile. "Send her in."

"Come in, Miss Strawbridge," Helen called, opening the door and holding it for Lucy to pass through.

Moe rose and greeted Lucy as she entered the room. "Well, well, Loocy!" He beamed and nodded to his secretary to leave them. " 'Sa pleasure to see ya! Thoughtcha'd fergotten us. 'Maybe,' I said to myself, 'she didn't think so much of us after all. Maybe Miracle Pitchers wuzn't good enough for her. Maybe'—oh, lotsa maybes; but here ya aré. . . . And it onney took ya four weeks ta make up ya mind. Not bad! Take a seat, Loocy, and tell me when ya wanna go ta work."

"Well," Lucy smiled, settling into the armchair in front of his desk, "there are a few conditions I'd like to discuss with you first."

Moe shook his head. "Conditions! Conditions! This business is lousy wid conditions! Have a cigarette." He thrust a mahogany box at her. She rummaged around and extracted one. "The boys gimme that," he said, handing the box to her so she could examine it. "See, it says: 'To Moe Korn, Our Vice-President, The Gang.'"

"How sweet!" Lucy minced.

He clicked a cigarette lighter and held the flame for her until she'd inhaled deeply.

"The boys give you that too?" she asked with doe-eyed innocence.

Moe smiled. "Naw," he protested amiably. "After ya been around here a while ya'll know why I'm proudda the gang. . . . Great guys!"

"I'm sure they think the same of you."

Moe settled down behind his desk and winked at Lucy. "They hate my guts," he said. "Now, what's with you?"

"Well, Mr. Korn, I've been talking to Willie about taking this job and I don't feel I know enough about pictures to just walk in and sit behind a desk. That sort of thing wouldn't be fair to you, or Willie."

"Uh-huh," Moe nodded.

"And I don't want to be a part of your organization just because I'm Willie's friend. I'd like it only if you felt I had something to offer. You see, I want to measure up to the standards of success you yourself have set for your studio, and in order to do that I must have some technical training first."

"You'll get it," Moe said. "You'll get it."

He studied the glowing end of his cigar and felt a sudden inexplicable dignity at being associated with the making of pictures. "What the movies need, Miss Strawbridge," he confided, leaning forward pontifically, "is realism, plus"—and he paused magnificently to emphasize his next point—"a touch from dramma."

Lucy looked at him incredulously and with quiet anguish collapsed in her chair.

"What I mean, Mr. Korn," she said simply, rousing herself, "is that Willie and I both decided, and hoped you'd understand, that it would be better if I didn't work for him."

Moe sat up. "Not work fa Willie?" he exploded. "Who else ya gonna work for?"

"You," she said quietly. "I think it would be more fun."

Moe jumped to his feet. "Excuse *me*! I gotta talk ta Louis. Stay here!"

He rushed across the corridor.

"Willie's in there!" Matilda called after him as he dashed past her into Louis's sanctum.

"A nut I got in my awfice!" he screamed before he shut the door behind him. "A reglah cockeyed nut! Your goil friend!" he

360

snorted at Willie. "Can ya imagine, she wantsa work fa *me*! Me—
not him, Louis! What the hell good's zat?"

"She'd make a good assistant." Willie mused. "Add a little tone
to your office."

"Shurrup, you!" Moe snapped. "It's all your doin', anyway—
don't think I don't know it!"

"Moe," Louis interrupted, "Willie was just telling me about that.
The girl's only worrying about her reputation, and quite rightly so.
She goes out with Willie all the time and if she works for him people
will talk. But if she works for you first, then everything'll come out
Kosher. All you got to do is give her a title, like assistant to Mr.
Korn, or something, and she can work with Willie anyway. Get it?"

Moe looked suspiciously at his brother-in-law until Louis reassured him with a nod and a cocksure wink.

"Okay!—But I'm against it!" Moe hedged, starting for the door.

"What's her salary?" Willie called after him.

Moe stopped in his tracks. "Ten bucks a week. She don't need it."

"Make it seventy-five to start with," Willie countered.

"Compromise on fifty," Louis arbitrated.

Moe winced. "Ya robbin' some poor awfice goil . . . but it's okay
by me!"

Willie grinned. "Wait a minute," he said. "I'll go down to your
office with you just to make sure she gets it!"

Overnight they put another desk opposite Helen Connally's and
painted "Lucy Strawbridge, Ass't. to Mr. Korn" on the door.

39

FROM HER DESK in Helen Connally's office Lucy deployed all
over the lot. Nothing was sacred to her. She pursued her investiga-
tions with a persistence that was devastating. She invaded the cutting,

sound, and camera departments. She met Raoul and learned that exaggerations are necessary when costumes are designed for the screen.

"There are very few really chic women in motion-picture audiences," Raoul explained, "and your movie fans like extravagance even though it makes a travesty of fashion. Of course," he added, "if we keep at it long enough they'll take us seriously and the travesty will become a fashion. However, it does help us to cover up the extra bulges . . . ." He smiled, one of those you-know-how-women-are-built smiles.

Lucy thanked him and proceeded to the paint shop.

At her own request, her guide on these explorations was Ace Luddigan, for whom she had had an abiding respect ever since the morning he had razzed Willie in the projection room. Ace seemed more than just an efficient cicerone. People actually appeared glad to have him nose through their departments.

"There's such a lovely spirit of co-operation here," she said, as they crossed the lot and headed for the property department.

"Yeah," Ace grunted. "Sure is."

"Well, they certainly go out of their way to be nice to us," Lucy insisted.

"They should. I give 'em plenty warning."

"What do you mean, Ace?"

"I call 'em up. I tell 'em you're Moe Korn's new assistant and you wanna know what's what. Yuh wouldn't a seen a thing if I hadn't."

"Why not?"

"They'd a thought yuh was an efficiency expert."

"Are there many of those?"

Ace looked at her owlishly. "Yuh never know, lady!" He laughed.

They stopped in front of the prop shop. "Two stories of junk," Ace said. "And still yuh gotta send out fa whatcha want!"

Lynn Carson, head of the department, took them around. It was like traveling through a museum of odds and ends. Sèvres china,

362

soda fountains, plumbing fixtures, clocks, chairs, period furniture, and paintings—all the magnificent and insane objects man spends a lifetime acquiring stood side by side in a jumble that made a mockery of the passion for possessions.

Carson unconsciously apologized for it. "Gotta keep everything. Everything from bric-a-brac to papier-mâché elephants!" he said, as he okayed them out of the building, which was constantly guarded by studio policemen.

"Let's go on a stage," Ace suggested, pausing before a call board.

"All right," Lucy said. "You know, it's amazing the amount of materials that go into the making of pictures."

"And the amount of brains that don't," Ace grumbled. "Everybody in this business gets a brainstorm some time or other. I had mine. I tried being an actor once. But summa these guys keep going round and round like they was perpetcherly living inside a tornado. Lessee, Archie Newbold's shooting a show on 7. Yuh been on a stage yet?"

Lucy shook her head.

"Come on, then! Getcha big thrill! Right this way!" Ace barked.

"What's the name of it?" Lucy laughed.

"*South of Singapore.* Wunna them tropical lulus. Cheap sets. Lanscape department puts up a lotta palm trees; cheaper'n walls."

The man guarding the entrance to Stage 7 stopped them. "Who ya wanna see?" he asked.

"Listen!" Ace roared. "You B punks been buried so long yuh don't even rekkanize A folks when yuh see 'em! Outta the way!"

The doorman mumbled, "Got a job ta do, 'at's all."

Lucy and her dragoman crossed the stage.

"They got a new tramp playing the second lead in this pitcher. Some hoity-toity sassiety tart wunna the Noo York bankers spotted in summer stock. Wrote to Moe telling him tuh sign her right away or else! So now we got her. And I hear she's sump'm! Name's Shirley Matson, and I dunno what experience she's got, but it ain't all been onna stage. Leastwise 'at's my impression. But they all go a little haywire when they're making their first pitcher. Either they're too nice and don't get nowhere, or they scream bloody murder if a cat walks across a stage. Yuh see, inna first pitcher they try too hard. And this one's lucky tuh have Archie directing her. He's certainly no rose, but he'll hold her down anyway. Le's watch."

The company was working on the far end of the stage. The painted backdrop, which suggested mountainous country in the distance, was suspended from the roof and curved around the entire rear corner of the stage. Palm trees and tropical plants were scattered before it in profusion, giving an illusion of lush vegetation leading to the hills. In a small clearing toward the foreground three native bamboo huts nestled behind the curved trunks of a few coconut palms. A sandy beach in front of the huts led down to a long, flat rock that extended out over a tropical lagoon. The rock formed a perfect diving ledge running the length of the pool about a foot and a half above the water.

A half-mist floated up from the tank. The water was heated and the entire set took on the humid atmosphere of a Turkish bath. Extras in the background, dressed in native costumes, had been sprayed with oil to simulate perspiration.

Diana March and Shirley Matson were rehearsing a scene on the rock. Shirley, clad only in an Oriental sarong, looked like a delicate, dusky savage. Diana wore a simple cotton frock. The cameramen, sound crew, script girl, electricians, and prop boys were gathered around the camera on the near side of the pool. The director sat in a canvas chair in front of them. Ace nudged Lucy right up beside Archie, who looked around and accepted Ace's introduction with a brief smile.

Fred MacGowan, the assistant director, turned to his gaffer and said, "Hit 'em all!" The lights went on and Fred nodded to the boss.

Archie leaned forward in his chair and called across the lagoon: "Okay, girls, let's take it! Just play it the way we rehearsed it. All right, Diana?"

364

Diana nodded.

"She's a peach!" Ace whispered casually to Lucy. "Stage star. Regular guy. Don't *haff* ta be high-hat."

"Mr. Newbold!" Shirley turned toward the director.

"Yes?"

"Is my make-up all right? I mean when I turn around just before Miss March hits me?"

"It'll be all right, dear," Archie reassured her. "This is just a long shot."

"Well, when she talks to me before she swings, she grabs me, you know, and that musses my hair. I think it might be better if she didn't touch me, don't you?"

The grips began to relax beside their lamps. The cameraman leaned forward burying his head in his arms across the top of his "blimp." The sound men took off their headsets and lit cigarettes.

Newbold stood up and walked to the edge of the tank.

"Look, Shirley," he said calmly, "just run through the scene. Miss March tells you off. You answer. Then she knocks you into the water."

"All right," Shirley called back, "but it might look better if I were sort of in front of her and backed away as she spoke . . ." She turned on emotion 26, the wistful one, as she heard Archie interrupting her.

"It won't! Let's make it. Okay?"

"Okay," Shirley admitted grudgingly, and she adjusted the shoulder strap of her jungle costume.

"Another Sarah Bernhardt!" Archie fumed softly to his camera crew.

Diana remained aloof through all of Shirley's jittery suggestions. She knew they were born of the hysteria that seizes some players just before they step into a scene. But although she felt a certain dignified compassion for the youngster's stagefright, she resented being delayed over trivialities and inwardly she was seething with

365

impatience. She controlled herself, however, with the bored assurance of an experienced trouper and when she heard Fred yell, "Turn 'em over!" she sighed and stepped into position.

The sync bell rang. The girls started the scene and Shirley immediately set about applying the military theory that a well-ordered retreat is often more desirable than a Pyrrhic victory.

It took her less than five seconds to maneuver Diana's back to the camera. Five seconds of apparently innocent, sincere acting.

Archie Newbold jumped to his feet. "Cut!" he yelled.

"False start," echoed the sound man.

"The retreat from Moscow—with trimmings!" Archie muttered. He tugged at his nose and paced slowly back and forth looking down into the water. "Miss March," he finally said shrewdly, "don't jump into the scene that quickly. Warm up as you go." And then, quite as though it were an afterthought, he added, "And, Shirley, don't back away from her."

"I'm afraid I can't help it, Mr. Newbold," Shirley apologized. "I'm always conscious of the slap. Maybe that's why I pull away instinctively."

"Well, darling, it may be instinctive, but I notice it's always toward the camera. Let's try it again."

"I'm sorry," Shirley said, stamping her foot and allowing just the tiniest note of rage to creep into her voice. Then she turned to Diana. "Darling," she cooed, "your lipstick's all out of kilter. Let me fix it."

Diana stepped out of range as Shirley reached for her face. She signaled to the make-up man to come over and repair the damage. God, what a minx, Diana thought. When people start worrying about my lips and not about my performance I'll be ready to turn in my dressing-room key. As though it mattered in a long shot. Oh, well! She smiled an intimate thank-you to the make-up man and turned and walked away from the lagoon toward the bamboo huts. She knew Archie would wait until she was quite ready to begin. There wasn't much sense in getting angry about Miss Matson. She was just a bold little thing with a terrific inferiority complex. In other words, a bitch.

366

Diana March suddenly looked up at Archie. He was biting his fingernails. She came back to the pool and nodded to him. As they took their places, one side of Miss March's mouth smiled at Miss Matson. It was a smile that was seared in acid. Shirley felt a cold chill run up her spine. She was suddenly afraid and contrite.

"Mr. Newbold," she called, "are we going to run the scene through where I get knocked into the pond?"

"No. We'll get a double for the fall into the water. Then you won't back away from her before she slaps you."

"That won't happen again, and I'd much rather do the complete scene. Really I would. Besides, it'll probably be easier for Miss March."

A quiet snicker ran around the stage.

"Miss March can take care of herself, thank you," Archie said tartly.

"I just thought it might help out."

"Okay, if you insist!" Archie grinned, shrugging his shoulders.

"Then I slap her now?" Diana's voice cut like a knife across the lagoon.

Archie nodded.

"That's all I wanted to know."

Fred MacGowan looked around the set, yelled, "Quiet!" and "Turn 'em over!"

"Action," Archie said gently.

They played the beginning of the scene like veterans with an eye to the niceties of timing and an instinctive regard for tempo. But Diana slurred her lines just before she was supposed to hit Shirley. It was done so delicately that only an expert could have detected the shading between accident and design. Tension gripped the crew. They leaned forward, staring at the girls in a sort of hypnotic trance.

It was too much for Ace. He giggled softly and touched Lucy. "Here it comes!" he whispered.

There was an awful moment of silence while Diana wound up like a baseball pitcher. Her arm almost described a complete arc and stopped abruptly only when it struck its target. The water rippled with the sound of the concussion. And Shirley, knocked off balance, found herself teetering on the rock like a tightrope walker trying to keep her footing. It wasn't at all what she had expected. She had planned to slip gracefully into the pool, and here she was poised on the edge of a rock, her body arched and her arms flailing like a windmill. Diana slowly reached forward, and with magnificent restraint poked her with her forefinger. Shirley collapsed and splashed backwards into the pool, looking for all the world like a crab doing a high dive.

"It's a lily!" the cameraman shouted above the laughter.

Miss March stepped out of character and came up to the edge of the tank. "Sorry I blew my lines, Archie," she said. "Let's try it again."

Then she leaned down and helped Shirley out of the water. "Hope I didn't hurt you, dear," she murmured casually.

Shirley tried hard to smile.

The script girl turned to the director. "The fall was swell," she suggested. "Now we could cut to the close two for the dialogue."

"Okay," Archie said and as he rose from his chair, he called, "New setup, boys. Close two-shot at the edge of the rock."

He turned around and murmured, "That's got her fixed!" to his cameraman, who replied by saluting his boss with Hollywood's conventional okay sign, a circle formed by the thumb and forefinger, snapped briefly toward the object of one's approval.

Archie strolled over to Ace. "How ya doing, kid?" he asked.

"Okay. Miss Strawbridge is Moe's new assistant."

Archie's eyes opened wide. "How nice!" he said frostily.

" 'Sa good job," Ace said, prodding the director's ego. *You* shoulda had it."

"Nonsense." Archie smiled casually. "I'm not equipped for it."

Lucy got the implication and frowned ever so slightly. Ace came to her rescue. "What equipment you talking about?" he snapped.

Archie lit a cigarette. "Brains," he said blandly, through the haze of smoke.

Lucy doubted that that was what he meant.

Archie turned, and out of the corner of his eye he saw Diana approaching. "Oh, Diana!" he called. She came over and joined them. "Diana," he continued, "this is Miss Strawbridge, Moe's new assistant."

Diana smiled. A warm, intimate smile. "You haven't been in this racket long, Miss Strawbridge, have you?" she asked.

"No. Why do you ask?"

"You're too pleasant-looking. You know, people in pictures acquire an awfully harassed look in no time at all."

"I think I know what you mean." Lucy laughed.

"Do you, though? Ace knows! It's a sort of nervous joviality. People look as though they're constantly munching dried-up fur and trying to swallow it with relish."

"You just had a mouthful yerself, didncha, Diana?" Ace grinned.

"Oh, Miss Matson? She's not bad. A nice girl, really. Slightly impetuous, but nice."

Archie put his arm around Diana. "March, ya kill me!" he said. She winked at Lucy. "I damned near killed her too, didn't I?" She freed herself from the director's embrace. "See you later, children!"

"Goodby!" Lucy called after her.

Diana waved cheerily over her shoulder.

"Nice person," Lucy said to Ace.

"Yeah. They're all nice till yuh work with 'em."

"Now Ace," Archie admonished, "you know she's really a swell guy."

"Too good for B pictures," Ace snapped.

"So am I," Archie said, quite seriously.

"Trouble with this business is everybody wants tuh be sump'm other'n what he is."

"I don't," said Lucy. "I'm content to be just a stooge."

"Le's go," Ace interrupted.

She turned and walked on ahead of him.

Archie grabbed Ace's arm and whispered. "Ya better look out for her. Anybody says anything like that's either honest or stupid, and one's as bad as the other."

Ace stopped in his tracks. He looked Archie square in the eye. "Listen, fella," he confided, "you been my friend fer a long time. I think yuh orter know this. They're grooming her fer your spot. Keep it quiet. So long, pal."

Archie shook his head and watched Ace disappear through the door. "It wouldn't surprise me," he muttered.

40

WITHIN A FEW DAYS the lot recognized Lucy as the new White-haired baby, the front-office prodigy. Everyone bowed to her, from the lowliest grip to the haughtiest director. Overnight she became privy to the private and mystic huddles of producers, directors, and writers on the studio streets. Whenever she walked past they called her over and asked her opinion on whatever matter they happened to be discussing, and in no time at all Lucy knew enough about horse racing to lose a fortune.

She picked up bits of information about everything going on around the lot, and pretty soon she became moderately flushed with her own importance. She began to really like the picture business and she gave ungrudgingly of her native intelligence. But she never for a moment betrayed anything she thought might be helpful to Willie. Her best suggestions she kept with unflinching and instinctive loyalty for the one person she felt it her duty to protect.

It was this very same feeling that led to her first open clash on the lot. One in which she learned that she had to fight for her ideas, essentially because her position entitled her to certain privileges of communication with other executives. A grip seldom talks to a boss. Most of them don't want to. But when two executives begin discussing a story or picture, one of them becomes a burglar. Lucy went into the fray unarmed. She still believed in the grammar school legend of honesty.

Willie wanted her to see the *Cellini* picture before the sneak preview. He and Dodge had already made most of the necessary cuts and Dodge was scheduled to run the picture for the music department in the morning.

"The music department's gotta have a running," Ace explained, as he was squiring Lucy up the stairs to the projection room, "so's the boys can pick temporary tracks tuh dub in fer the sneak preview, and also so's they can start composing the final score fer the finished version."

"Hold tight," he concluded, as his hand rested on the doorknob. "Yer gonna meet some more bums."

"Sounds like a Chinese riot in a tunnel," Lucy laughed.

Ace smiled weakly and opened the door.

The full impact of the voices inside struck Lucy like a tidal wave. She tried to identify individuals by their conversation, but it was impossible because, like most convicts, the boys had learned to talk out of the sides of their mouths. Gradually Lucy became conscious of the vague, sprawling shapes that lurked patiently behind the haze of cigar smoke. She stood in the doorway and looked around the room. These, then, were the men who made pictures. Strange men in shirt sleeves, lumped together in a mass like so many polyps waiting for someone to take hold and electrify them into a functioning organism.

" 'Lo, Ace!" one of them called.

Ace, standing beside Lucy, barely dipped his head to acknowledge the greeting.

John Dodge suddenly peered around the hips of the satellites surrounding his chair. "So," he said, "you got here at last!"

"Yuh don't need me!" Ace grunted. "I seen it faughty times. . . .

This is Miss Strawbridge, Moe's assistant, Mr. Dodge. Willie wants her tuh sit in on the running."

Dodge removed the pipe from his mouth, rose to his feet, and came forward. "You know this is only a rough cut, Miss Strawbridge. We're running it for the music department and—"

"I know," Lucy cut in quickly.

He shook her hand. "Perhaps you'd like to sit next to me. I'll fill in the missing inserts and montages for you." He turned to the back of the room and called Johnny Morelli, his cutter.

"Yes, sir?" Johnny answered.

"Any sequences left out?"

"Only the fight with the Germans at the lake."

Dodge motioned Lucy to a seat in the front row. "Sit here," he said, "and if anything puzzles you, don't be afraid to ask about it."

Lucy sat down and the director spied Ace making tracks for the door. "Where you going?" he asked quietly.

"Aw, Chris', John, do I hafta stay?" Ace groaned.

"You're in charge of the cutting on all A pictures, aren't you?"

"Awright. So I'll stay. But I won't *like* it!" Ace threatened, sinking into a chair. "Every time I see this Cellini louse it looks worse to me."

Dodge shook his head wearily. "Luddigan," he said, "you kill me! Miracle's little tough guy. Ever since you were an actor nothing's been good enough for you. This stinks, that stinks. Everything stinks. Dontcha like movies?"

A slight titter ran around the room.

"Some of 'em," Ace answered.

"Some of 'em? Well, that *is* something! Ace, why don't you stop being a miser with your praise? Loosen up! Why, some of the boys think you're so mean you'd swipe the nails out of a coffin to goose the corpse with!"

The gag worked. The boys in the back rows walloped their thighs with laughter.

Only Lucy heard Ace grumble, "If it was *your* corpse, mister, I'd buy u-tacks."

And then John Dodge showed the boys he was truly a great man. A magnanimous man. A man who was too big to resent criticism. "Stick around, Ace," he said, with a kindly, reassuring smile. "It won't be so bad."

"Seckon act curtain," Ace said, with a bitterness that sprang from his genuine hatred of phonies.

"Second act or no, let's go!" Dodge said, offering a cigarette to Lucy. "It'll help stifle the stench of my pipe," he explained, as the lights went out and the picture began.

"Hundred and fifty feet of main title!" Johnny Morelli sang out in the dark.

"Lotsa trumpets!" Dodge cautioned. "Where's Lou?"

"Right here!" Lou Shapiro, head of the music department, answered from a chair directly behind the director. As Dodge wheeled around to repeat his instructions, Shapiro interrupted him. "I know," he said, "lotsa trumpets!" He turned to Victor Kaufman, the composer, and yelled, "Hit the brass here, Vic!" Then he leaned forward and whispered confidentially to Dodge, "Kaufman's swell with trumpets."

"And tempo in the music!" the director shouted.

"Victor," Lou repeated, "don't forget tempo."

"What's a piece of music without tempo?" Victor groaned in the dark.

"Crap!" Ace snapped.

"All right, boys!" Dodge yelled impatiently. "We come out of the main here and— Sound effects! Where's the sound-effects gang?"

"Here, sir!" a voice answered hurriedly.

"We go right into a door slam as Todd comes into the shop. Got it? Oughta be effective as hell, Lou."

"Uh-huh."

"Be sure to fade out the tracks just before Todd closes that door."

"Okay!"

"Interesting way to look at a picture," Lucy mused.

"Huh?" Dodge grunted absently.

"I said it ought to make a very exciting picture!" Lucy cried above the dialogue.

"You ain't been in the business long!" Ace intoned mournfully.

"All right, boys. Shut up, Ace! Give the show a chance!" Dodge said, as impersonally as a Rotarian showing pictures of his baby to the boys.

Lucy tried hard to concentrate, but no sooner did she become interested in the film than Dodge would inevitably bellow admonitions to put hoofbeats here and march music there.

The running took an hour and a half, and Lucy, who had never seen a picture in which men were so prone to fight at the flicker of an eyelash, felt that she had just witnessed an interminable montage of clanking swords interspersed with dialogue by Shapiro which consisted for the most part of his oft-repeated advice: "Make here with tones like an organ!"

The lights went on and Lucy looked around. The boys were limp. Dodge stood up and strode to the center of the room.

"Well," he asked, "whadja think?"

A few quite timid souls cried, "Swell!" and others, "Great!" They smiled at one another and nodded reassuringly. Theirs was a fumbling, labored praise, a build-up for themselves and for the man responsible for weeks of work.

"He *knows*!" one man said, eloquently summing up the measure of their awe and self-deception.

And then a lone, small spectator, elated beyond caution by the security men find in mass reaction, betrayed the feeling of his fellows. "That's an awful lotta action for one picture!" he bumbled.

John Dodge ignored the criticism and turned to Shapiro. "Well?" he asked.

"Ya *got* something there!" Lou answered cryptically.

"Sure we have," Dodge snapped, instinctively taking the pleasant point of view, "and, Lou, this picture was shot with music in mind. When it came to those silent suspense scenes I said, 'That's for Shapiro, he'll fix it up fine.' And you will, too, I'm sure. The only thing is, remember it's a *big* picture. I want a big score. None of this piddling small-time stuff. It's gotta be big! Epic!"

"Victor," Shapiro grunted to his composer, "use only whole notes."

Then he turned back to the director and inquired innocently, "What else?"

"Wait till I clear the room. . . . Okay, boys! Thanks a lot!" Dodge said.

The boys edged toward the side of the room and began filing out silently.

"Not you, Ace! I want you and Johnny to stick around. You too, Miss Strawbridge, if you don't mind," Dodge added hastily as all three of them inched toward the door.

"Now, look here," he continued, "you see what I mean? I want this music to have a feel to it. The feel of courtyards clattering with the beat of snorting chargers—"

"The manure track," Victor muttered under his breath to Lou.

Dodge heard him. "You don't like it?" he asked.

"Not much," Victor answered.

Dodge turned to Lucy. "And you?"

Lucy shook her head.

"Why not?"

"I'd rather not say. And it's not my business."

"Please. Why didn't you like the picture?" Dodge insisted.

"Very well, then, because it's not honest."

"That's a critic's comment, not an audience's. Critics don't mean a goddamn thing in this business, you know that."

"I'm learning it. But if the public's money is your standard of criticism, beware of it—because the critics are teaching them to shop for their entertainment right now!"

"Well, young lady, *I'm* not going to worry about it. I know every-

thing about this business"—he paused and smiled self-consciously
—"except possibly music. The boys will tell you that—and I know
that honesty has no place in it. You can't make an honest picture!
Your beloved public's too vain to accept one."

Dodge suddenly stopped talking and sucked vehemently on his
pipe. Lucy watched him closely and shuddered. She had good reason
to expect him to become violent. After all, she was forcing a man
into the position of defending his failure and she had had no right
to do it. Except that he had asked her a question and she had been
fool enough to answer frankly. He sank into the chair next hers and
emptied the bowl of his pipe by tapping it sharply against his shoe.
Then he leaned back and unfolded his tobacco pouch.

"Why, this town hasn't even got the integrity of an infuriated
oyster!" he cried, scooping tobacco impatiently out of the pouch and
tamping it into his pipe. "And honesty and integrity are one and the
same thing. A luxury this business can't afford! It dresses its dancing
girls like cheesecloth gargoyles to please the kind of censor who'd
like to see Aphrodite draped in lingerie. Maybe that's why they do
it. Maybe it's to satisfy the bluenoses. Or maybe it's to convince the
hinterlands that even Hollywood chorines are madonnas. I don't
know."

He's so mad he doesn't make sense, Lucy thought.

"But . . . I . . . do . . . know," he continued, interrupting
each word with a staccato puff on his pipe until the flame on the match
almost burned his finger, "that when you talk honesty, young woman,
you talk art. And when you talk art, you DON'T talk motion pictures.
Remember that!"

"I wish I could agree with you," Lucy said quietly.

"You will someday," Dodge sighed. "Now what, aside from
honesty, do you think is wrong with the picture?"

As Lucy opened her mouth to tell him, he raised his hand and
interrupted her. "Now, just relax. And be careful of what you say.
If it's good I might take it."

"If it's good, I want you to."

"Just keep yer credits straight!" Ace snapped.

Lucy smiled and said, "I really think you've missed the essential point of Cellini's character."

"Which was?"

"The fact that he was a braggart. The greatest the world has ever known."

"And just how, in an action picture, would you pause to show him as a braggart?"

"You don't have to pause. Do it at the end."

"How?"

"After the last fight, cut back to Cellini dictating his memoirs, which he did when he was about sixty-five, and show him exaggerating the details of that encounter. You've got a narrator bridging the episodes with excerpts from the autobiography anyway. It would be simple to do. One shot and you'd have a—what do you call it, Ace? The end of the picture?"

"A tag," Ace said.

"A swell comedy tag. Really you would. As a matter of fact, it would be high satirical comedy."

"No, no, Miss Strawbridge," Dodge groaned. "Not in a million years, we can't do that."

"I wish you could. Just once," Lucy said wistfully.

"Once would be enough. Anything else?"

"Yes. Your music score. May I suggest that whoever does it forget the period, which they'll probably do anyway, and swipe a score from Strauss? Richard Strauss. I hear the boys are very good at that sort of thing. And I think music in this instance can make or break the film. You see, Mr. Dodge, I have a feeling that this picture should give one the feeling of 'Till Eulenspiegel.' Cellini striding through the sky and reaching down to knock over a grocer's stand. That's what most men are like, isn't it?" She smiled as she asked the question, and then looked Dodge straight in the eye. "They could be gods, you know. But they're always fumbling with mousetraps."

There was something so unconsciously intimate about her last

377

remark that Dodge looked at the floor and wondered momentarily if he'd been wasting his time in the picture business. Finally he straightened up and said, "Ace! What do you think?"

"I like that grocer stuff," Ace rasped. "And the mousetrap business too. That's pretty good!"

41

THE NEXT MORNING Willie told Lucy that Dodge had made a great suggestion for the end of the picture. Lucy smiled as Willie outlined the entire flashback idea to her.

"I don't think it's so good," she said. "It would make a high satirical comedy out of it, and we can't do that, you know. Not in a million years."

"I guess you're right," he said. "I'll tell him to forget it."

"And, Willie, tell him why," Lucy added, looking very owlish as she left his office.

42

THE CITIZENS of Long Beach, California, are a hardy race. The town is famous for its sailors, girls, oil, and sneak previews. All four are hard taskmasters. The sailors prey on the burghers' daughters, the girls on their sons, the oil fields stink up the town, and the sneak previews are enough to try anybody's patience.

The previews are, however, of more than a nuisance value to the townsfolk. They give them an incontrovertible check on the gallivantings of their youngsters, who through some psychic manipulation invariably ferret out the right theater for the night's festivities.

They come in droves. High school Lotharios with the first fuzz of youth on their cheeks. Peanut-munching sophisticates in gaudy polo shirts. Young girls in slacks and rouge, with a certain superior smugness born of having wrested nature's secret from under their parents' wary noses, peering through their laughter. With cigarettes and beaux and crunchy candy bars they come into the Temple of Art. Into the Holy Altar where, with a sort of furtive promiscuity, they neck in the second balcony.

Nor are they averse to matching their wits against the inanimate voices emanating from the screen. It's their opinion against that of Hollywood's master craftsmen. And the kids invariably win. Time and a certain amount of punishment have made them suspicious guinea pigs and they defy the efforts of producers to amuse them.

This open antagonism lends a sort of gladiatorial air to the occasion. An air in which the spirit of Roman carnival is further enhanced by the constant crackling of cellophane whenever a member of the audience relaxes his thumbs-down attitude long enough to peel another candy bar out of its sanitary socket.

Into this maelstrom of puerile malevolence Willie plunged the preview of *Cellini*.

The heads of the cutting and sound departments, Danny Gorlica and Dick Hemet, along with Johnny Morelli and Ace, arrived with the print around seven-thirty. They checked on the fader installation, which enabled Hemet to manipulate and control the volume of sound from a seat in the reserved section of the orchestra. They gabbed with the projectionist for another ten minutes. Then they walked outside the theater and smoked cigarettes until Willie and the other executives bustled into the lobby at eight-thirty.

Then they all barged down the aisle to the reserved section and sat through the newsreel in a haze of hushed expectancy.

Willie and Lucy sat together, flanked by Hemet with his fader on one side, Dodge with his wife on the other, and the various privileged executives of Miracle spread-eagled behind them. Louis and Moe squeezed in beside the Dodges. At eight-forty-five, the curtains parted and revealed the familiar title card that announces all sneak previews.

The Following
PREVIEW is presented for
Your Entertainment and Approval.
It has Not Been
Finally Edited.
Please Mail Comment Cards.

The audience, curious as to its fate, maintained a cautious silence. Then came the temporary main title: "Miracle Pictures presents Robert Todd [applause] in *The Life and Loves of Cellini* [tumultuous applause]. Directed by John Dodge [applause]. Produced by William Levinson [grudging applause]. Screenplay by Norman Schwarzkopf and Jack Dale [less applause]. Based on *Cellini, the Magnificent*, by Gregory St. Malden [no applause]. And so on down through the list of technical directors and craftsmen, at which point a lover of contrast perched in the balcony delivered himself of a full-blown and energetic razzberry. The house giggled, and as it settled back to its job of dissecting genius, a restless silence pervaded the entire theater.

Lucy suddenly experienced an uncontrollable shiver of ecstasy. This was really exciting. She felt Willie's hot hand anxiously searching for hers. She clasped it and they sat tensely through the first three reels. She also sensed his agony when people coughed or fidgeted in their seats. She leaned over reassuringly whenever a paying customer drifted up the aisle, and whispered, "Probably going to the bathroom or home to mind the baby."

Occasionally a ripple of applause for a spectacular scene or a well-thrust blade relieved their anxiety, but for the most part the house accepted Todd's swashbuckling heroics in painful silence.

When the fifth duel started in the fifth reel one of the balcony boys whistled impatiently and a few others stomped their feet but it wasn't until the seventh and next to last reel that all hell broke loose.

Dodge's pet shot was in the seventh. It was a long dolly shot taken from behind a gang of ruffians who had insulted Cellini in the street. The camera zoomed over their heads, across the street, and finally, picking Cellini out of the mob, resolved itself into a slow pan that continued beyond a full-screen close-up of his face. Up, up, up the camera crept. Past his chin, his lips, his nose, until nothing but his eloquently defiant eyes remained flashing on the screen.

The emotion of recognition overwhelmed one of the gallery gods and his lone, lusty voice roared down from the balcony as the camera finally came to rest on the bridge of Cellini's nose. "Hello, Joe!" he screeched, and then subsided.

The rest was confusion. The house rocked with derision and hardly another line of dialogue could be heard above their laughter.

The studio heads didn't even loiter for their usual sidewalk conferences after the preview. Willie just whispered to Gorlica to grab all the preview cards he could get and ducked out of the theater trying to look as much as possible like a cash customer himself.

The flight ended at the Levinson house. Max brought in highballs and the whole Miracle advisory staff settled down to a night's wrangling about the picture. George Tilden, Gorlica, Ace, Dodge, who'd dropped his wife at their house, Louis, Moe, and even Fritz Kornfeld, who had come to the preview at Moe's request, thereby committing the unpardonable crime of sitting in at the deathwatch of another director's picture—all of them sat and waited.

Lucy picked out a book and retired to a comfortable chair in a corner of the living room, from which she thought she could watch the wake without being asked to take part in it.

An air of solemn commiseration enveloped the mourners. Moe looked at each of his henchmen in turn and finally shook his head. "Willie," he sighed, "when they got nothin' ta say—there's nothin' ta say!"

"I know it stinks! You don't hafta remind me!" Willie snarled impatiently. "Let's see what we can do to improve it!"

"Store it inna vaults," Ace cracked.

"I'm with ya on that!" Moe seconded.

"Now, wait a minute, boys," John Dodge interrupted, ambling toward the fireplace. "That's not as bad a show as you think. I've seen plenty of good pictures come out of lousy previews. And I'm sure you all agree that we took it to the wrong theater."

"Who's agreeing?" Ace demanded defiantly. "Good preview, good house. Lousy preview, lousy house. You guys are all alike. If the show's no good, the audience stinks. All I gotta say is, if they don't like it—it ain't art!"

"Braffo!" Kornfeld cried in vociferous approval.

"You keep outta this," Dodge warned. "I don't know what you're doing here in the first place!"

"I ast him," Moe said.

"That's okay, then," Dodge conceded.

"Anybody got any ideas?" Willie asked.

Danny Gorlica nodded. "Let's take out the long pan shot to Todd's face."

"I'll buy it, Danny. Anything else?"

"We could drop out at least three fights. We're over footage anyway."

"Christ, yes!" Dodge agreed emphatically. "Take 'em out!"

Lucy thought his desire to assist in the dissection of the corpse amounted, by virtue of its anxiety, to an acceptance of sole responsibility for having perpetrated the crime.

"Next?" Willie looked around the room. George Tilden shook his head. Louis quietly puffed his cigar. Dick Hemet stared at the wall. Johnny Morelli sat poised with paper and pencil to jot down the changes. "No other suggestions?" Willie pleaded incredulously.

"Yeah," Moe grunted, "send out fer a story."

"You don't like the story?" Dodge exclaimed with querulous amazement.

"Ya gotta show me one first!" Moe snapped. "Then I can tell ya if I like it or not. All ya got's a lotta Greeks slingin' spaghetti at each other."

"Greeks don't sling spaghetti, Moe," Louis contradicted quietly.

"Wotsa difference who slings what! All I'm sayin' is, there's no coercion to the pitchure."

"Cohesion," Louis prompted.

"Fa Chrissake, Louis, shuddup! They know what I mean. . . . There's no excuse fa all this fightin' and squabblin'. It don't hang together. Thass what I mean."

"He's right!" Willie agreed. "It stinks."

"You said that before," Louis reminded him gently.

"So what? What're we gonna do?" Willie wailed.

Lucy, instinctively aware that Willie was too frightened by the specter of defeat to mold it into victory, tried to catch his eye. But Willie was so nervous that his eyes no longer focused. It was Moe who finally noticed her.

"Maybe Miss Strawbridge has a sudgestion. She ain't so mixed up in this business so's she's lost her common sense yet. How about it, Loocy?" he asked.

"Well," she confessed, tucking her book to one side in the crevice between the cushion and the chair, "it's true, I haven't been in the business very long, so if what I say sounds like a lot of drivel please forgive me."

"In zis crowt neffer abologice," Fritz interrupted.

Lucy smiled at him. "Well," she said, "I do think perhaps Mr. Dodge is right when he says it may not be such a bad picture. To-night's audience couldn't be a cross section of audiences throughout the country. It was too movie-wise for that. Most people just think a movie's either good or bad and that's all there is to it."

"Very sound, Miss Strawbridge. Very sound," Louis agreed dourly.

Moe turned around and grinned at him.

Lucy caught the byplay, hesitated a moment, and then added

impatiently, "The thing you *can* learn from a preview, and that was brought home tonight, is that a movie plays or doesn't play well before an audience. And this one didn't."

"Very sound, Miss Strawbridge. Very sound," Moe repeated, aping Louis.

Lucy looked at him and couldn't help laughing. She knew how pretentious she sounded and she was grateful for the interruption.

"You said so yourself." She smiled at Moe. "You complained it didn't hang together. Well, why didn't it?"

"Tell us," Moe prodded her.

"I will," she snapped. "Here is the most exciting story of the Renaissance. The golden era of modern man. The sixteenth century age of Pericles, and what happens? Somebody expectorates in the street and forty men drop dead."

The Board of Strategy roared with laughter and she raised her voice to regain their attention. Nor had she thought it was quite so funny as they did.

"Now, why," she demanded, "why does the picture fall apart? Is it because we don't go into Cellini's career as a craftsman enough? Or because he has so many love affairs a modern audience can't accept them? Or is it because he's just a Western hero done up in sheet iron? That's what I think's the trouble with it. The day's past when you can get by with a fancy-dress Western unless"—and she paused for emphasis—"you are unequivocally honest with it. A good picture is an honest one. And by honest I mean a picture that impresses its audience with the sincerity and integrity of its maker."

She looked directly at Dodge, who avoided her eyes, and she smiled quietly to herself. This, then, was power, and Moe Korn had suddenly, perversely, she suspected, thrust it upon her. Well, she'd make good use of it—and she suddenly realized that most of the people in the room respected power not for the terrifying responsibilities it incurred, but because it gave them the privilege of applying vengeance with impunity. It was a simple emotional reaction and one that Lucy had never really appreciated before.

She cleared her throat and watched Dodge as she spoke.

"Cellini, as I suggested before to Mr. Dodge, was a braggart. But you'd never know it now. And an audience should know it. I suggested a method of dovetailing it into the end of the picture, but I was wrong. I see now that the audience should be aware of the fact that they're witnessing the saga of a liar from the very first reel. And this fact should be hammered home time and again. *Start* with Cellini dictating his memoirs, *then* cut to the fight with the two brigands. *Then* go to the bedroom scene with the girl where he brags about holding forty men at bay. Set your contrast right away and keep at it. It will tie your picture together and turn it from a straight action picture into a human and, I hope, amusing commentary on bright men who brag about the things they do and appropriate unto themselves the things that other people have done. Don't you think so, Mr. Dodge?"

Mr. Dodge blanched. He didn't think so.

Willie saw the light. "Lucy," he asked, "did you originally suggest changing the end so that the audience heard Cellini dictating his memoirs, exaggerating his battles and his love affairs?"

Lucy examined her fingernails. The bird was flushed. Mr. Dodge looked like a frozen setter trying to maintain the dignity of a point.

"Well?" Willie demanded.

"Well," Dodge alibied, "what if she did suggest it? It's a lousy idea anyway."

"Lousy enough for you to come to me with it. Fine thing!" Willie snorted. "And you a high-priced director. How much we paying you, anyway?"

"Not enough."

"Not enough!" Willie screamed. "You swipe a young girl's ideas and tell me they're yours and you say we ain't paying you enough! Listen, Tootsie, for every dollar we're paying you we're insulting ourselves. But we're not doing that any longer! You're through! Scram!"

Dodge strode angrily across the room and paused at the threshold.

"As for you," he thundered at Willie, "my agent will see you in the morning!" Then he disappeared into the night.

"I seem to have heard that line before," Louis chuckled.

"And ya'll hear it again," Moe said, winking surreptitiously at his brother-in-law as another happy idea possessed him. He turned to his nephew. "Willie, if it's okay with you, let's try Loocy's sudgestion. It onney means a few retakes. Fritz can shoot them."

"Na, sure!" Fritz acquiesced. "Only I stippoolate my name shouldn't appear in ze credits."

"That's okay with me!" Willie shouted, beaming enthusiastically at Fritz and Moe.

Ace walked over to the fireplace and shook his head.

"What's eating you?" George Tilden asked.

"I never expected tuh live tuh see it," Ace chuckled.

"See what?" Willie interrupted anxiously.

"See it happen in this industry."

"What the hell you talkin' about?" Moe demanded.

"Justice, bejesus!"

43

"UNEQUIVERINGLY HONEST, my ass, Louis!" Moe shrieked, pounding an executive tattoo on his brother-in-law's desk. "The goil dunno what she's talkin' about!"

Louis shrugged his shoulders. "Then why did you turn a three hundred and fifty thousand dollar investment over to her? If you gotta fix things—at least fix 'em so we break even!"

Moe rolled his eyes heavenward as though asking the gods to visit compassion on an idiot. "Ya'll break even!" he moaned impatiently, slapping his forehead. "Fa the last time, Louis, listen ta me, will ya! The pitchure'll never make a nickel. So if it ain't no good ta the company, le's at least get sump'm out of it ourselves!"

"But the girl's a bright girl!" Louis protested.

"The goil's a dope. An arty dope!" Moe said. "And she ain't no good fa Willie. Fa Chrissake, Louis, the onney reason we got her around here is ta get rid of her. Have your forgotten 'at? . . . So, where wuz I?" He calmed down. "Oh, yeah. Tamorra she'll have the retakes finished and the pitchure screwed up—but *good!* So then what happens? So we say it's wunnerful. Then it goes out and gets panned and nobody gets ta see it and we stay ta Willie, 'See! See, what ya schicksa gotcha!' "

"And Willie'll say, 'See what *your* schicksa got *you!'* and where'll you be?"

Moe shuddered and decided to ignore the interruption. "So we tell him," he continued with an obvious effort at self-control, " 'Willie, if your last pitchure had been good, you'da been an important execkative tidday. The bankers wanned ta promote cha.' Then we show him the wires from Noo Yawk. Then he gets sick to his lousy little stummick and he gives the bimbo the air. You wait and see! I know that punk. He wantsa be president!"

"Someday I want him to be."

"Yeah. But not till we're ready fer him."

"He can have it tomorrow for all I care."

"Louis," Moe said, striding angrily toward the door, "you got no guts. Thassa trouble with you—no guts."

"Good day, Mr. Korn," Louis called pleasantly.

"Ah, fa Jesus' sake!" Moe groaned, slamming the door behind him.

Moe's predictions came true, with one exception. The critics were unanimous in acclaiming the production. Almost all the reviews mentioned that it was the first time the movies had approached a biographical film with an intelligent conception of its leading character. Newspapers, magazines, women's clubs urged their readers and friends to see the film. The New York advertising office, basing its campaign on the reviews, heralded it as a new departure in picture-making. Radio commentators lauded it with bells, gongs, stars, and all the other symbols they employ to simplify the process of selection for their listeners.

The ultimate evaluation of all this publicity, which takes place in the bookkeeping department, proved only one thing. The picture, as Moe predicted, didn't make a nickel. It broke even in the key spots or big cities and played to empty houses in the small towns and rural districts where the real profits accrue.

For a few days Moe sauntered around the lot sporting an unexpected and definitely unbecoming expression of satisfaction across his usually dour pan. Then on the afternoon they had planned to reveal the sordid truth to Willie, Moe's face froze back to normal and he burst into Louis's office screaming, "We been doubled-crossed! Read that. Read it!" Then, tossing a telegram on Louis's desk he subsided breathlessly into the nearest armchair.

Louis began to smile at the very first sentence:

BECAUSE WE FEEL MIRACLE NEEDS MORE PRESTIGE PICTURES WOULD SUGGEST CONTRACTING WM LEVINSON TO MAKE 3 OR MORE CLASS A PRODUCTIONS A YEAR STOP NO BUDGET RESTRICTIONS STOP WIRE CONFIRMATION.

CASE AND OGILVIE

"Well?" Louis asked, looking up at his brother-in-law.

"Ya can't trust them guys," Moe wailed. "Ya just can't trust 'em. Go ahead, wire the confirmation. What can we do? They got the mazuma and us too. It's all 'at goddamn dame's fault! We better pull in our horns and give her the silent treatment. Mebbe that way we can freeze her out!"

"You can't do that without having trouble with Willie."

"What the hell else ya been havin' with Willie? From the day he started sniffin' around that dame, what else? Ya see him around the house, mebbe? He comes home evvey night fa dinner, I suppose? Fa Chrissake, Louis, I know what's goin' on. I don't hafta be told. He's usin' yer house like a goddamn hotel! . . . Gimme a light." He leaned over the desk and stuck the stump of his cigar into the flame Louis held out to him. "'Sa truth, ain't it?" he demanded between puffs.

Louis had to admit that it was, that all of them were considerably upset by the change in Willie. "But," he concluded, "he's better off with her than with the tramps he used to run around with."

"Thass where ya wrong," Moe said, striding back and forth in front of the desk. "A man uses a tramp and he's done with her. Willie ain't usin' this dame. She's usin' him—and us, Louis! We walked right into it! We made a mistake and we gotta ratify it. He's so gaga about her he ain't listenin' ta nobody else, and she's pumpin' the poop so fulla crap about art in pitchures, somebody's gotta perteck him. Thass where we come in—and we're gonna get ridda that dame right now, buhlee me!"

Louis leaned forward. "Moe," he said, "whatever you do, you mustn't hurt her. She's a nice girl."

Moe glared at him and suddenly pointed to the telegram. "Who comes first?" he demanded. "Yer son and us, or 'at goddamn dame?"

"The boy," Louis answered, "and I still say you can't do this without having trouble with him."

"Oh, yes, we can. And besides, he'll help us."

"How?"

"Mind if I use ya dictograph?"

Louis, fascinated as always by Moe's manipulations, sat and stared at him through a fog of foreboding.

"Get Miss Strawbridge in here!" Moe shouted through the mouthpiece to Miss Mayer. He straightened up and grinned at Louis. "Just nod ya head and back me up in anything I say," he said. "This time I got a lulu, but a lulu!"

He paced the room and rubbed his hands together briskly while they waited. The prospect of giving Lucy the business without tipping his mitt to Willie filled him with satisfaction.

The buzzer finally rang. "Send her in," Louis said.

Moe greeted Lucy at the door. "Loocy," he said, "we just wanned you ta know that no madda how much the pitchure's losin' ya did a swell job of salvation."

"Salvage," Louis corrected.

Moe smiled. A wan, confidential, what-are-we-gonna-do-with-him smile. "If it wasn't fa you," he continued, "the show'd of lost money insteada breakin' even, as it's doin', and in order ta show our appreciation we're gonna give ya a slight raise and a real tough job ta do. Think ya kin hannel it?"

Lucy was startled, gratified, and very curious. Louis motioned her to sit down.

"Just what kind of job is it, Mr. Korn?" she asked, smoothing her skirt down over her knees as she sat on the edge of the nearest divan.

"It's kinda difficult ta explain. But I'll put it ta ya as simple as I can. We've discovered a lotta waste around here—"

"—An appalling amount of extravagance," Louis amplified.

"—And there's no way we can check it ourselves. Soon as we show our schnozzles the boys start coverin' up. Now, all of 'em—'cept Dodge, and we got ridda him—like you a lot. Furthermore, seein' as how they know you ain't inna business long they're kinda figurin' you fer a dope. Well, *we* ain't. We know a smart goil when we see one."

A thoroughly comprehending and therefore deprecatory smile came to Lucy's lips. "You mean you want me to spy for you?" she asked abruptly.

"Well," Moe protested, fixing her with a professionally confidential eye, "not exackly. Not spyin'. Sorta, say, an inefficiency expert. Yeah, thass it."

"No." Lucy shook her head. "I couldn't do that. Besides, I'd rather work directly with Willie now."

390

"Thass just it! Ya will! Ya see, the other perducers are kinda down on Willie, what with him gettin' the best pitchures, the picka the talent and all that sorta thing. Them guys is wastin' more time trying ta sink Willie than they're spendin' on their own shows. It's gotta stop, Miss Strawbridge!"

"After all," Louis said, "we have to protect our boy, and you're the one to do it!"

There, that got her, Moe thought, seeing the light in her eye. She's giving in now!

"Well," Lucy hedged vaguely, "if it will help Willie—"

Moe rushed into the breach. "Help him?" he expostulated. "It'll save him! Them wolves stop at nothin'! We know!"

"All right. I'll do it."

"You got a great thing, Loocy. Loyalty. A great thing! There's onney one point. We'll send out a memo sayin' yer Willie's new assistant, and ya'll be all set. Onney Willie mustn't know that besides workin' on his pitchers, yer doin' this—er—"

"Research," Louis suggested.

"Yeah." Moe beamed. "Research fer us. It'd hurt Willie's morals."

"Shatter his confidence," Louis explained.

"Ya see, the kid thinks people like him. He wantsa be liked. He trusts guys too much. Believes in 'em. You gotta check up on them guys and see that all their budgets and expenses is legitimate. We wanna have enough dope on all of 'em ta hang 'em if they start crucifyin' Willie. Get it?"

Although the prospect of her new assignment filled her with uneasiness, Lucy nodded calmly. Her voice did not betray her when she asked, "How am I to do these things?"

Moe, overcome by the emotion of the moment, came across the room and touched Lucy's shoulder paternally, and in a voice that fairly oozed sincerity, parted with his big secret. "Everything'll be fixed fa ya. Ya'll have access to the company's books—that is, those we keep out here. Ya'll sit in on alla budget meetin's. Ya'll know why the money's bein' spent and where it's goin'. Ya see, we trust ya, Loocy." He pulled himself up briskly. "Okay?"

"Okay, Mr. Korn."

"I'll tell Willie yer gettin' a fifty-dollar raise and startin' tamorra ya'll be his assistant."

"But as Willie's assistant how will I be able to sit in on other producers' budget meetings?"

For a moment even Moe was stumped. He walked to the window and looked out long and earnestly over the lot. Then he turned to Lucy. "Yer learnin' the business, fa Chrissake!" he explained, with a wave of his hand.

"Surely. But how do I actually get into these meetings?"

"I'll take care of that through George Tilden. He'll see thatcha get there."

"The studio manager? Won't that be a tip-off?"

"Nothin's a tip-off around here unless I wannit ta be!" Moe said irritably.

"That's it, then," Lucy said, accepting her fate.

"Still one more thing, Loocy. If Mr. Levinson and me gets actin' kinda rough with ya, it's because we dough wanna let them guys know ya workin' fa us."

"We wanna forestall any rumors," Louis appended. "It's just part of the game."

Lucy rose. "Very well, gentlemen, tomorrow we begin the game of espionage." She hesitated near the door and turned, looking directly at both of them. "For Willie," she added.

"For Willie," they chorused as she closed the door.

"Next?" asked Louis.

"Next we see that Dodge's agent learns Loocy's a front awfice spy. By tamorra the whole lot, 'ceptin' Willie, will know about it. From there on she'll be on her own."

"For keeps, I hope."

Moe walked to the door. "Thassa stuff, Louis!" he said. "S'long."

"S'long," Louis answered cheerfully. Then he turned, looked

out the window, and shook his head. It was a dirty trick—but, then, he supposed it had to be done.

And so, finally, Lucy saw the lot as others saw it—from the viewpoint of the lesser employees, the heads of small departments, the minor martinets who curry brief smiles from the higher-ups and rush home to tell their wives of their good fortune. She began to understand their psychology, for with the exception of Willie, Tilden, Ace, and her old friend Paul Kersey, the important people on the lot began to shun her as though she had suddenly become a victim of the spotted plague.

Eventually, because it was her duty to attend conferences, she became a party to both the confidences and the contempt of the various producers. But she was no longer privy to their gags. They never spoke to her unless it was absolutely necessary and after a few embarrassing attempts, she gave up trying to join in their discussions. Never having been exposed to the chicanery of cinema tycoons, she attributed their attitude to the natural disdain men have for women in executive positions.

There was no reason for her to be suspicious of Willie's family. She was a well-bred, well-educated young lady with an instinctive regard for the eternal verities and consequently believed in the family as the one measurable unit of loyalty and integrity.

Unfortunately she hadn't realized that Willie's ambitions were bound to conflict with theirs.

44

"OH, THEY'RE POLITE ENOUGH," Lucy lied, as she sat in Paul Kersey's office trying—and very obviously, he thought—to keep up her courage, "polite as Chinese executioners. Ace says that's the danger signal. They're only nice to you when they're sharpening up their knives."

"Then you don't really have to worry, do you?" Paul chided gently.

Lucy slowly lit a cigarette and glanced at the floor. There was no sense in bluffing Paul. He was her kind. And he knew her reactions almost instinctively. "No, I don't think I do," she confessed.

"You haven't *done* anything?" he asked, hoping to press her into revealing the secret they both knew.

"No," she said flatly.

"Well, it all seems very mysterious and strange."

She turned sharply. "What does?"

He looked at her softly, objectively, the way an intelligent man might regard his child. "Lucy," he said, "I feel responsible for you. For your being here. I introduced you to Willie and you haven't been the same person since. Something's wrong with you. You're not happy any more. Is it Willie?"

She shook her head and felt suddenly on the verge of tears.

Paul got up from behind his desk and ambled over to the window. "You like him, of course," he said into space.

"Yes," she answered.

He turned and looked at her. "Why?" he asked.

"Because he's been loyal."

"Loyalty must mean an awful lot to him. I don't think he's found it anywhere. Not even in his own family."

"Why, that's pure nonsense," Lucy protested firmly, secure in the knowledge that the family had enlisted her aid in keeping a check on Willie's enemies.

"It isn't nonsense, Lucy."

She watched him toying with the cords that adjusted the Venetian blinds, flapping the small weights idly against the wooden slats. There was something curiously knowledgeable and sympathetic about him, as though he held the key to her problem in his hands and was afraid to give it to her. As though he were waiting for her to ask him for it. She wondered why. Perhaps he knew. Perhaps in some vague, unaccountable way he had been apprised of her new position and the nasty implications behind it. But how, she pondered, how could he know? And then a sudden fear came over her. What if she had been tricked? Suppose Moe and Louis had duped her into believing in their sincerity and then betrayed her. . . . That would explain a lot of things. How simple it seemed. Too simple, though. They couldn't victimize their own kin. Or could they? Hadn't Willie said they were a pack of wolves? My God, she thought, how could I have forgotten that! "Christ!" she groaned.

Paul Kersey recognized the symptoms and came across the room. "I know," he said softly, standing beside her. "They've told everybody. Everybody on this lot knows you're their spy."

"Oh, God!" she cried bitterly. "No wonder they begged me not to tell Willie. They made me betray him!"

"No, darling. They just wanted to get rid of you."

"The swine!"

"That they are. But out of their secret conferences and cabalistic superiority one consolation arises—the term of their employment is indubitably short."

"That's not true. People like Korn and Levinson go on indefinitely in this business."

Kersey shook his head. "In the end they kill each other off like gangsters. They're no better than that. You can beat them, Lucy. We can. I like Willie, too. The three of us could do it. It's a cinch. Some of the executives in this business are more to be pitied than despised. They're so sharp and shrewd and sure of themselves —and still they fail. They think they're financiers and adept at the handling of money, but in reality they're just so many little boys huddled around a big table kicking a million bucks around as though it were a toy balloon. The figure means nothing to them. Their own salaries come too easy."

"The wonder of it," Lucy said, "is how in heaven they ever get their jobs."

"Sheer ineptitude and brag," Paul answered. "They prattle about showmanship as though it were a magic formula, a panacea for all the ills of a badly run business. Well, to me, 'showmanship' is just a word they hide their inefficiency behind. This bunch can be beaten. And for the benefit of the business they should be. A little of their shrewdness goes a long way. Willie's got a touch of it. But Willie also wants to improve himself. That sets him apart. They're beyond improvement. They keep themselves incommunicado in their little ivory towers and think they're superior when in reality they're merely untouchables. What this place needs is a little more humanity and intelligence. You can't ever sell either of those things short, and we can supply it. It's going to be quite a fight, Lucy. Do you feel up to it?"

"You bet I do," she cried vehemently. "And Willie will too."

45

"YOU'RE GOING to do *what*?" Rebecca demanded, dashing up the stairs after Willie.

"Move the hell outta here!" he shouted, slamming the bedroom door behind him. Rebecca, going full steam, smacked her nose against it and came to an abrupt, demoralized halt. For a frightening second she stood bundling up her energies, and suddenly the door separating her from her son symbolized the chasm that had grown between them. An instant later her feeling of impotence translated itself into a tantrum. The door quivered violently before her assault and finally burst open with such force that it came to a shuddering halt only when the doorknob cut a notch in the wallpaper.

Willie, grabbing a suitcase out of the closet, turned quickly and saw his mother framed in the doorway, looking for all the world like a spurned woman tottering from her deathbed to accuse her betrayer.

There was something comic about her fury. Perhaps it was the wisp of hair that persistently dropped back over her eyes as soon as she tossed it fitfully to one side. Perhaps it was the fact that secretly Willie suspected she was playing a scene. She was too furious to be concerned. The truth hadn't really sunk in on her yet. Willie paused momentarily and continued across the room, flinging the suitcase onto the bed and striding back to the bureau to invade the drawers and toss shirts, underwear, socks, handker-chiefs—everything he could lay his hands on—into the bag.

Rebecca could stand it no longer. She ran across the room, fell on the bed, and with one last, exhausting effort, pushed the suitcase to the floor. Willie walked over calmly, turned it right side up and scooped his belongings back into it. Rebecca began to weep.

"No hysterics, Ma!" Willie cautioned.

And then Rebecca gave voice to her indignation. "After all we've done for you!" she wailed. "All the things we've given you! How can you do a thing like this? . . . Another boy would be grate-ful—glad—but you—you're no good, Willie, no good!"

"Yeah, I know," he repeated mechanically. "I know all about it."

His lack of sympathy for her misery filled her with leaden-eyed misgiving, and then her strength returned. She ran to the door crying, "Louis! Louis! For God's sake, come up here!"

"The family's in the patio, Mrs. Levinson," Max announced calmly from the foyer below.

Rebecca composed herself with difficulty. "Send Mr. Levinson up here. Right away, Max!" she ordered. Then she ran to the win-dow and saw the rest of the family sitting in the patio beside the pool.

"Louis!" she called, before Max could get outside. "Come up here! Quick!"

Her voice burst upon the late-afternoon silence that seems to swell from the grass and substitute for twilight in Southern California. The response was electric. Three heads whipped instantly toward the window. Jacob and Momma were on the rear step even before Louis sighed out of his chair. He knew what was coming and was in no hurry to face it. He hadn't dared tell any of them and hoped he wouldn't have to. Now, he thought, trudging up the stairs, there'd be no way out. He pushed Momma and Jacob to one side, looked into the room and saw just what he was afraid of seeing—Willie packing his clothes. Louis suddenly felt quite bilious. His mouth became dry and feverish.

"Well?" he managed to say.

Rebecca pointed an accusing finger at her son. "He's leaving!" she cried dramatically. "We're not good enough for him any more."

"I know," Louis said flatly, "I know."

There was a long incredulous pause while Momma scowled at her son. "It's that schicksa!" she cried, hitting the nail on the head so hard it hurt.

Willie stopped packing and stared at his grandmother. "That schicksa, as you call her," he said quietly, "is a better friend to me than any of you."

Rebecca's hand fluttered to her heart. "Ugh!" she gasped, with pious indignation.

"Do you have to go?" Louis asked, his voice meek with shame.

Willie turned back to his packing.

"We really weren't finagling against you," Louis continued, "we just wanted to get rid of that girl."

"What makes you such bastards?" Willie groaned, slamming the lid of his suitcase.

"It's only when we're fighting to keep our own," Jacob apologized gently.

Willie smiled a quick, intimate smile at his grandfather. Jacob was the only one in the whole family with what Lucy called "the decent, sensitive reactions of innately cultured people."

"*You'll* understand," Willie said. "I've *got* to go. Louis will explain later, after I've gone . . . if he's got the guts," he added as an afterthought.

Louis glowered at his son. Willie's hand rested on the doorknob. Rebecca's face looked white and tense.

"If you go, you don't come back!" Louis threatened.

"I'm sorry I hurt you, Ma," Willie murmured.

Rebecca looked at him with startled eyes. And when she felt the tears come, the real, hot, honest tears, she buried her face in her hands and didn't feel them trickling through her fingers.

Willie dropped the suitcase and grabbed his hat from the bed. "Mind if I take my car?" he asked.

No one answered. He picked up his bag.

The door closed behind him and the Levinsons entered the last phase of their destiny.

BOOK 4
FINALE

1

"TO INSURE a continuance of unexcelled A product," Willie modestly wired Case & Ogilvie, "I beg you to extend me the right to conclude my own contracts."

"You may make any contracts in the name of Miracle Pictures you deem necessary," the bankers telegraphed. "Keep up the good work."

Willie lost no time in consolidating his own unit. With Lucy and Paul as a nucleus, he weaned Ace away from Moe, persuaded Fritz Kornfeld and Mel Price that their opportunities to continue directing A pictures increased in direct proportion to their fealty to William Levinson, and finally, at Lucy's request, he wheedled Richard Morse into tearing up his old contract and accepting a new deal as an associate producer attached to Willie's unit.

Bringing Morse into the fold lightened Willie's task by two or three pictures a year. Dick would receive the usual associate-producer credit on those pictures assigned to him; but Willie was also assured of a new and all-important inscription on the main titles of his pictures: "William Levinson in Charge of Production." And it meant that Willie had thrust his nose into the select circle of Hollywood's most important producers.

He was justly proud of himself. It had taken him only five months from the receipt of the telegram to corner the best brains and talent on the lot without incurring so much as an extra farthing of financial responsibility. They had pledged themselves of their own accord, without demanding increases in salary (which they knew would eventually be forthcoming), and their loyalty had the adhesive quality of an ingénue's youth. Of their own free will they had renounced positions of security and given themselves up to Satan. Willie alone dispensed the ultimate temptation: an A picture is the apple in Hollywood's Garden of Eden.

2

LUCY WAS secretly delighted when Willie moved away from the family. It was an inevitable schism and since it came on the heels of her betrayal by Moe and Louis, she took it as a personal vindication.

She was grateful for the opportunity to entrench herself even more solidly in his life. Now there would be no outside disturbances, no family interference. Willie was free. And out of his freedom she hoped to fashion a companionship neither of them had had together. It was a delicate operation, requiring patience. And she proceeded cautiously lest he misunderstand her motives, which were based not on revenge, as he might have suspected, but rather on a genuine desire to share more of herself than had previously been possible.

First she got him temporarily settled in a hotel room which they used as a base of operations to scour the town, evenings on end, in search of a suitable apartment for him. This was not easy, for there are only two kinds of apartments in Hollywood. The dank and the swank. The former reek of the efforts of cadaverous Hall Room Boys to preserve their identity in a town where great wealth and abject poverty are but a few short weeks apart. Living on allowances, wits, or slender remittances, men and women either sliding down or trying to find the ladder of fame leave in each room an aura of their own ineptitude. Somehow the walls reflect their simulated gaiety, their valiant, bitter-lipped defeat. The ghosts of women lie undone upon the beds. Here, for a moment, one stole ecstasy from failure—another, anodyne from pain. Here, for a moment, one could see men sitting quiet before typewriters, eying the keys and searching for the clue. Here, by a window, men stared at empty pages, probed for infinity, and found a word instead. Here, then, men sat and looked into the sun and took their bitterness to bed.

Of this misery, which is the core of Hollywood, Willie and Lucy saw none. Willie did what was expected of him and stuck to his income bracket.

But even the hushed elegance of Hollywood's more sumptuous suites exudes an aura of its own. Behind the haughty doormen, servile maids, and obsequious elevator boys, Lucy sensed the stealthy finger of impermanence. In the plushy softness of a new-laid rug, the dulcet unctuousness of a manager, the proud look accompanying the confession of an elevator boy that he had "been on the job THREE years"—in all these she sensed a tragic striving for solidity. A solidity that could never manifest itself in a town that reflected the emotional instability of its major industry, a business founded on evanescent shadows.

The past lived quickly in these places. So quickly and so vividly that the walls were permanently scarred with memories. Here in this angular, modern room sat ghosts of coatless men sucking cigars, deciding destiny through pudgy lips, and with a single word denying livelihood to those who were their betters. Here, in another room, ornate with Spanish oak, sat other ghosts, conniving with suspicious eye to oust their predecessors. Each in his time. Each to his own success. Each to his own demise.

She would have none of these. No ghosts for Willie's room. This was to be his home. A place that she would build. A sanctuary for a man who'd known no peace—and who, she hoped, would find it in her image.

They drove around town for three weeks until they found the right apartment in a new two-story Colonial building just off the Sunset Strip between Hollywood and Beverly Hills. The rent was quite high—two hundred fifty dollars a month—but that included maid service, linen, garage, electricity, heat, and water. And tenants were privileged to use the tennis courts and swimming pool adjoining the gardens in the rear of the building, without extra charge.

Willie thought it was all wonderful.

His own apartment had obviously withstood the onslaught of an interior decorator and come out quite well. The focal point of the living room was a large brick fireplace, on each side of which white bookshelves ran up to the ceiling. A mirror over the fireplace gave an illusion of greater depth to the room, and the furniture harmonized pleasantly with the striped wallpaper of the Regency period. The decorator had disguised the door to the kitchen by papering it with the same design as the rest of the room; and by putting a comfortable armchair with a lamp and end table beside it in the corner between the large bay window and the bookshelves, he had managed to give a semblance of privacy to a spot that was perfect for reading. It was one of those rare, warm, inviting rooms that immediately put people at ease.

The bedroom was large and masculine. No frills, but the closets had shoe and tie racks, and the bed was the kind that definitely kept its four feet on the floor.

This, then, was Willie's home, and Lucy determined to make the best of it. She lined his shelves with carefully selected books. Novels like *Jean-Christophe, Of Human Bondage, The Magic Mountain,* and *The Old Wives' Tale.* Biographies that scanned history from Plutarch's *Lives* to *The Autobiography of Lincoln Steffens.* The poetry of Walt Whitman, the English romanticists, Robinson Jeffers, and the modern American poets—all of them marched side by side down Willie Levinson's library and, but for Lucy, it would have been a lonely parade.

She began to arouse his interest quite casually, slowly, carefully. In discussing a script she would from time to time draw analogies and prove her points by referring to the volumes on his shelves, and gradually Willie found himself thumbing more and more often through his library.

406

Eventually they settled down to a routine of his own making. Three evenings a week, or more if possible, they spent in his apartment, and while he read she often worked on scripts. It was a warm, wonderful, and friendly relationship, of particular gratification to Lucy because she found her presence stimulated rather than disturbed him.

Occasionally they discussed the things he'd read and as they talked about the application of literature to daily life, she carefully instilled and nourished in him the conviction that each new volume, every author, was his own discovery. It was inevitable that he should become interested in books. He had been born with intelligent curiosity. It was part of his heritage from Jacob.

Out of this experience with the printed word came a new mind, nurtured on the premise that a man who puts his thoughts to paper knows more of moral and amusing conduct than his fellow man. If that premise held true, and it could be sorely doubted, Willie's metamorphosis presaged great things to come.

But Lucy had unwittingly fostered a galloping consummation with culture, and the results of it were far beyond her expectations.

To begin with, he became self-consciously impressed with his own superiority. His speech became a cross between the idiom of the studio and the ponderous syllables of time. It was obvious that his associates were destined for a new adventure, because his knowledge consumed him with a burning fervor and he felt it his bounden duty to spread the word.

Savonarola was off on a new crusade. Pictures became his pulpit and the ignorant children who made them, his unwilling acolytes. "Taste," he preached, "is the definable difference between a genius and a booby. . . . Our pictures must be intelligently attuned to the modern tempo!"

There was something unconvincing about a Savonarola who hitched up his cassock and took to roller skates. Something unconvincing, undignified, and ominous.

3

SOME OF WILLIE'S ACCOMPLICES began to discern the faint glimmer of a halo forming around his head. There was as yet no concrete evidence of his having been knighted by the immortals, but his step was livelier and his manner more vital and less recalcitrant than it had been in the heyday of his egomania.

He had three more successful shows under his belt. *Revoked*, a comedy for which he imported the entire New York stage cast; *The Whistling Man*, in which Fritz Kornfeld discovered that his directorial métier lay in exposing the neurotic impulses that drive sane men to murder; and *Peter the Great*, a supercataclysmic spectacle, introducing to the confines of the screen Walter Merrick, a celebrated stage actor. But Willie managed to take even the well-merited kudos for these pictures in his stride. He was beginning to unbend. He became more courteous to the unimportant people on the lot, who in turn came to adore him. Secretaries smiled honestly as he passed them. And when he walked on the set, the grips greeted him with a respectful "Morning, Mr. Levinson."

Young Mr. Levinson had acquired this new personality so painlessly that he wasn't even aware of it when Miss Holmby rang the dictograph one fine afternoon and announced, "Mr. Levinson would like to see you."

"If he wants to see me"—Willie winked at Lucy, who lay on the couch in slacks, with Raoul's sketches propped up on her knees —"let him come down. I'll be in the office for another half hour."

Lucy peered over the sketches at Willie and shook her head.

"Tsk! tsk!" she chided. "Your own father!" Then she yawned and gently allowed her feet to drop to the floor. She studied them

408

intently for some time before she turned and looked up at Willie. It was an abrupt, affectionate look. There was really nothing to say. She hugged Raoul's drawings to her bosom and started for the door.

"Please stay," Willie entreated.

"It will be quite awkward. You haven't really spoken to him since you left the house, you know. . . . I'd rather not."

"Please do, darling."

He looked at her earnestly for just a moment, then relaxed into the casual executive-assistant relationship that had gradually come to govern their business contacts.

Lucy was grateful for this barrier. It was friendly without being intimate, comfortable without being the least bit compromising, and informal enough to make her job fun. Their roles were instinctively reversed the moment they left the studio, but during the day they hid behind it like nocturnal creatures seeking refuge from the sun.

Lucy smiled softly at him. "All right," she said. "I'll stay if you really want me to." Then she became very businesslike and spread her sheaf of sketches across his desk. "About these costumes. I think we ought to go outside the studio for Miss March's clothes. Raoul hasn't caught them at all. And she's not the kind to complain about them. So it's up to us to protect her. Irene or Howard Greer, or any one of a dozen designers could whip up just what she needs. But not Raoul. She's just not his type. What do you think?"

"Whatever you say," Willie acquiesced impatiently.

He was nervous about the impending meeting with his father. It wasn't that he felt insecure or that he doubted his ability to cope with any argument that Louis might use to persuade him to come home; it was just that he realized that one has to be doubly firm with one's relatives. The blood ties are so strong that one's negatives seem to quail before them. And he didn't want to hurt Louis. Yet he was quite aware that he might have to, and the prospect of doing so disturbed him greatly.

Miss Holmby buzzed the dictograph. "Mr. Levinson to see you."

"Send him in. Sit there, Lucy. In the comfortable chair. We'll put the old man in the hot seat."

"Gently, Willie!" Lucy chided. "Gently."

The door opened.

"I thought we'd be alone," Louis said, crossing to the chair beside the desk.

Lucy got up, gathered her sketches, and tucked them under her arm. "Excuse me, Bill," she pleaded, "but I must go."

"Toilets and tombstones . . . if ya gotta go, ya gotta go!" Willie laughed uneasily.

"Your jokes are funny but your timing's bad," Lucy said, as she closed the door.

"Well?" Willie asked his father.

"It's about your mother. She shouldn't be made to suffer because of something Moe and I've done. She hasn't complained, understand. It's just that she's so—well, listless and tired-looking. She hasn't been the same, Willie. She misses you. And I do too. Come back with us. Please." Louis noted the look on his son's face and hastily added, "If you can't do that, at least come visit us on Friday nights for dinner."

"Nothing doing."

"It's just one night a week, Willie. That's not asking much."

"Friday nights for dinner!" Willie snapped. "So you can all sit around and make cracks about Lucy. No, thanks, Pop! I'm through. And at this point I don't owe any of you a damned thing!"

The blood ran out of Louis's face. His eyes narrowed and he suddenly looked as determined as a sharpened pencil point.

"You owe us nothing?" he repeated belligerently.

"From the day you started using my girl as a pincushion—nothing!"

"Let me tell you something, young man, you owe us everything!"

Willie lit a cigarette and nodded patiently.

410

"We clothed you, fed you, nursed you. When you were sick we held you in our arms. Your problems were our problems. Our hearts were yours. There was no division of ambitions, or instincts, or desires. We were a family!"

"You did nothing for me that other parents don't do—except that you did a little more. You connived with my uncle against me."

"Willie, I confessed to that and apologized for it. Perhaps I've been too easily swayed by Moe. Sometimes he's too clever for his own good."

"—and yours," Willie added, without malice. "He put you in the movie business, Pop, and we're in it for keeps. Blood, if necessary. You guys are old-hat now. You don't know what's going on around you. This industry's growing up. It's gonna do great things. And I'm growing with it! That's why I'm sticking to my guns."

"Willie, Willie, talk sense!" Louis pleaded. "Think of all the things we've done for you and forgive us this once."

"It's been more than once."

Louis ignored him. "We bought you the best clothes," he continued, "let you stay in pictures when you should have been at school. Sent you to the finest school in the country, and now look at the thanks we get."

"Thanks, me eye! An education is the inalienable right of every American."

"Inalienable right, poppycock!" Louis spluttered indignantly. "What's got into you, anyway? What kinda meshuggina talk is that? Inalienable right. The only inalienable right of every American is to be wrong!"

"In that case," Willie said, "the Levinsons came over with the Indians."

"Willie, for God's sake, this is no time for jokes! Your mother's a sick woman! I'm throwing my pride out the window! Begging you to come home and you sit there making wisecracks. For heaven's sake, Willie, think! Think way back! We love you. We love you because—well, because you're ours and if it wasn't for us you wouldn't

411

be here today. Sometimes you make me think it might have been better that way. Please, please come home. I won't ask you again."

Louis looked at his son and waited.

"Pop," Willie finally said, "don't misunderstand me. Try as I might, I can't help loving you and Ma and Jake, but I'm on my own from here in."

"We love you too, Willie. It's because we love you that this hurts so much."

Willie's voice suddenly became tense and strident. "Listen, Pa," he cried, "this is the way it's gotta be, understand. There's no way out. None. Unless you take Lucy into your house as gladly as you'd take me."

Louis drew back, frowning. The implication of his son's statement made him suck in his breath hard. He gasped, "Are you going to marry that girl?"

Willie hedged. He wanted to say yes, but he hadn't asked her and if she turned him down, they'd throw it in his face forever. He thought quickly, and finally said, "If I do, I want her to be as welcome as I am."

"She's got nothing to do with it!"

"I think she has."

Louis's lips compressed with anger. "Then you won't come home?"

Willie shook his head.

"All right," Louis threatened, "if that's the way you want it, that's the way you'll have it! We'll fix you, young man!" He pounded his fist on the desk, then turned abruptly and stalked toward the door. Halfway across the room he paused and looked over his shoulder. "But good!" he added in an icy tone.

The door slammed behind him and a curious late-afternoon silence filled the office. Willie looked straight ahead. Then he lowered his eyes and gazed aimlessly at the blotter for a long, long time.

412

4

PHINEAS CASE sat behind his mahogany desk thumping a leather-tooled paper knife end over end.

"An answer to Mr. William Levinson," Mr. Case grumbled to his male secretary, who adjusted his spectacles and notebook in a brusque gesture of preparation which had, with the passing of many years, become an unconscious ritual.

The metallic point of the paper knife continued clicking an obbligato against the glass-topped desk.

Mr. Case cleared his throat. "Messrs. Korn and Levinson, Sr., have no right to take you off the payroll without our consent. The matter was never discussed with us and I assure you that had we been consulted, you would have been immediately and properly advised of our decision which, in this case, would have been a negative one. In view of the apparently unsettled conditions prevailing on the West Coast you may expect Mrs. Case and myself in Los Angeles by the middle of next week. In the meantime your salary will be paid out of our New York office as of this date. Sincere regards, Case and Ogilvie, etc. . . . Call Mrs. Case and make the necessary train reservations. We'll stop at the Town House in Los Angeles."

5

THE TRANSPORTATION DEPARTMENT'S special cabriolet assigned to collecting important dignitaries sped down Sunset Boulebard. The Reception Committee sat in the back seat separated by an armrest. A cigarette jiggled nervously in the young man's hand and he kept looking at his watch. The young lady shook her head and laughed at him.

"There's plenty of time, Willie," she said. "Relax."

"I'm scared, Lucy. I never met a banker before."

"Don't let that worry you. My family's lousy with them. In big towns, they belong to the best clubs. In small ones, they're pious Rotarians."

Willie settled back in his seat. "Well, we'll make it all right," he said.

"If Moe and Louis knew what we were doing they'd die!" Lucy chuckled.

"They don't—thank God! Say, Case's wire didn't say anything about where they were going to stay, did it?"

"No. We'll settle them in the Beverly-Wilshire Hotel and keep them to ourselves for the next two days. Then we can spring them on the studio. I'm really looking forward to this. . . . I want to see Moe's face when you say, 'Mr. Korn, this is Mr. Case, from New York.' Incidentally, Mother thinks she went to school with Cornelia Case, but I wouldn't trust her. At times it seems as though Mother went to school with half the country."

The car pulled up at the station.

"We've still got ten minutes," Lucy said, looking up at the big clock.

414

"I hope they like us," Willie prayed through clenched teeth as he followed her onto the pavement.

They walked through the waiting room up onto the platform, where they leaned against an empty baggage truck and smoked cigarettes in apprehensive silence.

A redcap ambled up to them. "You Mister William Levinson?" he asked.

Willie nodded.

"There's a message foh yuh at the info'mation desk. This way, suh."

"What is it?" Willie demanded.

The redcap beamed apologetically. "They wouldn't tell me, suh."

"I wonder if those guys . . ." Willie speculated.

Lucy shrugged her shoulders. "It couldn't be. They don't know. It's probably from the Cases. Maybe they're not on this train. You'd better go."

"Meet me here."

"Right. Hurry!"

Lucy paced up and down the platform. It was deserted but for a few groups of redcaps standing in knots a car-length apart. She felt uneasy. Surely more people were coming down to greet other passengers. She stopped a passing porter.

"Could you tell me where Car A2 will be?"

"Jes' about wheah yuh standin', lady," he said cheerfully.

He walked on and she frowned. He had seemed to be—well, she wasn't quite sure, but he could have been laughing at her. It was a cold, foggy morning and she wished Willie would return.

Five minutes passed and then another five. She heard a train whistle in the yards and she became frantic. Here it was. And where was Willie? She saw the engine puffing toward her. Saw it nose like a blimp into its hangar between the track beside her platform and the one across the roadbed. Above the clatter of its pistons she screamed to a passing redcap, "Is that the Streamliner?"

415

"No, ma'am, it's five minutes late," he shouted. "Thass jes' a local. Thass ten minutes late."

She sighed. A loud, thankful sigh.

Five more minutes. She walked back and forth, pausing anxiously every time she passed a passenger ramp to look down for Willie.

She opened her bag and lit another cigarette. Then she looked at herself in the mirror and adjusted the angle of her hat, which was one of those pert, flowery straws. She gave her hair a final pat and rummaged through her change purse until she found a quarter. She gave it to a porter and told him to run down to the information desk and bring Mr. William Levinson right back to her.

She heard a long, low, honking noise. Something that sounded like a cross between a cow and a foghorn. For a moment she giggled, then she looked down the tracks. That was it. The Streamliner. It was coming.

She became so panicky her legs shook beneath her. The train was gliding past. It was stopping. She looked at the car numbers rolling by, but she could hardly read them. It was stupid to be this nervous. Was that Car A2? There, near the ramp? It was! She ran over and stood at the top of the ramp while the porters let down the step-section—and then it happened.

From nowhere, Lucy was suddenly caught up in a maelstrom of still photographers exploding flashlight bulbs as the Cases descended the steps. Beaming, scraping publicity men posed their victims alone and with studio stock girls in bathing suits. A brass band blared "For He's a Jolly Good Fellow!" And Moe and Louis, after bowing obsequious greetings and smiling for pictures, started down the platform with their banker. Lucy tried frantically to push her way through the band, only to run into the business end of a slide trombone. She got a quick, bewildering glimpse of a very frightened couple and found herself pinned against the wall half way down the ramp.

Lucy shook with anger and, blinded by her tears, struck out

416

furiously at the vague shapes parading past her. But it was useless. The band marched on. Cornets, trumpets, fifes, and bass drums slammed her back against the wall again. She kicked the last man in the line, who turned around and cursed her as she ran back to the platform. And then she saw Willie ambling slowly up another ramp.

"Hurry! Hurry!" she screamed, and then as all the fight went out of her, she sighed, "For God's sake, hurry!"

Willie just smiled and came over leisurely. "It's all right," he said slowly. "I just spoke to him. He's not coming on this train."

"All right, hell!" Lucy cried. "There he goes!"

Willie looked and saw Moe and Louis disappearing down the far ramp with a couple of very perplexed strangers followed by a band,

"They musta got the wrong guys," Willie giggled.

"Well, that trombone player got my hat!" Lucy growled fiercely, turning around.

Willie looked at her and began to laugh. "Don't tell me," he howled, "I know. It's been attacked by a lawnmower."

"Go ahead and laugh, you idiot." Lucy stamped angrily. "But that guy you spoke to wasn't Case. *They* got Case and I know his wife! She went to school with Mother. I met her years ago!"

Willie's face blanched. "My God!" he croaked.

He grabbed Lucy's hand and they tore through the station to the entrance. But the car wasn't there. Louis and Moe had taken it. In its place they left the band playing "For He's a Jolly Good Fellow . . . 'ta-ra-ra-boom-de-ay."

6

THEY SAT BROODING in front of Willie's fireplace. It had been a dismal, hectic day. Three hours to find out that the Cases were stopping at the Town House. A half hour getting there, only to discover that Moe and Louis had spirited their eminent guests away again. The rest of the afternoon frittered away searching for all of them. An entire day without a single contact or clue leading to the culprits and their victims.

Lucy sipped her third highball and stared into space. Willie moped and watched the flames sputtering up the chimney.

Even as a defeated general mulls over the sequence of events culminating in his annihilation, so Willie sat moodily reconstructing the steps that led to the fiasco at the station. His mind skittered back to his early days at the studio. His apprenticeship to Fritz. Meeting Lucy. His first big picture. The inevitable conflict with his parents—every step. But on one point and one alone, his intelligence came to grips with an impasse. There was no denying an accomplished fact. His rivals had walked off with the fruits of his labor. It was as simple as that. But *how* had Moe and Louis found out that the Cases were coming to California? That one recurring question infuriated Willie to the point of self-pity.

He sat staring into the fire, shaking his head wearily, shuddering with the ecstatic anguish of personal defeat and commiseration.

The other strategist, being a woman, occupied herself with the problem of turning a fait accompli into defeat for their rivals. Hers was the groping sulk of a fighter taking a count of nine and fumbling furiously for a bit of strategy that might floor his opponent. But no brilliant ideas came. So she began to consider the least of them—kidnaping Momma, parking in front of the hotel until the Cases returned, stalking the restaurants at dinnertime. Perhaps they were eating at the Levinsons'. She looked at Willie and smiled in spite of herself.

"I can't figure how they found out," Willie mumbled.

"Forget it!" Lucy pleaded. "We've got to do something."

"What?"

"There's a good chance that they'd be eating dinner at your family's house, isn't there?"

Willie looked at her incredulously. "Jeez, you're reaching, aren't you?" he said. "Dumb they are, but that dumb they couldn't be!"

"We've got to get to them."

"What for? We'd still have Moe and Louis around. Let's wait till tomorrow. They'll probably be at the studio."

"Willie, I've got it! You call the house and tell your father you've reconsidered and want to come home."

"No, Lucy, that won't settle anything. It's up to us. You and me. We've got to figure out one hell of an idea!" He turned back to the fire and kept muttering, "a hell of an idea," as though the words contained a magic formula that by mere repetition could solve their problem.

Suddenly he turned and put his hand out to Lucy, who took it in hers.

"We'll do it somehow, darling," she said.

"God, what a woman you are."

He looked at her intensely and the corners of his eyes wrinkled up in a warm, impulsive smile. Lucy dropped his hand and slid slowly to the floor in front of her chair, her legs curled up beneath her. She looked into the fire, and the flames glistened in her eyes, burnished her cheeks, etched their delicate dance upon her hair.

Willie watched her. Here, seated at his feet, was the woman he loved. Surely no other man had ever loved a woman with such

419

heartbreaking intensity. She had—without malice, he was certain—insisted upon continence in their relationship, and if that was the secret of permanence, he was willing to accept it. Far back in his consciousness he knew, and suspected she did too, that eventually they would have each other completely in the physical sense, and he realized that it would somehow be like no other experience he'd ever had. If she still thought it best to wait, he'd wait and gladly. Because he knew now that she loved him. And that was in itself enough. Words didn't matter. Words were a barrier to love.

He dropped to his knees beside her, turned on his back and put his head in her lap. She stroked his hair gently, affectionately.

"Lie still, darling," she said. "Forget it. Something will turn up."

"Lucy—" he arched his neck so that he could look into her eyes —"I wonder if knowing things, if being educated isn't a step toward self-destruction?"

" 'A little knowledge is a dangerous thing,' " she quoted, turning her head back to the fire. "One can be happy with it, but it's still dangerous. Real knowledge gives one a sense of the pattern of things. And that in itself is enough to make one sad—to expose one to a sort of Weltschmerz. The surprise is taken out of life and with the surprise, joy. One knows what's going to happen or has happened and one doesn't take arms against it. But in its place one acquires the luxurious privilege of intelligently condemning the things man does to man."

Jesus, what a lot of words, Willie thought! Intelligently condemn Moe and Louis . . .

So what? . . . So they got the Cases!

"Kiss me," he said, almost defiantly.

He felt Lucy stiffen instinctively and then relax. Her dress rustled as she bent over toward him. Her warm breath caressed his eyelids. He sensed her breasts pressing against the top of his head, and her moist lips closed over his. It was so soft, so dark, so all-encompassing. There was no other world but that created by the touch of flesh on flesh. Their breathing became short, staccato, restless. She tried to

420

raise her head, to break away, but his arm rose slowly and held her to him. Even as she shook her head their lips clung together and when they finally parted it was with the lingering quality of velvet caressing velvet.

Lucy sat motionless, dimly aware of the world outside, of auto horns and traffic noise and people in the streets. Willie stirred uneasily. He kept his head in her lap and shifted around so that his body lay at right angles to hers. Then he settled back and sighed. "Sometimes I feel very old and very wise, and others, I want to crawl right back into your womb and be born again."

Lucy cupped his face in her hand and gave him a look that was far more intimate than a kiss. Then she whispered, "I wish you *had* been my child, Bill." And she suddenly put her arms around him and held him very close. . . .

"Take me home now, darling," she said finally. "I haven't been home at all and Mother's probably waiting for me."

"Not now," he pleaded.

"Now, darling. I'm sorry." And then Lucy's face suddenly lit up. "My God, what fools we've been!"

For a split second he felt an anguished chill curdle his stomach and then a feeling of relief oozed through his bones as Lucy cried, "Mother's the answer to the whole mess! We'll have the Cases up to dinner. Let me handle this for you."

She saw a frown of protest and bewilderment cross his face.

"Please, Bill!" she continued. "I'll get Mother to call the Town House. Oh, Bill! It's a cinch. Only I think you'd better not be there. It might even be a good idea not to let them see you at all."

"Not see me at all?" he repeated incredulously. Then he became suspicious and angry. "You're ashamed of me," he cried.

She shook him by the shoulders. "Don't be a fool, Bill. I will be, if you don't behave yourself. I just don't want them to know how young you are. I wouldn't spend one single moment with you, if I ever became ashamed of you. And you see to it that that never happens, will you? Oh, Bill, if we can only get them to dinner, we're in

—I know it! They're unconscious snobs, just like Mother. I'm sure of it. By this time Moe and Louis have probably sold themselves down the river. If they haven't, we'd never have had a chance, Bill, really. Take me home, darling—and hurry!"

Willie shook his head, grabbed the keys to his car, and said, "Okay, boss!"

7

"VERY WELL," Mrs. Strawbridge said to Lucy, as they descended the stairs to greet the Cases, "but I should think you'd be able to find a better outlet for your energies than devoting them to the cause of *that* young man!"

The way she said "that" startled Lucy. There was genuine contempt in the word. Lucy stopped so short that her mother had to turn to look up at her.

"I know you don't like him," Lucy said. There was a note of challenge in her voice, and a challenge from her daughter always made Mrs. Strawbridge wary.

"It isn't that I don't like him, Lucy, it's just that I can never take him seriously. I suppose that amounts to the same thing."

"I'm afraid—and sorry—it does."

"You're quite serious about him, aren't you?"

"Quite," Lucy replied quietly.

"That's too bad. I'd hoped for better things for you."

"What better things? Boys out of Harvard with crew haircuts and good families? Chest-thumping suburbanites whose idea of a good time is a country club dance every Saturday night? Did you ever stop to think, Mother, that almost all the fun at country clubs is based on infidelity? No, thanks. Not for me. This thing with Bill is alive. It's real! I know it's dangerous, but I don't care. Really I don't.

422

There's so much in it for me. A career, and I've found I want one for myself now. Excitement, and I'm working every day beside a man I really care for. This is the real thing, you know—and you must help me tonight."

The doorbell rang, cutting Mrs. Strawbridge's answer down to a bewildered nod. . . .

"Power," said Lucy to Mr. Case as he drained his demitasse, "is a germ that breeds its own destruction."

"Quite so. Quite so," Mr. Case repeated amiably.

"And that is precisely the trouble with Mr. Korn and Mr. Levinson. They positively exude the will to power." Lucy smiled, her triumphant Q.E.D. smile.

"And my dear, they swear so terribly!" Mrs. Case protested across the table.

Mrs. Strawbridge shrugged her shoulders. "The epigrams of the riffraff, Cornelia, are confined to those that have survived the ordeal of time. People who swear lack imagination."

Lucy threw her mother a look that was a kiss of gratitude. Then she turned back to Phineas, and putting on her most engaging smile, which Mr. Case thought was just this side of coquetry, she asked, "People without imagination shouldn't be running a motion-picture studio, should they, Mr. Case?"

"Shouldn't they?" he asked blankly.

Try as she might, Lucy couldn't answer that one. She felt as though a piece of string attached to her lips might help to keep her smiling, but nothing short of that could.

Mrs. Strawbridge came to her rescue. "Well, Mr. Case, don't you think imagination is an asset in the picture business?" she asked from the head of the table.

"Perhaps."

"He's a cautious soul," Mrs. Case explained.

"I don't know whether he's cautious or cagey," Lucy said slowly, fixing the banker with a stern look.

Phineas winked at her.

She felt a warm glow creep through her and come to bloom on her cheeks. "Mr. Case," she said confidently, now that she knew he was suspectible to flattery, "there's not much use in trying to be subtle with you."

"Were you being subtle, Miss Strawbridge?" he inquired blandly. He lit a cigar and blew a smoke ring at the ceiling. There was a suggestion of a twinkle in his eye. "What are you trying to say?"

"Well, bluntly," Lucy cried, beside herself with impatience, "just what would you think of making Bill Levinson the head of the studio?"

"Think of it? I've never even met the young man."

"Through no fault of his," Lucy moaned.

"I imagine not. But who told the other two we were coming?"

"That's a question that is driving young Mr. Levinson to distraction."

"I'd like to meet him."

"I think it could be arranged. Tomorrow, if you wish."

"Pick me up at the hotel around ten in the morning."

"What sort of person is this young Mr. Levinson?" Mrs. Case asked.

"Oh, he's an intelligent boy," Lucy said. "He's not at all like his family."

"That's good," Cornelia sighed.

"And he should be the head of the studio someday," Lucy repeated, driving her point a little beyond home and into the next county.

"What do you think of it?" Phineas asked Mrs. Strawbridge.

"As an experiment in sociology, I'd recommend it."

Lucy lowered her cigarette and glared at her mother. The Cases were waiting patiently for Millicent to explain her remark. Mrs. Strawbridge chastised herself silently; it was high time she learned to control her tongue. She'd make a memo of it. Things to do today: Control your tongue.

424

"Well," she said hesitantly, "he's so young . . ." And then she picked up speed. "Perhaps his very youth might stand him in good stead. I often feel that youth alone is a reliable barometer of America's mass thinking. Somehow young people seem to reflect this nation's moods more readily than older ones."

"Older men hesitate," Lucy interrupted, "and in show business hesitation is death."

Mrs. Case smiled at Mrs. Strawbridge. "What a bright young girl you've got, Millicent dear," she said in a coddling stage whisper.

"Bright only half describes her," Mrs. Strawbridge said ruefully.

Willie had spent the night in his apartment anxiously waiting to hear from Lucy. It was his first evening alone in many months and he was bored stiff. Bored with anxiety, with trying to read, with waiting for Lucy's promised phone call as soon as the Cases left her house. He found himself harking back to the old days when he was diddling all the girls instead of just trying to hold hands with one. But the memories of those halcyon times didn't excite him any more. They had become a forgotten frenzy.

He toyed innumerable times with the idea of calling Lucy but thought better of it, and by two o'clock he had consumed a sufficient quantity of Scotch and soda to retire in a state of drowsy despair.

At eleven the next morning, Lucy dashed into his office. Her face was beaming and she could hardly contain herself.

"I've got him outside!" she cried, grinning with excitement.

"Got who?"

"Case, you fool!"

"You never phoned me last night," Willie sulked.

"Oh, I couldn't," she answered breathlessly. "Stop worrying. Everything's set!"

"Well, bring him in!" Willie cried impatiently.

"He's in the little boys' room."

"Well, Jesus, don't let him get away from you. Stand outside of it!"

Lucy pointed toward the ceiling. "They don't even know he's here!" she confided reassuringly.

"They don't, eh? You came through one of the studio gates and they don't know he's here? Don't think they don't! . . . Scram!"

Lucy bolted for the door and as her hand grabbed the knob, Willie called after her, "And when you come back I'll tell you how they found out the Cases were coming to California."

Lucy paused in the doorway, her eyes wide with curiosity. "How?" she asked.

"They steamed my mail open, and the telegram too!"

"How'd *you* find out?"

"From here on in I'm paying one of our messenger boys an extra twenty-five a week. Get out of here, will you!"

The dictograph rang. Willie pressed the key. Miss Holmby announced, "Mr. Case out here to see you."

Willie jabbed his finger excitedly toward Lucy, who turned calmly, opened the door, and said, "Come in, Mr. Case."

Phineas crossed the threshold. Willie advanced to greet him. Lucy introduced them and they shook hands.

"I'm really glad to know you," Willie said, with just enough fervor in his voice.

He actually seems sincere about it, Phineas thought with some amazement. But then, why shouldn't he? He's got nothing to lose. Looks older than he probably is, too. Dark beard. And he's got a brain. Sort of a quick gleam in his eye. If only he can be an honest man. Lucy said he was, but then quite obviously she cares for him. An honest man is much, much easier to deal with than a crook. He's easier to get rid of, for one thing . . . if, as, and when it ever becomes necessary. . . .

Phineas smiled in spite of himself and he became conscious of Willie's voice intruding itself on his privacy. He was saying something

426

like, "Our first meeting didn't turn out quite as we planned it . . ."

"I think it will," Phineas answered.

"Do sit down." Lucy bustled cheerfully, practically shoving an armchair through the back of the banker's knees.

There was nothing left for him to do but sink into it. Lucy walked over to the divan and sat down. Willie proffered his cigar box. Mr. Case shook his head and asked if he might smoke his pipe.

Willie went back to his desk and pressed the dictograph key. "Under no circumstances am I to be disturbed," he said, "by anybody. And I mean everybody, Miss Holmby. You understand me?"

"Very well, sir."

The key clicked and the three of them were alone. The great moment had arrived. And quite naturally it was met with a long and eventually embarrassing silence.

Phineas Case finally cleared his throat. "You're a very fortunate young man, Mr. Levinson," he said.

Willie raised his eyebrows inquisitively and a hesitant smile broke slowly across his face. "It's been a rather difficult climb, sir," he admitted magnanimously. "So far, I mean. The rest is up to you."

"Did you hear that, Phineas?" Phineas said to himself. "It's up to you." Quite direct, that. Damned near blunt. But interesting. I don't think he quite understood me. But then again, maybe he didn't want to.

Phineas smiled softly.

"I didn't mean that," he said. "I meant you were lucky to have a young lady like Miss Strawbridge around. I imagine she's been quite a help to you."

Lucy smiled, and the look of gratitude she gave Mr. Case was practically a curtsy.

"She's been a great help, Mr. Case. A great help." Willie got up and walked over to Lucy. He stood behind her with both hands on her shoulders and she raised her left hand from the arm of the couch so that she held his fingers even as they rested on her dress.

"That's easily explained, Mr. Case," Willie continued. "Lucy is me. We're one. She's my world."

Phineas Case looked up at his new protégé and felt like Cupid. There could be no question of the boy's honesty now. Not after such a forthright avowal of his affections. If only his own children had confided in him with the same simple honesty. But, then, at an early age they had become Cornelia's property.

Here at least were two youngsters toward whom, in a sort of off-hand way, he could play godfather without upsetting his equilibrium or theirs. Both of them at least seemed sensible, and besides, he felt at ease with them. Much more so than with the gentlemen who were still guiding the destinies of Miracle Pictures.

It was rather a shame that he couldn't give them everything they wanted: control of the studio and a goodly share of the stock besides. It might not be a bad idea, though, to tell them the truth and see what happened from there on in. To sort of let them handle their own destinies. With the new reorganization, Case and Ogilvie would be certain of their controlling interest—and if the kids bungled the proposed stock deal they could still run the studio, and the firm might even realize its original purpose of prying a good deal of stock away from Korn and Levinson. Besides, if that happened, the reorganization might not be necessary. Well, Phineas sighed to himself, let's try the truth. He cleared his throat again.

"Mr. Levinson—"

"Please call me Bill," Willie interrupted.

"Very well then, Bill—and Lucy. I have a confession to make to you. During the whirlwind courtship that your relatives thrust upon us, I advised them to buy in all the Miracle Picture preferred stock they could get their hands on, because, to the best of my knowledge, that stock is due for a rise. I also told them that there was going to be quite a block of stock up for sale in the near future. And I felt that you should be apprised of that fact, Bill, and act accordingly."

"You mean you want me to buy too?"

"Not at all. I want you to sell."

"Sell?" Willie's eyes popped wide open with incredulity. He'd been taken into camp before. But not this time. It had taken a lot of shrewd manipulation to build up his interest in the company and he wasn't going to dump his holdings on the market just to satisfy the whim of a guy who happened to own it. The hell with that. Why, his family had acted as though they were giving him a piece of the sun when, at each birthday, they gave him a present of some of their Miracle stock. If they thought so highly of their holdings, only a fool would part with his unless he had a damned good reason. Suppose this guy was trying to get rid of ALL the Levinsons? Then what?

Willie left Lucy and sat down behind his desk. "I don't understand, Mr. Case," he said innocently. "It's taken me a long time to add to the shares my family gave me, and you can't blame me for wanting to know why I should suddenly unload my stock."

"Why do you think I came out here, Bill?"

"To see what was going on?" Willie ventured tentatively.

"I knew what was going on. Your letter told me far more than, I'm afraid, you intended to. No. I just came out here to make sure."

"Sure of what, sir?"

"You," Phineas said, looking Bill right in the eye. "And what I'm going to tell you is in strictest confidence. I really didn't like your relatives, you know. . . . In a manner of speaking, I lied to them. The stock will go up a few points, but only because they'll be climbing all over each other to acquire your shares. Then in a month or so it will go down. And it will go down quickly. You see, we plan to reorganize the entire financial structure of the company. If you unload your shares now, they'll pay you slightly more than a legitimate profit. Then, when the new stock is issued, I'll see that you get a prior option on enough shares to give you control of this end of the business. I say this end advisedly, because, as you undoubtedly realize, we have an interest to protect in the east. By that time your relatives ought to be in moderately straitened circumstances and if you stage a private bear raid on their holdings, say selling short down to twenty from forty-five, you'll be in a position to convert what had been their holdings into new stock without incurring any loss on your own. Does that answer your question?"

"It certainly does, sir," said Willie, burgeoning with respect for a man who played the Levinson game for higher stakes than the boys in the studio had dreamed about. "But what makes you think they're going to sell?"

"They'll follow your lead, once they find out what you're doing. And by the time you let them know you've been selling, you'll be ready to raid *their* holdings."

"They're a smart bunch." Willie hesitated. "I hate mixing with them on anything as important as this. Besides—and please don't misunderstand me—what guarantees have I got from your end?"

"You mustn't question my integrity, Bill," Phineas said coolly. "I haven't questioned yours. You'll receive a letter from New York confirming our discussion as soon as I get back east. And the gentlemen upstairs will receive a wire from me relieving them of their responsibilities. Your pictures have been good, Bill. I've seen every one of them. And I hate movies." He rose and reached for his hat. "Coming, Lucy?" he asked.

Lucy got up quickly, rushed over to Mr. Case, and kissed him heartily on the cheek. "God bless you, Phineas," she said and her voice was husky.

"Er—Mr. Case—" Willie fumbled hesitantly—"I can't thank you enough. It seems silly to stand here and say thanks, but I've been wanting this to happen so much and so hard that now that it's here—well, here it is!" he concluded lamely.

Phineas shook his hand solemnly. "Just keep up the good work," he said, and started for the door.

"Er—Mr. Case, just one thing more," Willie called.

Phineas stopped and raised his eyebrows.

"Send the letter of confirmation to my home. Lucy will tell you why."

"I certainly will, boss," Lucy laughed as she closed the door behind them.

It was as simple as that, Willie thought to himself. And for the first time in his life he felt a queasy, billowing fear of responsibility. He looked success right in the eye and he had a frightening premonition that perhaps it was going to spit in his.

8

TELEGRAMS EXCHANGED three weeks later between the studio in Hollywood and the bankers in New York:

WHO EVER HEARD OF PROMOTING A GUY FOR MERIT IN THIS BUSINESS

MOE KORN

FINANCE OUR SOLE RESPONSIBILITY STOP WE ARE NOT IN MOTION PICTURE BUSINESS

CASE & OGILVIE

YOULL BE IN IT UP TO YOUR NECKS IF YOU DONT WATCH OUT

MOE KORN

KINDLY REFER TO OUR LETTER DEFINITELY PLACING WILLIAM LEVINSON IN CHARGE OF STUDIO STOP REGARDS

CASE & OGILVIE

9

WILLIE SUDDENLY FELT chicken-hearted. He had reached the zenith at which he could afford the luxury of remorse, but he hadn't had a chance to display his gentler self. It was moderately gratifying to see the Adelsteins and the Kleins falling all over themselves in their frantic effort to scramble over to the right side of the fence. And he had told them not to fear for their jobs. They would continue producing the B product. "Under Moe?" Well, of that he couldn't be quite positive. The bankers would have to make that decision themselves. The Adelsteins and the Kleins understood. They walked away not quite reassured by either Willie's smile or his words.

All the minor employees on the lot addressed him as Mr. Levinson now. Even the few who had retained the prerogative of addressing him as Willie became more circumspect in their usage of the familiar. People like George Tilden, the studio manager, began to terminate their remarks with "sir" until Willie put a stop to it. George had even gone so far as to ask him whether he would like to have Louis's bust taken down from the front gate. And what about the sign on Moe's door, or Louis's? Did he want them removed? "Never, as long as I'm running this place!" Willie answered coldly.

"Then they'll stay?" George asked, his face lighting up hopefully.

"They might. It depends on the bankers," Willie said.

He was curious about Moe and Louis. As far as he knew, they were camping out in their offices, carrying on as though nothing had happened. But the day the notice of his promotion appeared in the trade papers, most of the studio problems began gravitating toward his desk, and by the end of the week all the department heads had in one form or another pledged fealty to their new chief. Only Moe and Louis hadn't come around to see him. In fact, they'd avoided him like the plague. And he'd intended to be singularly pleasant toward them. Pride kept him from calling them immediately, but in the end he succumbed to curiosity.

"I'm sure they want to see you," Matilda Mayer said, "but they won't admit it. Why don't you just come up and walk in?"

Matilda was a businesswoman and her emotions were more reliable than those of her employers.

When Willie entered Louis's office he expected the boys to greet him if not with cordiality, at least with the courtesy generally accorded his new position. After all, he was the boss now; it was the shrewd thing to do, and shrewd they were.

He was mistaken. His greeting consisted of an almost hysterical silence. Louis sat behind his desk and his eyes followed Willie across the room. Moe, standing beside the window, only turned when he felt Willie approaching him.

Willie put out his hand.

Moe looked at Louis, gave Willie a withering glance, and turned back to surveying the lot without so much as a shrug of his shoulders. Willie retreated a few steps and watched his father get up from his chair and go over to Moe. Their backs looked ominous.

Willie grabbed a trade paper from Louis's desk and settled down in the most comfortable chair in the office. He was determined to wear them out by sheer patience. He could wait. Till Doomsday if necessary. Remembering that Moe always called it "Tombsday," he grinned. This was it, all right! But they'd come around. They had to, and the next move was up to them. He lit a cigarette, crossed his legs, and buried himself in the *Hollywood Reporter*. The next five minutes, he thought, will be devoted to silent prayer, after which they'll tell me to go to hell. They're going to force me to fight them, when all they have to say is, "You've won, Willie." That's all. Just a little common sense, a few simple words, and I could afford to be truly generous. But they won't give me that chance. Not in a million years.

He heard a rustle of clothing and looked up. Moe was turning toward him.

"Why don't you get out of here?" Moe asked.

"If I was going to do that, I wouldn't have come," Willie answered.

Silence again. It was Louis's turn. After a few moments he took it.

"Please go before I say things I shouldn't. After all, you are my son."

"It's high time you realized it," Willie said, "and both of you stopped acting like a coupla stumble-bums. Now, why don't you sit down and behave yourselves? I want to talk to you. Things aren't as bad as they seem."

Moe and Louis looked at each other, shrugged their shoulders, and sat down grimly. Willie got up, put the *Reporter* back on the desk and returned to his chair.

"You think I'm a louse, don't you?"

There was no response at all. No flicker of an eyelid, no emphatic shake of the head, nothing but silence. Good God, Willie thought, they're so mad they won't even swear at me! Well, here goes, it's now or never.

"Look, Pop, don't resent me, and that goes for you too, Moe. You should be grateful that I'm the guy. The studio's still in the family and that's the important thing. Think back: Did Case's letter say anything about your being fired? It didn't, did it? All it said was, Willie runs the studio. Well, you don't for a moment think I could run it without you, do you? Your experience is invaluable even though the parade passed you by. Yeah—don't look so hurt. That's what it did. You had things your way for a long time, but the business got too big for you. You're still making ten-twenty-thirt dramas when the movies are ready for important things. Yes, important! Things

434

beyond the Cinderella themes, the love-conquers-all, the to-hell-with-the-Indians, and the ain't-the-White-Man-a-wonderful-thing crap.

"This is the beginning of a new era! The movies don't belong to you boys any more. They belong to the people. The people who gave you a mandate to employ the greatest sociological weapon on earth for your own profits. And what did you do with it? You laid an egg from here to Timbuktu!

"The day has come when pictures have got to start telling the truth, and the truth is always ugly unless it's done with artistry. And that takes brains, background, and education."

Willie thought he detected the first flush of a smile on Moe's face. He paused and watched him intently.

Moe finally opened his mouth. "Ya gonna make them things?" he asked owlishly.

"What things?"

"Them artistic pitchures?"

"I certainly am."

Moe broke into a broad grin. "That's *good*!" he said expansively. "Go to it! We're all for ya!"

Willie's bubble collapsed ignominiously; he knew he was being ribbed. But he decided to ignore it.

"Well," he continued self-consciously, "that sort of important picture is necessary in the A product, but the things you excelled in, the ten-twenty-thirt dramas, are just what we need for the B's. So I'm asking you to stay on—at a slight salary cut—as executive producers in charge of the low-budget pictures."

"How much of a cut?" Moe demanded.

"Thirty per cent," Willie replied calmly.

"Never!" his father exploded, jumping to his feet. "Never!" he repeated, pounding his fist on the desk.

Moe looked at Louis and shook his head slowly. "When yer licked, yer licked, Lou," he said, with a finality that surprised even Willie.

"Not me!" Louis shouted. "We can always go to another studio. This business needs executives. Good ones, like us. We'd be welcome at any other studio in town."

Moe walked over and put his arm around Louis's shoulder. Louis shuddered and shook him away.

"Don't touch me!" he cried. "You're a traitor too. You said we'd fight this thing out together to a finish, and now look at you—quitting! You, Moe, a coward! In front of this—this rat that's my son!"

Willie's stomach suddenly zoomed down to his knees. He looked up at his father and saw tears of rage pouring down his cheeks. Willie closed his eyes and felt as though he was going to vomit. His face became cold and clammy and he breathed with difficulty. When he finally looked up, Moe winked at him reassuringly. "Don't worry, kid," he said. "It'll be all right."

The kid smiled weakly at his uncle, who put his arm around Louis's shoulder again to comfort him. But Louis would have none of it. He struggled violently to break away. The tighter Moe held him, the more Louis pushed and sobbed and fought to be free. When Moe's compassion finally became exhausted, he began to shake his brother-in-law, and Louis, his fury spent as quickly as it had been roused, slumped in a heap into the chair behind his desk and held his head.

"Relax!" Moe said, and began to rub the back of Louis's neck. "It'll be fun workin' here. More fun'n workin' anywheres else, I promise ya. We'll watch Willie make *important* pitchures and we'll make the ones that bring inna mazuma."

He winked at Willie again. One of those superior, a-man-has-to-be-humored winks. But Willie suspected that Moe meant what he said far more emphatically than was necessary for Louis's immediate welfare. He got up and poured a glass of water from the thermos bottle.

"Here," he said to his father, "take this. It'll make you feel better."

Louis lunged forward and knocked the glass out of his son's hand.

436

"Now, now," Moe said soothingly, "that won't do no good. Remember what Willie said? It's still inna family! We just got another podner, thass all. Ya boy's in business with us now—fa keeps!" He smiled reassuringly at Willie. "If it's okay by you, it's okay by us."

"It's okay by me," Willie said.

Louis shuddered.

"Relax, Louis, fa Chrissake!" Moe snapped impatiently.

Louis straightened up in his chair. "I'm all right," he mumbled. The glazed look gradually disappeared from his eyes. His brain was slowly beginning to function again, but he couldn't quite pick up the loose ends of the squabble. Best to let Moe handle it, he thought. Let him handle it. He's always right. Vaguely he heard Moe asking Willie just what Case had said about them.

"Nothing much," Willie answered.

"Whad he say the day he come to ya awfice?"

"Practically nothing. The first I heard about my new job was by letter. We never even discussed you."

"Yer lyin'!" Moe snorted. "But yer learnin'! . . . Whad else he say?"

"I'm telling you—nothing!" Willie protested, flaring up and subsiding just as quickly. "So I'm sure it's okay for you to stay on here."

"He didn't tell ya nothin' about the stock?"

"Stock?" Willie asked vaguely. "What stock?"

Louis's head snapped around so fast Willie thought he was going to break his neck. Obviously he didn't know what tack Moe was going to take next and was waiting breathlessly to see if their surrender was to be unconditional. Well, whatever happened, Willie wasn't going to be the patsy.

"Didn't Case tell you to sell yer shares?" Moe asked.

Louis settled back, looking decidedly relieved.

"No," Willie lied, drawing out the word so that it was more an expression of indignation than a statement of fact.

"Well, he told *us* to!" Moe snapped.

"Do you think I ought to?" Willie asked innocently.

"We're doing it. That ought to be enough for you," his father said coldly.

"Well, if you think so, I will!" Willie said, pausing at the door.

"Now's za time!" Moe said cheerily.

"And you'll stay?" Willie asked.

"You bet we will!" Moe grinned. . . .

"The lying bastards!" Willie muttered to himself as he walked down the stairs. "They're going to buy. They think they double-crossed me, telling me that they were going to sell, but they're going to buy!"

He felt quite proud of himself. Things were happening exactly as Mr. Case had predicted they would.

10

THE ANNOUNCEMENT by the brokerage firm of Stein and Salinger that they had eleven thousand shares of Miracle Pictures for sale at forty produced no startling effect upon the market. The offer was, as a matter of record, met with appalling lethargy. Two hundred shares were snapped up by quixotic speculators. But the expected quick sale failed to materialize. Moe and Louis sat on their money bags. If a man gave them the hotfoot in business, he could certainly be depended upon to do the same thing in a stock transaction. If Willie had the inside track to Mr. Case's affections, then the sensible thing to do was to follow Willie's lead.

The next morning Stein and Salinger offered fifty-one thousand shares at the market price. Miracle skittered down from forty to twenty-five in record time. Moe and Louis had dumped their holdings sooner than they were supposed to, and Willie, frantic and desperate, rushed home to telephone Case in New York.

"I know all about it," Phineas said quickly. "They're selling.

Well, we're buying. And we'll hold it. There will be no reorganization. We've got their stock and that's all we wanted. So don't worry about it. As long as you didn't sell your stock—and nobody bought it at forty, What have you got to lose?"

"Mr. Case," Willie almost sobbed, "I did what you told me to. I sold! I didn't know what in hell *they* were doing. I'm a motion-picture man, not a stockbroker. You bought my holdings too—and at twenty-five!"

"Well, as I said, don't worry about it. We'll reimburse you through bonuses—eventually. In the meantime, let your relatives think you bought them out. What they don't know won't hurt them. Now forget about it and go to work. Your salary will be three thousand a week—that ought to make it up to you in no time at all. Give my love to Lucy. Goodby."

"Goodby," Willie sighed and hung up slowly. He had sold out his family for keeps this time. And himself with it.

He called Lucy at the studio and told her to rush over to his apartment.

Meanwhile he stalked impatiently around the living room. Now that he had committed the first important blunder in his life, he felt that he should feel some quick remorse, rather than this numb awareness of the things around him—the titles of the books upon his shelves, the way the sun streamed through the blinds, a spot upon the lampshade near the couch, all these inconsequential things intruded on his consciousness. This, then, was one's reaction to catastrophe. This inability to balance things, to put them in their place, to file and catalogue belongings, ills, the trivia that fill one's daily life. This wasn't bad at all, this gentle lull of all activity—this absence of relationship. If only one could realize what it was. A sort of contrast. Conflict, that was it! Within oneself. Beyond projection . . .

But when he heard the key click in the door, the trance was broken and he felt penitence, and fear, and wild remorse.

Lucy stood before him and knew instinctively that he had been betrayed. "Oh, God, what now?" she asked.

He told her briefly, and was amazed to see her smile.

"You haven't lost a thing," she said, talking softly as if to a bewildered child. "The studio's still yours. Moe and Louis are out of your way for life. At three thousand a week you'll make up what you lost on the stock in a year or so. And besides, Mr. Case did say something about bonuses, didn't he?"

Willie nodded halfheartedly. A loss of a hundred and sixty-five thousand dollars, against a salary of a hundred and fifty-six thousand a year. He was out nine thousand plus income tax. That wasn't as bad at it could have been. He shrugged his shoulders.

"Then what are you moping about? Moe and Louis won't know Case bought up the stock. We'll see to that. And what do you care who owns the business? You're running it and that's what you wanted, isn't it?"

Willie looked up at her incredulously. He was half hysterical and his eyelids were fringed with tears.

"Sometimes," he said, "I don't know what's the matter with me. Every time I work myself into a corner, you come along, take me by the hand, and lead me out of it. I can't ever lose you, Lucy. I've a great fear that someday I may. And that must never happen." He looked at her intently. There was a curious directness in his eyes. "Sit down, darling," he said. "I'm going to ask you something now and I beg you not to laugh or be unkind."

Lucy sat down slowly. Compassion gave her face a poignant radiance and made her beautiful. She shook her head and asked, "Darling, when have I ever been unkind to you?"

"Never. But you can be terribly unkind by saying no to me now. Lucy—" he took a deep breath—"I'm asking you to be my wife."

He turned away abruptly and fled to the window. He wanted to watch her, to be next to her, to guide her answer, but he didn't dare. He was afraid she might say no, and what would happen to them then? They couldn't go on as they were. That was obvious. They were at the crossroads now. A mere question had brought them to it. And henceforth they would walk together either forever or never. . . .

440

A bird flashed past the window, wheeling earthward with wings outstretched, calling down the chromatic scale to its mate still lingering in a tree. "Follow me!" it sang. "Follow me!"

You're happier than I am, Willie thought. You, and the lowliest worker on the lot. They've got their wives, the women they love. And I have empty hands. He held them out before him, empty and open. A wave of great self-pity enveloped him and he shuddered.

It seemed as though he had been waiting patiently for an hour and still there was no sound from Lucy. Perhaps she'd left! Sheer panic struck him, and he wheeled around to find her standing in front of him, searching his eyes with hers.

"I know how old you really are, darling. And I'm five years older. Do you know what that means?"

"Not a thing," he said intensely, "not a goddamn thing!"

"Are you sure, darling?" she asked.

He nodded wildly.

"Well, then, of course!" she cried, flinging herself into his arms.

11

PAUL KERSEY looked at Willie and broke into a long, slow grin.

"Congratulations, Bill," he said. "You got a grand, great girl."

"You're telling me!" Willie said, so pleased with himself that he could hardly keep from shouting.

Bridegrooms, thought Paul, remind me of an effervescing Bromo-Seltzer. They bubble over with expectancy and then settle down to cure a long protracted headache. Little Willie's going to be a husband! Poor baby. He probably rushed right over to tell me just because I introduced him to Lucy. Well, I hope they'll never rue the day. I wonder if his family knows.

"Where's Lucy?" he asked.

"She went home to break the news to Mother." Willie grinned.

"Have you told your family yet?"

"Nope. You're the first."

"Then they don't know you're going to marry a schicksa?"

"Not yet. But they ought to have suspicions by now."

"They'll probably be madder than hell."

"What for?"

"Isn't there a tradition about marrying outside your religion?"

"Paul," Willie said calmly, "I'm sure the wrath of my fathers looks down on me with envy."

Paul smiled and tapped his chin thoughtfully. "Your fathers are in heaven. Your immediate forebears are just upstairs—which is a step toward your ancestors, but still close enough to be dangerous. Don't let them heap ashes on your enthusiasm, will you?"

"Paul, they'll come around without my doing a thing about it. They have to."

And they did, gradually, like little wolves wondering whether to harry or make friends with a small brown bear. They were sure of their strength, but not of his. Therefore, whenever the bear grunted or seemed the least bit restive, they retreated respectfully and sheathed their fangs behind obsequious smiles. But whenever he slumbered they scrabbled back again and gnashed their teeth and snarled encouragement to one another. But they didn't dare attack. This prolonged frustration raised havoc with their gastric juices and they all lost weight.

Especially Momma, who became quite sick and had a stroke.

The night she died, the family gathered round her bed. And when she asked for Willie they shook their heads and said, "Not in this house. Never again."

"Gat him," she sighed. "Is de end. Be kind."

They called Willie and he came alone. And when he strode into the room, his kin turned their backs to him.

"Jesus!" he cried. "Even in death?"

His grandmother motioned from the bed. "Comm here," she groaned. "Close by."

He took her hand and sat beside her. She looked up at him and in her tortured eyes he saw the last faint echo of a smile.

"Na, ledd dem hate." she said impatiently. "Vot kinda mensch are you dat dey should hate you so? A chailboid? A moiderer? Mebbe you killed a man?"

Willie smiled softly and squeezed her hand. Rebecca stepped between them and bent down over her.

"Now, Momma," she pleaded, "please don't excite yourself."

"Eggzite myself," Momma moaned, turning her head from side to side. "I'm dying en' she's sayink dun't eggzite chaself! Vot else should I do, please? Sing sonks?" She turned back to Willie and then she coughed and gasped for breath and the whole family rushed forward and stood around her, trembling.

When she recovered she patted Willie's hand.

"Please, Momma!" Louis sobbed.

"There's nothing we can do," the doctor said resignedly. Rebecca went over and held Louis close to her.

"Dey're happy." Momma nodded at Willie. "Dey got each odder. But you, you're a fine boy, Villie. I got no time fa hate. Nod me. Should I go op to heaven en' say 'Gott, I got on oid a grennson is a louse?' Nod me. Ven I see grempa, *olav hasholem*, you know vot I'm gonna say? I'm gonna say, 'Poppa, is no schlemiehl, dot Villie. Is a fine boy. Fomm him ve should be proud.'"

"She's losing her mind," Louis wailed.

Momma shook her head slowly and looked at her son. "Vot's a liddle lie betven me en' Gott, Louis?" She smiled.

"A good sport to the last," Moe said solemnly.

"Should ull be good sputz. Villie's a smott fella. A highkless goniff. So, hokay! Gibbim a chence! If he vants ta merry a schicksa, ledd him merry a schicksa! Vot's it to you? I'll fix it up vit Gott!

"Now, comm, kiss me goodby en' remember me vid luff. Comm,

Louis, mine boy. Rebecca, Yacob, ull uf you. . . . Den go. I vanna be alunn. Unly da duktah should stay vid me."

One by one they filed past the bed. Each kissing Momma. Each breaking into tears and rushing from the room. Louis was the last to go. And when he met Willie outside the door he put his arm around him.

Momma heard the latch click for the last time. "Duktah!" she groaned. "Da needle. Qvick! It hoits turrible!"

The doctor filled his hypodermic with morphine.

"You're a brave woman, Mrs. Levinsky," he said, swabbing the skin on her thigh and pinching it together.

"Da needle, duktah!" she gasped.

She didn't know it had already pierced her flesh.

12

ALTHOUGH PEACE OVERTURES were well under way by the time Momma had been lowered into her ultimate resting place, there had been no real intimacy between the family and Willie's "intended." If anything, the overtures were conducted with frigid politeness. Casual inquiries over the telephone and an occasional vague suggestion that he and Lucy come to dinner some night were the sum total of their hospitality.

Despite Rebecca's efforts to appear gracious, there was still a martial overtone in her attitude. And although she was conspicuously preparing the ground for a reconciliation with her son, that overtone crept into even her most insignificant conversations. Whenever she asked after Lucy her voice sounded tinny and flat. And it hurt Willie. The more so because his mother was unconscious of the power of her persistence. She wanted Willie home again, so much so that she was even willing to accept Lucy—with reservations.

But Lucy's daily experiences at the studio precluded the possibility of any immediate armistice. At one point, after Moe had given her what she called a "cowlick" smile in passing, she became so exasperated that she remarked to Willie how strange it was that her mother should have completely accepted him, whereas his family still maintained a fence around themselves. The kind of fence they probably leaned against and over which they undoubtedly indulged in some fine and fancy back-alley gossip. She herself had, after all, come from a rather respectable line of ancestors, much more so, in fact, than the Levinsons, and she hoped they had been apprised of that fact.

To this Willie replied that the only difference between their ancestors was that hers had had the time to acquire the quality of graciousness, while his had still been busy struggling for survival. Gently he persuaded her that they had best—temporarily at least—concern themselves with themselves and their work.

"When they finally come around, it'll be so complete that you'll find yourself annihilated by the very fervor of their affection. Now let's forget it and really get to work."

From that moment on, they began spending an average of sixteen hours a day at the studio, picking new stories, conferring with screen writers on the preparation of those already chosen for production, casting accepted shooting scripts, planning new productions, and supervising those already in front of the cameras.

Willie's pictures began to be distinguished by an overtone of importance. It was the importance that Hollywood attached to the unknown, hence impressive. When he announced a program of films including such names as Beethoven, Browning, and Byron, one wag quipped, "Here's where the three B's get lost in the Bronx and emerge as million-dollar A's." But for the most part, the town accepted him as an addition to that select group of "class" producers who indulge their fancies in filming features that Hollywood enviously identifies with Art.

Class producers are the town's showcase exhibits. From Gold-wyn to Zanuck, from Selznick to De Mille, the traffic in halos has been terrific. Their peculiarities have been exploited as a salable commodity, their phobias catered to, their major successes aped, and their talents ballyhooed to such a point that the gods at one time seriously debated the advisability of getting along with last year's laurel leaves or, at best, of having the old ones altered.

In due time Willie became a figure in the daily newsprint. In-terviewers often traced his connection with the picture business back to his babyhood, when he had been Billy Lane, the child star, and although most of the stories concerning him were legendary, some of them were based on fact.

The one he liked best concerned a story conference at which some of his assistants recommended filming all the great classics that had sold over a million copies. He had actually punctured their en-thusiasm by producing a list from which he rapidly rattled off the following names, "Charles Monroe Sheldon, Jesse Lyman Hurlbut, John Fox, Margaret Sidney, Eleanor Stuart, and Anna Sewell. Know them?" he had asked, looking around the room. No one knew them. Somebody guessed, "Famous murderers." Willie paused just long enough to satisfy his ego and then announced rather elaborately, "They're authors, gentlemen! And each one of them wrote a book that sold over a million copies! And, gentlemen, permit me to also inform you that a little opus called *America's Part in the World War* is still up there selling with the best of them. Any questions?"

There were none. And no more suggestions. Willie was the czar of the lot and Lucy his czarina. Ace Luddigan tagged along as a com-bination czarevitch and court jester, and the rest of the unit com-forted themselves within the range of authority vested in them by his Imperial Highness.

Only Paul Kersey remained vaguely outside the fold. He be-longed, but he managed to evade the rigid caste system mainly be-cause of his friendship with Lucy, to whom he was at once father confessor and a beloved link with the past.

446

She respected Paul. Since they had the same background, she could talk to him without being misunderstood, and did so whenever she had an opportunity. It was in Paul that she found refuge and comfort from the indignities inflicted upon her by Willie's family. She was too proud to discuss them with her mother and—except for her one outburst—too wise to say anything about them to Willie.

It was Paul with whom she had a long discussion of the fact that the picture business had undoubtedly done more *to* than *for* her. It is this depressing realization, in one form or another, that makes sensitive people eventually flee Hollywood. It comes over them in waves and they suddenly feel surfeited with palm trees, projection rooms, and drive-in hamburger stands.

It was while she was in the throes of this Hollywood neurosis that Lucy confessed to Paul that she had a vague hankering after friends who never wrote to her any more, friends she read about in literary columns or art magazines, people whose names were mentioned in liberal publications, people she knew and had grown away from and those she'd grown up with—those young country-clubbing people who were probably still having a wonderful time carousing around the east in station wagons.

"Lucy Strawbridge in five easy stages," she said wryly, "Vassar, Long Island, summers in Europe, literary cocktail parties, and Willie Levinson."

"An essay by the future *Mrs.* Levinson," Paul observed, and there was something savage in his observation—almost resentful.

Lucy hesitated a moment, then dismissed the absurd thought that flashed through her mind. She smiled at Paul quite seriously. "It wasn't easy for me to make up my mind to that," she said.

"I know," he answered quietly.

Did he, though? she wondered. Could he possibly know the agony she'd been through before she could bring herself to admit that she loved Willie? Just to admit it! The situation had been so patently ridiculous from the beginning that the absurdity of it had somehow contrived to keep her from being honest with herself.

And now, it didn't matter any more. Somehow, the difference in age, temperament, and heritage meant nothing in the end. Not a thing. What had begun as a promise to Dr. Lansburgh had become a situation in which the pupil had enslaved the master—only he hadn't realized it yet. And it was better that he didn't. It was too soon. There was still so much to do. And this knowledge made it necessary for her to insist upon still maintaining their pledge of continence. She was well aware that the time had come when it no longer protected her. She didn't need or want protection any more. *He* had to have it. From himself. Because she still instinctively feared his reaction to the sudden elimination of the barriers she had erected between them.

"You were thinking about your friends," Paul reminded her.

"Yes?" she asked vaguely, startled by his interruption.

"Yes."

"What about them?"

"How are they going to react to him?"

"I don't really care," she said. "I don't care a damn."

"Then why were you suddenly hankering for them?"

"It wasn't them, Paul. I think it was because we were all so irresponsible then. There was nothing to worry about. Nothing to be afraid of."

"What are you afraid of now?"

"I wish to God I knew. I wish to God I was a child again. I hate problems, Paul."

"Go on, you thrive on them. You want to be a gay young thing again because you've forgotten your youth. Memories are wonderful things. They re-create the world we loved, with practically no regard for the trouble we had living in it. But you, Lucy, you'll never be able to run away."

"Never before, but Willie's family could make me do it—*They* could make me run like hell. I've thought of it, you know. Often."

448

"You're not afraid of them," Paul said solemnly. "It's Willie you're afraid of."

"Don't be a fool!" she snapped.

"Why don't you dash off to Yuma, then, and get it over with?"

"I don't want it that way. Don't misunderstand me! I'd be married by any tank-town parson, but not until those hyenas really knuckle under."

"Lucy! What language!" Paul protested, rolling his eyes in mock horror.

"Hell, I'm mad, Paul! And you can't blame me. There's no springboard from which I can start to make them like me."

"Give Willie up and they'll positively worship you."

"Oh, pooh!"

"Settle down, darling. Give Willie time. He can't help fixing it for both of you. The more solidly he entrenches himself as boss of the company, the quicker they'll come around."

"If that were only true!" Lucy said bitterly. "But it isn't. They hate me, not because I'm a schicksa, but because they know that without my help Willie would never have been able to take over the business."

"Well, he's done that. They're out. He's got the power, the money. The more he makes, the quicker they'll heel to. They've got to! Christ, he owns the company. He can kick them out completely. Tomorrow, if he wants to."

Lucy took a cigarette from her case and lit it silently. The case clicked sharply when she snapped it shut. Wouldn't Paul be surprised, she thought, if he knew what Willie's interest in the company actually amounted to?

"Somehow," she said, smiling, "to hear you tell it, it always comes back to making better pictures. The bigger the box-office, the softer their hearts." She paused and sighed, the nervous sigh of a fighter nearing exhaustion. "It sounds logical," she continued, "in a business sense. And we're making three good shows right now. Maybe when the money starts pouring in, I'll be a bride."

449

13

WILLIE FINALLY had everything. Power, riches, the respect of the woman he loved, and the envy of his fellow men.

"Did it all himself, too," they'd say. "No hiding behind the old man's name for him!"

"Great guy, W. L., great guy!"

The great guy was beginning to believe in his own infallibility. It was inevitable that he should. Every day some little thing happened that made him feel vitally important to the industry and impressed by his place in it.

He became Miracle's representative at the councils of the Association of Motion Picture Producers.

His name began to appear in connection with the Community Chest, the Motion Picture Relief Fund, and various philanthropic societies around town.

The magnificoes from other lots began calling him up, asking his opinions, showing him special previews of their latest films.

The Academy of Motion Picture Arts and Sciences notified him that he had been elected to the Producers Board, which automatically made him a member of their executive committee.

In short, he was rapidly becoming a magnifico himself, and magnificoes leave genius behind them. They hire it. Therefore they are above it.

Willie's transition was gradual, subtle, almost imperceptible at times. He was still called by his first name, and when he was alone he responded as cordially as ever, but when he was in the company of other bigwigs, whether they were topnotch agents who no longer sent their satellites to deal with him, stars who laughed at his poorest jokes, or directors who took his advice seriously, he evinced a notable lack of enthusiasm when his own employees yelled "Hi, Willie!" as he passed them on the lot.

This was, of course, understandable. He wasn't snubbing anyone. He, more than others, realized that one of the greatest assets a studio can have is the excellence of its technicians. So he went out of his way to be nice to them—when he had the time. But he was definitely serving notice on all and sundry that when he was accompanied by other celebrities he would exact the tribute of his station.

After all, he was a national figure. And in show business national figures don't come cheap. They lose something in their ascendancy, even though it may be merely contact with the mob. They have a right to expect some recompense.

Secretly, Miss Holmby began referring to him as the "Rotogravure Kid." His new publicity director, Dean Johnson, fed the newspapers and magazines a constant stream of press releases in which Willie was invariably depicted as "The Man With the Omnipotent Touch."

That was the slant. "Omnipotence!" Dean invariably barked at his hirelings when they asked him for an angle upon which to "hang" their stories about the boss.

As a result of all this publicity the boss's mail became so voluminous that he had to hire another secretary whose most unpleasant job was heading off unimportant calls and callers. Although Miss Holmby, whom he retained as his personal secretary, continued to make all his appointments, he found it more and more difficult to keep them. The world, he felt from time to time, was beating a path to his doorstep.

But the boys who were invariably kept waiting in the projection room thought otherwise. They couldn't understand why he never arrived at a screening on time. They'd set a date, be assured that he'd be there, and then go up and wait. The aggregate salary kept waiting at the least of these runnings was about seven thousand dol-

451

lars a week. But if Willie wasn't going to worry, why should they?

Eventually they brought dice with them and some of the lot's wildest crap games took place while they were waiting for Willie. The boys took the precaution of posting an assistant cutter at the head of the stairs, and as soon as the boss started up to the projection room, the dice would disappear and Miracle's major and minor executives would greet him with their most benign smiles.

But Willie liked a long face better than he did a short one. A smile is an intimate thing and intimacy in Hollywood leads to salary raises, or at least to the opportunity to ask for them. Therefore, when the boss marched into the projection room, he always did so brusquely, in the manner of a harried executive begrudging his time to the very film that pays him.

The *Beethoven* picture was Miracle's most ambitious and expensive effort, pegged by the budget estimate at two million five hundred thousand dollars. It was an experiment, in which the action was to be subservient to the music score. The picture had been constructed around Beethoven's Seventh Symphony, and for the first time in Hollywood history, the music was transposed into a score for the entire picture and recorded by the studio orchestra before any scenes were shot.

From this track which, with the exception of blank spaces for dialogue, ran the length of the picture, Fritz Kornfeld was able by means of a playback to time his silent scenes so well that all visual movements bore a definite relation to the tempo and mood of the music. In place of the completed shooting script from which most movies are made, he had a mere skeleton indicating action and a few lines of dialogue.

Into this mold Fritz poured his real talent and emerged with one magnificent shot after another. However, these same shots, isolated from the music and photographed without regard to any chronological sequence, were bound to appear exceptionally dull at rushes. A day's work consisting of ten takes for a scene in Beethoven's study followed by interminable close-ups of a flute player silently whittling away at a solo passage couldn't be expected to set any executive's heart on fire.

So, when on the sixteenth day of production, Fritz shot innumerable angles of coyly lifted skirts, hand-kissing, sly winks, and girlish laughter, Willie exploded violently.

"Kill it!" he screamed, jumping out of his seat. "For God's sake, kill it!"

The lights went on. The boys remained tensely silent. Willie turned slowly around, looked at Fritz, and recited angrily:

> "Such shilly-shally stuff as this
> Is quite enough to make
> Anathema of bliss."

Then he turned on his heel and stalked out of the room.

The boys looked straight ahead and began thinking of their wives; of keeping them in mink coats or paying them alimony—and for what? For taking insults flat on their backs? For saying, "Yes, sir!" to some lousy bastard who knew it all or thought he did?

"Oh, well," Danny Gorlica finally sighed, "at least he's holding on to his ego!"

"Vis bose hants," Fritz said bitterly.

14

WILLIE WAS RAPIDLY turning into an intellectual snob. He became curt with his employees, imperious in his judgments, pained by argument, and precious about his knowledge. This, too, was not inexcusable. Youth learns quickly and wants to learn. But to know is not enough. To assimilate knowledge and translate it into action or living is the important thing, and that takes time. Time and innate humility. Willie had neither, and both are necessary factors to maturity.

Although he hurled stanzas of Byron, Shelley, Keats at the heads of his bewildered technicians, his love of poetry lacked depth, else he would have realized the incongruity of employing quotations from the romantic poets to help him settle arguments with men whose home lives consisted of raising chickens in the Valley.

By the same token he lacked the imagination necessary to clothe fact with fire, to give it color, life, or a personal equation to those responsible for carrying out his orders. And because he could no longer convey the full measure of his ideas to the men around him, he thought quite rightly that he was being misunderstood.

It was natural, therefore, that he should barricade himself in his office and become a brooding, impatient, reticent genius carrying the cross of his own inadequacy deep within his heart.

Lucy was the one person to whom he still responded. She knew what was happening to him and tried to act as his interpreter, but after he'd told her that what the Beethoven picture needed was "more Byron, something fluidic, exciting," she gave up in despair. She realized that unconsciously he was becoming a poseur, that he had to be set free from his newly acquired knowledge, and quickly, before the entire structure she had helped to build crumbled around them.

She was beside herself, because he no longer took her advice. He loved her, of course. But he was beginning to divorce himself from her influence. The pupil was, in fact, not above taking the teacher to task, and when she pleaded with him to change his attitude because people around the lot were beginning to lose confidence in him, he told her without malice that she had better stop worrying about a lot of jackasses.

"Who are they to lose confidence?" he continued, stalking around the room like a high school Hamlet. "Their eyes are like tachometers gauging the flight of others toward success. Envy is their solace, their one weapon, and it is the thing that in the end will destroy them."

454

"Too," Lucy added mournfully to herself, quailing before the realization that, like Frankenstein, she had created a monster that had got beyond her control. She was amazed that he could no longer see himself clearly, as he had always done, in relation to other people. The fact that he hadn't even noticed the change in himself added to her fears and she became desperate. Desperate enough to flatter him.

"Bill," she said, "you're probably the most brilliant person in this town today. Certainly you're the most talented man running a studio—"

"Thank you, Lucy," he interrupted, accepting the compliment with gracious sincerity.

She put her hand to her forehead and pursed her lips. "Bill," she continued, trying to ignore his egotism, "you've got to capitalize on those talents and you can't do it unless you express yourself on a level with your employees!"

"I'm surprised at you."

"What for?"

"For telling me how to run my business."

"Somebody's got to."

"I'd rather it wouldn't be you."

"Why?"

"I love you."

"What's that got to do with it?"

"Nothing, except that I want you of all people to see things my way. Sit down, Lucy. Can't you see what I'm driving at? What I am doesn't count. Doesn't matter. What my employees are, does. If my intelligence is on a higher plane than theirs, then they must learn to meet me on my own grounds for their own good as well as the good of our pictures. There's nothing more important than time and space and the future of man. If we can get that into our pictures, we've got something."

Lucy leaned forward and looked sharply at Willie. "What the hell's the matter with you?" she said slowly, and even as she asked, she realized what it was. "You're sick, darling—that's what it is! We've

been working too hard. Do you realize we've hardly had a moment together outside the walls of this place? Morning, noon, and night, on
the set, behind a desk, in projection rooms; stories, casting, budget
meetings until, so help me, I could scream! Good heavens, we're engaged, Willie! Let's get away from here. Let's go somewhere before
our formulas for life recede and celluloid becomes our food. Let's
go now—before it's too late."

He looked at her incredulously. "You mean you'd go away with
me?"

"I'm afraid that if we're going to make anything out of our
lives, we'd better go now."

"Good God! That'd be marvelous! Just the two of us—away on
a trip—" He looked at her surreptitiously to make sure that he hadn't
misunderstood her.

"Pack your bags," she said, "and we'll go tomorrow."

"Where?"

"La Jolla, Palm Springs, Victorville, anywhere. There's a lovely
ranch in Victorville. I know the people who run it. We could be quite
alone."

"Quite alone," he repeated contentedly. "You know, I've dreamed
of this moment. Dreamed of it a million times—and now that it's
here—"

She looked at him inquiringly.

"It's more wonderful than I thought it could be."

He walked over and sat close beside her on the couch. "But how
can we go now, darling?" he said. "We're just finishing our biggest
picture. We can't run out on that! Please understand. There's nothing in the world I'd rather do, but not now. I promise you as soon
as the picture's shipped, we'll go. And please, darling, please, don't
look so sad. It's not the end of the world."

"It's not worth it, Bill. Really, it isn't."

"What isn't?"

"Ruining your health for a lousy picture." She looked away

456

from him and spoke softly because she was near tears. "You've got to get away. You're sick now, Bill, believe me—inside."

"Nonsense." He laughed mechanically.

And suddenly she realized he'd brushed her aside. Unconsciously, perhaps, but as though she were a trollop who had propositioned him at the wrong time. It was the first time he had ever hurt her pride, and the first time she had hated him.

She got up and walked quickly across the room. Willie watched her uneasily. When she reached the door she paused and turned. "Willie," she said frigidly, "somebody ought to tell you that there's no particular social distinction to being the richest man in the cemetery. Good day."

The door slammed shut and Willie shook his head.

"Jesus Christ!" he moaned. "What have I done now?"

15

LUCY STAYED HOME for the next two days and resisted Willie's importunate bombardment of telephone calls, flowers, and telegrams. On the third day she capitulated and returned to the studio, but not to see Willie. Instead, she went to Paul Kersey's office, where she immediately launched into an indignant tirade concerning her latest difficulties.

Paul took it calmly, but when he finally interrupted her, his voice betrayed the fact that he was becoming slightly wearied by her problems.

"Businessmen make lousy lovers, darling." He sighed impatiently. "So why don't you just consider yourself well off and let it go at that?"

"Oh, stop being bright!" Lucy implored. "And tell me what to do. You know I don't want to leave Willie! I just couldn't. And I don't want to give up my job, either. I like it. But I also feel that something's got to be done about this mess before I go absolutely potty. Really, Paul, this is serious."

"Calm yourself! Calm yourself! There's always the imminent consolation that he'll wind up in that portion of heaven reserved exclusively for executives."

"What are you getting at now?"

"The Executives' Heaven, my dear, is a place where beautiful women continue to kiss our bosses long after their spasms of delight have become yesterday's pornographic dreams. I also firmly suspect that it's lined with plush."

"Very funny," Lucy said acidly. "What's that got to do with me?"

"Well, at that point, dearie, he'll practically scream for your restraining influence."

"You louse!" Lucy cried impetuously, and found herself laughing in spite of herself. Laughing gaily and intelligently because she had been deftly unmasked, because laughter is a most disarming weapon and the least embarrassing acknowledgment of defeat.

Paul smiled at her. "I knew you'd come round," he said. "You know, one of the worst things Willie's done for you is to make you take yourself seriously. You never did that before. Please don't do it now. Perhaps your pride and ego have been hurt a bit, but you know how unimportant they are. So relax. And for his own sake, give him another chance. He needs you. It's trite, I know, but he does; now more than ever, and if a little sex will straighten him out, don't hesitate."

Lucy stiffened instinctively, as though she'd backed into a sizzling radiator, and Paul thought, "She's the only girl I know who can fairly bounce with indignation."

"Good God!" he exploded, "don't put that boule-de-suif look in your eyes. You're not being led to slaughter, you know. A woman's got to go to bed once in a while even if it's only with an idea. And

458

it's a good idea, because your Willie's so tied up in knots that I'm afraid that's the only way you'll ever be able to unravel him."

"Paul, if you only knew how often I'd had that idea and tried not to admit it to myself, you wouldn't think it so funny."

"Who thinks it's funny? You love the young man, ergo, you have him. It's that simple. Get on with it."

"I wish it were that simple, Paul," she said quietly, "but I'm afraid it isn't. When he turned me down three days ago he did something I never thought would happen to me." She paused and lit a cigarette before she added, "And still I understand it. Willie's a worker; in his heart and soul, a worker. But this is important to me, too. This is our life, not his alone. And he should have thought of that; but, somehow, he didn't."

"Of course he didn't, and the whole point is you'll have to have him on his terms."

"His terms?" she asked curiously.

"Wherever, whenever, however he wants you."

Lucy breathed sharply and sat down on the arm of a chair. Even that, she thought, even that choice is going to be denied to me. She'd wanted everything to happen romantically, away from the goddamn beehive where workers were judged by the money they made and drones by their box-office draw. She wanted to get away from all that and go somewhere where both of them could find each other again and draw strength from each other and belong to each other. She'd wanted this to be a wonderful, rich, romantic experience, a foundation on which they could build a new life together; a life too strong to be disrupted by families or motion pictures or any of the horrible complications that had conspired against them.

But she was fed to the teeth with all the things that had happened to her—the things the Levinsons had done, that Willie was now doing, the innate differences she had had to reconcile herself to and compromise with—and this was their last chance together. They had to have it. If Paul was right and it had to be done on Willie's terms she would make even that compromise.

459

"I'm even willing to do that," she nodded. "But if anything goes wrong with it, God help us, it'll be the last straw."

Paul grinned at her. "Don't be so tragic," he said. "Just get on with it."

"I think I will," she said, and she stood up slowly.

"You'd better, before it's too late."

"Too late?"

"Yes, dear," he said, rummaging among the papers on his desk. "Here's a letter I just received from Ullman and Wolff. You remember them. Friends of mine. The only Broadway producers who ever made a commercial success of art. Seems they contacted a Mr. Case of Case and Ogilvie and sold him a bill of goods. Did a good job, too, even though they don't know much about pictures. We went to school together. Naturally, they used me as a reference, and at that point Mr. Case and I began corresponding."

Lucy wheeled sharply away from Paul and walked toward the window. When she turned, her face was livid with rage. "To think that you, of all people, should be spying on us!" she cried.

"In a way," he confessed, "that's true. But I've been spying for, not against you. The ship's sinking, Lucy. You and I know it. We all know it and it's every man for himself. But I'm loyal—"

"Loyal!" Lucy repeated, and her voice broke with anger.

"That's what I said. I really believe that if Willie were given a chance to lead a normal life he'd come around, and until you've given him that chance, I'm going to stick with you. Case asked me how things were going and I said, 'Swell!' Here's the entire correspondence," he added, handing her a sheaf of papers. "Most of them concern Ullman and Wolff, and what I thought of them. But in each letter you will see that my attitude is one of complete loyalty."

Lucy thumbed through them rapidly and had to admit that it was. "When are they coming out?" she asked.

"About a month. Willie will know in good time. Case will go through the formality of getting his opinion."

She handed the folder back to Paul.

460

"Lucy," he said, "this whole studio's going to hell and I hate to see it as much as you do. Really, I do. You know that."

"Paul," Lucy said slowly, deliberately, "if I couldn't believe in you, I'd feel as though I hadn't a friend in the world. You leave Willie to me. And wish us luck."

"Oh, I do, Lucy," he said, kissing her sentimentally on the forehead.

16

IN SOUTHERN CALIFORNIA the gentlest steady fog becomes a flood. And when the winter rains drift in and visit for a week or so, the ground eventually becomes a muck of lush and squidgy clay. But there is comfort in the rain. Romantic comfort for those who like to walk in it. Prosaic comfort for those who like to be protected from it. Melancholy comfort for those who like to listen to it splattering against the rooftops, gushing down the drains, glazing the windows with torrents of despair. For whether one is in or out of it, the mere sound of rain imbues one with a sense of peace, of loneliness, of vague, impersonal sorrow. It is the time for mourning, for consolation, and for love.

Lucy turned from the fire and looked down at Willie, whose head was cushioned in her lap. They had dined together and returned to his apartment.

Driving through the storm had been a high adventure. The top of Willie's convertible had jammed and they couldn't yank it free. So they had driven home with the rain swirling around the windshield, pelting their eyes and faces, but they had been gay about it, as only young people can be gay in the face of adverse elements.

After they slammed the door to Willie's apartment, they stood giggling breathlessly inside it, like mischievous children flushed with the excitement of having got away with something they shouldn't have done. Little pools of water formed at their feet and the rug began to give off the odor of damp wool. Instinctively Lucy looked down at her clothes. Her dress clung to her as though it had been poured from a mold. She suddenly felt dismally wet and exhausted.

"Could we have a fire and a drink?" she asked. "I've got to do something to get warm."

"Go into my bedroom and take off your clothes. My bathrobe's in the closet," Willie said, trying to make it sound as impersonal as though he were ordering ham and eggs. He noticed her hesitation and quickly added, "I'll have a fire and drinks ready by the time you get back."

"You're sure you won't mind how I look in your bathrobe?" she asked, quietly unfastening the top buttons of her dress.

He turned from the fireplace. "Darling!" he cried, advancing affectionately across the room.

She fled quickly.

When she returned he left her sprawled before the hearth, and after lighting the stove in the kitchen and hanging her clothes above it, he changed into the lounging pajamas she had given him for his last birthday.

He came back to the living room holding her hat before him, very much as though he had a dead mouse by the tail, and shook his head sadly. She looked up at him and smiled a wry, gentle smile. "Men have to drown them to appreciate them," she said.

"I liked it," he lied gallantly.

"A man that likes women's hats is either a fool or a pervert. A hat's the one thing women buy to arouse other women's envy. Come, sit down by me," she said, drawing her feet up under her robe.

"Where do you want me to sit?" he asked plaintively, like a little boy seeking reassurance.

"Put your head here," she said, patting her thigh.

He sank to the floor and laid his head in her lap and they listened to the rain in silence for some time.

After their last reconciliation, she had wasted an entire week trying by indirect methods to persuade Willie to go away with her. But in spite of his polite, almost pleading refusals she had managed to wangle certain concessions from him, as a result of which they had been leaving the studio every evening at seven. They had dinner together at least four nights a week, and spent more time with each other away from the studio than they had become accustomed to.

Willie had been more than amenable to all these demands, except leaving the studio by seven o'clock. But Lucy, well aware that the success of her scheme hinged on his acceptance of this one point, had held on tenaciously until he acquiesced.

It had become practically a renewed courtship, in the course of which she gradually permitted him more physical intimacy than he had ever hoped to achieve. She found herself vastly excited by these sudden, almost furtive, explorations of her body, and as Willie became increasingly impetuous, never having fully realized that Lucy had intended giving herself to him on their trip, she found it progressively difficult to keep the inevitable moment from occurring prematurely.

She was doubly gratified to know that their new relationship had already contributed to the restoration of his equilibrium. He was a saner, happier man and his assistants, though somewhat bewildered by this sudden transformation, were uniformly and unquestioningly grateful for it.

The time had come tonight, she felt, when she could give in to her desires and capitulate to his without jeopardizing their future. They were sure of each other now. As sure as they would ever be.

She looked down at his head in her lap and wondered what he was thinking. His eyes were closed and there was an amused, almost complacent expression on his lips. He was remembering their increasing familiarities, going back, toying over the first long kiss and her unexpectedly submissive response. It had been so exciting! Almost as exciting as the time he unfastened the top of her dress and fumbled so long and impatiently with the clasp holding her brassiere that she finally had to come to his rescue and undo it herself. She had held him close to her, giving him freely of the sanctuary he had himself created; had held him close and kissed him, softly, gently, like a mother, for what seemed an eternity.

And then, last night, the night she had permitted him the penultimate intimacy and succumbed with dark, ecstatic frenzy to his impassioned touch—what luxury it was to be beside the woman one loved! To know that one's mere presence excited her. To be gentle in familiarity, firm but kind in pursuit of the forbidden. To know that emotionally they had already completed the union which they had yet to achieve physically.

This wasn't the way it had been with all his other women. There was passion in it, yes, but it was a white, clean passion that, if anything, became more intense by virtue of its purity.

Love is such a simple word for such a complex thing, he thought, and he opened his eyes and found her face above his. She was looking straight ahead, thinking about the rain and the loveliness of this night which was to be theirs, and she bent down and kissed him slowly on the forehead.

He smiled at her impatiently and sighed, "You're the gentlest thing on earth. You know that, don't you?"

Her cheek caressed his and when she spoke she murmured in his ear, "Gentle? That's a deception, darling. Women in love belie their looks. Love makes us soft, if that's what you want of us. But our softness is a lie. Our fiercest desires are sometimes hidden in our gentlest kiss. Nature intended it that way. Surrender's more exciting to a man than passion of itself."

"Is it, though?"

"Think of last night," she breathed into his ear, and then her lips closed over his.

Kisses so short if measured by the years grow long when treasured by the memory. Even as time embellishes a dream, scenes of one's

464

youth, or anecdotes oft told with pride, so Willie knew this moment, this one kiss, would grow in ecstasy as years rolled by.

She'd never done this before. Kissed him and felt of his flesh. Caressed him with abandon and touched him with desire. And suddenly he shook with fear. The subconscious fear that assails all men when they come to grips with a passion so complete that it encompasses a world between its loins. It is a man's fear, based on envy, and Lucy became aware of it and slowly withdrew her lips from his.

He sat up and turned her around so that their backs were toward the fire. Then he lay down beside her and she came close to him so that he felt her body quivering against his through the folds of her robe. He slipped the robe down over her shoulders so that it pinioned her arms behind her. Then he kissed her breasts, fiercely, violently. She struggled and he was afraid that she was fighting him, but she muttered softly, "My arms, darling." And he drew away, wondering if he had hurt her. "I wanted to hold you," she explained, as the top of her robe slipped to the floor. He looked at her. The belt around her waist still clasped the rest of the garment to her body.

She leaned back and stroked Willie's head while he kissed her. He fumbled at the belt and tore it loose. She lay exposed to him and he drew back again to look at her exquisite nudity. She was so beautiful. Full, rounded breasts; her abdomen, curved just enough to cushion; legs, firm; thighs, strong and slender; skin, of an exciting slightly pinkish tinge. This was what he'd wanted, waited for, and now could have. He knew it the moment that her eyes met his.

He fumbled anxiously at his own clothes. He wanted to tear them off, but every button, every clasp became an obstacle. He stood up and angrily wrenched himself free. Then he crouched beside her and kissed her hungrily.

He felt her hands upon his shoulders, pulling him toward her, and then the force of his emotion diffused his strength, sapped his vitality, robbed him, as only sheer emotion can, of rapture. Suddenly, like a wounded, incredulous bird he paused in flight, and in the instant between thought and realization an icy fear assailed him and he fell to earth, stunned by his own incompetence.

For a frightening second he looked at her and his eyes told her what had happened. He fell on his face beside her and began to sob violently. She tried to comfort him, but her heart wasn't in it. He had let her down for the final time. Failed her completely, and though she understood that it had been brought about by the very intensity of his desire for her, she was too sick with exhaustion to succumb to pity.

She got up slowly, went into the kitchen and put on her wet clothes.

He was still crying when she came back to the living room. She knelt beside him and lifted his head from the floor. She kissed him gently and murmured, "It's all right, Willie. Maybe it was meant to be this way."

He turned away from her kiss and moaned, "I'm so ashamed. So ashamed."

"It's not a question of being ashamed, Willie."

"It is! It is! It's never happened to me before. Honestly."

She drew away from him and shook her head. A look of deep anguish came into her eyes. "Let me put you to bed," she said wearily. "You need sleep. You're all in. Come, darling. Come along."

She put her arm under him and helped him into the bedroom. She turned down the covers and got him into bed. His convulsive sobbing never ceased. She tried to smooth his forehead, but at the touch of her hand he turned and buried his face in the pillow. She left the room and came back with a double jigger of Scotch which she forced him to drink. Then she kissed him good night, put out the lights, closed the door to the apartment, and took a taxi home.

17

MISS HOLMBY TOOK one look at Willie as he walked into the office and knew it was going to be a terrible day.

"Good morning!" she said, as cheerily as possible. "Hard night?"

"Get Miss Strawbridge on the phone!" he said gruffly. "And see that I'm not disturbed."

Miss Holmby shuddered ever so slightly when he slammed the door behind him.

Willie went to the window, looked across the lot, and shook his head. It didn't mean a damned thing to him. Not a damned thing. Lucy's worth more than all of it, he thought, and I've failed her all the way down the line.

He crossed the room and sat down in his chair. His fingers drummed impatiently on the desk. There were a million things to do, and here he was, waiting for a phone to ring. Just a lousy telephone call. Why the hell wasn't she around? Why didn't she answer? Christ, Holmby was taking a long time getting her. Efficient woman, that. Wonder what kind of sex life she's got. Wonder if the boy friend can give her what she wants. . . . Well, even if he does, it can't be very interesting. Maybe I've got the only virgin secretary in town. That would be the pay-off. . . . Jesus, where's Lucy!

He clicked the dictograph key. "Well?" he asked.

"Yes, sir?"

"Doesn't she answer?"

"I haven't been able to locate her yet."

"Tell the commissary to send over some coffee."

"There's a letter on my desk from Case and Ogilvie. It's marked important."

"It'll keep. Get Miss Strawbridge and the coffee."

"I'm trying, Mr. Levinson."

He hung up and looked around the office. He'd had no sleep at all, or if he had, he hadn't been conscious of it, which is as bad as having none at all. He felt horribly empty in the pit of his stomach and he wanted his coffee badly—or thought he did. He was at once restless and depleted. He felt vaguely that things would be all right, but he had to *know*—and now. The buzzer rang.

"Yes?"

"Miss Strawbridge hasn't come in today."

There it was. As simple as that. Miss Strawbridge hasn't come in today. "Call her house," he said.

He twirled the dial of his phone absent-mindedly. Zero way over and let it spring back. . . . Back to your youth, which was sunlight, and your day now—which is night. What are you worrying about? What if she isn't around? She probably didn't get any sleep either. Poor darling, it must have been just as trying for her as it was for you. What can a woman think about a thing like that? Does she think I've always been that way, or will be? That's nonsense, of course. But does she know that? It couldn't have happened at a more inopportune time. No, sir! It would happen then! . . . Despite his anxiety, he laughed at himself, quietly and quite maturely. It was a kind of Olympian joke. What was her line about the God Priapus? Something about—

> The God Priapus astride his victims
> Standing and sneering, laughing and leering.
> Lewd is the mockery of
> Death through exhaustion.

Only there had been no success to his exhaustion. No satisfaction. It was negative. But maybe that was what she had meant. Maybe she realized long before—long, long before—that that would happen to them.

468

The phone rang. "I've got Miss Strawbridge's house for you," Holmby announced before she clicked off the wire.

"Hello, Lucy?"

"No, Mr. Levinson, this is the maid. Will you please hold the phone?"

Willie smiled. At least she's been getting some sleep. She'll feel better. God, it's silly of me not to feel sure she understood. It's a compliment to a woman to want her beyond one's ability to appease her senses. She must know that. What the hell's taking her so long?

There was a knock on the door. Miss Holmby brought his coffee in. He smiled at her. "I'm sorry I snapped at you," he said.

She put the tray on his desk and looked up at him. "Whatever it is, Mr. Levinson, I wish you luck," she said simply, and walked out of the room.

Willie suddenly felt like crying. Here was an impersonal automaton who worked for him day in and day out for forty dollars a week and suddenly, as though she sensed his unexpressed anxiety, wished him good luck—and after the things he'd just thought about her too. . . . What the hell was going on here? Five minutes and still no answer.

He sipped his coffee and sighed.

"Hello?" a voice said cautiously.

"Oh, Lucy, darling, did you sleep?" Willie asked anxiously.

"Willie—" the voice hesitated—"this isn't Lucy. It's Millicent Strawbridge. She's gone. Took the seven-o'clock plane to New York. Whatever happened to you two? She wouldn't tell me, and I've never, never seen her in such a state."

"She's gone" was all that Willie heard, and he stared blankly out the window while Mrs. Strawbridge babbled on. He was on the verge of tears, but somehow he couldn't cry.

"What's her address?" he blurted out.

"She didn't say. She only told me that you shouldn't try to find her. That she was all right and wanted me to thank you for everything. You've been most kind, you know. Most kind. If there's anything I can do . . ."

"I've got to see you right away. I've got to find her. I've got to!" His voice broke with emotion.

"I'm afraid you never will, Willie. She's made up her mind. You'd better try to forget her. Believe me, I'm sorry, and I too wish you well."

Mrs. Strawbridge waited for Willie to say goodby. But he had dropped the receiver on the desk and walked to the window. She waited a few moments and finally called, "Willie?" But there was no answer and she hung up slowly.

"He was such a young boy, such a young boy!" she repeated to herself, and her voice was tinged with genuine regret.

Willie looked across the lot again. Looked, and thought of all the time and fun they'd had together. Looked, and saw faint cracks on walls, stairs that needed painting, streets that needed to be repaired. For the second time in his life, insignificant details penetrated his consciousness with the amazing clarity that only comes in moments of blank despair, when the mind rambles disjointedly through kaleidoscopic memories, while the eye in independent, thoughtless focus perceives anew things that the mind accepted as reality.

"There was so much to do," Willie cried sadly. "So much, my Lucy. And without you—I don't know. . . . I swear I don't."

And he felt strangely unsure of himself.

18

IT IS A TERRIBLE THING when a man who has never doubted his destiny discovers within himself the first suspicion of inadequacy. It is terrible because it startles him into immobility. Willie should have pursued Lucy, but he couldn't. The fire had gone out of him, and he desperately needed sympathy.

The family is a well from which sympathy must flow as an eternal spring. But obviously Willie couldn't turn to his own family. Where, then? To Paul Kersey? To go to Paul would be an admission of his own failure, and that wouldn't do. To Richard Lansburgh? It wasn't the sort of thing he could write down on paper, in black and white.

There is nothing so personal as impotence, nothing so private, so devastating, and so seldom understood. It is more than a functional deficiency; it is a psychological maladjustment. And Willie, eventually realizing the hopelessness of going to somebody for sympathy, only to face the permanent curse of suspecting his confidant of betraying his confidence, tried very hard to get back to work.

In answer to Case and Ogilvie's letter asking his opinion about "Messrs. John Ullman and Casper Wolff, two well-known and successful Broadway producers who we feel might prove helpful to you," Willie wrote: "I have, as suggested, conferred with Mr. Paul Kersey concerning the capabilities of Ullman and Wolff, and as he is of the opinion that they would be of inestimable value to the company, and having hired Mr. Kersey as much for his judgment as for his literary ability, I can do nothing but concur with him. Sincere regards, etc."

Willie was slipping. His guard was down and the heart had gone out of his life and his work.

Beethoven was ready for its première. The publicity department had sent invitations, printed to resemble ancient musical manuscripts, to all the leading reviewers and stars in town. Every columnist had been persuaded that this was to be the press preview of the year. The Cathay Theater, famed as the scene of almost every important première in Hollywood, had been procured for the event. The inevitable searchlights that during the week heralded the opening of every new market or drugstore in Los Angeles, were rented in battalions to add to the festivities by scanning the sky like so many periods in search of a sentence. Grandstands for the fans had been erected along the line of march from the curb through the private park to the theater marquee. A national radio hookup had been arranged, and Willie, the master of this little show, had with a true humility foisted upon him by circumstance planned to go alone.

But he hadn't counted on the rapacious inquisitiveness of his relatives. On the afternoon of the première Moe and Louis came down to see him.

"Nu, no tickets?" Louis asked. "Is it so good your flesh and blood shouldn't see it?"

"Mebbe it's gonna disrupp their morals." Moe grinned. "Mebbe it's over our hats."

"Heads!" Willie groaned, pressing the dictograph key. "Miss Holmby, haven't any tickets been set aside for my father and uncle? . . . Well, be sure they get four good ones."

Moe and Louis looked at each other.

Willie hung up, saw their faces, and asked, "Not enough, boys? After all, I've only asked for one for myself."

"Just four?" Louis asked.

"Just four," Willie repeated impatiently.

"What about Jacob?" Moe asked curtly.

Jacob. Willie had completely forgotten him. Forgotten his only friend in the family.

"Tell Jacob I'd like him to go with me as my guest. Have him meet me at my apartment around seven."

"Just Jacob?" Moe asked, and he seemed slightly crestfallen. "Do you mind?"

"Not at all," Louis replied magnanimously. "It's very sweet of you to take your grandfather. He likes schicksas."

Willie looked up at them sharply. No. They didn't know. They must have known she'd left the studio, but not that she'd gone east. Well, that was something. The first piece of luck in over a week. He smiled to himself, but he felt suddenly depleted by this crumb of

472

good fortune, and he resented their captious good humor knowing how smug their attitude would have been if they had known the truth.

His smile vanished and he said, "Please go, boys," as pleasantly as he could.

"Good luck!" they said, but they made no move to shake his hand. . . .

Willie went home early, washed up, put on his dinner jacket, and moped around the apartment waiting for Jacob. At ten minutes after seven he became impatient. It seemed strange to want one's grandfather to be anywhere on time. But there it was. He was as nervous and irritated as he would have been had he been expecting a luscious blonde with a penchant for breaking dates.

Even as he assured himself that Jacob had never failed him, he wondered if now, after all these years, his grandfather too had inexplicably turned against him.

The doorbell rang and put an end to his fears.

"Jacob!" he cried joyously as he yanked the door open.

Jacob stood on the threshold, smiling softly and shaking his head. His eyes glistened a bit, and he made clucking noises with his tongue, intended to express his gratitude for having been permitted such an infinite pleasure. "Are you alone?" he asked.

Willie nodded, and felt the old man's arms around him. The stubble of Jacob's beard scratched against his cheek as they kissed each other.

"Come in. Come in!" Willie urged, grasping Jacob by the arm and leading him into the living room. "Sit down," he said, indicating the chair beside the fireplace.

Jacob sat down, hesitantly, like all old men who seem to doubt that their behinds will ever find the mark. Then he sighed and as soon as he found himself safely entrenched, he stretched his feet and looked approvingly around the room.

"It's nice," he said. "Where is she?"

"A little schnapps?" Willie asked, evading the question.

"So much," the old man indicated, leaving a space between his thumb and index finger so modest that a fly would have had trouble squeezing through it.

Willie poured himself a Scotch and gave Jacob a small glass of some very old brandy Lucy had bought for him.

"Na," Jacob pursued, "what's happened? She's not here and you don't answer me. That means she's gone. For good?"

Willie looked down into his glass and drained it in one gulp. As soon as he had finished smacking his lips, he said quickly, "I'm afraid she has, Jacob."

"So." The old man sighed. And there was a horrible finality in the sound. A finality that briefly recognized regret, then hurried past it to accept that which had been ordained.

It angered Willie by its very bluntness and when he turned to Jacob he spoke with resentment as well as hurt. "I loved her dearly, Jacob. Very dearly! And I miss her with a passion that amounts to hate!"

"To hate?" the old man asked. "You learned to hate before you learned to love. That was your heritage. She came to you with love. And all you found in it—now that she's gone—was the mirror of your own environment. You hate again. Have you learned nothing from this girl? Was she that big beside you?"

"Yes," Willie confessed, "she was." And there was anguish in his voice.

"I knew you didn't hate. She put her mark on you. You're a man now. Forget her. Her job is done. Well done, I'd say."

Willie shook his head. "That isn't it, Jacob," he said. There was a bewildered look in his eyes, because he was trying to tell the old man something he'd never confide in another human being. Something he so hoped would be understood. "It's just—" and there he paused, and shook his head again.

"Just what?"

474

"Just that I failed her so," Willie murmured.

Jacob smiled gently to himself. "Would a man be a man if he didn't fail a woman once in a while?"

"This was different," Willie said softly.

"Every man thinks it was different with him."

"Jacob," Willie said, and he tore himself to pieces trying to get the words out, "I failed her—physically."

"Well, what did you expect?"

Willie looked up quickly and smiled with relief. Here at last was the comfort he'd been waiting for. And from a source he least expected. Compassionate Jacob! But—of course! How silly of him not to realize that Jacob would be the one person to understand. Willie laughed at himself and sat tensely in his chair awaiting further reassurance.

"Look at the kind of life you've led. You think any man should be a Hercules after such goings-on? Drinking, carousing, sitting in an office—you think that makes a man strong? You should get out in the open. Get your health back. Exercise, go away for a while. What woman wants a weakling around the house—especially when she's got an independent income?"

"Oh, Jacob," Willie cried gratefully, "you're a lifesaver."

"So—be your own lifesaver. Go out and take lessons. Learn how. That's what you've got to do."

"Lessons?"

"Sure. Lessons. Only a schlemiehl gets into a fight if he doesn't know how to defend himself."

Willie groaned and looked at his grandfather for a long, long time before he shook his head and suggested that they start for the preview and have dinner on the way.

"Yes," Jacob agreed. "We'd better go. Only it hurts me to see you feeling like this. Tonight should be a big night for you. A happy night. And look at you, Mr. Longface, walking around with your shoulders on the floor. She's gone! Why weep your heart out for frail

475

woman? Remember: 'their poison, like a viper's venom, seeps through the blood exhausting one with love or trembling sorrow.' You can't win."

"Yeah," Willie said bitterly, locking the door behind them. "I know all about it."

19

THE PREMIÈRE had been a glittering triumph. And there is, for all its elaborate hokeyness, a definite electric vitality that communicates itself to the participants in a successful preview. There is a kind of pride at being connected with the industry; a sort of paternal smile for the producers who have lived up to their responsibilities; an intimate cheerfulness that pervades the naturally skeptical faces of rival producers and stars. A cheerfulness that is most gratifying because it is an honest expression of envy.

From the moment Willie stepped up to the microphone under the marquee and read a message summing up Miracle's hopes for *Beethoven* in fat, round phrases prepared for him by the publicity department, to the final spontaneous reception in the lobby of the theater, during which he received the congratulations of the entire picture colony, Willie knew that he had at last knocked Hollywood on its proverbially star-spangled ear.

The gang from Miracle stood in the background and smiled at him possessively, while people he had never seen before filed past him and bowed and shook his hand and murmured humble expressions of infinite gratitude. Stars from other lots, resplendent in jewelry and furs, inclined their heads and looked at him with an envy that amounted to adoration. The big names of the business patted him on the back and said, "Great job, Bill, great!"

476

And Bill was, for the moment, the happiest man on earth. He had done what he had set out to do and his triumph was complete. Complete even without Lucy, for excitement had momentarily purged him of loneliness.

Only there was that vague feeling of finality. Like saying goodby to the other members of the graduating class and finding one's exhilaration tinged with sadness. It was like waking up alone in a brand-new world and not wanting to wake up at all, like finding oneself a pioneer and discovering that one had unconsciously meant to play it safe. And now there would be no more safety. From here on in he'd set a standard for himself. A standard of such excellence that he doubted his own ability to maintain it. He'd have to have other men around him. Men as capable as himself of turning out great motion pictures.

And luck had given him those men. Toward the end of the impromptu reception Paul Kersey came up with Ullman and Wolff, who had arrived by plane earlier that afternoon.

"Bill," he said, "this is John Ullman, and this, Casper Wolff."

Willie looked closely at his latest acquisitions. They were both tall, slim, and definitely distinguished looking. He had no doubt that they were sizing him up even as he was forming his own opinion of them. An opinion that was instinctively favorable. Here was no fawning obsequiousness, no obscene deference to his position, but rather an immaculate reserve bordering on reticence, swamped by caution. And he respected it. They were the kind of men Lucy would have known and approved of, the kind of men Willie envied and never suspected of being far less sure of themselves than he had ever been.

Paul put his arm around Willie's shoulder. "Like to have a bite with us, or are you tied up for the rest of the evening?" he asked.

"No. Jacob's gone home with the family and there's a press party at Ciro's. I'll have to show up there sometime tonight, but we could go somewhere else now, if you'd like."

"Could we?" Mr. Wolff asked. "My first night here I'd rather not run into a studio party. I'm sure you understand."

477

"Of course," Willie agreed pleasantly. "There'll be plenty of time to meet the boys. Matter of fact, I loathe studio parties myself. Just go as a matter of policy. You know how it is. In the meantime, how's about driving over to the Brown Derby, the one in Beverly?"

"Right," Paul said. "Meet you there in fifteen minutes."

Willie smiled and walked toward the exit, stopping on the way to congratulate the house manager on his handling of the show.

As soon as Willie left them, Paul turned to his companions and grinned. "Well," he asked, blandly imitating Willie, "how's about it?"

The two men smiled vaguely.

"He seems nice enough," Wolff said. "I thought he'd be a little terror."

"He will be, when he starts fighting for his job," Paul warned them.

"Case didn't send us out here to fight Levinson," John Ullman answered. "He sent us out to help him."

"When we suggested ways of cutting operational costs in the management of the studio, he laughed at us," Wolff said. "He said he didn't care how the studio was run so long as it made money."

"A sensible point of view," Paul agreed. "But if *Beethoven* flops, this studio won't make money. Too much has been poured into it."

"For Levinson's sake I hope it's a hit," Ullman said. "It's a good picture. I'd hate to lose my job over a picture like that."

Paul looked at him quickly. "Then Case said if it flops you move in?" he asked.

"Not exactly," Casper answered coldly.

"He didn't suggest it?" Paul pursued.

"Well—vaguely. He indicated it was a possibility."

"That's all I wanted to know," Paul said triumphantly.

"Paul, listen," Ullman protested impatiently, "stop looking for trouble. We came out here to do a job. If it works out one way, we'll probably be producers. If it works out another, we *may* run the studio. The one thing we don't want is trouble."

"You won't have any trouble. None at all. He's through. Right now. He'll curl up like a sow bug and hope he won't be stepped on too hard."

"How much does he know about us?"

"Practically nothing, Casper. But it won't hurt to give him a vague hint. You see, he thinks you're both out here just to help him."

"That's all right with us."

"Well, it's not all right with me, John," Kersey said. "I want him to know he's licked."

"Good God, what's he done to you?" Casper asked.

"Nothing. I just worked for the sonuvabitch. It's what his whole family did to other people on the lot that gripes me. I want him to know what decent people are like, people who think about other people—even in business."

John Ullman shook his head slowly. "Whatever the Levinsons did," he said, "was because they were both power-conscious and stupid . . . and in that, they were no different from the robber barons of a previous period. We'll come along with you to the Derby, but don't expect us to suddenly look the guy in the eye and tell him he's a dead goose. That's not our job."

Maybe not yours, Paul thought, but I'm going to make it mine. And he said, "Okay, let's go. We've got some drinking to do before he joins us."

20

THE BROWN DERBY is a place where one can pursue privacy in full view of other celebrities.

Willie sat in the middle of one of the semicircular booths with Paul and Ullman on one side of him and Wolff on the other. They were a distinguished group, if only by virtue of the fact that, unlike the customers in other booths, they were intensely interested in each other.

The three of them had downed their third round by the time Willie joined them. And Willie, who had yet to make any specific commitments concerning the kind of job he had in mind, was still sizing them up. It was a decision he naturally assumed would be made by him. He felt quite definitely that in probing for their qualifications it would be best to keep the conversation on a grand scale; so he led off by asking them, with a smile of confidence born of his immediate triumph, exactly what they thought about the motion-picture business.

And as John Ullman answered his question, Willie found himself listening like an enraptured schoolboy to a man who not only enjoyed talking but, unlike most men, talked well.

"There's nothing the matter with it," Ullman said, twirling the stem of a half-empty brandy glass, "nothing. It's a solvent, going concern. It meets all its obligations except, perhaps, those thrust upon it by the common stockholders. It pays its employees, its stars, its amortization on equipment, and its interest on loans. If by any chance a motion-picture company finds itself in receivership, the receivers break their backs to hold on to it. But—does the industry as a whole need good management? I don't think so. It hasn't had it in years gone by and still it's survived. The trouble is, it's too good. It's too big for little men. Certainly the people who are actually making it hum—the stars, the directors, and some of the producers —are better than most of the men on top. At least they're trained to their jobs. And you can't say that about many studio heads, can you? No many. Of course, you're an exception."

"Don't believe him," Kersey laughed. And to Casper, Paul's laughter sounded about as contagious and genuine as a giggle in the morgue.

Ullman shook his head. "No," he said, "I mean it. He's tried, and hard. It doesn't take any great talent to spend a million dollars to hire brains, but executives are born meddlers and it takes real fortitude to allow those brains to function without interference. And it takes brains to convert life into drama. Really it does. And because most of your top men weren't up to it, they took refuge behind a barrier of their own making, the Hays Code. They didn't have to do it. They just ran that way. It was easier. So easy that today when you talk about such a simple fact as having a baby, you have to spell it out slyly, B-A-B-Y." He waved the brandy glass from side to side with each letter and then he shook his head.

"It's true," he went on, with a pensive smile, "really true. Audiences have been fed pap so long they've grown soft. Men stagger out of your theaters looking as though they've discovered butterflies in their balls. And have you noticed how quickly women snap their purses shut when they leave a theater? It's because they've found satyrs in them. Satyrs committing a nuisance in their handbags.

"They're all bilious, sick, green with bewilderment because you've got them half believing your lies. And it's your own fault, too. You've all been playing Dr. Frankenstein, Mr. Levinson."

"Just call me Bill."

Casper winked at Willie and put his hand on top of Ullman's glass. "Johnny," he said, "you're getting drunk."

"So what?" Johnny asked. "What would you do in a spot like this?"

"You've got nothing to worry about." Willie grinned.

"That's just it," Casper said wearily.

"They certainly haven't," Paul added. And he sounded so emphatic that Willie found himself laughing at him.

"Paul," he said, "at least let me make my own decisions, will you?"

Paul saluted Willie with his highball. "To the very last," he said, looking his boss in the eye.

Casper shook his head and turned to John. "Go ahead. You were coming to the Hays Code." He turned to Willie. "I've heard this speech before," he said. "It's very good."

"Thank you." John Ullman nodded with mock sincerity, and he

held his glass up to the waitress who filled it with brandy. "The trouble with the Hays Code," he said, taking a quick sip, "is not so much that it slashes good stories to ribbons in its effort to comply with the pattern of human behavior it deems advisable for our morals, but rather that this pattern is incompatible with human experience. It is giving us morality instead of truth. By which act it defeats itself, for the simple reason that there is no higher morality than truth—which cannot be afraid to mirror life because it is life.

"There isn't a man in the country who doesn't know that some women have had extramarital experiences whether he sees them on the screen or not. And more than one wife realizes that her husband is more of a villain than the man who promises her a trip to Europe for a fling at her virtue. At least, it's an intriguing suggestion. And not withstanding the protestations of the censors, it is still doubtful that her morals would be affected by such a proposition. . . . If she really wanted to get to Europe the chances are she would have gone alone and got into infinitely more trouble.

"But you can't say things like that in movies, can you? Because you've strapped yourselves down. Way down," Ullman concluded, upending the brandy glass and sighing deeply when he realized that he'd drained it. "More?" he asked Casper timidly.

"I wouldn't," Casper said. Paul shook his head and frowned at Ullman.

"Censors," John confided to Willie.

"Let him have more if he wants to." Willie laughed. "He's the most amusing guy I've run into in a long time. Maybe it's because he's so sure of himself."

"Sure of myself!" John snorted. "Listen, Casper and I have been in the theater for fifteen years and every time we have an opening we leave town. That's how sure of ourselves we are!

"No fooling, we leave town. After all, the theater is a fickle wench. The mistress of the arts, but a delightful, discriminating one—and gracious courtesan though she is, responding magnificently to intelligent handling, she is still a capricious female, essentially, I suspect, because she is still beautiful.

"But you movie people have taken the same gal and made her a trollop. You have been callous with her and she in turn has become venal with you and eaten out your soul.

"You have done this because your top men have been shrewd where they should have been intelligent. I think it's because they never realized that a piece of film is like a word. That one must approach it reverently to give it form and fill it with significance. It is the nucleus from which the story springs, the medium by which the tale is told, and like a word, it has its place within the symphony of sight and sound. Like a word, it is always pliant, supple, anxious to imply new meanings; like a word, it can convey myriad emotions with compact honesty, and like a word, so help me, it should never have to contend with amateurs.

"The sad thing is that film—or the motion pictures—has suffered such indignities at the hands of dilettantes that I'm afraid the damage can never be repaired, and the efforts of all the fine young men like yourself to create dignity in a field noted for rapaciousness will end in failure."

"I'm not a fine young man," Willie said with quiet sincerity.

"It disturbs me to realize that if you aren't, you could have been. But do you really think you've got a chance, trying to make intelligent, honest movies?"

Willie smiled and turned to Paul. "You knew how Lucy felt. What do you think?" he asked confidently.

"Felt?" Paul parried. "One would think she'd been buried."

Willie nodded slowly and then looked up at Paul. "One would," he said bluntly, and even as he spoke his face became contorted in a grimace of despair. He had been trying to avoid thinking back into the far too pleasant past and here it was cropping up again.

"Permanently this time?" Paul pursued.

"I'm afraid so," Willie answered reluctantly.

"Then I'm afraid we really haven't got a chance."

"Paul!"

"I hate to say it, Willie, but Lucy was more to you than just another woman."

"I know that!" Willie exploded. "I know it so well it makes me sick to think about it!"

"Why don't you try to get her back, then?"

"Get her back!" Willie shouted, flinging out his arms with such vehemence that he struck Ullman's brandy glass, and in his excitement let it teeter back and forth until Wolff reached over to steady it. "My God, man, don't you think if it were humanly possible I would?"

There was a long silence during which John Ullman hiccuped. When Willie spoke again, his voice was low but bitter. "We had a great preview tonight, didn't we? How do you think I felt? What do you think happened to me when I saw 'Lucy Strawbridge, Associate Producer' flash on the screen? You think I felt happy? I felt like kicking everybody in the theater. Including you."

"You can't kick me, Willie," Paul said grimly. "You're at the point where the only person you can kick is yourself."

"As long as nobody else does it, that's all right with me."

"Is it, though?"

"What do you mean?"

"I think that without Lucy you're through."

John Ullman hiccuped again and clapped his hand over Paul's mouth.

Willie fought hard against believing what he'd heard. He liked Paul. Liked him genuinely and couldn't reconcile this unexpected truculence with their friendship. He had hired Paul, believed in him, trusted him, and suddenly without warning his friend had turned against him. It was all so shockingly vicious that Willie half expected it would wind up as a joke. He waited hopefully for the pay-off to the gag, but there was none. Nothing but silence and the inevitable realization that Paul, too, had betrayed him.

Betrayal is a most confusing fact to face. It is so demoralizing that one usually blurts out the first thing that comes to mind, and it is inevitably defensive. Willie fairly shrieked, "My God, Paul, I'm your boss!"

Kersey brushed Ullman's hand away from his mouth and cocked his index finger at Willie. "That's a singularly transient phrase," he snapped.

"I'm afraid it is," Ullman agreed reflectively, "afraid it is."

Willie turned a withering look at Ullman and then lashed back at Paul. "Listen, you bastard," he cried, and his teeth chattered with rage, "I made lotsa pictures before Lucy was around. Good ones. And what's more, I'll make a lot more, only you won't be around to pat me on the back and tell me you're my friend. You're through, Kersey. As of today. This moment. Your check will be mailed to you at your house. I don't ever want to see you around the lot again, understand?"

"You won't, Willie," Paul said smugly. "You won't."

Willie grabbed all the checks on the table, pushed past Ullman, and stalked over to the cashier's desk.

"Oh, yes," he heard Paul telling his companions, "he made some good pictures, but his standards, which were Lucy's, were a little highbrow, and as for *Beethoven*, I'm afraid he'll find the great American public isn't really ready for it. You see, he's put his faith in an octopus. An octopus he thought he'd seen reading a book."

"Why don't you stop?" Wolff said curtly under his breath to Paul. He sat back and waited until Willie disappeared through the door, then he pursed his lips and leaned forward again, resting his chin in his right hand so that he faced his partner. "And you"—he shook his head—"you're no better than he is," he said, pointing at Paul. "Agreeing with him over that sticky 'transient phrase' slop. That was a hell of a thing to do!"

"I know, Casper, I know. But I felt so sorry for the guy. Someone had to tell him and I'm glad Paul did it. I was just plastered enough to agree with him. That's all."

"You bitched it, old boy. And doubtless it occurred to you that 'transient' is a word that might well apply to us someday?"

Ullman shrugged his shoulders.

"Never," Paul suddenly interrupted with a great deal of emphasis. "Never, to you two."

"You mean you *hope* it won't." Cásper smiled quietly at Paul.

21

WILLIE FELT BETTER the next morning when all the local newspapers raved about *Beethoven.*

"Sheer Film Wizardry," "A Magnificent Creation," "An Exciting Experiment with Art" were some of the headlines that greeted Angelenos at their breakfast coffee. And those who read further learned that the mantle of Thalberg had at last fallen on equally gifted shoulders. The trade papers also buttered up the adjectives, lauding everyone from Willie on down to the lad who patched torn sprocket holes. For a moment he was the "Man of the Hour." And for a week *Beethoven* was the "Film of the Decade."

Then the national reviews began to come in, and Willie quickly told Miss Holmby to stop sending excerpts to the other producers on the lot. The boys with the syndicated columns, the correspondents with the nation-wide news services were hedging.

Although they unanimously praised Willie for his daring as a producer and his willingness to stake two million dollars on a prestige film, most of them also expressed varying degrees of doubt about the advisability of spending so much money on something that was questionable box-office. They raised the point simply because they didn't feel enough of their readers were interested in classical music, which, they hastened to add, was a shame, because it was really a fine film and they recommended it heartily to those who knew that Beethoven wasn't a seaport on the Skagerrak.

But the New York reviews, which arrived after the picture was released, pulled no punches. Some called it ponderous, others unauthentic, but they all agreed that every time the movies tried their hands at art, they came out with sticky fingers.

Willie cried, "Smart alecks! New York reviews don't mean a thing! They'll love it in the sticks."

But the music clubs in small communities were good only for a day's business and a shower of letters thanking Hollywood for having seen the light.

And at that point Willie began bleeding out loud. "They're crucifying me!" he screamed. "The publicity stinks! Theaters don't know how to sell pictures! It's the double bills! We make a great picture and what happens? A house manager sits on his ass and expects the customers to come arunning!"

And the more he yelled, the more the boys on the lot knew that he knew he'd sired a white elephant. So they smiled at him indulgently and patted him on the back and agreed that it was all the fault of the "goddamn house managers."

And Willie felt very lonely waiting for the inevitable letter from New York.

It takes more than bad pictures to force a top executive out of his job. It takes bad pictures, plus dissatisfied bankers, plus the next candidate for the job. That combination is unbeatable—and the candidates were already camped on Willie's doorstep. Worse than that, they were in his lap. And they employed ignorance as the device whereby they could acquaint themselves with Willie's job.

"How would you handle this?" they'd ask.

"Why come to me?" Willie would parry. "The letter's written to you."

"It's not our fault," Wolff would apologize. "They just seem to like writing to us. I can't understand why."

"Why don't you ask your friend Kersey? He's still in town."

"Naturally if we need information we come to you. You're the boss."

"Then write to Case and Ogilvie and tell them so."

"We've suggested that to them, but it doesn't seem to do any good. You know how it is."

"I certainly do."

While this sparring act, which continued over a period of four weeks, enlightened no one. it successfully split the lot into two irreconcilable factions. The pro-Levisonites royally snubbed the anti-Levinsonites and vice versa until the day Willie finally heard from Case and Ogilvie. It was a brief, concise note, but it solidified sentiment on the lot with amazing rapidity. The note merely stated:

> Beginning next Friday you will be relieved of your duties by Ullman and Wolff.
>
> In consideration of your many excellent services, we have decided to give you an extra two months' salary check which you will find enclosed.
>
> > Sincerely,
> > Case and Ogilvie

Willie took the letter and walked slowly up the stairs to Moe's office. "Call Louis," he told Helen Connally, and to Willie the words sounded very much like the tolling of a bell summoning people to church, to a place where they could all be under one roof and receive strength from each other.

"You know your jobs have always been safe with me," he said quietly, when they were finally together. "Although I've taken the business away from you because I felt it had to be done, I never honestly hoped to see this day."

"What's up?" Moe interrupted.

"As of Friday, you're through."

Moe and Louis turned slowly toward each other. This time they were too surprised for recriminations.

"Why?" Louis asked, and there was a catch in his voice.

"Because I'm through too."

Moe was tense now, and shaking his head incredulously. "But thass impossible, Willie! With your stock! Who's gonna fire ya?"

"I haven't any stock," Willie sighed. "I sold it to Case and Ogilvie."

"You sold it ta bankers?" Moe screamed. "*Them* bankers? Jesus!"

Louis ran over and grabbed Moe's arm. "Let's have no words," he said. "This is the end. Let's meet it with dignity."

Moe patted his brother-in-law's hand and watched him walk across the room to Willie. Louis stood before his son and looked at him solemnly.

"At least in betraying us you betrayed yourself," he said. "That's just. That's final—and, in a sense, it's our victory. You should consider yourself free now. Free of any obligations to me—of blood, or heritage, or birthright. I excuse you from my life."

"If that's the way you want it, Pop," Willie said, and he hesitated a moment before he left the room.

"That's the way," Louis murmured, and he stood there looking at the closed door for a long time before he shut his eyes and turned away.

22

WIRE from William Levinson to Dr. Richard Lansburgh:

I MUST FIND HER PLEASE WRITE AND TELL ME
WHERE SHE IS I KNOW SHES COME TO YOU

Dr. Lansburgh's answer came Thursday morning. Willie sat at his desk and held the letter in his hand. He was afraid to open it.

His window was only half shut and he was dimly aware of the studio orchestra rehearsing on the music stage down the street. Probably the main title music for Morse's new picture, he thought. And he was vaguely familiar with the horn passage that swept into his office with a strange persistence as though demanding to be recognized. He listened, against his will, and suddenly his face turned white and he cried, "Oh, my God!" and buried his head in his hands, murmuring "The César Franck, the César Franck" over and over again. He wished he could weep, but somehow he couldn't, and finally he raised his head, looked at the ceiling, and whispered, "Oh, Lucy, my darling. You shouldn't. You shouldn't have." Then he opened the letter slowly, absently, because he felt that his closeness to her was so concrete, so real, that nothing the doctor said could ever come between them. He tore the envelope into little pieces as he began to read.

Dear Willie,

This is going to be an extremely difficult letter to write. Difficult because I'm well aware that whatever I say to you at this point will sound like so many words and so little understanding. Therefore I must ask you to glance through this letter now, if you wish—but be sure to put it in your pocket and read it in a week or two when the first flush of your extreme despondency will have exhausted itself. Then, perhaps, I can reach YOU. . . . At this moment, I doubt that anyone can.

Lucy came to see me, just as you thought she would. She brought a clipping which I thought you might like to see. Am enclosing it.

We wanted so much for you, Willie. Young as Lucy was, she had an awareness of your possibilities that paralleled my own. And believe me it was born of our love for you. Not the sort of love you thought you had for Lucy, which was a mere projection of your own ego. You looked into a mirror and thought you saw Lucy standing there. She wasn't. You worshiped your own image and if you had really loved her you couldn't have failed either of us.

I know there is nothing more annoying than people who take the long view of things when what you want is an immediate reassurance concerning a specific problem. But that which you think is immediate and important is really trifling. Lucy is not the answer. Going back and finding her resolves nothing.

For the second time in your life you're faced with the problem of asking yourself where, what, and how useful you've been. Not only to yourself, but also to the community. It is the sort of personal inventory that generally takes place on a deathbed. How fortunate you are that you are able to capitalize on it now!

You worked in an industry that by its very ruthlessness transforms great men to grasping ones. . . . The struggle for power was one of such intensity that you, too, lost sight of the simple humanities that are the foundation of social living.

Power, of itself, divorced from human sensibilities, is the pestilence, the plague, the horde of horrors that makes a shambles of this world. The whole bloody sum and substance of its tyranny reveals itself from time to time as the cancer festering the body politic. It is a fungous growth cultured in the test tube of humanity, nurtured in the will of every man who venerates it as an abstract goal.

This is the deity you worshiped. The Mammon that destroyed you; the altar on which you sacrificed our faith in you and disemboweled yourself . . . and this is the thing you must renounce!

I don't want to be too harsh with you and yet I want to shock you into accepting your responsibility this time. Years ago, I remember, you fled from it and you're facing the result of that cowardice now.

The sad thing is that you had to lose so much to bring you

back to yourself again. I'm really sorry for you. Sorry you lost Lucy, your business, and yourself; but in another way I'm glad, because the very impact of this tragedy may suffice to make you realize that you and you alone decide your destiny. Nothing conspires against you until you compromise with your conscience. Unfortunately I have a feeling you never even consulted yours. You just eliminated it from your existence, and by so doing you hurt not only yourself, but worst of all, your friends and those who loved you most.

I look forward to an immediate and permanent reconciliation with your family now that Lucy's out of the picture— together you can do great things.

If in the future you ever have need of me, please let me know.

I am firmly convinced that someday you will be a better man for this experience and I will be watching your new career with considerable pride. I still believe in you, you know, perhaps because in some strange way I feel as though you were my son. Who knows, in years to come you may even return a like measure of that devotion.

I hope so—fervently.

Richard

Willie put the letter down slowly. The headline on the clipping caught his eye: "LEVINSONS-KORN KAYOED" it read. He picked it up and skimmed through the article. It was a long one, a resume by *Variety* of their careers and only a few fragmentary sentences penetrated his consciousness:

Familiar faces passing from scene . . . Built Miracle into a major company . . . Hit pictures . . . Developed stars . . . William Levinson became production chief . . . "Beethoven" laid egg . . . Company on skids . . . Bankers take over . . . Ullman & Wolff . . . great plans . . . Variety's West Coast

492

representative says impossible contact Levinson or Moe Korn. . . .

Rumored they will go into Independent Field . . . 2 or 3 pix a year . . . No confirmation. . . .

Willie sighed, folded the letter and the clipping carefully, and put them both in his coat pocket. Then he got up, crossed the room, closed the door to his office, shook hands silently with Miss Holmby, and walked out of the studio.

. . . Friday was a busy day for the lot's sign painters and plasterers.

Down came the bust of Louis. Up went a new Miracle sign. Names were erased from the name plates and the Levinsons quietly passed into history.

PRODUCTION NOTES

DESIGNER: *Maurice Serle Kaplan*

TYPE: *Linotype* Bodoni. Futura bold condensed *is used on the title and part title pages and for chapter numbers.*

TYPESETTING, ELECTROTYPING, PRINTING, AND BINDING: *H. Wolff Book Manufacturing Co., Inc., New York City.*